ENDANGERED SPECIES

A novel by
Ronnie Tanksley

CHAPTER ONE

WHAT GOOD IS SHE if she can't tell me how I was as a kid? Isn't that what Mommies are for? Yeah, it was one-thirty in the morning and eight years later when I asked, but so what! But you know what, deep down I know, I really do know how I was.

That morning, I turned ten. We had a reddish-brown cat, a stinking cat. Can you believe it? Nobody else was home. I stayed home from school that day. That cat was all over the house— running, darting and clawing away from me. All I wanted to do was smash its guts out, sit them in boiling water and serve them to everyone for dinner. Oh, but of course I would tell them they were eating chicken gizzards.

Our kitchen was small, but it went well with the rest of the decor of our modest two-story home. We lived in the south end of Albany, New York. Actually, it's where I grew up. Although it was the capital of New York, you'd never really believe it. People from New York City referred to people from Albany as 'country'. I always thought that was okay, because I believed we were smarter and our environment was less crime ridden, that is, until I got loose.

I had two brothers, one older and one younger. We all got along well, sometimes. They were treated special because they were the first and last born. Me, I was the middle child and got less attention. That was okay because I believed it would make me stronger in the long run. I would never be a mama's boy.

I finally caught up to that cat. I grabbed it by its sweet little neck and put it in my arms, gently. I didn't want it to have any idea about the harm I was about to inflict upon him. We had this small walkway backyard between the house and our two-car concrete garage. It was about five feet wide and fifteen feet long. One fence was ten feet high, and separated the yard from the sidewalk of Myrtle Avenue. On the other end of the yard was another wire fence that actually sat on a short concrete ledge. It went to the same height as the sidewalk fence. This ledge-supported fence became my personal cat-smashing wall. I kept smashing that cat on the fence, because after the ninth time it still kept kicking.

I wanted cat soup for the family, so I had to hurry up because my brothers would be home at two-thirty from school, and I wanted to surprise everyone. I know Randy and Tony would tell if they knew what I was doing. You see, they were in competition with each other to get brownie points from my parents. Whoever got the most points got the bulk of "special" attention that I didn't get. It was almost one-thirty, and I had to hurry because I would need to skin the cat and clean up before anyone got back. I could easily say the cat, or "Max" as they called it, got out again. Max always got out and ran the neighborhood, that is, until dinnertime, then he knew where home was. Well, that time he *was* dinner.

After the twentieth smash, Max finally didn't move much. He twitched a little while I skinned him with Mom's razor-sharp kitchen knife, but soon he was motionless. None of this was poor Max's fault. He just happened to be the easiest thing I could get to to take out some of my frustration. I had learned how to skin a cat from watching my Uncle Henry once when he skinned a rabbit, after going hunting with him. I quickly wiped some blood off of the face of my Mickey Mouse watch to check the time. I wore my watch on the inside of my wrist, unlike everyone else. I just thought it looked cooler. It was two-ten. I had to work fast. I stood up from the concrete floor of my parents' two-car garage. Both cars were gone. I was dusty. Most of Max's blood was in an old mop pail that I kept stacked in the corner amongst the rest of the junk, near the automatic garage door. Shit, I had to hurry. There was blood all over the ground; the pail had a small leak. I picked up the pail and kicked some dirt over Max's blood. Damn, Max was pretty slimy. It was two-fifteen and my Mom's favorite big pot was filled with boiling water on the stove. I had one more leg to skin and cut up. Ten more minutes and they'd be walking down the hill of Myrtle Avenue, passing by the fence.

I did all the skinning and cutting in the garage. The garage was old and junky. I kept my knives that I'd found over the years, and one very sharp hatchet, hidden in the corner under the mass of stuff, which included toboggans, an old portable piano, two old car tires, lawn chairs--not that we had a lawn, and whatever kind of junk that no longer could fit in our first floor. Even our basement was full of junk. I couldn't stand it. I would clean it all up, and Mom would fill it with junk again. This made me mad.

Anger or no anger, I needed to hurry I was frantic. If I'm caught, I'm dead. Nonetheless, I needed to hurry. My two brothers, Randy and Tony, would be home soon, and Mom was known for skipping out of work early for whatever reason. I ran down the four wooden steps from the garage to the small backyard, through the screen door into the kitchen. I took a hard look at the small digital clock on top of the refrigerator. It was two-seventeen.

"Shit!" I said.

How stupid of me to waste time running to look at the kitchen clock when I was already wearing a watch. That's an indication of how confused I was. My nerves were shot. Mom had the clock set to her work time, so it could have been a little slow. It could have been 2:30 already. I glanced to my right after I ran to the yard and looked out at Myrtle Avenue through our small fence. The fence separated the concrete yard from us and the sidewalk. I had to hide my knives. I could feel Randy and Tony halfway down the hill.

Randy, who was thirteen and the oldest of us three boys, was halfway down Myrtle Avenue with my younger bother Tony, who was seven years old. They were both neatly dressed in their blue tie,white shirt, navy blue pants and black tie-up shoes. This was their school uniform.

"I hate Sister Landers. She always asks me to answer the question," Tony complained in a squeaky voice.

"That's because she's checking to make sure you're paying attention," Randy replied in a heavy tone.

They passed by the Myers' stoop.

"Kids learn anything today?" Mr. Myers asked loudly.

"Yes, sir," Randy said, mockingly as they kept walking.

Mr. Myers was in his sixties, and all he did was sit on the stoop. His house resembled the other two or three-story houses that lined the neighborhood. All he did throughout the day was mind everyone else's business.

"Where's Corey today?" Mr. Myers asked.

"Home sick," Randy replied.

"Yeah, he's sick all right. I know he faked it," Tony replied in disgust.

"Oh shut up. Cause if he did, he's the dummy!" Randy said.

"I'm tellin' if he's fakin'."

"Boy, shut up. You'd rat out your shadow if you could."

Tony knew he was right, and could only smile. They were only a few doors from our garage.

I ran from inside the garage to the gate and peeked out.

"Oh my God, here they come."

I tossed the green garbage bag with Max's head in it over the fence into our neighbor's yard, along with the rest of their trash.

I gotta be finished, I thought. Shit! Where's Mom? I hate having to do this. I stopped for a minute and thought about what I was doing. I must have been crazy. A tear rolled down my cheek. Max didn't deserve this. But I couldn't help it, I wanted to destroy something the same way I had been. I had to start somewhere.

I quickly wiped the dirt off of my blue jeans and cotton blue pull-over shirt. I looked down and saw that my black, high-top, canvas, Chuck Taylor Converse All-Stars sneakers were dirty and stomped my feet on the concrete so that I wouldn't track dirt through the house. I ran through the house, bumping into chairs and knocking over pictures on the buffet table. The pictures could wait. I looked out the Myrtle Avenue side window and there she was, driving down the street towards the house in her four-door white Honda Civic.

Just as my brothers were passing the fence, I was opening the screen door to the kitchen. Randy, the older one, was curious. But Tony, the youngest, was even more curious. You know, the pain-in-the-ass type.

"Corey what are you doing, I thought you were sick?" Tony snapped.

"I am, I was just calling for Max. He got out again."

Tony thought something was up.

"You let him out. I'm telling Mom," Tony said.

"Tell her and I'll cut your tongue out and feed it to the rats."

Tony stuck his tongue through the silver wire fence, teasing me. Randy frowned and rushed to the front door, and Tony followed.

They entered the house from the Grand Street, front door entrance.

I ran in the house and poured Max's remaining parts into the big pot of boiling water and covered it. Randy and Tony came to the kitchen. Randy tried to look in my pot.

"What's in there?" Randy asked.

"Chicken soup," I replied, standing in front of my pot, protecting it. "I'm making dinner for everyone."

"The little girl is making din din," Tony teased.

He teased me about how I kept clean and would occasionally make dinner.

At school, Tony got into trouble a lot for teasing and picking on the girls because they wouldn't give him the time of day. He wasn't good looking at all. Well, at least not like me and Randy. Randy, he was different. He was good looking, and muscular for a thirteen year old, and would always go to school looking sharp. He always made sure he re-ironed his clothes, even after Mom pressed them.

I was handsome, but my shyness would be the death of me. Randy could care less about how shy I was, as long as I stayed out of his way. Randy wanted to be a man before his time. We had a problem because I was ten and he was thirteen, so why should I treat him like an adult? I was protective of my cooking. Randy wanted to know what was in my pot. He motioned for Tony, stood near the kitchen entrance, to go around the other side of the round table to look. I held my ground in front of my pot. Randy, with his barrel chest, stood at one end of the table, and Tony came from the other I wasn't afraid of Randy. Tony made his way around the table where we had six cheap, plastic chairs surrounding it; one at each end and two on each side.

Tony decided he would use one of the chairs as a step ladder onto the table. I was a rock. I started to swing my butcher knife.

"All right, get any closer and you'll both pull back nubs." My eyes fixed hard on Randy's. "Randy, you know I'll do it."

You see, once when I was seven our neighbor's friend, a close friend, and another friend came into our area. I was coming home from school, walking through this alleyway that was one block in length. Mostly the bums hung out there at night, drinking and breaking their Thunderbird wine bottles. This was near our second floor Pearl Street apartment. Actually, we were not but three blocks up from Pearl Street heading west. But it was still far enough away to say we were out of the ghetto.

Anyway, this friend of my neighbor's friend must have been seventeen or eighteen and had the muscles of a Greek god, and the reputation of a slick, switchblade toting, scary bastard. As I walked through the alley from school one day, he pinned me against one of the buildings that was on each side of the alley. It was near the building fire escape. He held the six-inch switchblade close to my adam's apple. He wanted money. Little did he know, we had show and tell in school that day.

"Give it all to me!" the thug said.

I said, "No!"

He poked me lightly, drawing a little trickle of blood from my throat. Then he had the nerve to show it to me on the end of the blade. The sight of the blade excited me, and my blood being on the end of it was even more interesting. I thought, "Wow, so that's what it's like."

I suddenly got a thirst for blood. All my money and the remainder of my lunch was in a small brown book bag. That afternoon for the last class (English), we had show and tell. We had to bring in something and be able to talk about it. Four years ago I saw Dats, that's my father, cut his neck shaving. Thick red blood rushed from a small area near his adam's apple. It was my first time seeing blood. The blood was so thick and rich I became obsessed with the sight of it. I thought the whole class would be intrigued with what a razor could do. I swiped the razor from Dats' bag that he kept under the bathroom sink. As it turned out, the class wasn't as interested in the razor as I thought they would be. Soon after, I realized it wasn't the instrument, but the sight of blood that would have been of interest to them.

Dats told me he had decided a long time ago that if he was going to be a parent, he wanted to be called something different from the rest of the world. Dats came up with this name by taking the "d" off of the end of dad and replacing it with the letters 'ts'. When I was old enough to understand, I was all for it. Really, it's all we ever knew growing up, except when we were around our friends' parents.

As the thug still had his knife at my throat, I reached in my bag and I pulled out the straight razor, and in an instant I sliced, from the hand that held the knife, his index finger and thumb off completely. Blood poured from his hand. I held his right thumb and index finger, still grasping the switchblade in my hand as he ran down the street in horror, yelling. He never told anyone. Later that day, I got such a kick out of it. I returned his two fingers to him with the knife and a note saying, "Ever fuck with me again and I'll cut both your hands off and feed them to you."

Randy saw me washing blood off my hands back at home, so I was forced to tell him what happened.

Randy and I never told a soul.

There was only eleven cents in the bag, but it was just the principle of it. I didn't feel threatened that Randy knew my secret because I knew one about him. Years ago, he had told me that he found a real gun and kept it in a safe hiding place. I was sad when he told me about the gun, but I never said anything about it to anyone.

We heard keys at the front door. Sometimes Mom would walk from the garage to the front door, because she wanted to see if there was any trash building up on the side of the house. But mostly when she came home she used the back door. I quickly glanced at the small, ten-year-old clock behind Tony. It was on the refrigerator, which was the same age. It was two thirty-five. I thought to myself, Mom had saved my brothers from me taking them out. I was sick of them. Tony jumped down from the table and ran behind Randy to the front door. I stayed in the kitchen to stir my vittles. In his haste, Tony rammed his left big toe on the buffet table in our small dining room. He cried out in pain. The short hallway from the kitchen to the dining room was somewhat narrow. The buffet table took up two feet, so if one wasn't careful, you stubbed your toe. He used the dining table chairs as support to jump the remainder of the way to the hallway door, not far from the front door. Randy greeted her.

"Hi, Mom. What're you doing home so early?" Randy asked.

Mom was beautiful as a youngster, but Dats had run her ragged over the years with his beatings and verbal assaults. Even so, she still managed to maintain a bit of beauty, even at forty. Dats was the same age and still good looking, and was a good provider, which were probably the reasons why Mom was still with him.

"I wasn't feeling too well, so I left early," Mom said softly.

Tony jumped into Mom's arms. She was tall and strong, so she could handle it. She carried him as she walked.

"Hi Mom. Corey's cooking," Tony said in a tattle-telling manner.

"Do we have to eat his cooking--I hate it," Tony complained with a frown as he jumped down from Mom's arms. Using both hands, she tugged on the thigh area of her pretty black rayon dress to straighten it back to normal after Tony had gotten it out of order. The dress fit her full, shapely figure perfectly. She wore three-inch black leather pumps. Mom didn't like wearing stockings or pantyhose.

She never gave me all the attention, but she did stick up for me when necessary.

"Now, Tony, it's not my cooking, but Corey's cooking is still good. Pretty soon he'll be as good as me, if he keeps it up."

"How you doin', Mom?" Randy said as he gave her a big hug. Mom walked from the hallway to the dining room, and stopped at the table that had dark wood on the chairs. Then she looked at the pictures that I knocked over earlier in my haste. She went over to the buffet table and began picking them up, but not without words.

"Who knocked over these pictures?"

There was no answer for a few seconds, then Mom spoke again.

"I guess I'm talking to these four walls now!"

"They were like that when we walked in from school, Mom. Corey musta did it," Tony replied.

"How you gonna say I did it? You weren't here!"

"Who else was here then?" Tony snapped.

Tony got in my face.

"I could say you did it, too," I said.

"Shut up!" Tony yelled.

"All right, both of you shut up. Somebody shoulda fixed them."

Mom flipped through all the mail that was on the dining room table. The table was large enough for six chairs. They were brown and matched the wooden table. Mom had this gold tablecloth on it that draped over the sides of the table, almost onto the chairs. The chairs had the same gold-colored padded cushion as the tablecloth. The only times we ate at this table were Easter, Thanksgiving and Christmas, or other special occasions, which were rare.

I had neatly stacked all the old mail in piles by days—there were ten days worth of old mail. Then I'd stack them according to category. It was very neat. Then I put all the mail from six months ago at the other end of the table. I entered the dining area where Mom, Randy and Tony were. Tony had his arm around Mom as she read a letter from a creditor in silence, frowning. I leaned on the china cabinet at the end of the table nearest to the kitchen. We used this china on Thanksgiving and Christmas. I watched Mom read, and Tony stuck his tongue out at me and flipped me his middle finger.

"Hi, Corey."

"Hi, Mom," I said softly.

"What's for dinner?" Mom asked.

"It's my new recipe for stew soup."

"What kind of stew, chicken or beef?"

Tony and Randy wanted to know too because I hadn't told them.

"It's a surprise, Mom."

"Now you know I don't like too many surprises," Mom said.

"Mom, Max is out again," Tony said as he looked at me.

Mom looked at me, then at Tony.

"He'll be back for dinner, "Mom said, not really concerned.

I thought about how right she was, and smiled a little.

"Corey, have you cleaned up yet?" Mom asked in a matter-of-fact tone.

"Yes, Mom." I had to do all the chores when I stayed home, whether I was sick or not. She never made Randy or Tony do chores when they were sick. Mom knew I really didn't like school, even though I excelled in every class and even athletics. It was boring to keep doing something I knew I could do with ease. In basketball, football and baseball I always led the team. Our school teams always won. All the coaches called on me to play on their school teams. As a fifth grader, I had an easy time with school. I managed to get A's in all my subjects without really trying. School was not a challenge for me.

I knew how to work all of the computers in the school. A lot of times I was asked by my teacher to tutor my classmates, if the teacher couldn't. I loved working on the computers. Even though I wasn't very big like my brother Randy, sports came fairly easy to me. On my fifth grade basketball and baseball teams, I led the team in three statistical categories. I had conquered them, as far as I was concerned. I wanted to learn cooking. At the time, I thought I would pay back the person molesting me by cooking them some day.

Mom kissed Randy and Tony on their cheeks. She lightly rubbed my head as she walked by on her way to the kitchen. She went to her bedroom door, took keys from her small black leather purse, then unlocked the padlock that was always on their door while they were gone.

Tony sneered at me.

"No kiss for you Missy Pooh," he teased.

I used the dish towel I held as a whip and snapped him with it.

"Kiss this." Snap! I caught him on the arm as he tried to run to the kitchen.

"Ouch!" Tony said. He ran into Mom and Dats' bedroom, which was adjacent to the kitchen, and a bit junky, but not as much as the rest of the house. Once when I tried to help Mom clean her bedroom, I got hollered at because I found some of my Dats' red Trojans and blew them up at Tony's seventh birthday party, thinking they were a new kind of balloon.

Mom's full-size bed took up most of her room. They had a dresser positioned near a radiator against the wall on Dats' side of the bed. The dresser had two big drawers in the middle, and two small ones on each side of the big drawers. There was a black dresser about two feet away from the foot of the bed. This dresser had eight long drawers. It housed Mom and Dats' clothes. On top of it was a thirteen-inch color TV and old papers, envelopes and whatever else Mom could stuff there. They were useless papers that I tried to throw away. On the other side of the bed was a brown tin cabinet that stored my Mom's clothes--old and current. The room had a closet, but it was so full with Mom's and Dats' clothes that they could no longer close the door. What a mess!

My pot was boiling. I sat and watched Tony watch Mom try to relax as she sat on the foot of her bed, catching the last of the talk shows.

"Corey, don't let that pot boil over on my floor or you'll be scrubbing it for the next week," Mom said.

I thought, who does she think keeps it clean anyway?

"Yes, Mommy."

I quickly got up to check the cat. By then Max looked like any other boiling chicken part. Next I would put him in the oven and spread some hickory smoked barbecue sauce over him. They'd never know the difference. I sliced some potatoes and put them in the baking pan with the meat. For extra flavor, green peppers would go in with just two minutes left to cook, to make sure they wouldn't burn.

For openers, I wanted a nice tossed salad with all the trimmings. The big difference would be in the presentation. Instead of having everything in one big plastic bowl, everything would be separate.

Mom came out to assist, but I wouldn't let her. She still had her dress on, but changed into her fluffy white house slippers.

"Corey, you need to let me help. Your father will be home at four-thirty. You know he likes his meals by five o'clock."

The clock on the fridge read four-fifteen, and I had to hurry. But really I didn't care if the meal wasn't ready. Those rules applied when Mom cooked, not me.

"It'll be ready. You go call your girlfriends."

I smiled. Mom frowned. "Don't let yaself get a beating, okay? Cause if I get one, so are you. I'm sick of hiding bruises. I'm sick of you and your father. I can't even see my girlfriends because of bruises that I don't deserve!"

If dinner wasn't ready on time, there would be trouble. Dats would beat Mom, and Mom would beat me. I would get a beating anytime I stepped the slightest to the left of the line that Mom and Dats had drawn. But I swore that night there would be some changes made- -for good! I was through with being hit for no real reason. I was blamed for everything that went wrong.

The toilet wouldn't flush one day after I poured some garbage down it, and I was beaten. I had to use my six months worth of allowance to buy a snake tool to clean it out. Not only that, I had to clean in the cracks of the floor tiles. There was dirt from ten years of nobody cleaning; it was gross. I know they stuffed the toilet with Downey paper towels right before I dumped the food. There was no way everything would go down. It was a smooth move, but payback was right on track.

Not only that, one day Randy tied me up, slapped me around and stuffed my mouth with shit paper. This all, of course, was when I was too young to defend myself. I never told on him, and I know he thought that was a little strange. I was going to tell Mom, not because of the pain, but just for her to know of my new experience. Then I watched how scared he was when I was about to tell. I didn't understand the reason for his fear. After he did a series of things to me, I still never told, and he would probably have gotten away with it all, until today.

Before I get back to my cooking, let me expound on what they did. Once when I was five, on a hot summer night I was sleeping naked in my bed. Me and Tony shared a room. It was late, and I wasn't feeling too well, and Mom had just taken my temperature rectally. The pain from that wasn't so bad. It just made me feel like I had to take a crap. Mom was very gentle about the way she did it. Little did I know, Tony and Randy were watching through the small crack from the door being ajar. Later that same night, Randy decided he was going to have a little fun at my expense. Of course this was great news to Tony. I was sleeping hard. They tiptoed their way into my room. Randy had the same thermometer that Mom had used earlier than night.

"Shhh," Randy said as they crept through my bedroom door.

Randy whispered, "Are you sure he's sleep, 'cause if he's not I'm gonna use this on you!" Randy raised the thermometer towards Tony. Fear bulged Tony's brown eyes as he vigorously shook his head yes. Chill bumps covered his skin.

They slowly pulled the covers off of me.

Randy giggled as he looked at my small butt. Tony covered his mouth as he smiled.

"Quiet," Randy whispered.

Randy put the thermometer near my rectum. Then he smiled at Tony, whose face was inches away from his. Then he whispered, "Now when I say so, you hold his legs tight and then I'll shove this up his ass. This'll teach 'em." Tony smiled.

As he rammed the thermometer I yelled loud enough for the whole neighborhood to hear me. Randy covered my mouth and held me down. Tony laughed as Randy pulled the thermometer out.

Randy quickly put the thermometer up to Tony's nose. "Smell that shit," Randy said, laughing. Tony immediately pushed Randy's arm away.

I laid there crying for a few seconds as rage built up. Then I tried to grab Randy. He was too strong for me. He shoved me to the floor and walked out, laughing. Tony followed him.

The next day I was about to tell Mom what had happened. I decided not to after seeing the scared look on their faces. I didn't understand this. To me, if you had the balls to do something, good or bad, be accountable.

I thought I had encountered the worst pain ever, but it was later that same night that was the most horrible experience of my life.

My temperature was a hundred-and-two. I still to this day don't know why Mom didn't take me to the hospital. Anyway, late that night I heard footsteps. I thought it was Mom looking in on me, so I relaxed and went back to sleep. Then out of nowhere, I felt something jammed up in me . . . rectally. It was the same place where the thermometer was earlier, only it was bigger and warmer. Someone kept pounding. Back and forth, again and again with a gun forced against my head. I was gagged.

I couldn't stand it. I couldn't see or move. It happened more than once after that first night. I even tried to scream, but I was always gagged with a cloth and blindfolded after that first night. Sometimes duct tape was put over my mouth. When it was ripped off, it added to my pain — not from the strength of the person holding me down, but from the shock that I was experiencing. I knew it was wrong because it hurt, and also because the person wouldn't reveal their identity.

Ten minutes went by. I was aware of the time because we had one of those clocks on the night table between our bed that glowed. I didn't understand, where was Tony? He slept in the bed next to me most of the time, except when he got scared and ran to Mom's room upstairs. You see, our room was in the basement. I didn't mind the basement because it was cooler there during the hot, summer months, but that night was a horribly painful experience. That night would forever scar me, and I'd never forget. I'm still not sure who was on me that first night, or the other times for that matter. I do know that everyone was home. Randy was in his room upstairs off of the dining room. Mom's brother, Uncle Henry, who's a year older than Mom, stayed in the extra room. It was a small room to the left of the living room entrance. Uncle Henry's room really wasn't 'his' room. We considered it his because whenever he stayed over at our house late, either talking, playing cards or drinking, he would spend the night. Mom would sleep in there when she got mad at Dats, or Dats would sleep there if Mom kicked him out of the room when she smelled another woman's perfume on him from supposedly being out with the fellas. He hated that cot in there. It was rigid and cold. He deserved it though. How stupid could you be to come home to your wife with another woman's scent? He could have at least tried to hide his screwing around.

I felt so dirty that I decided to take a hot bath, even though it was the middle of the night. I remembered I had the water steaming hot and just layed in it with the lights on, but in my mind all that I could see was darkness. I didn't know what to do. Finally I dozed off to sleep, and Mom found me that next morning. I never told any one.

I didn't know who violated me, so I decided to just keep cooking for the time being.

Mom became impatient with the dinner not being ready yet. The potatoes were there, but the meat wasn't quite ready.

Dats was coming. I heard the garage door opening. He had this automatic door put on so that he could open it from his car as he turned up Myrtle Avenue from Grand Street. Our house was on the corner. We would race to the living room window facing Myrtle Avenue to see Dats' facial expression before he got into the garage. That way we could determine what kind of mood he might be in. Randy usually was the first one to the window, and that didn't change that day. I didn't race because I was cooking.

"Dats is coming," Randy shouted from the living room.

"He looks mad at the world."

Most of the time he was upset about something. When he was pissed off we stayed out of his way. And Lord knows, don't mess with his dinner. He always believed if he worked, no matter what mood he was in, he should be able to sit down to a good dinner. He felt nothing should ever get in the way of his dinner being prepared properly.

One time, he beat me with an extension cord because I burned the chicken trying to fry it the way he liked it. I had red marks on me for two weeks. That was the last time I really messed it up.

I heard the garage door close. It was very slow, and always sounded like it was about to fall off the hinges. I checked the stove to make sure everything was in place. I hoped that he wouldn't be too upset at my tardiness in preparation as long as the food was good.

Mom was nervous.

"Corey, how long before you're finished?"

"Not long," I quickly replied.

As she came to the stove and looked in my pot where I was boiling the potatoes, she rubbed her fingertips together like she always did when she got nervous. Everybody loved my mashed potatoes. I knew I wouldn't go wrong there. I wanted to make fresh green beans, but time had run out, so I went for the frozen ones instead. Sometimes I told everyone they were fresh. Everyone swore by them, too. My trick was the seasoning. First, I would boil a cup of water. Before I'd add the frozen green beans, I would add a chicken bouillon cube and let it simmer for exactly one minute with the cover on the pot. Then I would break the green beans apart from each other. That's why it's important to take the beans out of the freezer ten minutes before you begin to boil your water. That way, the beans are naturally thawing. If you throw them directly into the pot from the freezer you kill the beans' taste. After a minute, I'd put the beans in the pot one at a time and put the top on. I would let them cook for exactly five minutes. It was perfect. There were two reasons why I liked to cook: one, it gave me time to think; two, I had this notion that if I could cook meat from an animal real good, then human meat would be a cinch. Both species bled. This way, I figured, when I found out who was responsible for molesting me, I would chop them up and cook them. Or if I could outsmart that person, I could catch them off guard, tie them up, and cut one part of their body off at a time and let them watch in pain while the body part boiled in water. It was equal to the physical pain and mental anguish I had experienced for five years.

Over the kitchen sink were two small windows. Mom had dusty, white cotton curtains on the window, but I could still see Dats at the top of the garage stairs. He would always stand there for a minute, looking around to make sure everything was clean and in order in our small backyard. It was really only a walkway as far as I was concerned. He'd go from that top fifth step to the fourth, and get a better look while he continued to scratch his hair.

He would always greet Mom with a wave of his hat, because she was usually in the kitchen cooking. But he really couldn't tell who was in the kitchen, unless the person inside opened the curtain when they heard the footsteps on the stairs. He would even say hello when he was mad too, but would only manage a slight grin, not a full teeth and gum bearing smile the kind he would have after a night out with some tramp.

He waved to me with his hat. Saying "hey, Dats" under my breath, I nervously waved to him and glanced over at the pots as the meal was just about ready. He'd made it to the bottom of the stairs and pressed his nose on the window to get a better look at the stove. This was his silent way of asking if dinner was ready. Well, I was cooking, and his rules for Mom didn't apply at the moment. That is, as far as me giving him that `ok' sign to say everything was ready. I knew if I didn't hurry, Mom would take it out on me after Dats yelled at her.

Mom was an imposing woman. She was almost as big as Dats. She stood six feet and weighed one hundred and eighty pounds all muscle. Well, not quite as muscular as when she was NCAA Division I shot-put champion at Fordham University. She hurt her shoulder her freshman year. She also threw the javelin, and was the star of the varsity basketball team for three years.

Her scholarship was in track, but they convinced her to play basketball since she'd played in high school and had done well enough to get scholarship offers for that also. To say she was physical was an understatement. She loved track. After she graduated she met Jim, my Dats, who at the time worked nights as a mechanic at the local bus company in the Bronx and going to school in the day, full-time.

One day while doing overtime, Dats went to do repairs on a bus that had broken down. Sara, my Mom, was on that bus. They fell in love, got married after Mom graduated the next month and moved to Albany.

Mom wanted to try for the Olympics, but chronic shoulder problems wouldn't allow her to throw the shot-put or play basketball at such a high level again.

Mom was still very strong, though. She ran regularly and did aerobics, pushups and situps.

One time when Dats came home drunk and smelling of another woman's perfume they had a fist fight. When she met him at the dining room door, he started pushing her back as far as the kitchen entrance. Then with one punch she knocked him back five feet. Dats was out cold, because he bumped his head on the dining room wooden table while heading toward the floor.

Dats was from the Bronx. He had five brothers, and grew up practically on his own. His family was very poor. All he wanted was to work, go to school and get out to more peaceful surroundings. Since Mom was born in Albany, and Albany was considered "country" by New Yorkers, Dats went for it. He immediately got a job with the local bus company, Capital District Transportation Authority, as a mechanic. He worked days initially, but sometimes he had to go out at night to fill in for people. He hated that because he liked everything to be in a certain rhythm. Even so, he still managed to attend school part time and earn his Bachelor's degree in communications.

As Dats came in, Mom stood behind me with her hands on my shoulders. I looked at Mom's hands as she touched me. I remembered that horrible night when I was molested that the person's right hand was on my right shoulder holding me, while their left hand held my hand from fighting them off. My right hand was pinned under me, and my screams couldn't be heard because my head was buried into my pillow while my mouth was taped.

But it couldn't possibly have been Mom, her sex organs wouldn't allow it.

Mom was nervous as she spoke to Dats.

"Hi Honey, guess who cooked?"

Dats was half smiling and half frowning as he glanced down at me while I smiled. His grey cotton work uniform was a little dirty. Sometimes he would shower and change before he left work. That day he didn't.

"Now, let me guess," Dats said sarcastically, in a commanding tone that seemed to always carry throughout the entire house. He put his old, beat-up, brown Stetson on top of two old newspapers and two two-year-old telephone books that sat on top of our old steam radiator near the wall, next to the kitchen back door. At six feet-two, he was a little taller than Mom. For someone who didn't exercise, he kept his thick frame in decent shape.

"Corey, what did you cook for dinner ol' buddy?" Dats asked as he used his thick hand to lean on the radiator for a moment.

Dats sat in his favorite chair at the end of the table, close to the kitchen door. He turned his back to me as he took off his black, oil-stained boots.

"So what did you cook?" Dats asked again, in a condescending tone. I glanced up at Mom who was still standing behind me, nervous. I felt like bashing him upside his head. He pissed me off when he stood over me like some drill sergeant. He never cooked or did anything around the house. Then I rushed about checking my pots.

"I made mashed potatoes, fresh green beans." I figured, why not hype it up. They wouldn't know the difference. Oops, I said to myself. Right where he was bending to take his left boot off was the small trash bucket. And right on top were the empty packages the frozen beans came in. I ran from near the stove around the other end of the table, because Dats was blocking the shortest way. Then I lifted Dats' hat where old papers were sitting under it.

"Mom, why do you keep all these old papers?" I promptly threw two newspapers in the trash, covering the empty frozen food packages. I pushed the trash way down, making sure it couldn't be seen.

"Dats' hat will smell if he sits them on moldy paper."
I danced with joy back to the stove and peeked in the oven.

"And our meat for the day is a big surprise."

Dats stood, smiling that 'I don't care' smile.

"Some of it's baked right?" Dats said with cockiness.

"Yes, you could say that," I said with pleasure.

"Well, it better be good," he groaned as he walked toward the kitchen entryway, carrying his oily boots.

"Honey, where are you taking your boots?" Mom asked.

Staring in space, Dats replied, "Oh, I don't know. Hi, Babe."

Dats gave Mom one of his rare kisses on her cheek. This usually meant a wild evening of sex. They continually missed dinner, and would stay in bed for the night. Some hollering, moaning and groaning would follow. Dats would send Mom on a food voyage in the middle of the night.

Mom and Dats kept a padlock on their bedroom door when they were gone. They also had one on the mirrored cabinet that was in their room. My brothers and I tried many times to pick the locks. Dats escorted Mom to their room.

"Keep the food warm, Corey," Dats said with a big grin and a wink.

"Sure Dats," I said with a broken heart. I wanted them to eat the cat.

Randy waltzed into the kitchen with Tony. They both had changed from their school uniforms. Randy had put on a pair of old faded blue jeans that he had pressed and given a sharp-looking crease. His tight-fitting, white, crew neck T-shirt enhanced his already large muscles. His sneakers were old, low-top, white leather Converses, but he kept them clean. Tony had on some old, wrinkled, brown cotton pants and a grey sweatshirt. The shoelaces on his old, dirty white skips were untied.

"You know what they're gonna do now," Randy said as if it were routine.

Tony was right there, bright-eyed, wanting to know all the details.

"Are they going to make that slapping sound?" Tony asked, dumbfounded.

He didn't know anything. I knew what I knew because I would stay up late watching Dats' Playboy Channel after he went to bed. When I didn't understand something, I'd sneak a peek at Dats' old Playboy books in the garage that he thought he hid from everyone. Everyone except me. There was this store downtown that I called the Pink Pussycat. It had all these whips and other gadgets in the window that I would look at whenever I went for a bike ride. Downtown wasn't but about a mile from where we lived, so it didn't take long.

Randy and Tony slowly tiptoed to the bedroom door to eavesdrop. Dats had locked it from the inside. Randy was smiling, and waved for me to come over and listen.

We could hear moaning. We tiptoed into the dining room and smiled and giggled at this.

Then Tony motioned for us to go back and listen again. We were leaning on the door. The moaning and groaning was more pronounced. Mom must have said ten 'oh baby's' in a row. We were pressed against their door, really trying to listen. I thought it was locked. Tony and Randy stepped behind me, shoved me into the door, started giggling and ran as I fell inside the room. Dats hadn't put the lock on securely.

"What the hell is going on, boy?" Dats yelled.

"Corey, what are you doing?" Mom screamed as she quickly covered herself and Dats who was under her, laying on his stomach. I slowly stood from my knees.

"What . . . I . . . I . . ."

I was afraid for a minute, but more intrigued by their positioning. I'd never seen this in the books or on the Playboy Channel before. Mom was on top of Dat's butt.

"Tony and Randy . . ." I mumbled nervously.

"So you want to see, huh?" Mom asked sarcastically, while grinning.

I really did, but said, "No, Mom, no."

She used her hand to raise up and fix herself on Dats' butt. She let the covers drop from her shoulders, keeping her bottom half covered, exposing her large breasts. Then she raised up on her knees and turned frontal to me. I couldn't believe my eyes. Below her waist I noticed something protruding out. I got a sick feeling in my stomach. I wanted to run away, but I was frozen and couldn't move.

Dats was thrown for a loop.

"Honey, what are you doing?" Dats said in shock.

"He's ten, he knows."

"You're of age now. You know what it's like, don't you, Corey?"

Mom had terror in her eyes. I started to get scared as I gradually backed up, mumbling.

"No, no, no."

"Now get the hell out of here!" Mom shouted while pointing to the door.

I stumbled and ran out of the room. I pushed Tony and Randy out of my way as I ran for the bathroom. I fell to my knees, raised the toilet seat and vomited.

Randy and Tony laughed as they watched me upend my guts.

When I raised my head, Randy and Tony had stopped laughing as Mom stood behind them with her arms folded, angry. She was wearing black pants, an old burgundy Fordham sweatshirt and her slippers. "And you clean it up. As a matter of fact, clean the whole bathroom and our bedroom after you finish your dinner. And after that, go to bed!"

Mom was in my face, pointing her index finger as she talked.

"And don't you ever come near my bedroom again when that door is closed! Do you understand?"

"Yes, Mommy, I didn't mean anything, they pushed me."

"You just said you fell. Which lie is it?" Mom snapped.

"Yes," I said. I glanced over at Tony who pointed at me and smiled in delight at my predicament. For the first time in a while, I sensed a bit of sympathy from Randy, who popped Tony upside his head and motioned for him to stop teasing me as Mom walked away. Even so, payback is a bitch.

Dats even came out of the bedroom and showed some concern. He had put on his navy blue pants and an old, dingy looking, white T-shirt. His white tube socks got wet from the water on the floor. "You all right, Corey?"

I had this pitiful look, but I wouldn't let myself cry as I answered.

"Yes, Dats . . . Are you ready to eat now?" I asked. I was still one up on everyone. But it almost didn't matter anymore.

"Yep, but wash up before you touch the pots." He went into the kitchen.

I slowly stood as Randy and Tony watched. I let the warm water run down my hands to my fingertips. I washed them several times, then I washed my face. Then Randy stepped inside the bathroom, closing the door.

I was drying my face and looking into the small twelve-by-twelve mirror that hung from a wire spring attached to a nail above the sink.

"What did you see that made you sick?" Randy asked with a concerned look. I was still looking into the mirror while the hot water ran. Randy shook me softly on my shoulder, and I looked at him through the mirror. I turned the water up almost full blast so that nobody could hear.

"Corey!" Mom was calling me from the kitchen. "You aren't finished in there yet?" Mom yelled.

Dats sat at his favorite chair at the head of the table. A few feet to the right was Mom and Dats' bedroom.

"Honey, don't be so hard on the boy," Dats said. I heard this from the bathroom, as I turned the water off. I turned to get the towel from on top of the small brown hamper behind Randy. I cut my eye at him as I dried my hands. I threw the towel down on the hamper and walked to the kitchen. As I passed by their bedroom, I strained hard not to look. Randy was mad at me for not telling him what I saw. He stayed behind in the bathroom, slowly washing his hands and face.

"Honey, where is that ol' cat of ours?" Dats asked.

"I don't know," Mom replied as she opened the kitchen back door and called Max.

"Here kitty, kitty, kitty." Mom held the screen door open for a few minutes, and a fly got in. The sun was beginning to fade.

"Shoo fly, get out," Mom said as she swiped at the fly.

The doorbell rang. Tony ran from the kitchen entryway to the front. He almost fell going through the dining room door. We had a rug in the hallway that he got his feet caught on. The hallway had stairs leading up to our second floor apartment, where some strange people lived for six years. Who knows, maybe it was somebody from up there that molested me.

Tony peeked through the curtain on the front door leading to outside. He could see a huge man wearing a blue flannel shirt and old blue pants.

"It's Uncle Henry," Tony yelled. I went to the kitchen entryway. Uncle Henry hoisted Tony high into the air as he made his way through the dimly lit hallway. Before he entered, he always wiped his big feet. He had on his dusty brown work boots. For being a big man, he was light on his feet. He held Tony's chest high with ease. Tony's foot accidentally hit the dining room picture cabinet near the wall closet to Randy's bedroom. They stopped.

"Oops," Uncle Henry said, smiling, and wasn't overly worried about it breaking.

Tony climbed down from Uncle Henry's arms and knelt to pick up the picture. "I got it," he said.

"Come on in here. Just in time for dinner," Dats said.

"Why you eating so late?" Uncle Henry said.

"It's not late," Mom answered, rather suspiciously.

"I know why you're eating so late," Uncle Henry said with a huge grin.

Dats started to laugh. Mom was setting the table.

"Are you eating, Henry?" Mom said.

"Ah, what're you having?" Mom turned to me apologetically and ran her fingers through my hair.

"Ask the cook here," Mom said with a smile.

"Hi, Uncle Henry," I said, forcing a half smile.

"What's the matter, son, you look like you ate the cat? Where is that little cat?" Uncle Henry started to bend down and look under the table for it.

"Here kitty, kitty. Well, where is he?" Mom said.

Uncle Henry sat in the chair in front of the refrigerator on the side of the table nearest Dats. Uncle Henry was a big, muscular man. Even his face was chiseled. He needed a lot of room, and there wasn't much between the table and refrigerator. He almost had to squeeze in. There definitely wasn't enough room for anyone to walk by while Uncle Henry sat there. He was Mom's only brother. They were one year apart in age. While Mom went off to Fordham, Uncle Henry stayed in Albany and worked at the Port of Albany. It was mostly seasonal work. He loaded banana crates off the boats daily. Mostly the big men got picked to work there. Usually it took a person several times to get picked out of the twenty to forty men who showed up at the Port of Albany each day, trying to find work. The work was hard, but it paid fifteen to twenty dollars an hour, depending on how long you worked there.

It was perfect for Uncle Henry. He was intelligent, but more street-smart than anything. He finished high school, but barely. Mom's parents divorced when she was eight. Living with their Mom wasn't easy. Mom told me they got as much as anyone else. But Uncle Henry needed more guidance from a male figure. With him being a free spirit, anything was open territory. Even with this freedom, he managed to stay out of the way of the long arm of the law. He occasionally would get into fights. Mostly he won, even if it was two or three against him. When he was young, he once went to a local gym and tried to box to relieve tension, but soon realized he didn't have the heart to fight for the sport of it. He would rather fight in the street. He wasn't a big drinker either. Only occasionally would he and Dats go out to tie one on. I was surprised he had had a few drinks before he came over for dinner that day.

I hesitated to answer Uncle Henry's question, because Mom and Dats were present. It's not like we shared secrets or anything like that, but he was just a caring person. I did trust him somewhat.

"I'm fine. I hope you like dinner." I really didn't mean for Uncle Henry to eat cat, but unlucky for him he was in the wrong place at the wrong time. Oh well, I hoped it was as good as the Chinese make it. It was a delicacy to them. I found this out by reading up on the Chinese culture.

"So what's for dinner, kid?" Uncle Henry beamed. He called me kid mostly when he had a few drinks. That day he was a little more tipsy than usual.

"It's a surprise. I think you'll like it." I was starting to feel better. Uncle Henry always was able to put me in a good mood, even when I wanted to be somber

"Whatever you cook is good for me, Corey. In fact, anything anyone cooks is good for me," he said with a resounding laugh.

Mom put the green beans and potatoes in separate dishes. "Tony, Randy, come and eat," she called out.

Tony and Randy raced from the living room to the kitchen. Whoever got there first would get to sit in the prime seat at the other end of the table, opposite Dats. Randy won the race as he bullied Tony out of the way, knocking him on the floor after Uncle Henry got up to let them by. Randy, at thirteen, was already 5'11" and one hundred and eighty pounds. He was definitely big for his age.

Randy had grown very fast. At eight years old he was 5'7" and one hundred and sixty-five pounds. We thought he had some sort of disorder, but the doctor told us he was just growing fast. As far as I was concerned, he too became a suspect of my horrible ordeal. He already was watching Dats' old porno video tapes that he'd left around occasionally when he was too drunk to remember to put them away. Plus, he was reading Playboy Magazine at age seven. Not only that, but one time I caught him in the basement reading a gay magazine. Randy had gotten the magazine by bullying a rail-thin gay man who had tried to pick him up just outside the local candy store.

"Too bad," I teased when they got to Uncle Henry.

"I beat both of you." I was already in the hollowed chair. It was hollowed for a couple of reasons. One, Dats would tell us only the leader is to sit at the head of the table, and two, our kitchen was small. It seemed even smaller when we had company. If we sat on the sides of the table, we had to keep getting up if somebody had to get by. This was a pain in the ass.

Mom frowned at the way Randy bullied Tony.

"What's wrong with you, Randy? You coulda hurt Tony. Now sit down and eat!"

"Ah, they were only having a race like any boy would do," Uncle Henry said, laughing.

"I don't care. If he gets hurt, who's gonna have to take care of him? Me!"

She slung some mashed potatoes on Uncle Henry's plate.

"I'll take care of him if I have to," Uncle Henry joked.

"About the only thing you'll take is another drink or another one of your women."

"When are you going fishing again, Henry?" Dats asked.

"That's a good question," Uncle Henry replied, in thought.

"You want to go with us again, Corey?" Uncle Henry asked.

"No, I'm not getting sick again for nobody."

"That motion sickness is a bitch, isn't it?" Uncle Henry said in a teasing tone.

"Watch ya mouth!" Mom shot at Uncle Henry.

"Next time we should try a lake or pond," I suggested.

"You got it. I know the perfect place, Revena Lake. Maybe you'll catch something this time. But you gotta remember to keep your line in the water and not fall asleep," Uncle Henry said, laughing.

"I couldn't help it. All I wanted to do was keep still. Sleeping was the only way I could deal with the sickness."

"You're always getting sick, just like earlier," Tony said with envy. He hated the attention being on me.

"What happened?" Uncle Henry said with concern. There was a moment of silence as Uncle Henry waited. He scanned everyone's eyes for a second.

Finally, Mom spoke. "He was peeking in our bedroom and saw something he shouldn't have." She slammed potatoes on my plate. "And he better not make the same mistake twice or it'll be his last!"

"Naughty, naughty Corey. Caught ya doin' it, huh," Uncle Henry said with a joking tone.

"They pushed me into the door . . . I, I mean I fell then they pushed me in the room." I realized it was useless to plead my case.

Mom sat, and Dats blessed the food with his usual two minute thanks to God. We dug in and all you heard were forks and knives.

I watched as Mom uncovered the meat pan from the oven. My eyes followed the pan as she put it between the burners. She removed the top, and her eyes gave a questioning look.

"Mmmmmm, that smells damn good," Uncle Henry said with great anticipation.

"Corey, you should become a cook. I've never smelled such a good aroma before, and I've been to some of the finest of fine restaurants!" Uncle Henry said.

"I am going to be the best cook in the world," I blared out. Little did they know, my ingredients would consist of the human anatomy. "Uncle Henry, I'll come up with some of the best dishes you've ever heard of before," I said, bragging.

Mom studied the meat for a minute. "Corey, what kinda meat is this? It looks like you hacked it to pieces."

"Had to, it wouldn't stay still. You should of seen it before I skinned it." Everyone looked at me as I rambled.

"You know the best way to eat meat is without the skin. It carries all the germs and fat. Plus, Mom, I know you don't really like to have to cut the meat, so I did the honors."

"Yeah, but you can't tell which is the breast and which is the thigh," Mom said as she used the long-handled fork to take each piece out of the pan while examining it. All eyes were on the meat.

Mom passed a huge slice to Uncle Henry. "And gimme anything left over too," Uncle Henry said, as he wished time would pass fast. He glanced at his wristwatch. Uncle Henry was never one to have a dull moment. He had a hooker waiting, and that was that.

He could get any decent woman he wanted, but chose 'them' instead. But who am I to judge. I chop up cats. He loved the noncommittal part that came with dealing with a prostitute.

There was something strange that Uncle Henry said. I don't know if he slipped and tried to cover it up or if he was joking. But I know what I heard, and it made me think.

"Them 'nice boys' I run into at the job from time to time would love to have some of this meat!" Uncle Henry said as he ate his cat meat.

He had a strange look on his face with this comment. Randy gave me a strange look. Mom had finished putting meat on everyone's plate.

I watched as everyone began to eat.

"Corey, this meat is very tender," Mom said pleasingly.

"What did you put in it to get it this tender?"

"Pussycat juice," I said with a laugh that Uncle Henry followed.

"All right Corey, don't get smart with ya Mom."

"Yes, Dats."

"Mom, where's Max?" Tony asked while cutting his eyes at me.

"He'll be here in time for dinner." How right Mom was, I thought.

Randy finished his small serving first.

"This is the best meat I've ever tasted. Never had anything like it before," Randy said with wide eyes.

"Can I have seconds?" Randy asked as he held his plate up to Mom. I grabbed Randy's plate and put my meat on his plate. "He can have mine, Mom. A good chef always eats last." What a joke, I thought.

I sat and thought. Learning to cook animals would eventually lead me to learn how to cook humans.

I sat and watched as everyone cleared the meat pot clean. I heard my laugh echoing through my mind about how sick they would get if they only knew that Max was the entree for that day.

"All right, this is the last piece," Uncle Henry said as he held it up in my direction. I forced a smile, "Oh, no thanks. I'll make some more another time. I'll never forget the recipe."

I kind of wanted to stop them while they ate, but I couldn't.. They were having such a good time, I even thought about trying some. But that was okay, they deserved to enjoy their last cat supper. By preparing that cat dinner, it initiated some kind of payback for my woes. Out of everyone, Tony was the only person who I could not suspect, because when the attacks occurred he was just a toddler. No way could it have been him.

Tony couldn't have molested me. He wasn't big enough, nor would he know what he was doing. That left everyone else a suspect, as far as I was concerned. Even Randy, because he was big enough, and after I caught him reading those gay magazines I knew he knew what to do. After watching Mom on top of Dats in that disgusting position, I knew both of them were capable of molesting me.

Child molestation is wrong, and someone had to pay. But I had to be sure of who was going to pay. I hadn't ruled out the people who lived upstairs. They were strange, only coming out late at night. Someone from up there could have easily snuck down stairs at night and attacked me. Mom always left our brown wooden dining room door unlocked. I always thought that was kind of strange. Especially since those people weren't our relatives.

CHAPTER TWO

SOMETIMES AT NIGHT I would tiptoe to the upstairs apartment to listen at the front door. I have never seen the faces of the people who live up there. A couple of times, if I could stay awake, I would hear them leaving at about one o'clock in the morning. As I sat there waiting for everyone to finish eating, I looked at our dining room door and thought about going up there. But I decided to wait. Plus I had those stupid chores to do.

I remember when I'd come home from school early and watched a lot of unsavory people going in and out. Dats couldn't have known this was going on because he'd be at work when all the activity took place. They'd come up the ten porch steps, ring the second floor bell and be buzzed in without them even having to identify themselves. Once in a while, someone would come at night and follow the same procedure. Whoever it was up there didn't want to disturb Mom and Dats, so they knew never to have heavy traffic at night. Mom and Dats were the only ones who could be rowdy at night. Sometimes when I would sneak and stay up late, I would hear a cracking in the wood. I was very sure there would be about a hundred cracks, then it would stop for a minute or two and start up again.

The sound was coming from a room that was upstairs, between our living room and the side bedroom. But I still had those stupid chores to do. I knew the time was getting close for me to do what I was gonna do, so I had to get upstairs somehow to check things out that night. If I didn't do it soon, my situation would only get worse, because my night visitor was becoming more frequent. I'd learned to just lay there and take it, never knowing when it was going to stop. Once I tried to fight back, but whoever it was overpowered me.

Tony always seemed to be gone after the first time it happened. Either he was spending the night at a friend's or he was asleep in Mom's bed.

Randy and Tony stood at the bathroom entrance as I scrubbed the toilet.

"How's the shit smell?" Tony whispered teasingly. He'd heard curse words from Mom and Dats' arguments, so he felt safe in whispering them. Mom and Dats were in the front watching television with Uncle Henry.

"So are you gonna tell me what you saw Mom and Dats doing, Corey?" Randy whispered, almost desperate.

I stopped mid stroke, paused a second, rolled my eyes, then started back to cleaning. Randy grabbed my hair from behind, pulling my neck back as I held on to my brush. "Am I gonna have to tell Mom what you tried to do to me the other night?" Randy said, yanking my head back further.

"What? I didn't do anything," I said pleadingly.

"Keep your voice down," Randy whispered with agitation. "Are they looking this way, Tony?" he asked. Tony smiled, and shook his head no. Tony loved to see me get taken advantage of. I really believed he wanted me dead, if for no other reason than just to have me out of the way. Randy twisted my arm behind me. I wanted to yell out, but as hard as he was twisting, he probably would have broken it.

"Do you want me to tell Mom and Dats about the gay magazines you've been reading?"

"Those are yours," I shouted.

Tony looked at Randy with a questioning eye.

"Say what?" Randy said as he pulled harder on my black hair and twisted my arm.

"Whose magazines are they?" Randy repeated.

"Not yours, not yours." I did all I could not to yell out.

"I couldn't really see anything, they were covered!" I said.

"Well why did you barf?" Randy asked.

"I don't know, I just got sick because I was afraid. Let me go, please let go!"

Randy finally let go, and kneed me in the back. But I had had enough.

I threw down the sponge, began to scream, stood up and charged after Randy as he walked toward Tony, bowling them both to the floor. Blows were flying from every direction. Tony was beneath Randy as I continued my barrage of punches. Randy was almost helpless.

"Ouch! Ah, get off me you punk," Randy shouted. I heard footsteps coming from the living room, fast. I knew my time to whip them was almost up.

"Corey, what are you doing? Stop!" Mom said as she attempted to pull me off.

I was biting Randy's neck at the jugular vein and wouldn't let go.

Uncle Henry ran in, moving Dats out of his way.

"Henry, he's got him by the neck," Mom said frantically.

"Hold it, don't move nobody," Uncle Henry said with caution. Uncle Henry had spent time in the armed services, special forces and managed to learn and become very good at karate. He learned all the body's vital points. I knew them too. He had taught me.

"Now, Corey, you remember how we talked when we went fishing what would happen if the jugular vein was broken?"

"Mmmmmmmmmm," I replied as I held firm with my grip.

"Now, Corey, I'm just gonna kneel down to talk, okay? Don't move or you could kill your brother. We know you don't want that."

A tear rolled down my cheek. I was tired of it all. For five years I'd been talked about and molested, all by someone in my own home. Where would I find peace, I thought.

"Corey, I know it's hard, but this is your brother," Uncle Henry advised.

Tony was squirming, because he was on the bottom of well over two hundred pounds, with my seventy pounds, and Randy's one hundred and eighty.

"Tony, be still?" Uncle Henry pleaded.

Mom knelt down to me and rubbed my back.

"Honey, please let him go," she begged.

"Corey, we'll go anywhere you like, just let ya brother go. You could get in a lot of trouble if you hurt him," Uncle Henry said. I slowly let go. Not because Uncle Henry said we could go anywhere I wanted, but simply because this was my brother. No matter what he'd done, he was still my flesh and blood.

Randy rolled away from me and started to punch me in the face several times.

"Hey, Randy, stop it now!" Uncle Henry shouted.

"Randy, if you don't get off that boy, I'll beat ya ass. Where's my cord?" Dats growled.

Uncle Henry finally pulled Randy off me. Dats went into the kitchen, looking for his extension cord.

Blood dripped from Randy's neck. I wondered if I'd broken the vein.

I was in trouble, I thought. I'd really get beat. Tony gasped for air as he leaned on the dresser in the dining room, trying to catch his breath.

Mom looked at Randy's bite marks.

Dats returned promptly. He couldn't find his extension cord, because I had hid it earlier that day just in case he didn't like the dinner and got mad and wanted to beat me. He had a wooden board instead. It was three feet long and two inches thick.

"You okay, son?" Dats asked Randy.

All Randy could do was glare at me with the evil in his eyes, but I blankly stared right back, afraid of what I might do to him next, and he damn well knew it.

"Come into the bathroom. Gotta put some mercurochrome on these bites. Come on!" Mom said, pushing him into the bathroom.

"Corey started it!" Tony said, frightened as Dats stood before him with the board.

"Get in ya room," Dats said as he pointed the board at Tony in the direction of the basement door. "And don't come out the rest of the night."

Uncle Henry went into the bathroom with Mom and Randy, shaking his head in disbelief as he walked by me.

"You okay, Randy?" Uncle Henry asked.

"Yeah?' Randy said softly, obviously shocked.

"What were you doing to Corey?"

"He was cleaning the toilet and he got mad 'cause we were looking at him and he just jumped on me."

"Now come on, is that the whole truth?" Uncle Henry said incredulously. "You guys are always after Corey about one thing or the other. I knew he was gonna get tired of it sooner or later," Uncle Henry said with a sigh.

"Ouch! Mom, that stuff burns," Randy said. Mom pressed the gauze and kept pouring.

"Shut up, boy, you need this so your neck won't get infected. And I want you to leave Corey alone, you hear me?"

"But Mom, I wasn't . . ."

"Whack!" was heard as Mom slapped Randy upside the back of his head.

"Mom, that hurt, c'mon."

"Boy, don't lie to me. You can get away with it with ya Uncle Henry . . . *(whack!)* . . . and that's for lying to him. And don't let me ever catch you lying to me."

Randy thought the operative word was 'catch'.

"Yes, Mom," Randy said.

Uncle Henry rubbed Randy's head and said, "You'll be okay." Upon leaving the crowded bathroom, Uncle Henry walked Dats back to the living room.

"That boy of yours is a regular barracuda. Wish I had his heart, I would have been heavyweight champion of the world," Uncle Henry said.

I stood there waiting to be told what to do next.

"Dats?" I said, emotionless.

Dats turned back to me and said softly, "Go to your room, son." I was surprised I wasn't gonna be beat.

Uncle Henry smiled and winked as I made my way toward the basement door.

"Oops, no, you go into my room and watch TV," Dats commanded softly.

I was shocked. Dats had never allowed me in his room when they were in there. That day I was allowed to enter without anyone there. "Yes, Dats."

"Oh, here." He gave me the padlock key, flipping it in the air to me. What had gotten into him, I thought.

"I know you had a bad day, son, don't make it worse by going in my dresser drawers."

"Yes, Dats," I replied.

Uncle Henry put his huge arm around Dats' shoulder and turned him toward the living room.

"We need a drink tonight, whatdaya think?" Uncle Henry asked.

"I think I need one after that. But, I gotta get up for work in the morning, so I can't stay out too late."

Mom heard all of this, and spoke to them from the bathroom.

"You know you don't go out drinking on work nights, Jim!"

Uncle Henry snickered as he pointed with his thumb toward the bathroom, walking in the living room.

I was about to pass the hallway area where the bathroom was on my way to Mom and Dats' bedroom. It felt like I was moving in slow motion. I really didn't want to look into the bathroom, but my nerve wouldn't allow me to be a coward and look away. I looked as I passed. I continued to walk, but I felt like I was frozen in my footsteps.

Mom worked on the side nearest the bathtub as she applied the gauze to the left side of Randy's neck. I could hear my footsteps in my head and my heart thumping for more action. He was lucky I didn't finish him. Uncharacteristically, Randy only tilted his head slightly to the right, showing he'd had enough; for the time being, that is. Randy wasn't one to give up. But then, neither was I. He'd fight until he won the war. Randy cut his eyes toward me quickly, then looked back down, staring into the small sink at the bloody cotton balls Mom used to clean his wounds.

I felt his heart thumping as I passed by. Mom only glanced at me. Her eyes were questioning where I was going, but she already knew I needed to be allowed into her room at that moment to pacify me for the first time in years.

CHAPTER THREE

MOM, DATS AND UNCLE HENRY sat in the living room watching the eleven o'clock news. The newsman had just reported a story on how a child accidentally shot his baby sister. They were still thinking about what had happened earlier. Uncle Henry slouched further down on the couch that was lined with torn plastic in different areas. Even though he was slouched, his head could still rest on the mirrored wall behind the couch. The couch was upholstered with plastic because it was made of crushed white velvet with green floral designs. The plastic had been on for ten years. It was worn and torn in several places, and it was a disgrace. It was definitely time for a change. Too bad there wasn't enough money to get it reupholstered and new plastic applied. Uncle Henry played with a piece of the torn plastic in the seat area.

"Henry what the hell are you doing? The plastic's already in bad shape. Don't make it worse. I don't know what's taking Jim so long to get it fixed," Mom snapped.

Uncle Henry rubbed his index finger and thumb together, indicating money.

"Why don't you get it fixed, Sara? You work," Uncle Henry said with a slight grin.

"Shhh," Mom said as she watched TV intently.

"Did you see that? Guy killed his whole family. Crazy world out there," Mom said.

"I don't know about that drink, Henry," Dats said as he stretched in his favorite chair. "I'm gettin' awful comfortable," Dats said.

Dats bought the chair the same time as the couch, along with the love seat. Only it was more worn and didn't have any plastic covering it. Dats took it off years ago when he started complaining that the plastic made his ass sweat and inflamed his hemorrhoids. The only reason anyone believed him was because the doctor wanted to remove them, but Dats wouldn't allow such an operation on his precious butt. At any rate, he was always complaining about one thing or another. He said if God put them there, God would take them away.

Dats sat in, ate in, and slept in this chair or, I should say, 'his' chair. We never sat in this chair while Dats was home. If we forgot he was home and were sitting there and he walked toward the living room, all he had to do was give us that 'look' that said, 'get up, and I mean now!' It was positioned directly in front of the television, about ten feet away. From his chair he could look from the living room through the walkway of the dining room to the kitchen. He couldn't see all of the dining room or kitchen, but we could never talk loud if we were in one of these rooms dogging him out. He constantly watched the activity in the house, or he'd fake sleep and listen. Dats swore he slept better in his chair than in his bed. The chair was a rich green velvet that was easy to get comfortable in. Even Uncle Henry could fit in this chair, but it was a tight squeeze because he was so large. But for Dats it was perfect. Dats kept a colorful knitted quilt on the chair that Mom made years ago. He would either wrap his upper torso in this quilt or sit on it when his hemorrhoids felt extra sensitive. Dats never washed the quilt. I can't imagine how many times we smelled fart gas from that quilt.

Dats smelled the quilt.

"Honey, when's the last time you washed this?"

Mom looked at him in a sarcastic cross-eyed manner, then rolled her eyes. Then she sat up and looked at the dirty white lamp shade that sat on the wooden end table with white marble top. This end table sat between the love seat and Dats' chair. Even the plastic that covered the lamp shade was dirty.

"The last time you put it in the hamper. You too lazy to put it in, I'm too lazy to wash it!"

Mom had to keep lifting her legs because she was wearing shorts and her legs were sweating on the plastic. It wasn't hot outside yet because April in Albany was cool but that damn plastic made you sweat no matter what time of year it was. Plus Mom was a sweaty person.

The plastic on the love seat was in the best shape of all the furniture. Mom leaned over to the almost ceiling-high window and peeked out of the blind to see who was blowing their car horn across the street.

"Why don't they go ring the doorbell? It's stupid to sit out there blowing the horn waking up the whole neighborhood," Mom said.

I don't know if we're gonna get that drunk tonight, Henry I'm kinda tired."

"You don't need to drink on a work night anyway, Jim. A bunch of crazy people out there," Mom said as she watched two gunmen shooting at the police on the news.

"Sara, please, I don't need it," Dats said.

"Look at that, honey. You don't need to go anywhere," Mom

said as she rubbed her legs from her toes to her thighs successively, then stopped.

"Wow, look at that. Them Albany police don't play," Dats said with excitement.

The color in the TV set kept going from black to color, again and again.

"I thought I asked you to get the color fixed?' Dats said pleadingly to Mom.

"You didn't give me no fixin' money."

"I did, I left it on the kitchen table the other morning before I left for work. I left thirty dollars . . . yes I did, now."

"Well, I didn't see it. Maybe one of the boys got ahold of it. Probably how Corey bought that meat we had for dinner. Boy was it good."

"It sure was," Uncle Henry said with appreciation as he rubbed his washboard stomach under his blue flannel shirt.

"That boy can cook," Uncle Henry said, praisingly. "Maybe he's gonna turn out to be a cook or something. Nah, I see him maybe writing cookbooks and creating, not working for someone. He's too independent."

"Yeah, he almost killed his brother earlier this evening?" Mom said with concern. "If he's not careful, he'll wind up in jail before he turns eleven."

"Oh, they just had a little fight. All boys fight. He'll be all right. They're always teasing him and picking on him because he likes to cook and do things boys don't normally do. Sooner or later he was bound to explode," Dats said, brushing it off.

"What happened to him in your room anyway?" Uncle Henry asked. Mom and Dats looked at each other with straight faces briefly, then Dats cracked a smile.

"Well," Dats looked around as if to see if anyone was listening. He even got up to see if anyone was in the bedroom next to the living room.

Little did they know, I was listening to their every word. I was in the basement in the front part of my bedroom. I had snuck back downstairs to my bedroom. Part of the room was partitioned off with this long, brown, sliding, curtain-type cardboard that pulled together from one side of the room to the other. I would often close off the front part of the room from the back where our beds were. The basement room was about thirty feet long and twenty feet wide. The door to the entryway of the room was made of cheap wood. We had to fold a piece of cardboard and put in the doorknob area to keep it closed.

We never forgot to close it because our house was on the corner of Grand Street and Myrtle Avenue. It had a major sewer line on the corner. We once found a rat as big as Max, dead, in the basement bathroom.

Tony was fast asleep, so I could easily close the bedroom area off. He was a hard sleeper. It would take an earthquake to wake him--the devil that he was. Directly below the upstairs living room radiator I had cut a small hole, about three inches in circumference. If Mom and Dats were talking loud I could hear them as far back as the dining room. I cut the hole in the ceiling after I was molested. I used a small razor and Dats' drill to make the hole. I kept it hidden by putting the wood back in the hole after I used it. The wood fit snug back into the hole. The only thing between me and them was the dirty, gold, wall-to-wall carpet that ran from the living room to the kitchen entrance.

If they were shouting I could hear them as far back as the kitchen. I had this five-foot steel pipe that was open from end to end that I kept hidden behind the radiator in the basement.

I would sit in this cheap, green, floral-colored, cotton-pillowed chair that had its back against the radiator. We had another one that was similar to it against the wall. There was a thirteen-inch black and white TV that sat on a portable stand near my bedroom door. I would sit in 'my chair', like Dats and his living room chair, to watch TV. 'My chair'. Ha! What a joke. My green chair sat in front of the radiator almost, but not quite below a sandy-colored bookshelf that Randy had made in shop class at school. There were all kinds of books jammed on the shelf that Mom, Dats, and me had already read, from *To Kill A Mockingbird* to *Raisin In The Sun*. The bookshelf was positioned between two windows. Through these windows you could look right onto the concrete sidewalk and see only the legs of someone walking by and our front stoop. If you looked across the street, you could see people walking sometimes. The windows were almost always dirty, except when I took the time to clean them. The windows were always closed shut, even in the summer because it was the coolest place in the house during the hot months. It was like we had an air conditioner on.

I sat in my green chair and listened. To my left, near our TV, was a large, floor-to-ceiling, brown cabinet that housed our clothes and some of Mom and Dats' clothes. It was twice the size of an average refrigerator. Attached on the left front door of the cabinet was a full-length mirror. I looked at myself momentarily. In front of the chair was a small wooden coffee table that stood about three feet from the ground. I propped my feet on the table to listen more comfortably. After glancing at my Mickey Mouse watch, I started thinking about sneaking back to Dats' bedroom before he realized I was not there. If I didn't, I know he'd wonder. Especially since he knew I always wanted to get into their room, and with them finally letting me in, why wasn't I there. But I still needed to sit and listen for a while longer. My heart began to race a little faster.

It was weird how I could hear everything being said in the entire house through a stupid five foot long steel pipe. But on the other hand, it was great because this same stupid pipe was going to help me find out who was molesting me, no matter how long it took.

They weren't saying much. They were always careful with what they said at all times when they were in the house or in the car, or anywhere around us.

One day they would slip and I would finally know.

"Well, he saw ya sister and I having sex," Jim said.

"That's all?" Henry said. "I mean did he actually see you humping?"

"Yeah, a couple of times!" Jim said as he hesitated to answer.

Jim was still smiling and he glanced at Sara.

"Not exactly."

"Well, what does that mean?" Henry said.

Henry became a little irritated at Mom and Dats holding out.

"What were you doing?"

Then it hit Henry.

"Noooo! He didn't see that."

"No, not really," Sara said in a bothered kind of way.

"Look he shouldn't have come in there anyway He knows our room is off limits," Sara said.

"He said Tony and Randy pushed him in the room," Jim explained.

"No wonder the poor kid went off on his brother, his cup runneth over. Now you got him in your room watching TV like it's okay, and tomorrow you'll be locking the door on him," Henry said.

"That's right," Sara said pointedly.

"Well you better watch how you treat him because he didn't want to let Randy go. I saw it in his eyes. I've seen crazed men in the service before. They get that look in their eyes and they're capable of going on rampages and killing everyone."

"Oh Henry, please, he's just a boy."

"You'd be surprised how kids think sometimes. I mean, with all the violence in the street and on TV you can't get away from it," Henry said. Sara waved her hand at him dismissively.

In complete silence, I tiptoed up the basement stairs. It was dark. I had to feel my way toward the area facing the dining room door near the table. I deliberately stuck my head around the dining room hallway area and noticed that the living room door was closed. The door was made of thin wood squaring around glass. With the sheer white curtains attached to the door from top to bottom, plus it being dark, it would be hard for Dats to see me sneak back even if he was awake; as long as I was quiet. And that I was, quiet as a rat pissing on cotton. As I entered Mom's room, there was a small glow of moonlight inching through an opening in their dirty brown cotton curtains. I gently sat on the foot of their bed and sighed softly.

All I could do was pick up the remote and flick the channels on the TV. At least they had cable. After years Mom finally let Dats get it. But only after he got a good raise from his job. If that's true, I wondered why they didn't fix the torn plastic on the living room furniture.

I flicked to a James Cagney movie and kept it there. I glanced at the old papers, magazines, bills and other junk Mom had packed on the sides of the TV.

I cut my eye toward their bedroom doorway, then I looked to my left toward the head of their bed. On the floor near their famous cabinet, Mom had a pair or her black high-heeled shoes. My eyes stopped at the cabinet. I really wanted to see what was in the locked cabinet. I had to think, how?

The wind blew our kitchen screen door and it opened and slammed shut. I scanned Mom and Dats' long, wide dresser that was on the side of the bed, closest to the entrance of their room. I looked at myself in the large mirror that ran from one end of the dresser to the other. The mirror was big enough to see yourself only if you stood or sat on the side of the bed near Mom's locked cabinet. Through the mirror's reflection, my eyes keyed in on the padlock on the cabinet once again, then back at the junk on their dresser. To them, it probably wasn't junk. But they kept all their jewelry, Vaseline, keys, papers, old pictures, several lotions, hair grease, combs and brushes all so unorganized that it looked like a pig sty. My eyes shot back to the keys.

"Keys," I said softly.

I looked at the locked cabinet again, then back at the doorway again. I would have to move fast if I was going to look inside the cabinet.

I tiptoed quickly out of the room to the dining room inlet way, which was also the kitchen entryway. I peeked around to see what

Mom and Dats were doing. The door to the living room was still closed. I rapidly tiptoed back into the bedroom and went to the dresser where the keys were. I started to breathe heavy. I gently picked them up and ran back to the doorway to peek again to see if the living room door was still closed. It was. I quietly hurried back to Mom's side of the bed, turning down the TV as I walked by so that I could hear if anyone was coming. I noticed my palms were sweating a bit.

I bumped my shin on the wooden post at the foot of the bed as I turned the corner, making my way toward the cabinet.

"Ouch." I fell in pain on top of a pile of clothes that Mom and Dats had coming out of their bedroom closet. I held my shin and looked towards the bedroom doorway, hoping nobody would hear me as I gasped to keep from yelling out in pain. I rolled over on all fours and got up slowly, using the bed as support. I swiftly made my way to the cabinet. I looked at myself in the long mirror that was attached to the side of the cabinet door, which the lock was bolted to. I breathed deeply. Beads of sweat were forming on my forehead and my armpits were getting sticky. I slowly tried the first padlock key; it didn't work.

"Dammit!" I whispered. I looked at the bedroom entryway quickly, then I fumbled with the next key.

"Bingo." Victorious music played in my head as I was about to turn the lock open. A sense of victory, finally. Then as I turned the lock open, I heard loud voices from the living room.

"Yeah, don't come back in here slobbing all over me either. N'you know you gotta get up early for work tomorrow," Mom said, warning Dats.

Mom's footsteps were getting closer. It was easy to tell when anyone was coming in or out of the kitchen, because years ago Mom and Dats had this hard plastic put on top of the carpet. The plastic ran from the kitchen entrance to the dining room hallway door.

"Shit!" I whispered.

My body tensed up. Mom was almost at the kitchen. After inhaling and exhaling deeply, my mind relaxed then my body followed. In one swift motion I was able to snatch the key from the padlock, run to the foot of the bed and continue watching the TV on the dresser. Using the remote, I flipped from channel to channel. The eleven o'clock news was just going off. Mom waited at her bedroom entrance with one hand on her curvy hip and the other leaning against the refrigerator with her back to me. She yelled back at Dats.

"Jimmy, I'm not playing, don't wake me up when you come staggering back in here," Mom warned. Mom only called Dats Jimmy once in a while. Mostly when she was irritated. He hated being called

Jimmy.

"It's Jim," Dats shot back.

"If it's too late, he'll stay at my place, woman," Uncle Henry said, chuckling.

Dats and Uncle Henry made their way out of the kitchen back door. They shut the thin wooden door. Uncle Henry looked back through the small window that was the same width of the door, but only about a foot long. The window was located near the top of the door. Uncle Henry smiled and waved at Mom, who was frowning. Uncle Henry slammed the screen door as he ran out.

They were gone. Mom, standing in the same place, pivoted towards me. My breathing was back to normal. I was doing all I could to avoid looking at Mom's crotch area to see if there was a bulge there like Dats had. I was a little confused. How was Mom a Mom with a penis, I thought. Cutting my eye towards her, I could see there wasn't a bulge. I studied her, or him, from it's feet to it's face as she, well I guess it's Mom, stood there. I wondered because I had heard on the news about men having sex changes. But then she had a penis, so was Mom really a man? No, can't be. I decided to keep my cool. Being down here she could overpower me, and who knows, maybe molest me.

Nope, I'll stay cool and let her make the first move. if I had to, I was prepared to put up a good fight against her. She took one slow tep toward me while flicking the kitchen light off. The on/off switch was on the wall behind the refrigerator. The only light was coming from the TV. Mom took two more steps and was beside me with her arms folded and a mean look. I took a deep breath.

"You okay?" Mom asked in a caring tone.

I closed my eyes, said a one-second silent prayer, sighed, and opened my eyes.

"Yes, Mom."

"I forgot to put the food away. Do you want to eat, Corey?"

"No thanks, Mom."

Mom rubbed my head with compassion for a few seconds. I looked up at her, then down to my feet. She stopped rubbing and headed towards the kitchen. She reached behind the fridge and switched the light back on. I thought, why did she turn it off in the first place, or was it a mistake? For then, it was what it was.

She made her way over to the stove and lifted up the top to the meat.

"Phew. Smells like cat shit!"

"It's probably from sitting out, that's all. It needs to be in the fridge," I said.

"I don't know. There's not much left. I might as well leave the rest for Max." I could hear Mom raking the few small pieces of bone and meat into Max's dish. It sat near the fridge on the side adjacent to the kitchen back door.

"Corey, where did you get that meat from?" I began flicking the channels fast, searching for an answer in my mind.

"And how did you pay for it?" I could've easily turned in Randy and Tony for stealing the thirty dollars off the kitchen table to cover myself, but I was not a rat.

"I used some of my savings from my piggy bank."

"What store did you get it from? I want to try it sometime."

I put the remote down and went into the kitchen. I had to think of a quick lie.

"At the Ta . . ." I almost said the Tamarkies, which was an Italian grocery store on the corner, two blocks away. I couldn't say there because they knew me and Mom so well.

"From Price Chopper."

"Who took you there?"

"I walked." She believed this because I sometimes would go out on my own and take a walk to Lincoln Park, which was about a half a mile from our house. Mom and Dats used to take us there after a snowstorm and we'd ride our toboggan down what everyone called 'Dead Man's Hill'. It was a hill in Lincoln Park that from top to bottom measured a steep forty yards. At the foot of Dead Man's Hill was the street and a sidewalk that encircled a hill. This high grassy hill led to two football fields and two baseball diamonds. This small grassy hill was like a bowl surrounding the football and baseball fields. That's why we referred to this section of the park as the "bowl". The bowl was about a mile in circumference. Usually during the summer months and before it got too cold, people lined the manicured hill to watch whatever sport was going on. Sometimes the city held rugby games when there weren't football or baseball activities.

Next to the bowl was a large, public, round pool, and a pool house for people to change. During the summer months it was packed with vacationing school kids and adults.

Sometimes when I went running, I would run around the bowl and swimming pool. Combined, it was about one and one-quarter miles. At ten o'clock at night this wouldn't be good to do in gangland Los Angeles, but in pristine upstate Albany, New York it was quite alright. I really didn't like lying to Mom or Dats, or anyone for that matter, but this time I had no choice or I would have been caught.

Actually it was fun lying, just to see what I could get away with.

"How much was the meat?" Mom asked, calmly.

"Ten dollars for everything." I remember Mom and Dats paid ten dollars for Max, his food dish and litter box. They got their money's worth.

After what I did this evening, I felt sorry for Max. It wasn't his fault, it was theirs. They were the ones mistreating me.

"Next time let me know you're going to the market, I'll drive you. I know you like to walk, but you're still a little boy Okay?"

"Yes, Mom."

"When I finish washing these dishes I'm going to bed." She glanced at the small radio clock on top of the dirty white refrigerator.

"It's twelve o'clock," Mom said, surprised it was that late. "You go to bed, you gotta get up for school tomorrow."

"I'm still not feeling so well, Mom."

"You're going to school. You just told me you were feeling okay."

"But Mom."

'Don't but me. Now go to bed!"

As I turned I smiled and looked toward the basement door. I turned on the dining room lights. As I was about to open it, I heard footsteps coming down the second floor stairs. I quickly turned the lights off and inched open the dining room door that led to the hallway. It was dark and I couldn't see their faces because they were headed out. As the front door slammed, I closed it and sat in the corner with my back to the basement door. I sat there in the dark until I saw Mom go to bed. It was strange but one of the guys was carrying a ten-speed bike. I guess if he didn't have any other transportation, he did what he had to do.

I had been in that corner for the past thirty minutes. Mom was asleep, and she slept hard. It would take a Mack truck and bulldozer to wake her up.

I sat with my knees to my chest and my hands folded across them, making sure that my legs didn't slip from under me. My legs were starting to cramp a little from sitting like this for so long. Randy's door, across from the dining room table, was slightly ajar. He was a hard sleeper like Mom. I heard Randy moving around in his bed.

"Shit!" I never believed in sleepwalking. Seeing it done on TV in old Abbott and Costello movies was one thing, but to have Mom talk about Randy doing it was another. I thought it was a joke until I saw it firsthand. Was he awake or sleepwalking? In a minute I would know. He walked towards me. I leaned on the small radiator to my left. The radiator was beneath a ceiling-high window that was on the side of the dining room table opposite Randy's room. He gradually and methodically made his way towards the radiator. I could only see a silhouette of him as he slowly made his way towards me. It was almost as if he knew exactly where it was, even in his sleep. He loomed large as he passed by me. I crunched down in the corner, about two feet away from the end of the radiator. Suddenly Randy stopped walking and stood for a moment. He stood motionless. Then like he did when he used the bathroom, he placed his hands in his pants and took out his large penis. I couldn't see it, but I'd seen it many times before because he would moon me from the front, especially after he read one of those gay magazines he keeps hidden in a torn out space in his mattress. He thought nobody knew about this hiding place, but I did. He placed his left hand on the wall, leaned forward toward the radiator and held his penis with his other hand and began to urinate. Little sprinkles were hitting me as he pissed hard for about fifteen seconds. He finished and wiped his hands on his pj's two times, as if he'd washed them and now was drying them. He stood momentarily. I slowly wiped my shoulder and arm where the piss had splattered. He turned and slowly walked back to his room. There wasn't a heavy smell of urine, so I doubt that he pissed there regularly.

"Ran . . ." I whispered.

He didn't answer. I knew he was sleepwalking. Could he have sleepwalked to my bed and molested me, I wondered. Randy got back into his bed. I would have to wait for awhile again before I could make my move upstairs I wanted to make sure Randy wasn't trying to fake sleepwalking to catch me.

I hid in the corner, still making sure Randy was asleep and not trying to fake me out. Maybe he saw me when he got up and pissed on the radiator. I don't know. I heard a noise coming from Mom's room.

"Shit." She was getting up. I was stuck there in the darkness in the corner. Surely she would see me when she turned on the kitchen light to make her way to the bathroom. On came the light in the kitchen. She turned the corner from her room, and all I could think of doing was to kneel. I dropped down and bumped into the doorknob. I know Mom heard it, but she must have really had to go because she didn't break her stride into the bathroom. She quickly closed the door.

She cracked the bathroom door. I could hear her urine running hard into the toilet.

"Randy, is that you?" she asked loudly through the cracked bathroom door.

"Huh?" came from Randy's room as he was awakened.

"Dammit," I whispered as Randy sat up in his bed. He was awakened by Mom's call because in his bedroom there was a thin pipe door that only had a flimsy wall and tile separating it from the bathroom. The head of Randy's bed faced that door.

I ducked sideways, closer to the pee-stained radiator. All Randy had to do was turn his night light on and he would see me. I couldn't go any further to my left because the dining room table was right in front of the radiator, and I was too big to fit between the chair legs to crawl to the safer end of the dining room. I probably would have a hard time fitting anyway, since Mom had three boxes of junk stored near the head chair and the china cabinet along with dishes that, according to Mom, were too good to be used on a daily basis.

Mom flushed the toilet, turned off the light and felt her way toward Randy's room in the darkness. Randy was still sitting up with his feet on the floor when Mom got to his doorway.

"Randy," she whispered. My heart began to race. Mom felt around for the wall light when he didn't answer. I began to breathe hard. I knew she would see me once she flipped the light on. I heard the switch go 'click', then saw a flash and it was still dark.

"Shit, damn light blew," Mom grumbled. I was saved by the light. I sighed silently. Mom went to Randy's room. She laid him down on his bed. He was still asleep, sitting up. He groaned as she laid him down. I could see the silhouette of Randy reaching for Mom, trying to pull her down with him.

He must have been having a dream about sex because he humped toward her a couple of times.

"Randy, it's your mother I'm not part of your dream," she whispered, and looked around over her shoulder. Still not seeing me, she felt Randy's butt as she put the covers back over him. I was shocked. Mom molested me. No, she couldn've, I thought. She tiptoed to the light switch and flipped it on and off a couple of times, checking to see if it worked. When it didn't come on, she made her way back to her bedroom. I heard their old bed creaking as she climbed into it. Damn, I was sweating again and my right leg was asleep. I was deliberate as I uncoiled myself, stretching my legs out, wondering if this was the night I should try to get in upstairs. Another unexpected interruption and I would have a heart attack. I waited about ten more minutes before I made another move. Plus, I wanted to make sure everyone was back asleep. I slowly turned the dining room doorknob. The door creaked a little as I gradually pushed it open wide enough for me to squeeze out. The more I opened it, the more it creaked. I gently began to close the door behind me, all the way, slowly, letting the knob turn so that the lock would catch silently. I was in the dark hallway, tiptoeing towards the front door, and I stumbled over some shoes that were lined up against the hallway wall. When I stumbled, I didn't fall because I was able to hold onto the stair railway. I started to walk gently up the stairs, and they cracked about every other stair. I didn't care because one, Mom would think it was the tenant, and two, I was too far gone to turn back. The only thing that would stop me would be if the tenant was coming, and hopefully he wouldn't be home anytime soon.

I started to sweat all over, even in the palms of my hands.

I looked to my right, and on the open banister area were two dusty ten-speed bikes. I'd never come up these stairs before. I could smell something. It was strong. I always wondered what that smell in the hallway was from. I took a deep breath and slowly turned the doorknob. I felt the sweat running down my armpits. It was locked. But I still had the keys from Mom's dresser. I only brought the two I didn't recognize. Hopefully one of them would work. I pulled both of them out of my pocket. I tried one and it didn't work. There was a car across the street blowing its horn.

"Who the hell is that?" I whispered. Surely this horn blowing would wake Mom and Randy if it kept on. I stood there for a moment to listen for footsteps from Mom or Randy. Finally, I heard the car door slam and tires screech as the car sped away. I put the correct key into the lock and turned it delicately. It was so quiet you could hear the steel lock through the hallway. The lock rubbed the loose siding and finally it was unlocked.

I carefully pushed open the door, and there was a dim red light on in the kitchen. The light hung from the yellow painted ceiling. The smell was horrible. I covered my nose and mouth with my hand as I crept in. My adrenaline flowed swiftly. I stopped as I reached the four-chaired table. It sat below the red light that hung down from the ceiling. The table was pushed against the wall. There was soft instrumental music playing at a low volume from the antique radio clock that sat on the table. The table had four neat and clean place settings, but dirty dishes lined the small sink on the opposite side of the refrigerator. It was a small kitchen, proportioned like ours, but a lot neater. No newspapers piled on the radiator. I couldn't figure out what the smell was. I opened the door on the stove and found nothing. The stove was between the refrigerator and the sink. I glanced on both sides at the floor to see if there was a dead rat or something. Nothing. There was a back door that had cherry colored cotton curtains on the window that occupied the upper half of the door. The wooden porch beyond the door was hardly ever used, except for some storage boxes that I saw as I peeked between the two curtains. To the right, about ten feet away, was the bathroom. The door was closed.

Little did I know, Justin was on his way home. He was about five minutes away on his ten-speed bike. Justin loved his bike. It kept him in shape, and it didn't draw attention.

I opened the door and felt around on the wall nearest me, looking for a light switch. There wasn't one. I took baby steps past the toilet, thinking maybe there was a linked chain light similar to what we had in our bathroom on the first floor. I felt for the sink and finally touched it. I sighed and reached above the sink near the wall that had a medicine cabinet attached to it. On the door of the cabinet was a small mirror. I felt the mirror by running my fingers up to the top. Nothing. I slid my hand from right to left. Nothing. I took my hand down and was about to give up on this room. Then I decided, one more try. I remembered our chain was a little higher above the mirror, so maybe theirs was like that. Bingo. It was there. I breathed a little heavier as I slowly pulled the chain down, its links rubbing the side of the container. This was even a little too much noise for me. You could hear it throughout the apartment. As the bright light came on, I squenched my eyes because I'd been in the dark for so long. I looked around and it was spotless. It was so clean I couldn't imagine why there was such a smell running throughout the house. I heard a car driving up the street on the side of our house, Myrtle Avenue. I turned the light off just in case it was the tenant, because there was a window that was on the wall above the bathtub. There was no shower stall. I cautiously tiptoed out to the back porch door to see if Dats was pulling into the driveway. He wasn't. I turned and faced the front of the apartment and went to check things out, but I knew it was getting late and Dats or the tenant might be coming home soon.

Justin was at the corner of Pearl Street and Madison Avenue.

"The hell with it, I'm up here now," I whispered. I felt my way around as I tiptoed past the kitchen table, feeling the chair tops with one hand and the refrigerator with my other hand as I guided myself between the two in the dark. At the end of the table was a bedroom, just off the kitchen. The door was closed. I reached above my head with my right hand and slowly inched open the door. There was a residue on the door. It felt dry. I smelled my fingers and it smelled like baby powder. That was strange because I'd never heard any kids running around up here. I could see a lot better in this room because there was a tall street light on the comer of Myrtle and Grand. A beam of light shined through the venetian blinds. There was a twin bed with what looked like children's clothes folded neatly on top. I moved cautiously toward the dresser at the foot of the bed. On my way, I kicked a child's toy. It started to chime. I grabbed it. I banged on it a couple of times to get it to stop, but it wouldn't. If I didn't hurry it would wake the entire household. I put it under the pillow on the bed and it wasn't as loud. It finally stopped chiming. I looked around and there was a large picture of a clown on the wall opposite the bed. I wanted to hurry to get to the remainder of the apartment. I'd left the door slightly open and as I turned fast to leave, I didn't know it was as close and "whack," I bumped my nose. It hurt. I checked to see if there was any blood or if I'd broken it. Nothing. It hurt more from the surprise of the blow and the fact that I was scared as hell.

I carefully left the room, since this room was directly above Randy's. There was another bedroom to the left in the hallway leading to the living room. I turned the knob on the door and started to open it. I only opened it about an inch when I noticed it was padlocked. But why, I thought. There was only one person living up here. I walked slower towards the living room because the floor squeaked with every step. The street light glowed a little brighter through the venetian blinds. I could see better than the first bedroom. There was a black leather sofa, a coffee table, and a TV. It looked to be pretty clean. I touched the windowsill and it wasn't dusty. Their living room was a few feet smaller than ours. There was a large steam radiator separating the two large ceiling-high windows on the Grand Street side of the apartment. That wretched smell was even stronger. I had to hold my nose. It was coming from inside the last room, off of the living room. I heard a groan. It startled me because I thought I was alone. My heart pounded faster. The closer I got to the doorknob, the more my heart raced. The moans were more prominent now. Whoever was on the other side of the door knew I was there. I opened the door to a slight crack, just enough for my eye to see. Light shined in through the bedroom window from the Grand Street light pole across the street.

"Oh my God," I whispered in terror at what I witnessed. There was a boy, who could not have been older than me, tied up and gagged on a twin bed. He wore white underwear. I walked in. I couldn't see clearly, but he looked pale. He was thin. He had had a bowel movement at least a couple of times. His hands and feet were tied with leather at the four bedposts. The leather was so tight there were brown circles around his wrists and ankles from the dried blood. The boy lifted his head as I knelt towards him. I noticed that I had put my hand in some kind of powder near where the boy was laying. I smelled my hand. It was baby powder. I took the gag out of his mouth.

"What's your name?"

The boy gasped for air. I began to untie the boy's wrists. Then I heard footsteps coming up the front porch steps. I ran to the window and looked. It was the tenant.

"Shit!"

I froze for a second. Then I thought that for the boy's own safety I'd better retie him. I did so. I darted to the apartment front door. The boy's moans became louder, almost strained. I looked down the stairs and could see this large man opening the front door. I was trapped. The hallway light would automatically come on whenever the front door opened at night. I went to hide in the bedroom and saw my fingerprint on the door. There wasn't time to wipe it off. I heard heavy footsteps coming up the stairs. I ran inside. I went into the bedroom off the kitchen. There was a closet next to the dresser. It was full of toys. I stayed on the floor, damn near pissed on myself, and closed the door as the apartment door opened. Lucky I was skinny and could fit. I had to cover my mouth because I was starting to hyperventilate. I was scared, but if I didn't control my breathing I would surely be caught. I'd heard Mom and Dats talking about this man as if he were a killer. He flicked on the kitchen light. He didn't move for a few minutes. Then he slowly walked toward the bedroom door that I was hiding in. He put his hand up against the print, measuring the size. Then he ran to the bedroom off of the living room. I'd heard him go inside. I heard the garage door lumbering open as a plane flew above. Was that Dats coming? Did the plane trip the automatic door? Sometimes when planes flew lower than normal the garage door would open. Something to do with the airwaves is what the garage people told Mom and Dats.

"Shit, they need to get that door fixed," I whispered to myself.

I couldn't wait any longer. I had to get out of that closet. I quietly made my way to the bedroom door. I peeked toward the living room. I didn't see anyone. All I could hear was interrupted moaning coming from the bedroom.

I hurried toward the stairs. I knew he would hear me if I walked down the crackly stairs. I heard footsteps coming from the living room. I had to do something, quick!

I hopped on the banister and slid to the foot of the stairs. Justin came to the doorway and listened. I crawled to our door in a flash. I opened it enough for me to get in. Justin closed his door. I was safe as I crawled inside and tiptoed down to the basement. I was huffing and puffing. I walked around in a circle for a minute, wondering if he saw me.

I pulled my eavesdropping bar from behind the radiator, stuck it into the hole above and listened. Tony was fast asleep with the divider closed. I listened intently and didn't hear any footsteps. Obviously a plane had caused the garage door to open. I sighed in relief.

Justin entered the boy's bedroom, looked around, then sat on the foot of the bed. His immediate thoughts went back to his childhood days.

He envisioned himself in his tiny bedroom, being taken advantage of sexually by his father. He covered his eyes and hung his head. He knew he needed to clear his mind and take care of the business at hand.

CHAPTER FOUR

"OH, COME ON, have another one. What the hell, you're out now," Henry said joyously as he chugged down another Heineken.

"Yeah, why the hell not," Jim said as he glanced at the large clock above the mirrored wall of Tibby's bar.

"Hey, Tibby's give us another round," Henry yelled gleefully. Tibby's first name was John, but everyone called him Tibby. It just had a better ring to it. Tibby was the owner and operator of Tibby's Lounge on Central Avenue in the uptown section of Albany. The Harris' lived on the south end, better known to Albanians as Lower Albany. Tibby had owned the place for ten years. He was medium height and had a thick build. He'd been through three wives and had a new wife of one year already. He had two children by his first wife when he was twenty-five and one each during his two short-lived marriages following his first. He was a bit worn looking from the long nights, but he still looked good, which is part of the reason his new twenty-six-year-old wife wanted him. The other part was his money and stability.

"Boy you're gettin' prettier and prettier every time I see you," Henry said, flirting playfully with Tammy, Tibby's wife.

"Thank you, Henry," Tammy said.

"He treating you okay?" Henry asked, fatherly.

Tammy patted Tibby on his shoulder affectionately as he passed two beers to Jim and Henry.

"Couldn've picked a better husband," Tammy said as she lovingly ran her finger's through his dark, curly hair. Tibby smiled and his hazel eyes glowed as he looked at Tammy. His stare was followed by a sexy wink. Using both hands, Tibby leaned on the bar in front of Henry. Tibby wouldn't look Jim straight in the eye. Word around town was that Tibby was Corey's real father.

"How ya doin', Jim?" Tibby asked, painfully. Henry could see the tenseness in Jim's eyes.

"Well, bottoms up, Jim," Henry said as Jim slowly downed his bottle of Heineken. Jim wouldn't answer Tibby.

"Beatcha again," Henry said victoriously as he slammed his bottle on the wooden bar, almost breaking it. He belched.

"Wasn't racing," Jim said as he suddenly became serious. Tibby went to attend to one of the customers at the other end of the bar. Henry knew he had to keep the peace.

Tammy went to serve a customer at the other end of the bar. Soft oldies by the O'Jays played on the juke box throughout the small cramped bar. Patrons ranging from age twenty-five and up occupied the six round tables that were in a section of the bar.

"You shouldn't let some stupid rumor come between you and Tibby. You guys used to be friends," Henry said. Jim turned to Henry and looked at him with an evil eye.

"He was always Sara's friend before I knew him."

"Look, you took a blood test and every other test to prove Corey is yours, forget about it. Enjoy the music." Henry began to snap his fingers and move to the smooth beat. A trashy looking woman who stood next to him began to move with him.

"Wooo, now this is what you need, Jim."

Jim rolled his eyes and peered down at Tibby who was at the far end of the bar. Tibby glanced at Jim and grinned. Jim gripped his beer bottle tighter with every wrinkle of Tibby's smile. Tammy stopped to wait on Richard. Richard was an older guy who frequented Tibby's especially when he knew Tammy was there. He and Tammy had become good buddies and talked. Secretly Richard had a crush on Tammy. "Hey, how's my bundle of joy today?" Richard asked.

"Fine," Tammy said as she served Richard his usual draft beer.

Richard admired Tammy as he spoke. "How did such a pretty thang get hitched up with an old crow like Tibby?"

"Oh he's not that old. He's only forty-four."

"Well I'm with what ya daddy said--Ya sellin' yaself short!"

"Tibby takes very good care of me."

"So can I," Richard replied with a big smile.

"But you're an old fart too," Tammy said laughing.

"The older the wiser. See I'll know what to really do for ya."

Tammy rested on the bar with her face in her hands and her elbows on the bar.

"Yeah how's that?"

"Wouldn't you like to know," Richard said smiling.

"That's okay. Tibby's good enough for me."

"No way. He'll never be good enough for you."

Richard downed his beer and left.

"See ya later Richard."

"Next time babe."

Tammy liked the idea that Tibby had money. However, she fell for him before he had money. When Tammy was a teenager she would sneak into his weekend parties at the local Mason Hall. She tried college and other odd jobs before she realized Tibby was the love of her life. They had a sixteen-month old son named Jason.

Tammy spotted the way Jim peered at Tibby.

"Hey, Jim, what's on your mmd?" Tammy asked.

"What're you doin' in a place like this, Tammy?"

"I'm here with my husband."

"He doesn't need you for this. Besides, what are you even doing with him, he's scum."

"If you're gonna keep talking like that, I'm outta here." Tammy wiped the bar in front of Jim. "What is it with you about him anyway?"

"Before your time," Jim answered sharply.

"Anyway" . . . Tammy shrugged and was about to move on.

"So how are the kids?" Tammy asked, changing the subject.

Tammy stayed in front of him.

"Good."

"Hey, Jim, come and dance," Henry shouted as he grooved to the up-tempo beat of The O'Jays on the jukebox. Jim waved him off without looking as he continued talking with Tammy.

"The kids are fine, gotten bigger, eatin' up the house. Tony's really starting to learn fast. Randy's becoming a regular ladies' man. I don't know what I'm gonna do with him."

Jim looked over both his shoulders and to the back, then shielded a side of his mouth so that his next statement wasn't heard. "Think he's already having sex, too."

Tammy raised her eyebrows and had a slight grin.

"How old is he . . . thirteen?"

Jim nodded.

"Boys will be boys," Tammy said.

"I got him a box of condoms a long time ago--Magnums."

"Whooooo, ummmm," Tammy exclaimed.

"How'd you know he was having sex?"

"Came and told me."

"He ever have sex education at school?"

"Nah, only what he's learned from all those books he reads."

"What books?"

"Books he gets from the library"

"Jim, I notice you didn't say how Corey was doing." He shot Tibby a quick look at the other end of the bar.

"Well, he's doing fine. Loves to cook."

"Yeah, at least his wife won't have to worry about that."

"He cooked the best . . . I don't know whether to call it chicken, beef or whatever." Jim shouted to Henry, "Hey, Henry, what was that meat Corey cooked for dinner?" Henry laughed hysterically and said, "pussy meat." The same girl he was dancing with from earlier gave him a playful slap on his arm. Tibby made his way to Tammy and Jim.

"Looks like you two are having your own little party," Tibby said jealously.

"Oh, now don't be jealous, Honey, just friendly conversation," Tammy said.

With envy, Jim said, "Yeah, just gettin' to know your new bride a little better, Tibby. The same way you know my wife."

"Who?" Tammy said, interested.

"Oh, didn't he tell you? He and my wife grew up together. Why, Tibby, that's not nice. I'm a regular customer and good friend, and your wife doesn't know you grew up with Sara?" Jim said sarcastically. Tibby was a bit unnerved.

"Pour me some of that," Tammy went to reach for Jim's glass. Jim gave Tibby a wicked look.

"No, I want Tibby to get it, Honey!" Tammy realized she was in the middle of something very bad.

"Look, Honey, why don't you cover that end of the bar," Tammy said, trying to separate the two.

A small man entered and shouted, "Hey, Tibby, gimme two quick shots in my favorite glasses."

"Oh, hi Charlie," Tammy said, relieved and ushering Tibby halfway down the bar. "Go take care of Big Mike, okay, Honey?"

Jim took a look at the wall clock. It was three in the morning. Jim downed the Heineken that Tammy had just gotten him.

The front door swung open again. This time Justin Lord, a tall, clean shaven, muscular man in his mid-twenties entered. He let the door slam, which got the attention of Tibby, Tammy and several others sitting at two tables off to the side of the door. Jim did a double take on Justin, and smiled as Justin walked towards him. Justin's walk was confident and erect. He wore black cowboy boots. His tasteful all-black attire added to his presence. His black, rayon, button-down shirt and black jeans were neatly pressed as usual. He never dressed flashy. In his black eyes you sensed this man was no one to mess with, and his deep base voice seconded that. Justin nodded at Tibby.

"Gimme my usual," Justin demanded, winking at Tammy as he passed her. Tammy forced a smile.

"Hey, Justin, how's everything?" Jim said, sounding a tad intimidated.

"Faucet's still leaking at the apartment," Justin said.

"You gotta let me get up there in the evening sometime, I'm working during the day," Jim said apologetically.

"I'm too busy at night."

"Anything else wrong up there?"

"Few things," Justin said as he turned his shot of Jack Daniels up while he slowly scanned the room.

"No new troops in here tonight," Justin said with disgust.

"What kinda work do you do anyway, Justin?" Jim asked.

"Did you get the rent?" Justin asked, totally diverting Jim's question.

"Yeah, always on time, too."

"Good." Justin put his glass softly on the bar and was about to remove his hand as Tammy got the glass to take it away. He smothered her hand with his as he gently took hold of it and the glass. His eyes shifted from her eyes to her tight white turtle-neck sweater, which enhanced her small breasts, then to her tight black jeans covering her small hips, and back up again.

"How you been, cutie?" Justin asked.

Tibby was forced to wait on a calling customer, but glanced back and forth from the customer to Justin's hand. Tibby's eyes shffted to Tammy's eyes. She looked nervous, but smiled and glanced at her husband.

"I'm fine," Tammy said, looking down at the shot glass.

"Did you want another?" Tammy asked. Justin smirked toward Tibby, then looked at Tammy with his piercing eyes.

"Whenever you finish with that old crow, let me know. I wouldn't want to see you go to waste." Tammy tried to take the glass away, but Justin wouldn't let go.

"I'll have another later." He let go of the shot glass. "Oh, by the way, nice tan, sexy. But you look a little thin. Is Tibby feeding you enough?"

Tammy turned and inconspicuously glanced into the bar mirror, wondering if it were true.

Tammy would occasionally go to the tanning hut. Earlier that day was one of those occasions.

"Wash it out for me . . . please." Justin was not one to say please to anyone. For him to bestow such kindness upon Tammy was truly a gift and a come on, and Tammy knew it.

"Me and Corey will come up to fix that when you're available," Jim said.

"No kids," Justin snapped as he made his way by Jim.

Henry watched the entire exchange, and passed by Justin giving him a long, hard look. Justin gave a slight grin and flinched his toothpick at Henry. Henry went to swing at Justin, but Jim caught his arm as Tibby ran to the end of the bar and pulled out his extra long barreled .357 Magnum. He had it strapped to his side, under his full-body black apron. He wore it over his white, cotton, button-down shirt with the sleeves rolled up to his elbows and baggy khaki pants. He liked to wear black, low-cut Asics basketball shoes while he worked because they were comfortable on his feet.

"Not in here," Tibby declared.

Justin smiled and walked away saying, "Like I said, *Mr.* Jim, no Corey in my apartment."

Tibby reholstered his gun, and the patrons looking on went back to their drinks and conversations. Tibby went to the other end of the bar to a customer who motioned for him with a wave of his hand, but not before cutting his eyes at Jim. Tammy began to wash glasses in front of Jim and Henry.

"What was that all about with Corey?" Henry asked.

"Doesn't want kids in his apartment," Jim replied with suspicion.

"Why does he live above you anyway? I know he can afford to buy his own house," Henry said.

"Yeah, I wonder sometimes, too. Drives a regular ol' car most of the time, when he's not on his ten-speed bike. Probably on that bike tonight. Says he gets good exercise from it."

"Something strange about him, Jim. I'd be careful with the kids around him. Some of the guys at work think he's into some strange shit."

"He's pretty quiet in the apartment, so I got no complaints, Henry."

"Well, I don't particularly care for him and that comes from way back when I watched him grow up as a kid--stealing, loafing and whatever else he could get into. Always intimidated everyone because he's always been tall and muscular and he scares most people. Never seen him with a woman. Heard he's got plenty, but he might be into some kinky shit, too."

"I got no problems with Justin. I think Corey asks about him more than I care for. He's never met him."

"I would too if I had someone in my second-floor apartment and I never even talked to the guy much less hardly see him. Corey's a smart kid. He wants to know everything. And I don't blame him for wanting to keep tabs on the guy."

"This is one guy he won't get to investigate," Jim said assuringly.

"If I know Corey, he'll find a way," Henry said with respect.

"Hey, Tam, give us two more each," Henry said.

"Nah, come on, Henry, I gotta get up for work, and it's three-thirty and you gotta get up, too."

"Hey, I'm up. I punch in at six. No sense in going to sleep now. Just wasting time."

Tammy looked for the go-ahead from Jim. Henry waited with open arms and a big smile.

"All right, two more and we gotta get outta here," Jim pleaded.

"You got it, buddy," Henry said, and patted Jim on his back.

Two 'fine' women came up behind Jim and Henry. This was right up their alley.

"Hey, what can we do for you two vampires?" Henry joked. The two women continued to smile. They glanced at each other, then moved closer to Jim and Henry.

CHAPTER FIVE

TIBBY'S LOUNGE was closing as the last light went out inside. There were a few bums trying to get Tibby to let them back in for one last drink. Henry and Jim were carousing on the side of the building with what looked like two hookers. Both women were in their late twenties. They weren't dressed trashy, but they had that working girl "vibe" about them.

"So, what's up ladies?" Henry said, cheerfully. Henry took a closer look at the one with the tight mini skirt on.

"Don't I know you from somewhere?" Henry asked.

"You know who this is, sucker?" Sally B asked sharply.

"Is that Sally B? Oh shit, it damn sure is. Gimme a hug." Henry gave her a big hug.

"I remember when you were a little girl," Henry said. Sally B smiled affectionately.

"Where you been?" Henry asked.

"Oh, here and there, mostly New York," Sally B said in a sultry voice that matched her walk.

"Doin' what?" Henry asked.

"Don't ask," she said with a chuckle.

"Gotcha," Henry said.

"So who is this with you? Never seen her before," Henry asked.

"She's from New York. Why you askin' so many questions?" Sally B shot back.

"Well if you really wanna know, you ask," Henry said with a big smile.

"Who's that?" Sally B asked in a retaliatory way while pointing at Jim. Jim eyed the New York woman from head to toe, with a slight grin. Henry and Jim were quite drunk. Even though the girls weren't beauty queens, anything would look good. They were pretty though.

"This is Christina Johnson. She's staying with me for a while." Christina was about five feet five with very full breasts, wearing a bustier bra she didn't need. She had smooth, thick legs. Street life had stolen most of her youthful looks, but there was still a slight trace of prettiness left. No matter how small amount of beauty there was, Jim would find it and exploit it.

"My name's Jim Harris from Brooklyn, New York," he said while stumbling towards Christina to shake her hand. Jim accidentally bumped into her and held onto her shoulder for support.

"Guys had a little too much to drink tonight, huh?" Christina said in a sweet, soft, child-like voice.

"So where's the after-party tonight, Sally?" Henry said with anticipation. Sally B looked at Christina, who smiled back at her.

"Party's over at my place," Sally B said.

"Hey, I gotta be to work in a couple of hours," Jim said in a garbled voice as he turned toward Henry.

Tibby was locking the door, and Jim saw him glance their way.

"What're you looking at, scumbag?" Jim said, angrily. Tibby escorted Tammy to his new silver Cadillac coupe. Tibby looked toward Jim again and shook his head as he opened the passenger door for Tammy. He walked around the front of his car and waved his hand at Jim as he got into his car. Jim stumbled towards Tibby's car as he drove off.

"Fuck you, son of a bitch." Jim could hardly get the words out. These antics tickled Christina.

Jim looked at her and grinned. He walked toward her and put his arm around her.

"This is my girlfriend. Just so ya know, I got a mean bitch of a wife at home. So tell me right now if I need to leave you alone because I can go home and jack-off and be done with it."

Sally B smiled at Christina and spoke.

"Little rough around the edges but at least he's honest, Christina." Christina nodded in agreement and put her arm around Jim.

"Your place it is," Henry proclaimed.

"Henry, if I'm late for work, you're gonna pay me what they dock me."

"Yeah, sure pal," Henry said, playfully.

I've gotta tell Mom and Dats, I thought, as I sat in the chair staring at nothing. Then I heard footsteps coming down the stairs. I immediately got up and quietly peeked through one of the blinds. It was the tenant carrying a large, green, plastic trash bag in his huge arms. I couldn't tell if it was a body or not. I knew for sure the city trash trucks weren't coming in the morning. Garbage was picked up on Monday mornings. He looked over both of his shoulders as he took it to the sidewalk, quickly glancing at our first floor window. Then as if he knew someone were watching him, he paused and leisurely looked down at the basement window where I was watching him. Our eyes met for an instant, then I released the blind and jumped back away from the window. I stared at it momentarily as my heartbeat ran frantically again. I wondered if he knew it was me.

I slowly walked back to the window and pulled the blind open a half an inch to see if the tenant was still there. He was gone. I sighed in relief and sat in my eavesdropping chair.

He hadn't even taken the time to put a jacket on. It was a chilly Tuesday night. I thought about following him. But how? I was too small to drive, even though Dats would take me driving with him and Randy on payday. I decided not to try to follow him, instead I would tell Dats and Uncle Henry. Hopefully they would believe me and check things out upstairs.

CHAPTER SIX

"I DON'T KNOW if I should be doing this with you!" Sally B said.

"Why?" Henry asked.

"Well, I don't want you trying to get attached. My boss wouldn't like that."

"Who is ya boss anyway?"

"I can't say."

"Why?"

I just can't."

"Is it somebody I know?"

"Maybe." This caused Henry to quickly sit up in Sally B's full-sized bed.

"You don't need to live like this anyway. You deserve better. I mean, look at it."

Henry's eyes panned the cluttered small bedroom. "I mean, you've got books above the bed on a shelf. Books everywhere. Have you read any of them? Is it worth it to you for your pimp to take all the money and you live like this?"

Sally B's eyes slowly scanned the dusty desk that sat adjacent to the alleyway window. She stared at the old newspapers piled three feet high on the floor near the wooden desk. A cushioned chair with no back and a pillow as the seat sat in front of her wooden desk. The walls were covered with Polaroids of her friends, along with posters of Whitney Houston, Miles Davis, Luther Vandross, Elton John, Sammy Davis Jr., Kenny G, and Frank Sinatra. You name it, she had it plastered all over her walls.

"I mean, look at your walls. Full of all these great artists and you don't even have a stereo," Henry pleaded.

"I mean, it just doesn't make sense, Sally B. You were a queen, had so much potential. How could you just let it go to pot? Is this guy really worth it?" Sally B looked at Henry with sad eyes, no longer able to hide her pain and frustration over her plight.

"I mean, it just isn't fair, Sally B." Sally B slowly scanned her cluttered dresser with clothes strewn about. She looked at her open closet near her dresser. Her clothes were thrown on top of many pairs of old shoes that occupied the floor of her closet. On the top shelf above the hanger rack were more clothes, unfolded and dumped about. The hangers were pressed together because of all the old dresses and coats that were both hers and Christina's.

"I mean, have you ever thought about giving up this life and having kids?" This drew a sharp look from Sally B.

"Like ya friend Jim," Sally B replied as she gestured towards the closed door where Jim and Christina were.

"How'd you know Jim has kids?" Henry asked, intrigued.

"I don't," Sally B said, trying to hide that she knew something. "I mean, don't all married men have kids?" Henry straddled Sally B's lap as she lay in the bed on her back.

"No, you said that like you knew him and his kids. Come on, give it up. How do you know about them?"

"I don't," she said, trying to hide but not doing a very good job of it.

She sucked her teeth and pushed Henry off of her to his side of the bed and got up. She took her Marlboros from the small wooden night table that was the same height as the bed mattresses. Sally B searched for matches on the disheveled night stand.

Then she opened the drawer and angrily searched through some of the old papers that were squeezed into this small drawer. She began throwing the papers out on the floor, obviously nervous over Henry's line of questioning.

"Look, are we gonna do this or not? I thought we came here for sex. Isn't that what you want? I'm here to work. You haven't changed, always into my personal life. Even when we were growing up." She'd found her matches. She lit her cigarette and threw the match into her small, tin, overly worn ashtray that was bent at an angle between her dirty rotary telephone and a black Bible.

"I always wanted kids. Then after the car accident that killed my folks, I found out the blow I took in the stomach damaged me. I miss mom and dad so much." Sally B picked up a five-by-seven framed black and white photo from on top of her desk and looked at it. "Nothing's been the same since they died in that car crash. Why me? Why did I survive? To be left to live for this? I can't even bear children." She stopped, reflecting a moment. "I can't believe I sold their house they worked so hard to buy for a few measly dollars, and I blew it all on a good time."

"Sally B, I know you've had it hard, but we've taken our blows. You gotta get going, and you can start by getting outta this lifestyle."

A tear rolled down her cheek. "I need to know how you know about Jim's kids?"

She turned toward him, her eyes red and tears flowing. She wiped her eyes with the palms of her hands.

"It's Justin. Justin Lord. He told me, and he's the boss." Henry had a shocked look. Sally B sat on the side of the bed and Henry slid to her and put his arm around her.

"How'd you get mixed up with him?" Henry used his shirt to wipe her wet cheeks.

"After I blew all the money I got for the house, I roamed around New York City for awhile living on the streets. He was there recruiting. He offered me money, a roof, and a job in Albany, so I took it."

"So for all these years you've been working for him?"

"Between here and New York."

"Jeeeeese. He's got a lot of things going on, but you'd never know it."

"I never did like that guy. He's the kinda guy who looked like trouble, but you could never put your finger on it. Even when we were growing up he was very secretive. Hmmm, I wonder what else he's got going?"

Jim and Christina lay cuddled on Sally B's sofa bed that occupied most of the small room. There were black sheets covering the two small windows that were inches from the foot of the sofa bed. So close that if there were shades, they could open and close them with their feet. There was an unframed picture of Jesus above the sofa. On the night table, near the head area of the sofa bed, was a small light that was too dim to make a difference in the dark.

"Boy, oh boy, I gotta get going. It's time for work," Jim said as he glanced at his watch. He threw the covers back, and as he was about to get up, Christina grabbed him softly by the back of his neck and pulled him on top of her. She smiled shyly.

"You're a great lover," Jim said softy.

"You're so good, this one's on the house."

"Well, so are you." He rolled her on top of him. "Now I gotta go make some money," Jim said.

"Oh, come on, just take a short nap. You've been going all day and night, I bet?"

"You won the bet, but I gotta go to work." Christina again gently pulled him back, and she began to kiss him passionately on the mouth. With her sexy full lips and endless lust flying, he couldn't resist.

"Okay, thirty minutes, then I gotta go," Jim demanded.

"How many kids do you have?"

"Three boys. Thirteen, ten and seven."

"You have big boys?"

"In more than one way. My thirteen year old has the body of a grown man. His name is Randy. He's just starting to have sex. Tony's the youngest. He's a little spoiled, but he's a good kid." He abruptly stopped talking, and Christina motioned for him to continue.

"You said you have three boys."

"Yeah." He paused in thought momentarily.

"Yeah, Corey, he's ten." He paused again.

"Well, go on, what else? What does he like to do?" She held Jim tighter.

"I don't wanna talk about it anymore." Christina shrugged it off. Jim stared at the ceiling in thought.

"Hey, Jim, are you gonna be angry now?" Jim looked at Christina blankly. He kissed her on the lips, then took her in his arms and they kissed more passionately.

It was six o'clock in the morning. Henry came running from Sally B's bedroom into the living room, pulling his pants up and dressing himself.

"Hey, Jim, come on, get up, we're late." Henry shook Jim on his shoulder. Christina rolled over away from the commotion, not wanting to awaken.

"Huh, huh," Jim moaned.

"Come on, Jim, get up, we're late." Henry shook Jim harder, got his pants and threw them on Jim as he crawled to the edge of the bed and sat up.

"Damn, what time is it?" Jim asked as he rubbed his eyes.

"Time for us to get outta here. You know the story now, we came in but left back out for more drinks. Got drunk and slept it off in the car. Gotta say we slept in the car in case the wife came by my apartment looking for you."

"Doubtful. Probably glad I wasn't home." Jim finished putting his pants on. Henry helped with his shirt. He squenched his forehead.

"Damn, did we have that much to drink? My head is killing me." He rubbed his temples with both hands.

"Any aspirin?" Henry looked up, then ran into the bathroom. It was cluttered with women's toiletries. Two matching white towels hung from the rack on the shower stall. He opened the door to the medicine cabinet above the soiled white sink. He took the aspirin from the cabinet.

"Here, take four, it'll help attack that tequila we had on our way over here," Jim took all four and swallowed them without any water. Jim patted Christina on her butt. He then pulled the covers down. Her light skin glowed, and her medium frame seemed out of place in the sofa bed. Jim gently kissed her on her butt cheek. She turned on her side toward him. Upon seeing Henry staring and smiling at the view, she pulled the cover above her as fast as her fatigue would allow her. She gave an affectionate smile as Henry pulled Jim away and they left.

Jim hung his head a little trying to hide his face as he opened the passenger door of Henry's white, four-door Buick.

Henry, smiling, patted his hair while looking in the rear-view mirror. He got the sleep out of his eyes, then rubbed his face with both hands, making Jim wait.

"Come on, Henry, I know you're doing that shit on purpose," he grumbled.

Henry laughed boisterously. "Get in, scaredy cat." Jim quickly got into the car. He looked back up at the third story window where his new lover slept. The red brick on the building was chipping at the edges and the four wooden steps leading to the entrance were falling apart. This was not one of the better houses in the lower middle class section of Clinton Avenue. This area was considered the uptown section of Albany.

Henry drove off in a hurry, jerking Jim's head back slightly.

"So how was Christina?"

"Best pussy I've had in a long time."

"Suck ya dick?" Henry asked, wide-eyed.

"She did marvelous work. Come on, I gotta get to the job, Henry," Jim said, glancing at his watch.

"Look, she comes from a nice family in Westchester. Parents are pretty well off. She rebelled against everything they stood for. She told me she wanted to practice Judaism, but they made her go to the Catholic Church. Dropped out of college. Twenty-six years old and she still doesn't know what she wants to do with her life."

"You gotta stop all that shit between you and Tibby. You make yourself look like a chump," Henry said.

"I'm gonna get to the bottom of this Corey thing once and for all. I don't know how, but I am. Sometimes I wanna break that Tibby's neck. Seems like he's just rubbing it in my face with his little smirks and grins," Jim said.

"You and Sara need to be more careful around Corey. I would hate to see something bad happen," Henry said.

Sara stood at the kitchen entrance on the phone that was attached to the wall, about the height of her shoulder. She leaned on the wall with the phone tucked between her ear and her shoulder, anxiously awaiting for someone to pick up at the other end after several rings. Finally she got tired of it and slammed the phone back on its wall unit. She was pissed.

"Dammit, Jimmy, where are you staying out all night?" she sniffed, inhaling a rank smell. Then she said to herself, "What the hell is that smell?" She sniffed two more times, then headed out of the kitchen.

She charged by Randy's room shouting, "Everybody up!" Randy abruptly sat up in bed. She yanked open the basement door and yelled downstairs.

"Everybody get up down there, time for school." Randy crept towards the bathroom and was almost mulled over by Sara as she stormed into the kitchen.

"Mom, what's up?" Randy exclaimed as he stood in the kitchen entrance.

"Nothing, just go do whatcha gotta do while I cook break-fast." Sara looked under the kitchen sink cabinet, pushing pots around, making all kinds of noise.

"Where is that frying pan?"

Randy went over to the kitchen sink and took the frying pan out of the strainer where the dishes were put to dry. Randy held it up to her.

"Mom, is this what you're looking for?"

She stood from her kneeling position, saw Randy holding the frying pan, sighed, rolled her eyes and gently took the fryer away from him.

"Thank you, Honey, I didn't see it."

"You're welcome, Mom," Randy said as he walked toward the bathroom erect and mummy-like, with his hand at his crotch area.

"I gotta go get washed up," he said, rubbing his eye, then sniffed the rank smell. "Something stinks in here, Mom." Sara sniffed and frowned from the smell.

As Randy was about to enter the bathroom, so was I.

"I was in there first," Randy shouted.

"I gotta pee, come on," I said.

"Go downstairs," Randy retaliated.

Neither of us would let go of the doorknob.

"It's broken and won't flush downstairs."

"That's not my fault. Get lost."

"You get lost!" Randy shoved me away with his shoulder. I looked in the kitchen at Mom.

"Mom, can't I use the bathroom while he washes up?"

"You wait!" Mom said with an angry tone.

"Shoulda got ya behind up when I called you."

"Now, sit there and wait." Mom slammed a small pot down on the stove and added three cups of water.

"Mom, that's too much water for grits for three of us. They'll come out too watery."

Mom tried to cover. "Well, maybe that's how I want them this morning." Mom looked at me pointedly. "You're just like your father. Always trying to give directions."

"Dats doesn't like to cook, Mom."

"Don't give me no smart mouth." She came toward me. I stood in the kitchen entryway, swaying back and forth from having to pee so bad. She pointed her finger in my face.

"I'm doin' this, you understand? You think you're the only one who can cook around here?" Tony slowly walked into the kitchen, rubbing the sleep from his eyes and squinting to adjust to the kitchen light.

"Morning, Mom!" Tony said, barely audible. "Ehhh, Mom, something smells in here. Must be a dead rat somewhere."

"Yeah, I smell it too."

Mom went over to Tony, gave him a kiss on the forehead and then hugged him.

"Hi, baby," Mom said affectionately.

"Mommy, I have to go to the bathroom," Tony said, baby-like.

"Randy, open that door so Tony can come and use the bathroom," Mom shouted towards the bathroom direction.

Tony went into the bathroom. I shook my head at the disparity, then folded my arms.

Mom put six slices of bacon in the frying pan, which was full of Crisco grease.

"Mom, bacon will produce its own grease, just let it fry slow. We're gonna be eating grease."

"Don't get smart." She took the fryer by the handle and poured the grease back into the Crisco can. She put the fryer back on the burner and turned the fire down low.

"If you put a top on it they will fry better and faster." Mom cut her eyes at me as she bent down to the sink cabinet and got the top for the fryer. She got it and covered the frying pan.

Mom poured two cups of grits into the boiling water, then walked away.

"Mom, you gotta keep stirring them or they'll be lumpy"

"Why don't you help me, then?" Mom shouted back.

"I can't."

"Why, you're always wanting to cook any other time."

"I haven't washed up yet." I held up the palms of my hands to Mom.

"Randy and Tony, hurry up so Corey can get in there," she shouted.

I looked over at Max's bones in his dish. "Mom, can I throw Max's bones out now? I don't think he's gonna eat 'em. They're smelling up the whole house."

Mom had a relieved look with my discovery of what was smelling. "That's what that smell is. I thought it was a dead rat." She opened the kitchen back door and yelled, "Max, here kitty, kitty, kitty, where are you?" She waited a few seconds to see if Max would show up. "OK, come home when you're ready." Mom closed the door and went back inside. "Yeah, throw his bones away. I guess he's not hungry Maybe he found a girlfriend."

I put the bones in a brown paper bag and took it out to the trash can in the garage. Then I went back inside.

"Umh, Mom, I saw something last night."

"What kinda dream was it this time?" she said with a grin.

"It wasn't a dream, Mom, it was real."

Randy and Tony moved from the bathroom groggily and entered the kitchen. Both sat in their respective chairs.

"So what did you see?" Mom said, only going along with the story.

"It was upstairs." Anger came over Mom's·face.

"I thought I told you not to ever go up there." A blank look came on my face. Mom got in my face.

"Didn't I, didn't I now? Don't ever go up there again. And you're grounded." Randy and Tony chuckled. I shrugged it off.

"But, Mom, something smelled bad up there. I think Dats or you should check it out. You gotta check it out. I heard moans like it was a little boy in the room!" This got Mom's full attention.

"Whatdaya mean, a boy?" Mom asked.

The grits started to boil and bubble up.

"Mom, the grits." I pointed to them.

"Never mind. Randy, stir the grits, I'll be right back." She took me by the arm with a hard grip, pulling me into the living room and closing the door behind her. She pushed me down in the love seat. Randy and Tony watched from the kitchen entryway, but couldn't hear anything.

"Now, what did you see? And I want the truth," Mom said with a concerned look.

"It was dark and I couldn't see anything really, but it smelled horrible, like somebody died or something."

I thought I'd better lie. I got the feeling she wasn't going to be on my side.

"Where's Max?" she asked, then looked around.

"Here Max, here Max."

"Mom, I haven't seen Max, not even yesterday when I was home all day," I said with a scared look.

"Maybe he got in a fight with some rats and they killed him or he killed a rat and that's what I'm smellin'. Yeah, that's probably it." I had to lie to cover so that Mom would take the pressure off of me. She was concerned about the child part more. It seemed like it was more like I'd discovered something that I shouldn't have. She kneeled in front of me.

"Have you told your father any of this?"

Obviously Mom was rattled because Dats hadn't been home all night, and she had forgotten she was mad at him.

"Mom, I haven't seen Dats."

"I'll tell him when he gets home tonight. And you stay away from up there. How'd you get in there anyway?"

I shrugged. "I don't know, I just pushed the door open." Whack! Mom slapped me hard on the face. I didn't move. "Oh, that didn't hurt much?" She was about to slap me again when the phone rang. I wouldn't let myself cry that time. Randy answered the phone.

"Mom, it's for you," he yelled from the kitchen. She picked up the phone in the living room. Randy hung up.

"Jim," she yelled into the phone. "Where are you?" She glanced at me. "I need to talk to you. Oh, wait, I'm changing phones. Corey, hang this up when I get to my room." Mom rushed to her bedroom and closed the door. I was listening on the phone.

"Okay, Corey, I know you're listening, so hang up." I put the phone down in anguish.

"Shit, the key!" I ran downstairs to find Mom's keys. I went to my bed where my pants I was wearing the night before were neatly folded. I rummaged through the pockets, but I didn't find the keys. I was frantic as I looked all over, taking my just-made bed apart, then checking under the bed.

Mom was on the phone.

"Look, Jimmy, where have you been? I've been up all night waiting for you to come home."

Jim laughed loudly. "Now, I know I was out all night and I ain't gonna lie about it, but if you tell another lie like the one you just told me, I'm gonna hang up. I know you wasn't up all night waiting on me. Tell that to ya other one," Jim said jokingly.

"Oh, shut up." she said.

"Me and Henry got too drunk to drive anywhere so we slept in his car right in front of Tibby's."

"Where are you?"

"I'm at work. Where else would I be?"

"What time did you get there?"

"On time!"

"Honey, listen."

"What is it?"

"Corey got in upstairs."

There was a brief silence. All Jim could hear were the buses starting and going at his job.

Jim frowned and punched the air in anger as he spoke on the garage phone. He covered the phone more to try to hide his emotions from the other workers. There were twenty bays for buses in the garage at Capital District Transportation Authority (CDTA). Three-quarters of the bays were full with buses that were being repaired. The garage entryway was open and buses were going in and out.

The foreman walked by Jim while he was on the phone.

"Hey, Harris, you gonna make a living out of that phone call? Come on, let's go, back to work."

Jim rolled his eyes and mumbled to himself, "Shut up, you bald headed, fat gut, high school dropout."

"Huh, what did you say?" Mom said on the other end of the phone while Jim debated what to say to her.

"Oh nothing, Honey, I was talking to that redneck foreman of mine. Look, I gotta get back. You know what would happen if anyone found out?"

"Yes, of course I do," Mom said.

"Does Justin know?" Jim asked.

I don't think so. I'm not sure, I haven't heard from him."

"Look, make sure the door is locked. Wait, how did he get in?"

"I don't know." Mom looked on the dresser for her keys. She didn't see them, then she looked near the thirteen-inch TV. Didn't see them.

"Look, I don't know how he got in up there, but I have an idea how. I gotta go. Bye."

Jim hung up the phone and walked back to his bay where a bus was up on the rack. Jim pondered in thought for a minute, then the foreman walked up to him.

"Nothing wrong, is it?" the foreman asked.

Jim was startled a bit.

"Oh, no, nothin'."

"Well, then get back to work. Buses need to be running, not sittin' in the garage."

I plopped down in my eavesdropping chair. Tony and Randy walked in, both smiling.

"Mr. Neatman, what happened? Did ya lose something?" Randy said teasingly as he got Mom's keys from Tony and dangled them in front of me.

"Lookin' for these?" I tried to snatch the keys, but Randy was too fast as he pulled them away.

"Give 'em to me. I gotta put them back," I started to breathe heavily.

"That was a vicious bite you put on my neck yesterday." He softly rubbed the bandaid that covered the wound.

"Were you trying to kill me, Corey?" Randy asked as he walked toward me. Randy held the keys inside his clenched fist. I didn't back away as Randy stepped in my face, looking down at me.

"Gimme the keys, Randy." He had put the two keys back on the key ring and dangled them in front of me.

"If I don't?"

"Gimme the keys, Randy."

Randy sensed a danger in my voice, but didn't give in.

"No. You're gonna tell me what you saw or I'll tell Mom about the keys and you'll be grounded forever."

"I'm not tellin' you nothin'! I'll just be grounded."

Unbeknownst to me or Tony, Randy pulled a knife from his free hand and flicked the six-inch switchblade open and put it near my eye.

"How's about if I cut your eyes out, you won't be able to see anything again. Tony was scared, he thought this was going to be fun and games. He began to sweat, and so was I. I stood my ground even though I was terrified, not of what Randy might do but of what I would do once I took the knife from Randy.

"Do it," I urged with disdain. We looked at each other, eyeball to eyeball. Tony was scared as hell. He watched, and pissed his pants in the process.

"Don't tempt me, Corey."

"You don't have the balls." Randy began remembering his neck bite.

"That's what you think." Then suddenly Randy jabbed me near my eye. I fell to the ground in agony, covering my eye as blood poured out. Tony tried to run upstairs, but not before Randy grabbed his arm, dragged him in the hallway and looked him in the eye.

"It was an accident, you understand? That's what you tell 'em. An accident. Or you're gonna be in trouble too." Tony nodded and forced a scared half smile.

"Mom, hurry. Hurry, Mom," Tony rambled as he went running up the stairs.

Saint Peter's was located in the upper southwest part of Albany. I laid on a stretcher in the emergency room behind a curtain in one of the large rooms. There were seven other beds with curtains around them. Each room had the normal hospital oxygen tank, blood pressure, gauzes and other materials.

Two doctors looked at my eye as I continually blinked. It was a mess.

Dr. Allen, a boyish looking doctor doing his residency, and Dr. Bill, an older man in his fifties who was an expert with eye injuries, worked on me. Dr. Bill was brought in at the request of the resident.

"We're going to have to operate immediately," Dr. Bill surmised. Mom was shocked.

"We're gonna have to work fast to save this boy's eye," Dr Bill said as he worked feverishly while Dr. Allen assisted him.

Hopefully, we can do something with the damaged nerves," Dr. Bill stated.

"Or what could be the worst?" Dr. Allen asked.

"A life long twitch!"

In the waiting room were Sara, Tony and Randy. Tony and Randy sat nervously.

Sara slowly paced, her mind divided in two places: one on Corey's eye and the other, the more grave to her, was that Corey might know what was going on in the second floor apartment. Randy gradually swung his foot back and forth, not looking that overly-concerned about what he had just done to Corey. Tony read a Superman comic book. Jim, still in his work clothes, stormed through the waiting room door. He shot Randy a sharp-eye glare, and Tony, scared, never raised his eyes from his comic book.

"Hi, Dats," Tony said with a quiver in his voice.

"Yeah, yeah," Jim said in a undertone. Jim waved at Randy.

Randy swallowed hard, knowing he could be in big trouble if the truth ever got out.

"What's going on?" Jim said in a hushed, agitated tone while taking Sara by her arm and escorting her out of earshot of Randy and Tony, outside the waiting room.

"Did Corey say what he saw?" Jim asked with a concerned look. Sara had a frown and was not pleased with the line of questioning. A thick plate glass window, which was encased in the wall near the front door, separated the waiting room from the outside hallway. Randy could see Jim pointing his finger at Sara in a scolding fashion as he talked to her. The door to the waiting room was closed, so Randy and Tony couldn't hear.

"Don't you even care about what is going on with Corey's eye?" Sara said, with a loss of respect for Jim at that moment.

"Of course I do. But do you realize what would happen to us if it got out what we're involved in?" Jim said. Sara stared at Jim blankly and pondered. She knew he was right.

"Yeah, sure," Sara said, obviously upset.

"Did Corey see the kid up in Justin's?" Jim asked.

"He said he heard moaning, but I think it was too dark for him to see anything."

"Well, what else did he say?" Jim asked impatiently.

"He didn't get a chance to finish telling me because you called and then all this happened."

"Have you heard from Justin?"

"No."

I wonder if he knows Corey was even up there?" Jim said to himself as he lightly bit the fleshy part of his hand, knowing that if Justin did know, there would be trouble for Corey

"So how did all of this happen anyway? Were they playing or fighting?' Jim asked.

"Randy and Tony said they were playing with the knife and when Randy flicked it open, Corey walked into it as the blade shot out."

"Have you spoken to the doctor yet?" Jim said, half concerned. "He's been nothin' but trouble since the day he was born. Always sick a lot, everything. Sometimes I wonder about that boy."

"Now what is that supposed to mean?" Sara shot back.

"It means what I said. I don't know if Corey's mine or that no-good rotten Tibby's." Sara walked away with her arms crossed, embarrassed and looking around, not wanting to argue about this for the hundredth time.

"Well is he?" Jim asked in a raised tone, eyes watering. Sara turned around and looked at Jim stoically.

"I'm not answering that. Every time something happens you bring that up. You figure it out," Sara snapped. "If you and Henry hada been home, none of this woulda happened," Sara yelled.

"What! am I not suppose to work now?"

"You're suppose to work, but you also have a responsibility to me and these kids, one that you're not living up to lately."

Henry hurriedly came up behind them. Sara and Jim stopped arguing and looked at Henry.

"I left work as soon as I heard from you, Sara. How is he?"

"We don't know yet," Jim said.

"Well what happened?" Henry asked.

"Apparently they were playing with the knife and Corey got cut. That's how Randy says it happened," Jim said in an agitated tone.

Almost on cue, Henry looked through the waiting room glass window and Randy looked at him directly in the eye.

"I think Randy's lying," Henry said as he looked back at Sara and Jim.

"What makes you say that, Henry?" Sara asked.

"Because of what happened earlier yesterday evening."

"I don't think it has anything to do with that, Henry," Jim said.

"Corey took a pretty big plug outta Randy, wouldn't you want to retaliate? Maybe you should talk to Randy to see where his head is, Jim," Henry suggested.

Jim looked at Henry, then Sara, realizing Henry was right. Jim sighed and went inside the waiting room. He sat next to Randy, putting his arm over his shoulder. Tony saw this, and Jim motioned for Tony to sit beside him. Jim put his free arm around Tony's shoulder. Tony had a nervous, tight grip around his rolled up comic book.

"Boys, I want you to tell me exactly what happened," Jim said in a fatherly manner.

Back outside in the hallway, Sara was interrogating Henry.

"Where were you last night, Henry?" Sara said with anger.

"Didn't Jim tell you?"

"I'm asking you, Henry."

Henry smiled. "We went to Tibby's like we always do."

"Why didn't Jim come home? More time with ya whores?"

"Now look, Sara, we got drunk and slept in the car, and from there we went to work. That's it. We didn't want to have an accident driving."

"Well, why didn't you just call me to pick you up?"

"We didn't want to wake you. It was so late."

"If Jim had been home when he was supposed to, none of this would have happened because he wouldn't have to call me from work to check in and I could have kept my eyes on these kids."

"Look . . ."

"No, you look, Henry" Sara was in Henry's face. She tried to slap him, but he blocked it.

"I'm sick and tired of all the drinking and hanging out. You're suppose to be my brother. How can you carry on like you do with Jim doing what you do and here I am your sister? Don't you have any sense of 'blood'?"

This touched a nerve in Henry. His grin slowly faded. He slouched as he walked to a nearby leather cushioned bench. He patted on the empty seat for Sara to sit. Sara, arms folded and head down, slowly walked to the bench and sat next to Henry. Henry looked at Sara in the eyes briefly, then put his large arm over her shoulder. They slid back on the bench, putting their backs to the wall. Henry looked from one end of the hall to the next, trying to get up the nerve to say what was on his mind.

"Look, you're right. I carry on this way because I don't have any other friends, or should I say 'real' friends. Jim is my only buddy. I like him a lot and love him for who he is."

Sara sighed, and was stopped from turning away by Henry.

"And, I know you're my sister, too."

"You do realize that?" she asked sarcastically.

"Come on, sis," Henry pleaded as he moved Sara close to him. "Don't I always look out for you?"

There was silence for a few seconds as Sara's thoughts came together.

"Don't I?" Henry repeated.

"Yeah, I guess."

"You know I do. Like when Mom and Dad died and you couldn't stay at Aunt Helen's because you thought she was wicked. Remember that?"

"Yeah."

"But those foster homes weren't much better," Henry said.

"They were better than Aunt Helen's," Sara said with conviction. "Aunt Helen was a witch," Sara said.

"I guess I didn't like when they separated us. Henry, some horrible things happened that I never spoke about." Sara's eyes began to water. Henry put his arms around her, consoling her.

"It's all right . . . Look, I'm not too proud of some of the things I did either. That's why I ran away as soon as I got the chance. Brooklyn was crazy. Albany was the perfect place for me. I couldn't get in too much trouble here. But I wish we never got split up. I didn't really want to leave you in Brooklyn, but I knew if I came for you they would have caught me."

"But Henry, we're different. I mean, some of the things that have been done to me by those people."

Henry had a concerned look on his face.

"What things?"

"They raped me, Henry, did everything humanly possible to me, Henry. At first I didn't know what to do because I wasn't sure if they were supposed to be doing these things. Then I realized that it was wrong. They were very twisted, Henry." Tears rolled down her cheeks. "Do you miss Mom and Dad, Henry?" Sara asked sadly.

"Sure do. Ever since they died it's been all about survival. Then gettin' over how they died. That horrible fire. To me, there's no worse way to die than that. All I could remember was Mama's screams and those firemen wouldn't let me go back in to help her. Daddy, with his asthma, never had a chance in the smoke."

"I still have nightmares about Mama's screams."

Through the glass window where Jim stood, he saw Sara crying. Sara looked at Jim very sadly; he knew she was about to break.

"Henry, I have something else . . ." Sara said.

Jim came out of the waiting room like a locomotive, directly to Sara and Henry.

"What's wrong, Sara?" Jim said, taking her hand and ushering her up from her seat. He embraced her.

"Henry, everything's gonna be all right." Jim looked at Henry over Sara's shoulder as they embraced.

"What's wrong with her, Henry?" Jim asked.

"We were just talking about old times."

Jim looked at Sara with a questioning eye. He took her and pulled her close to his face.

"You okay?" Jim asked.

Sara nodded and put her head into Jim's chest passionately. Henry rubbed his chin a bit, perplexed at what Sara had told him. Henry stood and put his arms around both of them.

"We need to be concerned with what's happening to Corey," Henry said as he checked his watch for the time.

"My God, he's been in there for almost two hours," he said.

"Hopefully they can fix his eye," Sara said.

"Do we really know what happened?" Henry asked.

There was brief silence as Jim walked over to the waiting room window and stared at Randy. Randy gave Jim a quick look, then looked around the room. Tony's face was still buried in the comic book. But Randy had something to say.

"Don't ever say anything except what I told you," Randy said out of the side of his mouth in a whisper to Tony.

Tony didn't even look at Randy, only grunted in response. This angered Randy just a tad as he went over to Tony's couch and plopped down next to him.

"Look, this isn't a game this time," Randy said, as he snatched the comic book from Tony. Jim saw this and walked away from the window shaking his head.

"If you ever say a word, I swear I'll . . . I'll . . ."

"You'll what, cut me like you cut Corey? You didn't have to do that," Tony snapped.

"Shut up or I'll do you right now," Randy said as he slowly turned toward the waiting room window to see if anyone was watching. "Now do you understand, Tony?"

Tony hesitated a few seconds before answering. Randy, without overdoing it, considering that his parents and uncle were nearby, lightly nudged Tony on his shoulder to make his point, forcing a quick reply from him.

"Yeah, yeah, all right!" Tony answered in a urgent whisper.

Justin sat in his easy chair talking on the phone, "I think one of the kids from downstairs was up here snooping around last night. I'm not too sure. I'll find out from Jim. if he was, I'll take care of him, don't worry!"

Justin put the phone down and changed the TV channels on his large screen. He scanned the room from his black sofa that lined the wall, opposite his two Grand Street side windows. He settled on the Flintstones. He glanced at the door that Corey peeked in several times. He had his pink fly swatter handy. Occasionally he swatted at flies that circled near the coffee table that he had his feet on. He could hear cars driving up and down Grand Street.

Justin looked up toward the ceiling and scanned it. He then got up and went into the room that Corey had peeked into. Just above was a ceiling door and latch. Justin walked to it and used a wooden cane to check the lock on the ceiling door. It was definitely locked. He looked around the spotless room. No boy and no smell. Only a twin bed in the center. The ceiling door was one place Corey didn't know about.

CHAPTER SEVEN

HOURS LATER DATS, Mom, Tony, Randy and Uncle Henry were in my semi-private hospital room. The room was dimly lit. It was late afternoon. The sun peeked through the half-closed blinds shining on my bed from nearby. They couldn't be opened totally because my patched eye couldn't take the light. The room was well equipped with the usual hospital stuff. There was a brown leather lounge chair at the foot of my bed that Randy and Tony shared. Mom stood near the drawn curtains at the head of my bed that separated me from my teen-age roommate, who was just wheeled in from stomach surgery. Dats stood near Mom. Uncle Henry stood near the head of my bed on the side near the window.

Mom shook my shoulder lightly, trying to help me become more coherent.

"Corey, Honey," Mom whispered. I moaned and blinked my uncovered eye, trying to get a fix on the voice.

"Corey," Mom whispered again. I moaned louder this time.

"Honey, we're all here," Mom said reassuringly.

I squinted my unpatched eye and scanned around my bed. Upon reaching Randy and Tony during my scan, I rolled my eye and glanced at the off television that sat on a rack. The rack extended from the ceiling that was about eight feet from the ground. I then turned my head slightly to the left to look at Uncle Henry, who was smiling. I forced a short grin as I closed my eye.

Uncle Henry glanced at Mom and sat in the leather chair behind him. Dats paced along the side of the bed to the wall near Randy and Tony

Dr. Bill entered the room, followed by Dr. Allen. Mom immediately went to the foot of the bed where they stood with Dats beside them. Uncle Henry stood waiting to hear the prognosis.

Dr. Bill rubbed the top of his curly silver hair, from the front to the back. He was in pretty good shape, and still handsome for a man of fifty-five who worked all the hours that he could. He loved his wife, work and all children. Dr. Bill was well established in his field and no longer working for the money, but for the love of the job. But he never turned down his weekly salary. Dr. Allen, on the other hand, was single, white, doing his residency, and wanted all the money he could get. He sighed deeply.

"Well," Dr. Bill paused and said, "I think we saved the eye."

There was a deep sigh of relief from the family, especially Mom.

"Thank God," Mom said with a smile.

"But it's early and we have to keep a close watch on him for a couple of days. After that, he should be able to go home if the healing goes as planned. Myself, Dr. Allen, or a nurse will be in to check on him around the clock. It's important that he get a lot of rest. He doesn't need to be overworking himself trying to see everything right now." I glanced at everyone with a smile.

"Mrs. Harris, if you'd like to stay longer with Mr Harris, it's okay. We'll be talking to you." Dr. Bill walked toward the door in thought, with his head slightly tilted down. Dr. Allen was thin and stood erect and ready as he walked on his toes, following Dr. Bill. He was waiting anxiously for his next command as they left the room.

Mom tiptoed back to the head of my bed and patted me lovingly on my head.

"Jim, why don't we take the boys home and we can come back later to pick up Sara," Uncle Henry said. Dats looked at Mom for agreement.

"Sure," she said quietly. "You can grab something to eat or wait until I get home," Mom said in one big breath.

"We'll probably get something on the way home, Honey," Dats said with some affection.

Randy and Tony stood, almost in unison. Randy headed towards the door with his usual hip-hop walk, shoulders moving slightly from side to side.

"Oh, Honey, make sure you call the boys' school to let 'em know what's going on. The phone numbers are on top of the refrigerator," Mom said.

"I'll take care of it," Dats replied as he walked out of the room.

Uncle Henry went to Mom in his usual chest-leading walk, open armed. He gave her a big hug and whispered in her ear.

"I'm not going back to work, so I'm available if you need me to do something for you."

Mom leaned her head back from Uncle Henry's shoulder and looked him square in the eyes, straight-faced.

"Yeah, stay out of the bars."

Uncle Henry frowned, then sighed.

"And keep that husband of mine out, too." Uncle Henry chuckled and gave Mom a big hug and kiss on her cheek. He jogged lightly on his toes to catch up to Dats. Dats was at a phone around the corner from the two elevators. Randy and Tony were standing away from the phones, waiting for Dats as Uncle Henry approached, breathing heavily from jogging from my hospital room.

Jim was shouting on the phone.

"Now you listen to me! Nobody said he was even up there."

Justin was on the other end of the phone speaking in a smooth, breathy tone. "The kid said he saw somebody peek through the door, and when they heard me coming in, they ran. And you know my kids don't lie to me because they know the consequences of such acts," Justin said menacingly.

A brief silence followed because Jim knew what Justin was capable of doing at any given moment, to anybody. He knew this because he watched Justin burn his own brother's tongue out for giving out the wrong information on a number that cost him a million dollars. Then he sent him away and never heard from him again. Jim suspected Justin had his own brother killed. It wasn't that he needed the money, because he was already rich beyond his means. It was just that he was a ruthless son-of-a-bitch without a conscience, who had to make his brother an example. Corey had seen something that might cost him his life. Even Jim had his doubts that Corey was his, he still cared and loved him in a strange way.

Justin was smart. Nobody even knew what he did for a living, except Jim and Sara. Poor Corey, all he wanted to do was find out who molested him and try to do something about it. Jim knew Corey's life might be in danger because he knew Corey was the only one who had access to his keys, which included a key to Justin's upstairs apartment.

"Now, like I said, I want you to find out which one was up here or I'll take care of all three, you included," Justin reiterated.

Henry saw Jim in this down state of mind after hanging up the phone.

"You all right, buddy?" Henry asked.

"Yeah, it's just Corey." Henry threw his arm over Jim's shoulder.

"Oh, he'll be all right. He's a survivor," Henry said with a small smile. But little did Henry know, there was a lot more at stake than a cut eye. Jim motioned for Randy and Tony to follow them as they got on the elevator.

Justin had been in business, mostly illegal, since he was fourteen. He was involved in everything from selling Koolaid on the corner to marijuana in school. He'd been caught once as a teenager in high school, selling to someone he thought was a school pal, but was really an undercover cop posing as a student. He was sent away for a year and came back to Brooklyn and started all over again, this time adding prostitution and number running to his activities. He made enough money to send himself to Fordham University in the business administration program. By the time he graduated, his illegal business was booming, but after a few more years in New York, he decided a change was due because it was getting "hot" in Brooklyn.

Justin had a decent upbringing in a lower middle class environment, but took to the streets because he liked the excitement of it. Because he was so handsome, with his thick dark skin covering his well-muscled body, he never had a problem with women--or children. As a child, he was always the leader in games and in school events, and carried himself that way with his erect posture and gliding stride. He was an athlete for a while in high school, but his love of money was his passion, even though he later still prided himself on being in great physical condition, readying himself for what he called the revolution. That revolution meant being prepared for whatever changes might come. He was raised a Catholic, but these days he was not religious. He only believed in the almighty dollar, and forever bearing the thought of jail.

At times he was short tempered, but was obsessed with perfection. And when the few people around him did make mistakes, it was their last. Except when money was involved, Justin mostly kept to himself. When he was lonely, which wasn't often, he would call one of his many women to remind him of his God-like qualities, which he proudly possessed.

He always felt the key to his success was his subtleties. Being an only child was what strengthened him, along with having a sense of not caring about the rest of the world--only his. This was why he would go to any length to eliminate anyone who he felt was causing his "world" to crumble. This coming from a man who graduated at the top of his class and possessed an IQ that said he could accomplish anything he wished. That biggest wish being that he'd forever remain cautious and careful, after being locked up for a year. He swore he'd never go back to jail and that he'd build his empire glitch free.

I was half asleep in the hospital bed. At about midnight, a pretty, dark-complection nurse named Sandy came in to check on me. It was dark and quiet in the room. Mom was gone. Sandy was very voluptuous. I remembered her from earlier that evening. She didn't know I was awake. I just wanted to keep my eye closed and visualize how she looked.

Sandy was in her mid-twenties, at least. I'd been in the hospital once before to have my tonsils out, but my nurse then was nothing like Sandy. I just wanted to lay here and embrace her smooth touch. She strapped the blood pressure device around my right bicep and her fingers were warm and a little moist. I wondered if her adrenalin was running wild like mine. She gently took a hold of my hand, counting my pulse beats. I could feel her pulse from her index finger merging with mine through my wrist as she held on. My pulse seemed slow, then began to accelerate. Then hers began to pick up speed. I could see her breasts, medium and round, her thin waistline curving down to her shapely hips, her thighs, perfect to her calves that bulged with the shift of her hips. Our hearts were racing to that moment of truth as she laid my hand by my side and dried my perspiring forehead. She cupped her hand and rubbed the back of her fingers on my cheek to check my temperature. Then she stuck the thermometer between my lips, finding the area below my tongue. My hand became suspended, touching her hand as it rested on the bed railing. I felt her smile. I was "there" at that point where I knew she liked me and sensed what I sensed. After all the times I had snuck and watched Dats' Playboy tapes late at night, I was feeling real emotions from a woman who cared. Someone other than my Mom, who couldn't quite possibly think of me in these terms . . . or could she? Sandy would never harm me or molest me. For that moment was my birth in just sensing and being in my own little world, whether Sandy was with me or not. I opened my good eye. There Sandy was, standing there with her hand on the rail on top of mine with her warm smile.

"Hi," I said in a whisper.

"How ya feeling?" Sandy asked in a low, soft tone.

"Better, much better." My eye still hurt but my spirits were up. I was at that point where you're in pain, but because of Sandy, she anesthetized the hurt.

"You rest and we'll get that eye back in shape," Sandy said as she patted my hand.

Sandy stared at me for a few seconds, then with what felt like slow motion she began to lean towards me and I knew it would be a kiss. I closed my eye and she kissed me on my cheek. But I imagined it on my lips. Mom would use Spellbound perfume from time to time and Sandy had it on. Sweet, sweet smelling Spellbound perfume ran through my nostrils to my brain and through my spine, giving me shivers. Shivers that I felt for the very first time. When I opened my eye, the thermometer was out of my mouth and she was gone. For then, I felt safe, and if that was what a woman could do to a man, then I couldn't wait to grow older and try to leave behind those horrible molestations.

CHAPTER EIGHT

"SO DID YOU FIND out anything?" Justin asked.

"No, I don't think Jim's told Henry anything!" Sally B said.

Justin got up from his kitchen chair and slowly walked behind Sally B's chair while she puffed on her Marlboro cigarette. Her eyes followed him until he was out of her sight, behind her. Justin ran his thick fingers through her hair and down to her neck area.

"Did you get the boy back to New York okay?" Justin asked.

"Yes."

"No screw ups?"

"No."

"Too bad we had to separate the twins like that."

"What happened to the other one?" Sally B asked.

"Of course you know what happens when somebody screws up, right?" Justin's grip became a bit tighter around her neck. Sally B tensed up a bit and her cigarette fell to the floor. She nodded, as much as Justin's grip would allow.

He eased up, then let go and walked in front of her. He stamped out the cigarette and picked it up. He put it in her face.

"You see, Sally B, this is how I can crush things. You wanna make sure this doesn't happen to you."

Sally B was terrified of Justin. Justin had helped Sally B when she was living on the streets. He put her in charge of his New York prostitution, gambling and numbers businesses. Everything was done by her. All she would do was report to and pay Justin. He kept his face and name out of it. She was no longer one who worked the streets, unless it was for somebody special. She was indebted to him forever. He made her feel like she had a sense of worth, something her home life never gave her. She knew the city well because as a teenager, she had run away from home and got around and looked for acceptance from everyone. Until Justin, there was nobody. Justin knew how to get the most out of her, or anyone, for that matter. He trained Sally B exactly as he wanted her. Justin believed he was a genius, and Sally B felt the same.

They were in a room above Justin's kitchen, but only half the size. Justin stood up and glanced at the seven foot high ceiling. They had it set up like a kitchen. Sally B rested her elbows on a small square table in front of her. There was one other matching wooden chair on the opposite side of the table. A small brown portable refrigerator sat in the opposite corner of the table. On top of the fridge was a brown microwave. There were three portable cabinets on wheels that sat adjacent to the fridge.

He went to the refrigerator. He opened it and scanned the many different all-natural fruit juices that were there on the bottom shelf. He took out a grape juice and popped the can open.He took a sip and offered Sally B one. She rolled her eyes at him and he smiled. She got up and knelt beside him, taking her own orange juice from the fridge. He took it from her and popped the can open. He took a plastic straw from the side of the fridge door, stuck it in her can and gave it to her, followed by a kiss on her forehead. Justin stood up and pressed a button on the wall behind the telephone. What appeared to be a wall was sliding open from the center and enclosing itself in opposite sides.

"Aren't I a genius?" he said, praisingly.

Beyond the wall were two IBM computers, each with its own printer attached. The room was dimly lit. The screens of the consoles were illuminating their green light. Two automatic paper cutters were beside each printer. One computer was for his numbers running, and child selling, the second for prostitution. Each covered the entire New York State plus his other business interests abroad.

"Look, somebody from Jim's got into my apartment. It was one of the kids I think, and I need you to find out which one," Justin stated.

"How do you know?"

"Don't question me!" he snapped.

"But they don't know anything," Sally B said, timidly.

"Somebody was in my house and I need to know who. This is why the Roman Empire fell--slip ups! I've been in business for over ten years. The last time I was in a detention center was when I was sixteen, I spent one year in there, and it wasn't a pleasant experience. And I will not," he pounded on the small wooden table near one computer, "I repeat, I will not go back to jail for anyone! And if this Corey knows something, I need to know. If he does, I'll take care of it from there. Am I clear?" Justin said, pointing his finger in her face. "And if you can't handle it any more, I'll get somebody else! Understood?"

"Yes," Sally B answered, meekly.

Sally B oversaw everything. Justin gave her the freedom to

make decisions without having to consult with him. The only person who knew about Justin was Sally B, and he paid heavily to keep it that way. And he sure wasn't going to let a ten year old boy bring down his entire operation after years of doing business, illegal or not.

"Now, where were we," Justin said, smiling a sinister smile. He keyed in on his IBM portable computer, pressing key number one. On the screen appeared:

B for	Borough	: Br for Brooklyn
S for	Street	: Flatbush Avenue
	Date	: Saturday, April 28, 1993
SA for	Services	
	available	: 20 *(Women available)*
NW for	Numbers	
	worked	: 20
D-Dollars	Dollars per hr.	: $100
	Min. hours	
	worked	: 4
	Total intake	: $4,000
	MANHATTAN	
	Street/hotel	: Park Avenue Plaza Hotel
	service	
	Available	: 20
	Numbers	
	worked	: 200
	Min. hours	: 4
	Total intake	: $16,000

"Well look at that, and that's just two streets and one hotel for one night. That's millions of dollars a year on just one hotel." He nodded in satisfaction. "I control ten with the same profit." He turned to Sally B with a straight face. "I need to know if that boy or any of those kids know what's going on."

Jim arrived home late that evening from work. Randy, Tony and Sara rested at the kitchen table. Everyone was quiet. Jim had said the blessing and everyone was digging in, except Jim.

"I need to ask a question of you and Tony." Tony heard him and stopped in mid-bite of a fried chicken leg.

Randy looked at Jim with that 'I'm scared' look.

"Have either of you boys been upstairs lately, or ever?"

"No Dats," Randy said quickly, then sighed.

"Me neither, Dats." Tony said nervously.

"Good," Jim said with a half smile.

"Now we can eat comfortably." Jim cut his eyes at Sara.

"Dats, why did the person up there say someone was in his place?" Tony asked.

"Someone was up there, according to Justin, and only three people have the key. That's Justin, your Mom and me.."

Jim leaned towards the boys. "Now are you boys absolutely sure there was no visit? You might have gone up there and forgotten. Randy, we know you sleep walk, but I guess you wouldn't remember that anyway."

"But Dats, how would I get the key? You keep that with you all the time." Jim sat up in thought for a moment.

"Corey. I let Corey watch TV in my room the other day and I left my damn keys on the dresser."

A fearful look came across Sara's face.

"You don't know that Corey was up there, Jim," Sara said with deep concern.

"You're right, but I'm sure gonna ask him once he gets outta that hospital tomorrow." He looked at Randy and Tony scornfully.

"And what are you doing playing with knives anyway, especially you, Randy?" Jim nudged Randy hard on his shoulder.

"You're old enough to know better. Knives and guns are not play toys. Now what if you had killed him, you'd be looking at some possible time in detention or worse."

CHAPTER NINE

BRUCE BANES WAS A LOCAL, small-time Democratic politician in Albany. He'd won the job of Alderman for thirteen years. He was a fifty-year-old, fair skinned, jovial man who didn't look a day over forty. He had always thought of himself as a 'ladies' man'. Over the years he kept his medium build somewhat tight and in shape by eating right. Exercise wasn't his best friend. Luckily, his genes worked well with his mind. He had a wife and ten kids, all grown and on their own. Bruce had the uptown section of Albany to govern, and he made it his business to always know what was going on. Wherever Banes was he considered it his stage and he always put on a show in a fun loving, boisterous way, speaking in his rich baritone voice. Bruce, along with his wife Ella, owned and operated a hole-in-the wall, greasy spoon restaurant called 'Banes' Place'. Most mornings by seven there was a line out the door.

Sally B was a regular customer, when she wasn't in New York taking care of business for Justin. She always sat at the sixth and last stool at the small counter. That day was an exception though, because she was nervous and scared for Corey, whom she didn't even know, but she knew Henry and the destruction of which Justin was capable.

Sally B sat at the rear of the four booths that lined the wall near the front door, nervously smoking a Marlboro cigarette. She could see whoever walked in the front door. She waited anxiously for Henry to arrive.

Evenings weren't as crowded as the morning, but there was still a steady flow of customers coming in for take-out orders.

Every few minutes Sally B would look up at the front door when it was opened to see if it was Henry.

"Hey, Sally B, do I have the chicken pox today or somethin'?" Banes said from behind the counter, in his usual boisterous manner.

"Come sit. What's wrong, is your stool broke or something?"

Sally B forced a smile and mouthed that she was waiting for someone.

"Oh, new man, huh?"

Ella, Bruce's wife, walked from the small kitchen area. It was farther behind the counter area and blocked off by a wall with a small window-like opening. Honcho, the restaurant's bald black cook, was snatching order slips; off of the circling turnstile that held them from the window. Ella worked between the kitchen and the counter. For a woman in her late forties, she was still attractive and shapely, even though she was a bit overweight. Many a man tried unsuccessfully to lure her away from Banes, as he was known to everyone in the neighborhood. They were hard-working middle class people who kept a roomy, one bedroom apartment upstairs for political reasons. If Banes was going to represent uptown Albany as an Alderman, he had to have official residence. Their more spacious home was in Colonie, twenty minutes from Albany by car.

Ella came from the back carrying at least four bags of to-go orders.

"If you'd stop yapping so much, we could get these to-go orders out the door," Ella said to Banes. Ella looked to see what Banes was smiling at.

"Oh, hi, Sally B. How are you today?" Ella said. She was always cheerful and articulate.

"Fine, and you?" Sally B replied.

"Trying to keep this lazy husband of mine working." Ella nudged Banes lightly and he gave her a kiss on the cheek.

"That's not gonna do it, gimme some work. We'll take care of that later."

Some of the waiting patrons laughed as Ella handed them their orders in small to medium brown paper bags.

With his usual smile, Henry walked in.

"Hi, I'm home," Henry said to anyone who was listening.

"Hey, Henry, your usual?" Banes asked.

"You got it," Henry said as he looked around and spotted Sally B in the corner booth.

"Hi, Henry," Ella said.

Henry went to Ella, leaned over the counter, gave her a kiss on the cheek and said, "How's the first lady of the house this evening?"

"Just fine, busy as usual," Ella said.

She wiped sweat bubbles from her forehead using Banes' apron.

"Hey, gotta pay that phone bill," Henry chuckled as he made his way through a couple of waiting customers to Sally B's booth.

Henry slid on the well-kept leather booth seat sitting next to Sally B.

"Hey, what's up, Ms. Sally B?" Henry said with a big smile, followed with a kiss on her forehead.

Even though she felt secure in Henry's presence, Sally B had to strain to smile.

"Glad to see you too, big fella," Sally B said.

"So how's Corey doin'?" Sally B asked as she lit another ciga-rette. Henry looked in the ashtray as Sally B put the match away.

"That's five. Sally B, what's wrong, got a nervous twitch to-day? Get it?"

Henry let out a boisterous laugh, but Sally B wasn't in a joking mood.

"What, cat got ya tongue today?" Henry said, trying to break the ice.

"No, just things on my mind."

"Is it that bad?"

"Bad enough," she replied.

"Do you need something?" Henry asked.

"Yeah, I need to get away from all of this." Sally B looked around and waved her hand.

"How's Jim?" she asked.

"Hey, you asked me about Corey. How'd you know something happened?"

"I know lotsa people, remember?"

"Yeah, but you seemed to be too concerned, Sally B. What is it?"

"I was just asking how the boy was," Sally B said with frustration.

"Well, he's gonna keep his eye if all goes well during the healing."

"Good. How's Jim holding up?"

"Hey, since when did you get so concerned about Jim and his family?" Henry said with a slight frown.

"Nothin, it's . . . I just know he's your nephew and I care about you. Just showing some concern, that's all."

Henry smiled and put his arm around Sally B, and rested it on the back of the booth seat.

"Wow, I didn't know you care so much about little ol' me."

"Well it's about time, Banes," Henry said, smiling as Banes put a plate with a half of a barbecued chicken, mashed potatoes and salad in front of him. Banes put another plate in front of Sally B that had a cheeseburger and french fries on it.

"There ya go, enjoy," Banes said cheerfully as he headed back towards the counter, excusing himself past the four customers waiting for take-out orders.

Henry closed his eyes and said a silent blessing over his food, then looked at Sally B who was staring into space. Henry looked at her food.

"Yeah, that stuff'll kill you. I don't blame you."

Henry began to eat. Sally B still hadn't touched her food. With his mouth half full, Henry said, "If I wanted to eat alone, I coulda stayed at home. Now are you gonna eat or what?"

Sally B looked at Henry, then managed another smile and took her burger and slowly took a small bite, her mind still on the inevitable question she had yet to ask Henry, regarding Corey being in Justin's apartment.

"Henry" Sally B said, with her voice almost trembling.

"Was . . ." Sally B said and was about to pop the question when she was surprised to see Justin walk into the restaurant front door. He stood at the entryway and looked around with his usual sinister smile. Henry was engrossed in his food.

"What were--" Henry said, then looked up at Sally B and saw that she was staring at something; Henry saw Justin looking at Sally B.

"What's wrong?" Henry said as he went back to eating. "Don't you know him?"

Justin gave Sally B a subtle nod, then in his usual shoulder swaying glide, he made his way to the counter wearing his usual all black modest garb.

"No, no, no. . . well--"

"You know what's so sweet about you, Sally B? You're such an honest person and you almost always wear your feelings on your sleeve when you're around me. That's how I can tell when you're lying. Now that Justin made you more nervous than you already were when I walked in, are you gonna tell me about it? The other day you mentioned that you worked for him." Henry said nonchalantly as he continued to munch on his chicken breast.

"No, it's just that he looks so spookie, that's all. I was looking straight ahead and it was like I almost didn't see him come in the door."

"That's because your mind has been in another place since I came in here." Henry stopped eating and wiped his hand thoroughly with his napkin.

"Now, I don't particularly care for that guy and he knows it. Now, if you got something going on with him and I'm causing you trouble with him, let me know and I'll just go. You can take care of whatever it is you need to do with him, okay?"

Sally B took Henry's hand, put it in her hand and looked him in the eye.

"No, actually, let's get outta here and go to your place for awhile. I just wanna be close to you." Henry liked this request. He smiled.

"Okay, okay. That's fair, I can live with that," Henry said as he slid out of the booth seat, followed by Sally B.

At the counter, Justin turned away from Banes and watched Henry and Sally B make their way toward the entrance. Sally B couldn't help but cut her eye to catch one last glance at Justin who was smiling. Henry rolled his eyes at Justin.

"Nice couple, huh Banes?" Justin said as he turned back toward the counter and leaned with his forearms folded on the counter.

"Who said they were a couple?" Banes said, with raised eyebrows. Justin heard the door slam and said under his breath, "Nobody."

CHAPTER TEN

"HONEY, I HAVEN'T seen Max in a couple of days. Honey, Honey?" Sara said. It was dark and quiet as Sara laid wide awake in bed next to Jim, who was asleep. "Jim, I'm scared. Jim, wake up," Sara said, almost pleading as she nudged him. Jim moaned and groaned as he rolled over on his side facing Sara. She stared at the dark ceiling.

"What, Sara?"

"I'm scared and I want . . . Honey, what if Corey was in Justin's apartment?"

"Don't worry, Honey, nothing's gonna happen."

"He's ruthless, ruthless, and you know it," Sara said. This awakened Jim more, and he sat up in the bed with his back against the wooden headboard area.

"Listen and hear me good. I'm not gonna let anything happen, okay?"

Sara nodded and Jim, with his hand, gently turned her face toward him.

"You need to relax, and so do I." Sara, her eyes watery, looked lovingly into Jim's eyes. He kissed her passionately on the lips and they embraced, kissing again and again as they began to unclothe each other. Their hands fondled each other about their bodies. Then after a short while, Jim stopped, looked into Sara's eyes and smiled a knowing smile. Sara knew what this meant, as she rubbed the back of his neck wanting desperately to make love to him. Jim slowly got up and got his keys off his side of the bed. He felt around the key ring for the key he was looking for. He located the cabinet key then, still in the dark, walked gingerly around the foot of the bed. He got to the cabinet on Sara's side of the bed and unlocked the padlock.

As Jim reached for the small light switch inside the cabinet, Sara lightly grabbed his other hand.

"Not tonight, okay. Just make love to me!" she said with desire.

Jim dropped the keys. With his adrenaline flowing triple time, he got back into bed on top of Sara and made love to her aggressively. They threw each other from side to side. She clawed him several times on the back. He in turn thrust hard and heavy into her. She cried out several times, enjoying the pleasure that came with the pain. It was rough, but they both liked it that way.

"Honey, we have to, I can't stand it anymore," Jim said, out of breath.

"Please, baby, stay in me, I love you so much, I need you in me, don't stop."

"I'll never stop. I need it, Honey. I want you to put it in me, to give it to me, oh, I love you so much," Jim said.

"Anything. Get it," Sara said, giving in.

Jim slowly got to the cabinet. Ritual like, he took the equipment and put it on Sara.

Loud groans were heard as the front door to the house slammed shut. It was Justin going upstairs to his apartment. Even he heard loud cries from Sara and Jim's bedroom.

Justin smiled and continued upstairs.

Sara was on top of Jim as he continued to yell, trying to mute his noise by burying his head into his pillow as Sara thrust back and forth with all her hundred and sixty pound strength that she could muster up.

Sally B and Henry had decided to stop in Tibby's for a quick drink before they would go to Henry's place. But what was supposed to be a quickie turned into a three-hour drinking fest.

"Down the hatch," Sally B said.

Henry's boisterous laughter filled the near empty bar. On a Thursday morning at 2:00 a.m., this was normal.

Sally B had put her glass up to her mouth and poured her drink in, but when it came time to swallow it, she'd fake it and spit the shot of Tequila back into her Heineken bottle, feigning that she was chasing her shot. Henry was plenty drunk.

"Gimme another, Bibby, I mean Tibby," Henry said with laughter. Tibby smiled at Sally B. She waved him off, signaling that was enough. Sally B slid her chair close to Henry.

"Hey, you comin' closer, huh?" Henry put his arm around the back of Sally B's chair.

"Henry, about Corey," Sally said.

"What about him?" Henry replied with a big laugh.

"Has he ever been upstairs?"

"Upstairs? What, to heaven?" Henry laughed to the point of him bending back and forth in his chair.

"No, I mean in Justin's place," Sally B said.

"Sure he has, he lives in the house, doesn't he?" Henry said again with laughter.

"Henry, are you sure?" Sally B said, pleadingly. Henry put his head down on the table to rest.

"Of course I'm sure," Henry said, mumbling.

"Henry, are you sure? It's important now."

Henry turned to look at Sally B and his eyes rolled back in his head. He gave Sally B a slight grin, reached out and tried to rub her face, but his hand never got there. He passed out on the round table.

Sally B looked around and saw that the bar was empty. She motioned for Tibby to come to her. Before Tibby moved over to Sally B, he went to the front door and locked it, then turned off the front window advertising lights. He pulled the chain for the Miller Beer sign light and it flicked off, then the Heineken sign light and finally, Coors. Tibby looked out the window to see if anyone was out front standing around or trying to look in the bar

Someone came to the front door and started to bang on it. Tibby stopped and looked over to Sally B, who waved him off. Tibby unlocked two of the locks on the door and opened it, only the distance that the short chain lock would allow.

"Look, I'm closed for the night, I got an emergency."

"Come on, just one drink," the older man said. He was a bum who normally went to the liquor store during the day and hustled what drinks he could at night.

"Nah, you're broke and we're closed," Tibby said as he closed the door in the man's face. Tibby put the double locks back on the front door and hurried over to Sally B.

"Is he out?" Tibby asked.

"Yeah," Sally B said with dejection.

"What're you trying to find out from him?"

"It doesn't concern you. Come on, help me put him in your back room."

Tibby got Henry from the back and gripped his hands across his chest. Sally B picked up Henry's dragging feet and they carried him to the back.

"Look, Sally B, Henry's a nice guy and I don't want to get involved in nothing that's dangerous or gonna hurt somebody."

Tibby kicked opened the office door that had a sign that said 'private' on it.

"Look, whether you know it or not, you're in deep and it's very dangerous," Sally B threatened.

"Sally B, look, I'm with you and your call girls, but that's as far as I go. I got a family and a business," Tibby said nervously.

They put Henry on the sofa near the wall of the small office.

"Look, Tibby, if it wasn't for me, you would have lost this business a long time ago. I gave you the money to keep this joint open and I can shut you down."

"Well, what is this all about with Henry here? I need to know."

"Look, the less you know, the longer you'll live, okay? Let's just keep it that way. I was just trying to get information out of Henry. Let him sleep it off. I gotta go."

Tibby, sweating, wiped his brow with the palm of his right hand and took a seat behind his wood desk, staring at Henry as he snored.

There was an IBM personal computer on one side of the desk with a printer. The office was cluttered with old business files, but it was clean. "And if you want to keep that sweet little young wife of yours happy, I'd advise you to do just as I say and nobody'll get hurt. Don't you forget that I hold the deed to this place, and you wouldn't want to let Tammy get wind of that, now would you?"

Sally B started out the door, then stuck her head back in.

"Wake him at six so he can make work. I'll talk to you later."

Sally B left. Tibby looked bewildered, wondering what he had gotten himself into.

CHAPTER ELEVEN

BY FRIDAY MORNING at approximately ten o'clock I sat in a chair waiting at the foot of my hospital bed. I was fully dressed and ready to go home. Both of my parents stood near the door. They began to whisper to each other.

"I hate missing work, Sara." Jim said with annoyance in his voice. She rolled her eyes. "Whether you know it or not, I had to take a personal day to do this. You gotta keep a better eye on the kids."

"I don't even wanna talk about it Jim. Lets just get Corey and go.

"Yeah, it's easy for you to say. You're not the one who has to pay for my mother's living expenses."

"She had you didn't she!" Sara snapped.

"Yeah okay. Just so you know, even with insurance, this incident cut into that little vacation I promised you. You can bet on that."

Sara waved her hand at Jim in disgust.

While I sat and waited, I thought about Randy cutting me. I was angry with Randy and Tony. I was glad that they were in school. They were the last two I wanted escorting me home.

The only other thought that dominated my mind was being molested. I tried to forget the pain from that abuse. I couldn't. I was glad to be leaving the hospital but I really didn't want to go home. The only thoughts I had were the nights that I had suffered as a result of someone else's pleasure. I hated knowing that there was someone in our house waiting to attack me again. At that moment, I despised everyone. I wanted the abuse to stop. Even though I was afraid, angry and defenseless, I knew I had to stop it.

I was flanked by Mom and Dats. Mom was rubbing my back, happy that I was going home, and Dats obviously had something other than my release on his mind. I always knew this because he would pace while in thought. I was still a little scared about my eye. The patch would have to stay on for another week. Dr. Bill wanted to make sure that it didn't get infected during the course of it healing.

"How long before Dr. Bill gets here, Mom?" I asked. I was becoming impatient. I'd been up since seven this morning, waiting to get the hell out of this place, although I did have a good time with Sandy.

"We have to wait for Dr. Bill to give us some last-minute instructions. He left a message with the nurse that he wanted to talk to us before we left. He did say he might be a little late."

"How's it feel, son?" Dats asked.

"It doesn't hurt as much as before; but at least I'll be able to see."

Sandy, the nurse, walked in; my eyes lit up. Damn, she's sexy, I thought. I got a little boner again. I put my hands inconspicuously over my crotch area. I was kind of happy and sad. Sad because I was not going to see Sandy again, but happy to be leaving. What I wondered though, was would I get a boner every time I saw a beautiful, sexy woman or was I really in love with Sandy, because along with the boner came these butterflies in my stomach.

As Sandy walked toward me, I could hear her white pantyhose rubbing together at the thigh area. This turned me on even more.

"Hi, Mr. and Mrs. Harris," Sandy said cheerfully. Mom and Dats both spoke.

Sandy knelt in front of me, took both of my hands and held them. I quickly closed my legs. I did all I could to not stare at her breast area where her white uniform was unzipped, exposing part of her cleavage.

"So, Corey, are you ready to go home?" Sandy asked, with a big smile.

I drowned in her Spellbound perfume, sucking in every ounce of her air. God, was she beautiful.

I really wanted to see her again, but I guess I was too young and she might not take it right if I asked her for her phone number.

Besides, Mom and Dats were within earshot. I didn't want to get all embarrassed.

"You were very nice to me. I have something for you!" I said.

I reached into my shirt pocket and gave her a note that I had written. She read it aloud.

"Thanks for all the help you've given me. You are the best nurse I have ever had. Thanks again. Love, Corey."

"Oh, you're so sweet." She folded the letter and put it in her breast pocket. Then she gave me a big hug, and of course, I returned it. She pulled me close to her and her breasts rubbed my chest. God was that a thrill. I think she knew it too, or maybe I was wishing she thought she was giving me a thrill. Probably the latter. Sandy stood up and I sat back in the chair. Just like a woman to leave me hangin'. Dr. Bill entered in a big hurry.

"Sorry I'm late, everybody. Is everything taken care of, Sandy?"

"Yes, he's all set to go. I'll go call the orderly up to wheel you downstairs, Corey."

As Sandy exited, I listened to her muscular thighs rub together and watched her butt switch in her tight uniform. She wasn't wearing a ring, so I thought maybe I might have a chance. But a woman like that doesn't stay on the open market for too long. I knew she would be long gone and married by the time I was of age.

"Okay, we're giving Corey some medication to take and to apply to the cut area. Now, Sandy showed you how to redress your dressing when you have to apply the medicine. Don't worry about the discoloring in his eye. It'll take a while for that to clear up. It'll be black and blue for a while, too, so don't be alarmed. If pus starts to accumulate in or around the eye, you need to wash it clean quickly because this can cause infection. Do you have any questions?"

"No, and thank you for your help," Mom said with a smile.

"Thanks, Dr. Bill," Dats said as they shook hands.

"I'll see you in my office next week, Corey," Dr. Bill said as he waved good-bye and left the room.

The orderly arrived with the wheelchair. I got in and away we went down the corridor toward the elevator. We stopped at a bathroom because I had to go.

"I'll get the elevator," Dats said as he kept walking. Mom stayed with me and pushed the chair into the bathroom.

"Mom, I can do it."

"Okay," Mom said as she waited outside the bathroom. The orderly waited with her.

Jim pressed the button for the elevator. From around on the side of the elevator, Justin appeared. Jim was shocked.

"I see Corey's coming home. Hate for him to wind up back in here before he went to the morgue, if you know what I mean." Jim was motionless. He peeked back towards where Sara and the orderly stood in the corridor at the other end.

"Look, I haven't had a chance to talk to him yet. Get off my back, will you," Jim said as they both stared straight ahead of them, looking at the elevator. Jim was scared.

"You do that soon," Justin said as the elevator door opened.

"Going up, sir?" Justin teased as he walked on the elevator, leaving Jim standing there.

"No, thanks, I'm going down," Jim said.

"That you are if you're not careful," Justin said, with his ever present evil smile. The elevator door closed.

The down elevator came and Mom wheeled me towards it. Dats had a bad look in his eyes.

"You okay, Honey?" Mom asked him.

"Yeah, let's just go."

"Mom, when do I have to go back to school?"

"Monday, maybe. We'll see how your eye is."

The elevator stopped on the third floor. The door opened, it was Justin. He had dark shades on this time. Mom and Dats grew very silent. They seemed to be afraid. They didn't know whether to talk to Justin or not. They were scared. I wasn't sure who this man was because of my eye. Even my good eye was a little blurry. Mom and Dats chose to be quiet. They felt the less I knew, the better.

"Going home, too, huh, sonny?" Justin said, with false care.

"Yeah." Mom and Dats were just looking straight ahead.

Justin turned his back to them and faced the elevator door. After I looked at him, I had a flashback to the night I sat in my eaves-dropping chair, I remember seeing a man carrying a black bag down the stairs.

"Excuse me, sir, you look familiar," I said as I tapped Justin on his back near his waistline. Mom tried to stop me, but it was too late. Justin turned around to face me as the elevator door opened.

"Maybe you have met me. I'm your neighbor, Justin," he said as he walked off the elevator backwards.

Mom and Dats got off the elevator behind me. Mom pushed my wheelchair and the orderly walked with us. I got out of the wheelchair.

"Corey, you're supposed to be in this chair," Mom said.

I turned around and looked at Mom, then at the chair and sat back in it.

"Mom, where does he live?" I asked as she wheeled me to the exit door. Mom looked at Dats and he shrugged his shoulders.

"He lives upstairs from us," Mom said with hesitation.

"Upstairs," I blurted out. "That's what I wanted to tell you, Mom. I . . ." Mom covered my mouth with her hand.

"Honey, can we talk about this later, I'm very tired. I've been in this hospital too many days."

"But, Mom . . ."

"Corey, not now," Mom said sternly. Dats walked along silently; I knew he knew that something wasn't right.

"You just worry about getting back to school and catching up with the rest of the class."

"But, Mom, I saw something the other night."

This was just what they didn't want to hear. But I had to say something, even though it meant getting in trouble for taking Dats' keys.

"What do you mean you saw something?" Dats growled.

"Well . . ." They had that look in their eyes, like they didn't believe me, but I could tell they knew something but didn't want me talking about it.

"I mean, I *thought* I saw him, that Justin guy, carrying a bag down the stairs the other night. It was real late and dark, so I really couldn't see that well. It probably wasn't even him."

I thought, now what am I gonna do? I know what I heard and saw, but Mom and Dats didn't want to hear it. I thought to myself. Did they know? Were they involved? I guessed I would find out for myself. I decided to just play along, for the time being.

"Don't worry about things that don't concern you, son. You just worry about getting back to school," Dats said.

Whenever he called me or any of us "son," that meant he was bothered. Mom and Dats walked close and whispered.

"He's an evil sneaky bastard," Dats said, disgusted.

"Yeah he is," Mom replied sadly."

CHAPTER TWELVE

IT WAS LUNCH TIME, and everyone was on the front terrace running and playing at Cathedral Academy Elementary School. Kindergarten girls were playing hopscotch, and jumping rope, and other boys and girls were chasing each other playing tag. First through fourth graders joined in the fiasco. Some boys and girls were standing around in their little cliques, brewing up trouble with their counterparts. A couple of boys played stick ball with a tennis ball and old wooden stick. Some of the fifth and sixth graders sat on the school bars that were in front of the school about twenty yards from the front entrance.

The school housed grades kindergarten to eighth. It was a private Catholic school, located on the corner of Park Avenue and Eagle Street, two blocks up the hill from our house. It was a racially mixed school, with a few more African Americans than whites. The girls wore pretty blue and white checked dresses with wide shoulder straps. The dresses came to just below the knee. They either wore a white or navy blue blouse underneath their dress. The boys wore navy blue slacks and white shirts, with a navy tie or bow tie. Everybody had to wear black shoes. You weren't caught dead without this ensemble or you were sent home. The nuns and priests were very strict about this. It was very different from the public school I'd gone to from kindergarten to fourth grade. At Cathedral students weren't as hostile, even though Giffen Elementary was only two blocks away. I remember the kids at Giffen used to pick on me all the time because I was quiet and off to myself. Randy would stick up for me when things got out of hand, like a big brother should. But then he changed when we started going to Cathedral.

I don't think he liked how organized it was. But he always enjoyed playing football at lunch time on the side of the school, in between the gym and the place where the nuns lived. It was all concrete. The nuns had an eight foot high wooden fence around their building. Randy crashed into the wooden fence as he caught the pass and ran to the end of the building, eluding a two-hand tag by an opponent to score his second touchdown.

Tony watched from the end zone where Randy just scored. Tony was always impressed with everything Randy did, especially football because Randy was bigger, stronger and faster than the other guys in eighth grade.

Tony smiled as Randy raised his arms triumphantly after scoring. His eight teammates congratulated him with the usual pats on the back. Their team was up by two touchdowns. With the school bell due to ring any moment, ending the lunch period, they were safe with the win.

"You guys wanna try one more down? If you score, we can call it a tie. We'll give you that, but we doubt you'll score. Right, team?" Randy said, shouting down to the opposite end of the playing area that led into a parking lot for the nuns on Park Avenue.

The other team looked haggard and whipped with their school uniforms disheveled, ties undone. They looked at each other, then at Randy who smiled confidently with his teammates looking just as ragged as their opponents, but they knew they had an ace in Randy. They waved them off and decided Randy was too much for them to overcome that day.

"Nah, tomorrow we'll start over," one of Randy's opponents said. It didn't matter anyway because lunch time was almost up and everyone needed time to gobble down their lunch. Some of the guys would eat before the game so that they could play right until the bell rang.

Everyone started to take a seat on the school's silver rail that was in front on Park Avenue. Randy tucked his shirt in and fixed his tie as he walked toward Tony, who waited in the end zone.

"You think Corey will tell what really happened?" Tony asked. Randy, his breathing getting back to normal, looked at Tony for a few seconds, then looked around to make sure no one was within earshot.

"Even if he does, nobody's gonna believe him. But I doubt he will anyway. He's not like that. He'll keep it to himself. But that's what bothers me, 'cause he's always cookin' something up."

"I know, sometimes you don't know what he's gonna do," Tony said.

There were some guys Tony's age playing basketball at a hoop near the football end zone behind the school. The ball bounced toward Randy. He grabbed it, took one dribble and shot a three-point shot from the corner, it was all net. The kids were impressed as they looked at Randy, who appeared to them to be a giant, and were very much in awe of him. Calling out to him, one of the boys said, "Just like Dr J."

Randy said, "No, like Randy Harris." Randy could play football, basketball and baseball very well, but football was his favorite. He liked the banging part of it.

The school bell rang and everyone scattered. All the kids ran in the door that was in back of the school on the Eagle Street side. Tony followed his second grade classmates in the corner door. Randy followed, going against school policy. Third through fifth also entered there. Kindergarten through first entered in the front with the sixth, seventh and eighth graders.

"As long as you never say how Corey really got cut, it'll be our secret. So don't get scared and tell," Randy warned.

"Randy, Corey doesn't know I know this, but he was upstairs in that guy's apartment the night before he went to the hospital and I know we were warned to never go up there by Mom and Dats."

"I know because I woke up from a bad dream and heard footsteps going up the front porch steps. Then he ran into the bedroom, sat in the chair he thinks is his and looked around not saying anything. I made believe I was sleep. I guess after a while we both went to sleep."

A young nun in a sky blue dress and white blouse with a white veil on her head motioned for Tony to come into his homeroom. The halls were almost empty then, as class was about to start.

"Aren't you supposed to be in front, Randy?" the nun asked with a knowing smile.

"Yes, Sister!" Randy said. If we didn't know the nun's name, we were told to address them as just `Sister'. Randy hated it.

After Randy gently pushed Tony inside his classroom, he ran out the back door and then to the front of the building., Everyone was entering the building. The front yard area was almost empty.

CHAPTER THIRTEEN

IT WAS JUST AFTER NOON and Henry was just waking up from the noise of Tibby slamming his office door. Henry's head was pounding. He rubbed his eyes and squinted at the bright light that Tibby just turned on. Henry held his head as Tibby sat behind his desk, opening and closing the desk drawers, looking for a working ink pen. With each drawer slamming, Henry's head hurt more.

"Shit," Tibby said. Henry held his head, trying to provide some insulation from the noise.

"Come on, Tibby, my credit card was here."

"What are you talking about, must be still drunk!" Tibby teased.

Henry slowly scanned the walls that had 8 x10 black and white photos of famous entertainers and athletes. Pictures of Whitney Houston, Michael Jackson, Stevie Wonder, Muhammad Ali, and Joe Frazier hung on the wall. Not that these famous people came to Tibby's. Some of the singers performed at the Star Light venue in Latham, New York, which was twenty minutes away by car.

"What time is it, Tibby?"

Tibby looked at Henry and smiled, then he looked at his watch on his left wrist.

"One."

"Oh, man, work . . . where's Sally B and what was all that about last night?" Tibby had a concerned look.

"Wha . . . what are you talking about? She wasn't even here last night."

Henry pulled his handkerchief from his pocket. On it was Sally B's lipstick he had wiped off his cheek from earlier that night. Henry held the handkerchief up towards Tibby.

"Then what's this?" Henry said.

"How am I supposed to know."

Henry put the handkerchief back into his pocket and stood, heading for the door.

"I don't know why you act so strange sometimes, Tibby. You got a beautiful wife, a profitable business, children, and you're always acting like you got something to hide, loosen up. You know damn well I came here with Sally B last night. And if you are hiding something, you're giving it away." Tibby frowned and waved Henry off.

"Yeah, okay, whatever you say. I'm outta here," Henry said as he left.

Tibby dropped his ink pen and pondered his thoughts momentarily. Then abruptly, he picked up the Sony portable phone and dialed a number. It rang twice.

It was a squeaky female voice that answered.

"Hello."

"Sally B," Tibby said.

"No, this is Christina."

"Where is she?"

"I don't know."

"Tell her to call me as soon as she gets in. I'm at the bar. Tell her I'm at the bar." Tibby nervously hung up before Christina did.

CHAPTER FOURTEEN

I WAS IN THE LIVING ROOM looking out the window onto Grand Street, watching the cars go by. A black four-door Honda Accord pulled up in front of the house and parked. The windows were tinted. I moved a little to the side of the window near the love seat. I peeked through the corner of the blinds so that whoever was getting out wouldn't see me.

A few minutes went by before anyone got out of the car. I grew a little impatient, and just when I was about to leave the window, Justin emerged slowly from the passenger side of the car. After he closed his door, he stood beside it and looked up and down Grand Street. His eyes scanned the cars that were parked on both sides of the street. Then he glanced up toward the window that I was looking out, and I darted back. I wondered if he saw me looking. I waited a few seconds, and then I heard the other door opening from the car. I kneeled down to a lower blind and peeked out, this time even more carefully than the first. I'd never seen this woman before. She wore a scarf over her head and had shades on. She had a long black raincoat on, which I thought was strange since the sun was shining and the sky was clear. What were they doing? Justin went to the trunk. Again Justin looked over his shoulder and then side to side after he opened the trunk. This was the first time I'd seen Justin outside during the day, and he'd been living upstairs for at least a few years. Of course I was always at school at this time, just like most of the other kids, and the adults were at work.

The streets were quiet, except for a few cars passing by occasionally. Justin had the keys in his index finger and thumb as he handed them to the woman in the large dark shades. She quickly trotted up the stairs. Justin then took the same black sack from the trunk that I saw him carrying down the stairs a few nights ago. I could see it clearer. It was a plastic, extra large garment bag. It also resembled one of those black body bags that I remember seeing when there was a nasty car accident in front of our house.

Justin threw the bag over his shoulder like a sack of potatoes. He headed up the stairs, occasionally glancing at the window I was peeking out. I needed to know what he had in that bag. I had an idea, but I wasn't sure. Mom and Dats had stepped out to get some groceries a while ago and weren't back yet. There was no way I could get upstairs while Justin was home.

Our living room had a door that led to the hallway. I peeked through the keyhole, and the woman with the shades was blocking my view because her back was to me as she held the door wide open for Justin.

The woman closed the door lightly and followed Justin up the stairs as he whistled pleasantly. I thought about calling the police, but then I wasn't positive of the contents of the bag. Plus, I wasn't exactly sure about the kid in the bedroom that night. I couldn't identify the kid. I know that would be the first question that the cops would ask, and I would look like a fool if I couldn't answer them. But then if it were another kid, what torture would he be going through while I'm here being unsure? I usually followed my gut on these situations, and my gut was telling me to call. I knew there was a kid upstairs, and who knows what was being done to him or her.

I went to the phone that hung on the wall near the kitchen. My adrenaline flowed, my heart thumped, and I was nervous. It would be a crapshoot, but I hoped I'd be correct. If not, I was dead. Or maybe I could make an anonymous call and they wouldn't know who called. But that wouldn't work because they trace all the 911 calls and they would find out it was me anyway, so why not just say it was me. Somebody had to help that kid. I picked up the phone receiver and dialed 911. The operator asked, "What's the problem?" I told them that, "A kid was being kidnapped in the upstairs apartment at 139 Grand Street." I hung up.

In minutes there was a squad car there and an officer ringing the upstairs doorbell.

"Who is it?" the woman yelled from upstairs.

"Police, open up," the strong male voice yelled from outside the front door. I sat in the love seat and listened. Then I heard the door close upstairs momentarily as the woman went back inside. Then I heard another car pull up outside the house. I peeked outside the blinds again, and it was another black and white squad car. The two officers got out of the car immediately and took their night sticks from the door holders, then they looked around the Myrtle Avenue side of the house. One stayed where he could see the Myrtle Avenue side of the house and the other stayed on the side on Grand Street where he could see if anyone was going to try to escape from the Grand Street side out of the upstairs back porch or window.

Finally, after about three minutes, I heard the buzzer ring, opening the door to let the police in. I quickly tiptoed to the dining room door that led to the hallway front door and gently cracked it a bit so that I could see the two uniformed cops going upstairs. I knew I did the right thing. Hopefully, the cops wouldn't let on who called them to Justin. Really, I don't think they could because this was considered a criminal activity, and for the police to tell the potential criminals who ratted on them was like signing my death warrant. The two policemen made it to the top of the stairs and I heard Justin's door squeak as it was opened.

The policeman talked very loud.

"Ma'am, sorry to disturb you, but we received an emergency call that there was a kidnapping in progress. What is your name, please?" I heard the cop take out his small notepad.

"Sally Bellows," she said with a blank face. She'd taken off the scarf and long coat.

"Ma'am, may we come in? We'd like to look around."

"Well, do you . . .

Before Sally B could say another word, Justin, who played in the bedroom off the kitchen yelled, "Sure you can, officer, come right in." The two officers cautiously walked in, unsnapping their gun holsters and keeping their hands on their guns.

"I'm just playing a video game in my little game room here." The two officers walked near the room just off the kitchen. It was the same room that Corey left his hand print on the door the night he snuck up there. One stayed a little further in back of the other and began to look around the kitchen.

Sally B stood by the front door, leaned on the wall and frowned with her arms folded.

"Oh, please, call me 'J', that's my nickname," Justin said politely, with his hand extended to shake.

"Sure," the cop said guardedly, shaking hands.

"What can I do for you gentlemen? "I'm the first to always want to please Albany's finest."

"About ten minutes ago, we received a call that there was a kidnapping in progress. That a man was seen carrying what looked like a child in a black bag over his shoulder."

Justin smiled. "Excuse me, officers. If you don't mind, I'll be glad to get the bag that the caller saw me carrying."

"Sure," the overweight officer said with caution. Justin slowly headed toward the living room, followed by the heavy officer, while the other short, muscled cop watched the front door area. He followed them slowly to the living room. The officer found an empty room. He made his way back.

"Sir, we have to respond to all of our 911 calls," Tom said, a bit agitated. Justin emerged from the bedroom off the living room, carrying the same black bag. "Officer, this is what your caller saw."

Justin laid the large garment bag on the sofa and unzipped it.

Inside the bag was laundered clothing. Officer Tom inspected the clothing. After taking a good look, he looked at Justin.

"I'm sorry to have bothered you. But, as you know, we're required to check out all 911 calls!" Officer Tom said.

"It's quite all right, officer, probably some kid playing a prank," Justin said with a smile, cutting his eyes at Sally B who looked on, blank faced.

Justin began to lead the officers toward the front door.

"Again, sorry for the interruption," Officer Tom said.

The officers slowly walked down the stairs, their keys and belt utilities jingling. Officer Tom's radio transmitted another call, and they picked up their pace going down the stairs as he responded by talking into his shoulder walkie talkie.

"Go ahead," Tom said.

The front door slammed as they exited the door. Justin slammed his apartment door. He had that evil look.

"We were lucky," Justin said, then looked at Sally B with a questioning glare.

"Now, who could've known something was going on here?" Justin said.

"Do those kids know anything?" Justin asked.

"Not that I know of," Sally B said.

"Justin, I think we need to go to New York for a while. Let things cool off. We need to make a pick up," Sally B suggested.

"Now would be a good time to go, I guess," Justin said.

From the living room window, I watched the squad cars take off as their sirens rang out. I guess they didn't find anything because if they would've, they would be arresting them. Where did they put the bag? I know someone was in that bag. Mom and Dats were taking a long time at the grocery store. My mouth was dry from anticipating what they might have found. I had to go to the kitchen to get a glass of water.

A thought crossed my mind. I remembered that in the yard next door there was a parking lot for the neighbor on the Grand Street side of the house. Leading down into the parking lot were steel steps mounted on the side of our house, coming from Justin's back porch.

I was on the kitchen phone. "Hi, Uncle Henry. Yeah, I'm okay. There's a little pain, but I'll be okay. Fishing? Yeah. No ocean. Revena? Yeah. But I need to wait for Mom and Dats to get back so I can ask them. You'll be here in thirty minutes? Okay, they should be back soon. They've been gone for a while now."

After I hung the phone up, I heard footsteps coming down the stairs in front. I ran lightly to the front window and knelt down. I heard the front door slam. It was Justin and the woman with the scarf and shades on. Justin was carrying that black bag again. This time it wasn't as full because he had it slung over his right forearm.

"Put this in the trunk," Justin said as he handed the black bag to the woman. Justin must have felt my eyes because he suddenly looked up to the window I was looking out, and our eyes met through the blinds. It was too late for me to run away. He began to smile. I was scared again. Somehow I knew he knew it was me who was in his apartment and called the cops. It was just my gut feeling. But he wouldn't try anything until he was absolutely sure. Even though he knew I knew, he wouldn't do anything to himself that would be too risky. I didn't care. All I was concerned with was exposing my abuser. I dreaded being violated for all those years. Justin walked around to the driver's side of the car, occasionally looking back at me in the window.

Mom and Dats were coming in the back door as Justin was getting into his car. He pointed his finger at me as if he were holding a gun. He clicked his finger as if he were pulling a trigger. Maybe I was getting to him. I don't know. Maybe he had something to do with me being molested. I was going to find out.

"Corey," Mom called from the back door as she entered. I got out of the window. I quickly glanced over my shoulder and saw Justin drive off with the woman wearing the scarf.

"Yes, Mom," I said as I walked toward her. She gave me a hug. She seemed nervous. Dats was at the back door, staring at me.

"Hi, Dats."

"Hello, Corey. How's your eye feeling?" He was trying to act concerned, which he may have been. But there was something bothering him.

"It's okay" Mom and I separated from our embrace.

"Mom, the police were upstairs."

"Really, I wonder why?" Dats moved closer to Mom and I.

"What happened, son?" Dats said.

"I don't know, they came and went up there."

"Did you see them take anyone out in their police car?"

"No, Dats."

"Humm. I wonder what the problem was? There's hardly any noise up there and he's always to himself. Eh, probably nothing. Did the police knock on our door, Corey?" Dats asked.

"No. But they had their hands on their guns like there was big trouble up there."

"Did you see anything before the police got here?" Dats asked.

I looked Mom in her eyes and she had this scared look. More scared than when her and Dats would finish their little fights. Then I looked at Dats' eyes, and he wanted to know now. I wasn't sure if I should lie or tell the truth. There seemed to be this long silence and tension that lasted forever.

"No, I didn't see anything. I just saw the police come and then they went upstairs!"

Mom sighed. Dats had a blank look. I think he knew I was lying. I had been caught in lies before. Especially since I had just told them I saw something upstairs the other night. But only because my brothers would tell on me.

"Mom, can I go fishing with Uncle Henry today?"

"He's working."

"No, he's not. He just called and said he would be here in a half hour"

Mom looked at Dats.

"If it's okay with your father, you can go."

Dats looked at both of us momentarily as he scratched the top of his head where his hair was thinning.

"I guess it can't hurt. Where's he going to, Ravena?"

"Yes."

"No playing in the water. You can't get your eye wet. It might get infected. And we want it to heal right," Mom said as she kneeled in front of me, tucking my shirt in my pants. It was her way of reaching out and telling me she loved me. I loved her too, even though I was mad at her for what she did to me the day Randy and Tony pushed me into her bedroom.

I ran to answer the doorbell. It was Uncle Henry. I opened the curtain and he gave me the thumbs up sign, along with his usual big smile. He had his blue jeans, blue flannel shirt and black boots on. He was definitely ready to go fishing. I opened the door for him and he lifted me up like I was a piece of paper in his huge hands.

"How's that eye?" he said as he put me down.

"Good. The police were here today." We headed into the kitchen where Mom and Dats sat.

"What were they here for?" I wanted to tell him the truth, but I thought it would be best to wait.

"I don't know. Four cops came. Then Justin left."

"Hey, people," Uncle Henry said to Mom and Dats. He leaned over and gave Mom a kiss on her cheek.

"What's this about the police being here?" I could tell Mom

and Dats really didn't want to talk about it.

"Well, come on, what's going on up there?"

"I don't know. We got here as the police were pulling off," Mom said.

Suddenly, the front door slammed shut. We all heard footsteps running up the stairs. Then keys were heard opening the lock at Justin's. The door squeaked as it opened, then it was slammed shut.

"What did he say was going on?"

"Henry, we really don't want to know," Dats said with agitation.

"Oh, well, excuse me for asking or even caring for that matter," Uncle Henry said, definitely taken aback by Dats' tone.

"Okay, okay, I'm gonna stay out of it. If you need me, you know where I am," Uncle Henry said, backing off. "Sis, you sure you don't want to at least ask the guy why the police were here?" Mom looked at Dats quickly, then back at Uncle Henry.

"Maybe we should know. After all, it is our house, Jim."

Mom abruptly pushed her chair away from the table, banging into the fridge.

"That's my sister. Take over." Uncle Henry said with a big grin. Uncle Henry followed directly behind Mom, with his hands massaging her shoulders like a boxing trainer leading his champion fighter into the ring for the fight of his life.

He kissed her on the cheek again and rubbed her arms. Mom smiled.

"Will you stop. You're so silly," Mom said as she laughed. But deep down inside she knew it was no laughing matter. Mom motioned for Uncle Henry to stop at the hallway door. She closed the door lightly in Uncle Henry's face and he sighed. He leaned his ear close to the door to eavesdrop as Mom made her way up the stairs. I went to the door to try to listen with Uncle Henry.

We heard footsteps heading up the stairs. She paused at the top of the stairs. Then we heard three knocks and the door being opened. "Hi, uh, Justin, uh, my son said he saw the police come up here and I was wondering if everything was okay?" There was a brief silence. Justin looked at Sara strangely. Then she walked inside.

"What's this all about, Sara?" Justin asked in a whisper.

"My brother urged me to come up here to find out what was going on with the police. I'm just doing this to keep him from suspecting anything." Sally B came from the bathroom.

"He doesn't suspect anything, does he?" Sally B asked as she lit a Marlboro.

"No, not at all."

"That brother of yours is a busybody, Sara. Keep him out of your business."

"No problem. Look, I'm gonna get back downstairs."

"You do that. I'm gonna find out who made that call. I don't know how, but let's hope it wasn't that son of yours."

"We might not be around for a couple of days. So if you don't hear from us, keep an eye on the place. And make sure the keys don't get into the wrong hands." Sara nodded and slowly walked out of the door nervously, and realized the depths of what she'd gotten into.

Sara walked briskly down the stairs to liven her spirits, trying to camouflage her fear. Uncle Henry opened the hallway door for her.

"Well?" Uncle Henry asked.

"Oh, it was just some prank call made," she said.

"Prank call, Mom?"

"Yes, Corey. Kids make prank calls to the police all the time. That's one of the reasons the police don't respond to calls as quickly as they could because kids are always playing games."

"Oh," I said.

"Well, Corey, I guess we should go fishing now that that's over with."

"Yeah, let's go now."

"You be careful with your eye, Corey. Henry, don't let him get water in his cut. I'm holding you responsible."

"Gotcha, Sis."

Uncle Henry and I headed out the front door while Mom watched. She occasionally glanced at the top of the stairs toward Justin's apartment, wondering what was next.

CHAPTER FIFTEEN

UNCLE HENRY AND I climbed into his old 1984 Chevy pickup flatbed truck. It was his transportation, which he usually used when he went to work. Its red paint was faded, and the corners of the truck were rusting as a result of Albany's long, cold, snowy winters. The fishing poles were in the back.

Uncle Henry headed south on Pearl Street.

"We going to Revena to fish, Uncle Henry?" I asked. Uncle Henry's attention was definitely divided.

"Yep. That's the best place this afternoon," Uncle Henry said, while he smiled at me and kept an eye on the road.

"What's wrong, Corey? You don't look too happy about going."

"It's nothing, my eye just hurts a little."

"It'll get better. Oh, man, I forgot something at the house. We're gonna have to make a quick run to my place."

Albany was a small city compared to New York City, even though it was the state capital. During the mid-afternoon, you could go from uptown to center downtown in five minutes. Even during their rush hour, which was calm compared to New York's, you could make it anywhere from uptown to downtown in approximately ten minutes.

Uncle Henry lived at 273 Ten Brook Manor. It was a quiet neighborhood, right on the border between uptown and downtown. The area was quiet most of the time, except for the Fourth of July or an occasional domestic dispute. Uncle Henry pulled up in front of his modest two-family house, which he didn't own. He didn't want to run a home yet. He felt he wasn't ready financially, nor did he want the responsibility that went with ownership. He liked the idea of being able to pick up and leave when he got ready, even though he hadn't left Albany in over twenty years, except when he went away to serve in the Army.

Uncle Henry ran up the ten concrete stairs to the front door of the building. I was right behind him. He unlocked the door and walked into the dimly lit hallway leading to his one bedroom first floor apartment.

Uncle Henry liked a well-lit apartment, so he always kept his shades open during the day and a light on at night. He went into his bedroom. It was very neat and clean. He definitely didn't take after his sister.

I went in the kitchen to check the refrigerator. It was always full of goodies. Mom wouldn't let us have a lot of sweets. I grabbed a piece of apple pie.

"Uncle Henry, can I have some pie?"

"Yeah, eat all you want."

Uncle Henry brought out his gun case from his bedroom and sat it on the kitchen table. He had a small arsenal of guns that he had stockpiled since his days in the Army. This was a new one.

"What's that?"

Uncle Henry pulled back the chamber and a bullet fell out. Then he took out the six-round clip.

"It's a Beretta Cougar 9 millimeter. Brand new."

I was bright eyed. I liked Uncle Henry's other guns, but this one looked different. It looked like it could fit my hand like a glove. "And guess what, I'm gonna teach you how to shoot," Uncle Henry said gleefully. "But you can't tell anybody, okay?"

"I won't." I never really was interested in guns, but suddenly I felt the need to want to learn how guns worked. I only wanted it for protection from my molester.

"But we're gonna fish first. Then we'll shoot for a while," Uncle Henry said with a smile.

Uncle Henry packed the gun back into the case. I was finishing up my apple pie. Uncle Henry went back into his bedroom and brought out a Hustler magazine. I smiled as he slid the centerfold page in front of me on the table.

"One of these days you'll have somebody like that."

All I was thinking about was Sandy, my nurse. I pictured her face on this body, then I got excited. Then Uncle Henry snatched it away.

"Enough of that. Don't wanna give you a heart attack. We gotta get going."

Justin sat at his kitchen table with Sally B, contemplating his next move.

"I need to know who made the call," Justin said as he rubbed his chin lightly with his thumb and index finger.

"It was probably just a coincidence," Sally B said.

"All the time I've been here and the one time someone sees me with a black garment bag. A hand print was on my front door the other night. The kid we had says he heard somebody up here, and now the cops. No, this was no coincidence. I've remained free from problems for over ten years, and I'm not about to start slipping now. I have a good idea who it is, but I gotta be sure. I need you to do something for me."

"Are you sure it's worth it? Could be opening up a can of worms," Sally B said.

Justin gave her that evil look, and she knew to just follow instructions.

"Okay, what is it you want me to do?" Sally B said.

"Nothing, for now."

* * * * *

We parked on Gates Road in Ravena. It was a narrow dirt road. There were no other cars parked there at that time of day. We got out of the truck. Uncle Henry grabbed both of the fishing poles and the bucket of bait from the flatbed of the truck. He then went back to the cab of his truck to get the Beretta.

It was a mile walk from the roadside to Gates Pond where we would fish. The fish that we usually caught weren't very big. We just went fishing most of the time to be together.

"So how's things at home, Corey?"

"Fine."

"Mom and Dats been fighting much lately?"

"No."

"What about you and Randy? You guys okay?"

"Yeah, I guess. We really haven't seen each other since we fought. That next day is when he -- I mean, is when I cut myself in the eye."

"By the way, how did that happen?"

"Well, it was like we said. I kinda walked into it." Uncle Henry stopped in his tracks and stepped on a twig. All you could hear was that twig snapping under his big foot. He just stared at me for a minute. He knew that there was more to the story. And I knew that he knew.

"You hear how that twig snapped when I stepped on it?"

"Yeah."

"That's gonna be your little neck if you don't tell me the truth. You know we don't lie to each other."

"What if I do lie to you, how are you gonna know it's a lie?"

Uncle Henry started to walk down the narrow path again.

"I won't know, but if you do lie, it will be on your conscience forever, not mine. And sooner or later, I'll find out the truth some-how, like I always do." I sighed and decided to talk.

"He stuck me on purpose, I think, anyway. I think he was still mad about the bite on the neck I gave him. Sort of like a payback. But I don't think he meant to stick me in the eye. I think he really wanted to just give me a little nick on the arm or maybe in the neck."

"You're still mad, aren't you?"

"Yeah, kinda."

"Why?"

"Because we're brothers and he shouldn'ta tried to cut me."

"You bit him, and at last count, I believe he was your brother then, too."

"They're always picking on me for no reason, just because I'm different."

"But that's no reason for you to try to take him out with one of the moves I showed you. I mean, you shouldn't even be fighting to try to hurt Randy like you were. It's dangerous."

"What about him, he cut me!"

"Yeah, he was wrong too. Now both of you need to shake and forget about it. We'll do it when I get back."

"I'll think about it. He probably won't even want to shake on it."

"Believe me, I think he's had enough at this point. The next step, somebody's gonna seriously get hurt. No, he'll shake all right." We walked through a muddy area.

"How's the eye?"

"It's okay . . . . Uncle Henry?"

"Yeah, I'm here."

"If you think you saw something but you're not quite sure what you saw, should you say anything about it?"

"Depends on what it is. Is it serious? Is it something that you saw with your friends?"

"What if somebody's maybe getting hurt?"

Uncle Henry stopped and looked around at me.

"What do you mean?" he said in a very serious tone.

"Well, I'm not absolutely sure."

"Well, maybe you shouldn't say anything if you don't know for sure what you saw."

"I didn't say I saw anything, Uncle Henry."

"Did or didn't?"

"I guess I didn't then, because I'm not sure."

We finally reached the pond area. Uncle Henry cleared an area with his foot for him to put the equipment down. I put the pint-size white cardboard box of worms on the ground. I pulled a huge worm out of the box and watched it squirm as I hooked it. I threw my line into the pond and sat on a nearby rock. Uncle Henry gathered some small kindling and put it in the area near where he cleared away.

"What are you doing that for, Uncle Henry?"

"If we don't catch anything, we're gonna shoot us a rabbit and skin it, cook it, then eat it," Uncle Henry said as he pulled up his pants. "Damn pants are too big. I must be losing weight."

I laughed.

"What's so funny?"

"All you need is a good belt, Uncle Henry."

"Eh, belt, smelt. They just get in the way."

My fishing line began to tug.

"Hey, looks like I might have one, Uncle Henry, and you haven't even gotten your line in the water."

"That's because I'm preparing for our dinner while you try to catch it."

I began to give my pole a little tug to snag the little fish. I reeled the wagging fish in. It was my first catch of the day I unhooked it and threw it in the empty pail next to me. I felt sorry for the fish as I unhooked its mouth.

"Poor fish. Swim around looking for a bite to eat and it winds up getting eaten."

"Kinda what happens in life sometimes to people who are looking for help. They think somebody is trying to help them and the next thing you know they are being used and abused by the person they thought was gonna help them."

As I re-wormed my hook and threw my line back into the water, I could only think about the noise I heard that night I snuck up to Justin's apartment, and the times I'd been molested. I kept wondering if I should say something. Would Uncle Henry believe me? Would he think I was making it all up for attention or because I'd watched so many mysteries on television?

Uncle Henry threw his line into the water and sat next to me. We were both more silent than usual.

"You okay, Corey?"

"Yeah."

"How many you think you're gonna catch today?"

"Who knows. Let's clean out the pond, then get that rabbit."

I turned my head slightly toward Uncle Henry, who was staring out towards the pond. I wanted to say something.

"What's on your mind, Corey?" he said, without looking at me.

I wanted to tell him badly about what had been going on, but I wasn't sure he wasn't a part of it. If he was, who knows, he could kill me and say I ran off or drowned in the pond. I decided to tell him about the noise I heard upstairs in Justin's apartment to see how he reacted to that. Then I would do what my gut told me regarding being molested, I thought. What the hell.

"I didn't actually see what happened. But I heard something more than I saw it." Uncle Henry yanked on his pole trying to hook a fish, acting very nonchalant.

"Are you listening?"

"I'm right here. Keep talking."

"Okay. You promise not to tell?"

"I promise.

"First, I thought you were gonna show me how to shoot the Beretta?"

"I am, but you gotta promise you won't tell your Mom and Dats."

I smiled, "I won't." Uncle Henry knew what I was getting at.

"Okay, so I'll keep my promise. You want me to show you how to shoot first, that way if I tell, you'll tell about the guns?"

"Not exactly, but sort of. I didn't say it, you did. It's kinda scary what I have to tell you, so I need to be able to defend myself just in case someone tries to attack me."

Uncle Henry put down his pole with a fish tugging on his line.

"You got one, where are you going?"

He waved me off, heading toward his gun case. I grabbed his fishing pole and reeled the bugger in. It was small and wiggled like crazy. I unhooked it and threw it in the dry pail. I looked at the two fish in the pail for a moment, then decided to scoop some water into the pail so the fish could continue to live for a while longer. Maybe forever, if we never cooked them. I could think of many ways to cook them, but for some reason, I didn't want to.

After a few minutes, Uncle Henry was back from his truck. He handed me a brown grocery bag.

"Set these cans up on those rocks in front of that tree."

"That's not very far, Uncle Henry."

"I know, it's your first time. You gotta get comfortable with the gun first before you try to shoot distance."

I walked to where Uncle Henry told me and set up the four cans. Each had about two inches of space between them, lined up side by side. Uncle Henry loaded the gun. I looked in the case and there were three six-round clips, four counting the one he just loaded into the gun.

"Stand on my right side." I moved as he instructed.

"You pull the safety pin off." He took off the safety.

"You load the chamber by grabbing this, using your thumb and index finger and click it back." He clicked it back.

"Now you're ready to fire." I looked at him in the eyes.

"You wanna go first, Corey?"

"No, I don't know how."

"Good answer. Never try to shoot a gun without someone showing you how. All those stories you hear about having accidents with guns are accidents because people don't know what they're doing and they've never been taught properly." He'd gotten my attention, fully.

"Okay, now stand to the side of me and a little behind, but not too far to where you can't see the targets. First, move the cans from in front of the tree. We don't want it to ricochet off the tree. Not that it will, but you never know, safety first."

I moved the four beer cans to a rotted log, putting them on top spreading them about three inches apart. In rapid fire, Uncle Henry shot the cans off the log, using only four bullets. I went to take a look at the cans and was amazed at what I saw.

"All four, dead center." I picked up all four cans and brought them back to Uncle Henry for him to examine. He stood about fifty feet away. I showed the cans to Uncle Henry, and he blew the end of his gun imitating the way Clint Eastwood would do it in his old western movies.

"Now, why don't you just line'em up again and let's see what you can do." I smiled and hurried to put the cans back on the log, lining them up exactly the same. Then I went back to Uncle Henry.

"First, never point this thing at anyone unless you're absolutely sure you're gonna use it. Second, always put the safety on while you check the chamber for the bullet. Then you pull the chamber back and load your round. And you slap the round in. Like this." Uncle Henry took the clip off and put it back in, slapping the butt of the gun with his palm, making sure it was in.

Uncle Henry got behind me, knelt down and looked over my left shoulder. He had his hand on the gun while I held it.

"Now, look at your target. Remember, when you shoot, your hand always jumps up from the power of the gun. Aim dead center of the can."

"Uh huh." I was a little nervous.

"Okay, now I'm gonna take my hand away and you pull the trigger when you're ready. Put both hands on the gun and spread your legs shoulder width apart. Go ahead." I fired one shot.

"That wasn't too bad, just a little more to the right the next time."

Two shots were fired.

"Better, better, at least you're gettin' closer."

"Uncle Henry, I'm missing though."

"Remember to aim and concentrate. You'll get it."

"Okay."

"There ya go. Three down and one standing. Now that's the way you shoot," Uncle Henry said with a smile.

"Next time you'll get all four." I twirled the gun on my finger and put it back in my imaginary hip holster.

"Wow, a regular gun slinger are ya. You better gimme that now before you shoot yaself in the toe."

I handed the gun to Uncle Henry. A jack rabbit came from in the bushes and just stared at us.

"Dinner?" Uncle Henry whispered.

I smiled at Uncle Henry and raised my eyebrows.

"And I'll cook it, okay, Uncle Henry?"

Lightning fast Uncle Henry nailed that poor rabbit. This would taste a lot better than the cat I fed to Uncle Henry, I thought.

"What are you smiling at? Didn't you think that was a good shot? Right between his eyes," Uncle Henry said.

"You shoot'em and I'll cook'em."

"You do that, kiddo. By the way, what was that you cooked the last time I ate your cooking?"

"Cat."

Uncle Henry laughed boisterously. "Yeah, sure it was."

I walked toward the pond, then glanced back toward Uncle Henry who had a bewildered look.

"Whatever it was, it tasted great."

"Wait'll I cook that rat from the basement," I said to myself, smiling.

"Huh?"

"Nothing. Thanks for showing me how to shoot. Maybe someday it'll come in handy."

"Don't even think about it. And don't tell a soul what we did here today."

"Now, since we both have something on each other, I can tell you what I saw, Uncle Henry."

"What?"

"Actually, I was upstairs in Justin's apartment one night. The night me and Randy had that fight. I can't say that I really saw something. It was more like I heard somebody but never had the chance to look because Justin was coming."

"Oh, so you snuck upstairs?"

"Well, yeah. I'd never been up there and I wanted to see what it looked like. I wasn't trying to steal anything."

"So what'd you hear?"

"It sounded like a little boy."

"Where? Which room?"

"In the room near the front, next to the living room. It sounded like he was in pain. I don't know, maybe he was saying help in a cracked voice." Uncle Henry put his pole down, took me by the arms, turned me toward him and looked me in the eyes.

"Have you told anyone else this?"

"You're making me scared the way you're looking at me, Uncle Henry."

"Well, I don't mean to, but if you heard a kid and this guy Justin doesn't have any kids as far as anybody knows, it just doesn't sound good."

"How'd you know his name, Uncle Henry?"

"Well, I do come to your home, Corey. Don't tell anyone else this. I'll talk to your father and see if he's heard anything or seen any kids up there. But I won't mention anything about you, don't worry."

"Why is it such a big deal? Maybe it was his niece or nephew having a bad dream, Uncle Henry."

"I know he once told your dad he didn't have any family. That he was the only child. Eh, it's probably nothing. When are you gonna cook our rabbit dinner?"

"Ah, now, but you gotta skin it first."

I thought about how I didn't tell Uncle Henry the whole truth, about how I actually saw the boy. But I had to be cautious with what I told him. For the time being, Uncle Henry knew enough. I decided to just watch and see what happened. No matter what, the culprit had to die for molesting me!

CHAPTER SIXTEEN

AFTER THAT VISIT from the police, Justin and Sally B decided to take the first plane available to New York City. Justin didn't spook easily, but then again, the police had never visited his apartment in Albany before, or anywhere else for that matter.

Sally B drove a Hertz rental, a four-door black Tempo, fast, headed west on Flatbush Avenue in Brooklyn, New York. They could have taken a faster way to Manhattan, but Justin needed time to think.

"You think the kid made the call, Sally B?"

"Maybe. If he did, maybe it was a prank. You ever done anything to make the kid mad?"

"Nah. All I said to him at the hospital was 'hello'."

"Hospital? What were you doing there?"

"Paying my respects to Jim and Sara."

"Maybe Corey thought it was strange you being there especially since you two never met and you live upstairs from him."

"No, it was Corey. It was his hand print on the bedroom door and it was him who the last boy we had was mumbling about that night I couldn't find you to help me get him out of town."

"What'd you do with him anyway?"

"I threw him in the Hudson River."

"But why? You coulda waited and I could have brought him back and lost him in New York."

"Couldn't take that chance." Justin's voice began to rise.

"And if you're that interested in him, I can easily help you find your way to the bottom of the Hudson."

Sally B knew Justin was serious, but had to at least show she wasn't totally terrified of him.

"Then who you gonna get to run ya nursery pen?"

Justin grabbed her by her throat, causing her to make the car swerve, almost side-swiping two cars.

"Don't ever talk that shit to me."

Sally B slammed on the brakes bringing the car to a stop. Justin let go of her neck and pushed her head into the window.

"And open your window, it's hot in here," Justin said. Sally B reluctantly rolled down the window. She rolled her eyes at Justin.

Car horns blew loudly in succession behind Sally B as traffic backed up. It was peak traffic time at six o'clock and people couldn't change lanes so easily. As drivers passed Sally B they flipped her the finger and cursed her in true New Yorker fashion.

They were quiet the rest of the way to Manhattan. Sally B had experienced these outrages by Justin before, but they were mostly verbal, with occasional slaps on the face. She wasn't about to become another abused and battered woman, she thought. As they drove from the east side of Manhattan to the west side down Chambers Street, traffic was murder.

The sun was going down. It was still spring and the weather was very pleasant. The sidewalks were full. People walked to and from stores and to and from work. They were driving toward 42nd Street.

"Look, I'm sorry all right?" Justin said as he touched Sally B's shoulder.

Sally B lightly adjusted her shoulder so that Justin's hand fell off.

"You're gettin' a little too physical for me. It wasn't my fault that the cops were called. Anybody could've called them. You gonna kill another innocent kid just because he may have seen something."

"Look, your hands are dirty with every crime I commit. So

don't make yourself out to be so saintly. You only run my entire operation for me. Now let's get to Truman quickly!"

"I thought you wanted to go over to Tenth Avenue!"

Justin glanced at his ten-year-old Timex.

"I changed my mind. I need to do something!" he snapped.

Sally B hooked a right onto Broadway, causing them both to sway to the right in the car.

"Hey, slow down. You trying to kill us both?" Justin said, laughing. "You women sure do know how to get mad."

Sally B sped up Broadway, catching almost every green light.

"You need to calm down, Justin. Everything is fine. Let me find out about this boy." After a few blocks, she took a left onto Park Avenue and flew, catching all green lights. Justin looked at her with slanted eyes and a smirk.

"Woman, I ain't stupid. You better follow through. You don't even know this kid, so why you like him so much alla sudden? You just think I'm a cold-blooded killer, don't you?"

Sally B gave him a 'you said it, I didn't' look.

"Oh, woman, please. Look at all the kids I've given jobs to. Otherwise, they would be on the street sellin' themselves for peanuts, workin' for some nickel and dime pimp. Me, I put them in nice hotels." He gestured with his hands and looked around at the well-kept buildings as they headed uptown. "Park Avenue, Ritz, you name it, they've worked there. Got to stay there, too, maybe not for long, but it's all the same."

He was feeling good about what he had done. His smile widened with every verse. "Shiiittt! Look at you. You were a piecea ass whore sellin' ya ass to 'nobodies' until you met me. My goodness, woman, give me some credit. How many thirteen-year-olds out there wish they had what our girls have? Thousands of them, that's how many. I'm a businessman. It's the American dream. Yeah, it's illegal, but so were the Rockefellers and Kennedys and Contra Scan."

"Scam," Sally B said, grinning.

"Scan, scram, whatever. Hell, this whole goddamn country was built illegally by slaves. You know it just as well as I do. So tell me, what's so wrong with givin' a kid a chance to make some real money?" Sally B frowned.

"I'm talking about a kid whose already out there on the streets, begging and stealing and hustlin' whoever they can, huh?" Sally B was silent as she sped up.

"Uh-huh, that's what I thought. You know I'm right." He chuckled as Sally B had calmed down.

"Now gimme a kiss, baby, 'cause without you I'd go crazy."

Sally B looked at him with her big baby brown eyes and leaned over to kiss him. Justin tilted forward and pecked her lightly on the lips.

As they drove up to the valet section of Truman Towers, Justin put on his dark sunglasses and his blue Mets baseball cap. He put the cap so that it covered most of his forehead. The valet driver came to Sally B's side and opened her door. Another valet hastened to Justin's side and opened his door, but he didn't get out.

"Ten sixteen," Sally B said. "Oh, that's all right, he'll ride with the driver to the garage," she said as she handed the valet a twenty dollar bill.

The valet closed Justin's door, and the other valet got in and drove down the runway. Justin was hunched down in his seat, concealing his face as much as possible from the driver.

"How are you this evening, sir?" the valet driver asked.

Justin nodded and barely said hello.

"Beautiful night," the valet said, trying to start a conversation.

"I guess you're not doing too good," the valet said and shrugged his shoulders as he pulled into the space provided for condo number ten sixteen.

The valet driver got out.

"I'll get it, sir."

"No need," Justin said quickly.

The valet took the stairway back up two levels to the front of the towers.

Justin got out of the car and walked to the glass double doors. On the clean, white concrete was a black telephone used to call for help, if needed.

Justin pushed the numbers ten sixteen, then spoke into the intercom near the telephone.

"Sally B, it's me, buzz me."

The building was immaculate. The door buzzed and Justin pushed it open, went in and stood in front of the gold-plated elevator door. The elevator arrived in about a minute. Justin took out a plastic card key and slid it in the golden key slot for the penthouse. As he rode up, he smiled and inhaled deeply the fresh rosebud smell, enjoying the scent. He leaned back on the gold rail that was attached to the three walls of the elevator. He rubbed the golden walls with his fingertips, enjoying how clean and well-kept they were. He took his right foot out of his black loafer and rubbed his toes in the thick burgundy carpet.

"Ah, home," Justin said as the elevator door opened. He picked up his shoe and exited the elevator. The floors of the tenth floor were marble and very clean. There were only six condos on the tenth floor. From the tenth to the twentieth were glamorous condos. Residents on these floors included rock stars, athletes and movie stars.

As he approached door number ten sixteen, it opened. The floor was black marble. He stopped and scanned the beautiful decor of his opulent condo. He sighed and sniffed the cool, water-like cologne that perfumed the air. It was home for Justin, and it was fabulous. Whatever he lacked living incognito in Albany, he definitely made up for it with his lavish lifestyle in New York City. Justin walked down two steps that were a few feet from the front that led to the spacious living room. It was only a small part of the five thousand square foot penthouse. All of the furniture was imported from Spain, but it didn't have a Spanish feel to it. Justin sat on the white oval sofa located in the center of the room.

"Gimme the phone," he said. Then he took his small pocket calendar from his back pocket. He keyed in some numbers and leaned back on the sofa, sighing. Sally B returned with the black Sony portable telephone. She handed it to Justin, but he didn't take it.

"Here," Sally B said.

Justin opened his eyes and looked at Sally B.

"No, I want you to dial this number and ask for Captain Lee. Dial this number." Justin showed Sally B the number.

"Why are you calling Albany?"

"Just dial it."

Sally B sighed, then dialed the number. Captain Lee was an old running buddy of Justin's while they were growing up in New York. Lee and Justin used to pull scams together to make money when they were in their early teens. But Lee moved from the neighborhood and lost contact with Justin. Justin found him after Lee graduated from college, and they kept in touch from time to time.

Lee moved to Albany with his wife to get away from the fast pace of New York. He joined the force when he couldn't find a job in public administration after graduating from college.

Lee was two years older than Justin. He knew Justin lived in Albany, but he didn't know what he was really into. He was a tall, slender man with rough looking light skin, short dark hair, and a very square jaw.

"Captain Lee, please," Sally B said in a bothered tone. She folded her arms and held the phone to her ear with her shoulder.

"She heard a male voice say, "Lee.""

"Captain Lee?"

"Yes, who's this?" Sally B motioned to Justin for what to say next.

"Tell'em it's 'J'," Justin said with a smile.

"It's 'J'."

"'J'? This isn't 'J'. He's up to his old tricks, huh? Put'em on." Sally B handed Justin the phone.

"Hey, how ya doin' my good friend? Long time!" Lee said.

"Yeah, I'm in New York for the day. Just to see my family. Ya know what, I need you to do me a little favor. My friend has been getting some prank calls at his house. I think it's just kids, but somebody went a little too far when they had some of your boys come to his house on a 911 call. Can you check your records and lemme know who did this so the guy can at least ask the kids' parents to discipline whoever it is?" Lee was a little hesitant.

"Well . . . sure."

"Thanks, Lee. When I get back to Albany, let's get together."

"Okay, talk to you later."

Justin clicked the phone off and sat it on the solid gold top coffee table. He looked up at Sally B, who leaned on the edge of the white sofa.

"Well, now what? You just can't ease up, can you?" Sally B said.

"No, why should I? We gotta talk business. Are we increasing every week?"

"The gaming is picking up big and so are the girls. Do we really need to keep up with the kids? I think we should maybe lay off with them for a while, especially with what happened today in Albany."

Justin smiled. "Oh, so you do think it was more serious than you're lettin' on."

"No, I just think we need to back off." Sally B went and sat next to Justin.

"I always go with my gut and I think we should get out of the kid-selling business. It's twice as risky as the prostitution and gambling. Kids are just so fickle. All it takes is for one to get away and talk and we're goin' down."

Justin abruptly stood up and looked down at Sally B.

"No! You are goin' down if even one of those kids talks. The only way I'm goin' down is if you rat," Sally B frowned. Justin cupped her chin in his hand.

"N'you wouldn't do that, would you, Sally B, huh? Huh?" He yanked her head up a couple of times before she answered.

"No, I wouldn't." She jerked her chin from his hand and he grabbed it back. He kissed her on the lips, then he let her go and began to laugh loudly.

"Let's go take a look at the books," Justin said, leading Sally B to one of the six spacious bedrooms that had been converted into a full scale office. He took her over to his large, leather, black sofa. He began to kiss her, and she pulled away.

"Oh, I see I've been gone too long."

"Justin, we don't have time for this. We gotta get out and get that next kid like you wanted. Isn't that what we came here for in the first place?"

"Yeah, but don't you miss me?" Justin said as he kissed her lightly on the cheek.

"I thought you wanted to take care of business first?"

"This is business." He put his arms around her. Then he began to caress her butt and back.

"How do you figure this to be business?"

"Who knows? One day we may go broke and I might have to put you back out on the block with the kids." Justin began to stare deeply into Sally B's reluctant eyes. She knew what was coming. She tried to look away but couldn't resist as she stared back. He knew just what to do to put her under his complete control.

"You love me, you love me. Keep me, separate me, feel me, be me. Piece by piece I shall never cease," Justin said softly.

This was Justin's hypnotic call to Sally B.

She slowly repeated his words.

"You love me, you love me. Keep me, separate me, feel me, be me. Piece by piece I shall never cease."

She was at his mercy.

"Come with me," Justin commanded softly.

Sally B's gaze was deeper in Justin's eyes.

Justin pointed at her blouse and she unbuttoned it, fully exposing her breasts. He lightly kissed her nipple peacefully. His tongue slid to her naval. Small bubbles of perspiration started on her body. She unzipped her pants and took them off.

Throughout the night she ushered his bare body on top of hers from the soft couch to the plush carpet. Not another word was said.

CHAPTER SEVENTEEN

SALLY B DROVE CASUALLY along the seedy part of downtown New York on the westside. She scanned the many prostitutes that lined each corner. She spotted what appeared to be a teenager alone in the corner of a building. The brunette wore a skimpy, short red dress with white pumps and clutched a white patten-leather purse.

The teen had a gloomy look as Sally B pulled up to the curb.

"Excuse me, are you lost?" Sally B shouted from her car.

The young girl raised only her eyes toward Sally B as she continued to sit on the building ledge. Then she shifted her eyes back to the ground. Sally B got out of the car.

"What's your name?" Sally B asked. Then she sat next to the girl on the ledge. "Is everything okay?" The girl shook her head no. "Is there anything I can do to help you?" She glanced at Sally B in her eyes.

"Maybe me and my friend can help you. Are you lost?"

"No."

"Did you run away from home?"

The girl hesitated, then spoke.

"Are you the police?"

"No."

"How do I know that?"

"I guess you'll have to take my word."

She turned herself away from Sally B. Sally B got up and began to walk back to her car. The girl looked at Sally B as she walked.

"Wait," she said.

Sally B stopped and smiled.

"How can you help me?" the girl asked.

Sally B lost the smile and turned toward her.

"First, you must tell me your name and how you got out on the streets like this?"

The girl sighed.

"My name is Mary"

"You run away?"

"Maybe."

"Been workin' the streets?"

"You could say that, maybe."

"Ever done this before?"

"Few times."

"Well, why no luck?"

"I just got here and it seems like everybody has a boss."

"Well, so it seems. You wanna make some real money?" Sally B asked as she stood over Mary.

"Who doesn't?"

"You'd be surprised."

"What does that mean?"

"Nothing. Well what are you gonna do? Coming with me or what?"

"For what?"

"Get you cleaned up first. We gotta get some of that dirt off of you to see if you even qualify to work for us. Looks to me like there's a pretty girl underneath, maybe." Actually, Mary wasn't dirty at all. It was Sally B's way of telling Mary that things would be different if she came to work with her. Mary was silent.

"Who's us?"

"I'll tell you what, I'm walking back to my car, and if you're coming you'll follow me and get in, if not, I'll see you around kid."

Sally B quickly made her way to the car, got in and pulled off. Mary saw this and went dashing down the street after her. Sally B saw her through the rear view mirror, stopped, picked her up and drove off.

Sally B arrived back at her plush hotel suite. She escorted Mary directly to the shower.

"Get in and I'll get you some clothes. And don't take all night."

Sally B moved from the bathroom and Mary entered the shower, fully dressed. She was in a hurry, and still a little unsure.

Sally B returned with a new short, black tight-fitting dress and matching black pumps for Mary. She hung the dress behind the door and put the shoes nearby. By then Mary had undressed in the shower.

"Give me those wet clothes," Sally B said.

Mary gave Sally B the clothes, with thoughts of leaving behind the old and starting new. She went back into the shower.

"Hurry up now, Mary. We've got something to do."

"Almost done," Mary said.

"I want you dressed when I come back in. Five minutes. Got it?"

"Yeah," Mary answered, excited.

Sally B cautiously entered a nearby bedroom that was very dark.

"Is she ready?" a deep voice asked.

"Just about."

"Hurry up, we don't have much time."

"I'll be right back," Sally B said as she backed out the door, then closed it behind her.

Sally B entered the bathroom.

"Are you—"

"Yes," Mary said with a smile.

Mary was fully dressed and her shoulder-length curly hair went well with her new outfit.

"How do I look?"

"Good. But you didn't wash your hair?" Sally B asked as she got a closer look.

"Didn't have time. You said to hurry up."

Sally B smelled it. It didn't stink.

"Don't worry it's clean. I took a shower at the mission earlier today."

"Okay. Now listen," Sally B said with a stern look. "And take that grin off your face."

Mary's smile vanished.

"This guy does not mess around. He's gonna ask you some questions. Just answer them and don't talk smart and you'll make a lot of money. Got it?"

"Got it," Mary replied. She knew this was serious business. Her heart began to pound faster.

"Follow me."

Mary cautiously followed to the room door.

"Go in and don't say one word. Find the chair and sit."

Mary entered the bedroom slowly. It wasn't as dark as before, but she still couldn't see well. She could see a chair and a large figure sitting in another chair on the other side of the table.

"Please, have a seat," the deep male voice said.

Mary slowly sat down, never taking her eyes off the direction of the voice.

"What's your name?" he asked.

"Mary," she said, nervously.

"Relax. I'm not gonna hurt you. I'm here to help."

She sighed and relaxed a bit.

"Where you from, Mary?"

"Utica."

"Small, scrappy town. Why'd you leave?"

"I just left."

"Something going on you didn't like?"

"Sort of."

"Like what?"

"Just things."

"You have brothers and sisters?"

"No."

"You have a boyfriend?"

"No. Yeah, but my parents don't know."

"Why?"

"Said I was too young and don't need a boyfriend."

"How old are you?"

"Fourteen."

"Why did you leave home?"

"My parents beat me." Mary said as she started to sniffle, holding back tears.

"Don't feel bad, my parents beat me too. My father used to do weird stuff to me."

There was brief silence.

"You don't have to worry about anyone here beating you. I just wanna make you feel comfortable."

He moved his chair next to Mary's. "If me sitting this close to you makes you uncomfortable--"

"No, it's ok."

"Sure?"

"Not really, but I'm not nearly as nervous as I was when I came in here. So I guess it's ok."

"Good. I can see you and I are gonna have a nice, long, working relationship. All you have to do is, do as I suggest and everything will work out fine for you." Justin put his arm around her. "Don't worry about a thing. Are you hungry?"

"Thirsty?"

"Well, what are you?"

"To be honest—"

"I'd hope that you'll always be honest."

"I will. This is the first time I've felt somewhat comfortable in a very long time."

"Good. You tired?"

"A little."

"Why don't you go lay down over there on the bed."

"Where?"

"Let me show you. Take my hand."

Mary gradually found Justin's hand. Justin slowly stood and Mary followed his lead. They went to the bed.

"Have a seat or lay down, whatever you like. I'll just be right outside."

Justin began to walk away.

"Well, aren't you gonna stay with me?"

"Sure, right outside the room."

Justin stopped at the door.

"No, I meant in here."

"Would you like me to?"

"I thought maybe that's what you wanted?"

"No. Not at all. I'm only here to help you. I don't think it's a good idea that I stay in here with you."

"Please . . . would you?"

Justin thought for a few moments.

"Look, I'll stay in here until you fall asleep," Justin said as he walked to the bed and sat next to Mary.

"Will you lay down with me?" Mary asked.

"Why?"

"I just want you to."

"Are you sure?"

There was brief silence. "I'm sure."

Early that morning, after Justin had had his way with Mary, he decided that it was time to take care of business. It was still dark outside and Justin had it dark in the living room where the three of them sat. He wanted it dark so that Mary could not get a good look at him. Justin glanced at the large illuminated clock behind the small bar. It read four o'clock.

"Mary, we would like to give you a nickname. Is that okay?" Justin asked.

"Why?"

"With the kind of work you're doing, it's better that people don't know your real name. When you make a lot of money you might want to give up this business and do something else. To protect yourself you might not want people to call you the same thing as now."

"What name?"

"How about something real simple, like May. I always liked the month of May. It's when everything starts to bloom and the weather begins to warm up."

"That's sounds fine. I like May."

"What do you think, Sally B?" Justin asked.

"Sounds good to me."

"Then it's settled. May it is," Justin said.

"Sally B, what time did you tell Racine?"

"Four."

"You okay, Mary?" Justin asked.

"Yes."

"You'll be working with this guy, Racine. He's very good and he's fair. Work closely with him and do what he says. Everything'll work out okay. He knows the business well."

"I thought I was gonna be working with you?"

"You are. Racine works with us. He'll be your daily contact. If you have any problems, contact us. You will always be able to reach Sally B or me. That okay?"

"As long as I can still talk with you."

"No problem. I'm here to help you. That's what me and Sally B are here for."

Mary nodded.

"Just keep in mind that if I'm not available, Sally B will be, and she can take care of everything. I trust her with my life. If there is any problem with Racine, which there shouldn't be, call us immediately. Understood?"

"Yes."

"He may require you to work out of town from time to time. Don't worry it'll only be for a short while, and you'll be paid very well for your efforts."

"Don't worry I'll be alright. And thanks."

"Now Sally B will take you downstairs to meet Racine. Good luck, and I'll be seeing you soon."

Sally B stood from the sofa. Mary promptly followed. Mary went and gave Justin a hug as he remained seated in the dark.

"Take care." Justin said.

"Wow!"

"What is it?" Justin asked.

"We spent a whole night together and I never ever saw your face."

"That's okay. One day we will meet for lunch," Justin said.

"Let's go, Mary," Sally B said as she moved toward the door. Mary followed.

Justin knew he would never see Mary again. Sally B tended to daily matters. But she too may never see Mary again. That's how she had it set up. Racine was the man in the middle, and the one Mary would work for.

In the lounge, Racine waited patiently for Sally B and his new worker. They exchanged greetings and instructions. Racine ushered Sally B to the side, away from Mary.

"How's the boss?" Racine asked.

"Good, as usual. Got the right amount?"

"Here, I know this will make him even happier," Racine said

as he handed Sally B an envelope. " I'm outta here," he said. Racine went to get Mary. She waved goodbye to Sally B, and the gesture was returned. Mary didn't realize it, but she had just been sold.

Sally B returned to the suite. Justin remained in the chair, waiting patiently.

"Everything set?" he asked.

"Yes."

"How much?"

"Sixteen grand, just like you said."

"Good job. Take care of the cash later. Let's get back out there."

CHAPTER EIGHTEEN

IT WAS 5:00 A.M. A girl no more than twelve came up to Justin's passenger side as Sally B drove slowly south on Tenth Avenue near 42nd Street. She was not that attractive.

"Nah, get outta here," Justin said, smiling.

"We need something about ten years old. Something we can mold. I don't care if it's a boy or girl."

"Yeah, sure, Justin," Sally B said, irritated. A group of about five young girls approached Justin's door.

Justin was wearing his dark shades and his customary casual, all black clothing.

"How you like my new shirt, Sally B?" Justin asked with a smile. Sally B slyly glanced at Justin's shirt.

"It's just like all the rest of 'em."

"Now see, it's a new one."

"Don't understand what you're trying to say."

They passed by 35th Street and Tenth Avenue and they saw a girl getting into a new white Cadillac Seville. It was driven by a silver haired Caucasian man.

"Look at that. She is fine and young. Look at that trim body, every part is perfect. She's gonna kill that old bastard. But she's the type we need."

"I thought you wanted a boy?" Sally B asked.

"I do, but I want a girl, too. We can get a lot of money for her over in Japan. Follow the car."

"Justin, there are plenty of girls out here."

"But not like her. Now follow the car, woman!"

The Seville picked up speed after the girl got in. Sally B was about a half a block behind her when it turned right onto 29th Street.

"They're turning, don't lose'em," Justin warned.

"Whaddaya want me to do, tailgate, broadcasting that we're following them?"

Justin gave her a mean look.

"Ya know, you're running off at the mouth a little too much lately. What's gotten into you, woman?"

"You."

"Me! Nah, you got the wrong guy. Now, we ain't in love and never will be."

"Don't stroke yaself too much. I wasn't talking about being in love. I meant ya nasty attitude at times. You're so on edge about this boy in Albany."

"No, I'm on edge about the idea of facing jail again. And whenever I'm paid a visit by the cops for no reason that I caused, I'm concerned."

"Whaddaya care? Every aspect of your business is in false names that lead back to me. The only way you'll get caught is if I drop a dime on you." Sally B cut her eye at Justin, who pondered his thoughts. She knew that he may be contemplating getting rid of her. It would be hard for him to do it, but she knew if he was pushed, he'd do it in the blink of an eye.

"Look, just keep up with the Cadillac," Justin said. The Cadillac pulled half way down the block on 29th and parked.

"Stop right here," Justin said.

Sally B was not far from the corner of Tenth Avenue on 29th Street when she pulled over.

The silver haired man got out of his car, and the girl did too. He came on the sidewalk near her, and she motioned for him to follow her up the stairs at 215 29th Street. The silver haired man quickly looked up and down the street to see if anyone was looking. Sally B and Justin sat near the corner with their lights out. The silver haired man was obviously nervous because he pointed at Sally B and Justin's car. The girl gently grabbed the man's hand, bringing it close to her. The girl knew it was a dead giveaway to point or make any other sudden movements. The key to it was to act like you belonged in the neighborhood.

"Looks like the kid knows her stuff," Justin said, impressed.

"Sure does," Sally B replied.

"Don't move or her trick is gonna get scared off," Justin said. Sally B and Justin `froze' still.

"Sure feels strange being back out on the streets. I haven't looked for a kid in a long time," Justin said.

"Nothing like working for a living," Sally B said sarcastically.

"Yeah, and that's what I've done since I was ten." The silver haired man followed the girl up the stairs.

"Now we just wait," Justin said as he eased down into his seat.

"This won't take long. And what are we gonna do when they finish?" Sally B asked.

"Well, maybe I'll buy a piece. Then sell it off," Justin said with a smile.

"So, who's your Japan contact?" Sally B asked.

"Asoto Ki."

"How does he know you?"

"He doesn't. He knows Sally B."

"Yeah, I told him I was your contact person and that you'd be taking over the deal 'cause you liked to wrap things up," Justin said.

"Where do you get these people from?" Sally B asked.

"You'd be surprised how popular the name Sally B is in New York. So you see, Sally B, you're in this thing deeper than I'll ever be," Justin said.

"I'm powerful, yet doomed," she said.

"That's the way all people in the public eye are. Eventually they all fade to the back. Me, I'm already in the back, but I'm really in front without being noticed. And it'll go on as long as I live."

"Then what's gonna happen when you die?" Sally B asked.

"Well, I guess it'll all be yours, Sally B. I will have played the game and won. 'Cause that's all this is, Sally B, the game of buying and selling, only we're not chaired on the stock exchange. And to be honest with you, as good as I got it, I wouldn't want to be."

"You still can't change the fact that you're a cold-blooded killer--you'll die with that."

"JFK, Lyndon B. Johnson, Eisenhower and Hitler were all cold-blooded killers in their own way. And they made them out to be heroes. Look at Lyndon B., he kept the Vietnam war going for purely financial reasons and look at how many lives were lost. The Vietcong kicked our ass right outta there. Senseless. Then you got Watergate. Cheating at the highest level—he got greedy and got caught. And North and Reagan and all the contras. All the illegal shit that goes down at that level is amazing. And they get away with it. Why? Because it's what this country was built on. Stole land from the Indians, brought black people over here to be slaves and lynched 'em when they felt like it. So tell me, who goes to their grave a saint, Sally B? Dying's probably the easiest thing I'll ever do--livin's the hard part!" he said with a chuckle.

Sally B's attention was drawn to the silver haired man coming down the four concrete steps of the house.

"There he is. Now where's she?" she mumbled.

"Oh, she'll be coming out. What I want you to do is get in the trunk when she does come out. Matter of fact, why don't you just do that now because if I'm calculating right, she should be coming out just as old silver hair pulls off."

The twelve-year-old came out. She stood at the top of the steps of the old, dilapidated, red brick, two-story building. She looked up and down the street, then began down the stairs. She hit the concrete and walked in the direction of Justin and Sally B's Hertz rental.

"Never mind, just drive off. You'll have to get back there later," Justin said.

Sally B drove off, headed west on 29th Street. She could not make a U-turn because the street was one way.

"Hopefully she'll be heading back up Tenth Avenue," Justin said as they passed the girl.

"Damn, she's beautiful. Better than I could ever tell from far away," Justin said as he turned around in the seat and got on his knees to look at her.

"Slow down, slow down."

"Damn, look at those hips. She's like a woman. Look at that ass."

"You would say that. Why don't you just marry the ho," Sally B said sarcastically.

"Maybe I will."

"Yeah, right. What would you tell her you did for a living?"

"She'd already know 'cause she'd take your place, smart ass," Justin teased.

Sally B sighed. "Not hardly!" she griped.

"Okay, she turned the block. Hurry up, get around there. She's headed up Tenth."

Sally B put the pedal to the metal so fast that Justin went flying on her as she made the turn on Eleventh Avenue.

"Damn, don't kill us," Justin said as he picked himself up and sat back down.

"Now pull over to that garage area and hop in the trunk!" Justin commanded.

Sally B stopped and got out of the car. She yelled to Justin, "Don't forget I'm in here."

Justin popped the trunk.

"Don't worry, I won't" Justin said.

Sally B climbed into the large trunk and closed herself in. Justin pulled the brim of his baseball cap over his forehead almost to his eyes and sped off up 28th Street. Upon approaching the corner of 28th and Tenth Avenue, he looked to his left, then to his right. She walked up Tenth Avenue on the right. She was in the middle of the block. Justin whistled at the pleasure she gave him as she approached. He took a right onto Tenth Avenue and slowly drove in the girl's direction. He stopped the car and leaned over to the passenger side to roll down the window.

"Hey, come here," Justin said in a very persuasive tone.

The girl looked up and down the street, then across to make sure there were no cops. Then she went over to the front passenger side window of the car. She leaned over and her small cleavage showed from the top half of her dress. Justin couldn't help but look hard from behind his dark sunglasses and Mets baseball cap.

"So, are you a cop?" she asked.

This was always the first question.

"Do I look like a cop? Even if I was, do you think I'd tell you?" Justin said.

The girl walked on up the street. Justin neatly threw the car in drive and went after her. She wouldn't stop. He blew the horn a couple of times, but she still wouldn't stop. He reluctantly stopped, got out of the car and went after her up the block.

"Hey, look, I'm not a cop," he said in a convincing tone.

"Well, what are you?" the girl asked.

"A man who knows beauty when he sees it."

"That's what they all say," the girl said and she began walking again. After a few steps, he caught up to her.

"Look, I just wanna have a good time. I can pay you double of your biggest week," Justin said as he pulled out a wad of hundred dollar bills that amounted to about ten grand. If this didn't lure her, nothing would.

She reached for the money and Justin pulled it away.

"Not yet," Justin said seductively. "And not in no hell hole. We're goin' someplace nice."

The girl got into the car after Justin opened the door for her. Justin hurried around the back of the car and knocked twice on the trunk. Sally B tapped lightly as Justin made his way around the side to the driver's door. He yanked his baseball cap down again and got in the car. He headed uptown.

"So, what's your name?" Justin asked.

"Mimi, why?"

"Why not?"

"Usually nobody asks," Mimi said.

"Well, I'm not nobody," Justin replied.

"I see."

"How long you been on the streets?"

"I'm not on the street," Mimi snapped.

"Testy tonight, huh?" Justin said.

"How old are you?" he asked.

"Thirteen."

"Where you from?"

"Look, what's with all the questions? Let's just go do this," Mimi said, snapping.

Justin abruptly stopped the car

"Get out," he yelled.

Mimi looked at him sheepishly. There was silence for a few seconds.

"Look, I'm sorry. I've had a rough day. I haven't made any money and I gotta give what I made to my pimp."

"How much have you made?" Justin asked.

"Not enough."

"Like I said, I'll pay you enough to cover for a week. Come on, what do you average a week for yourself? One, two, three thousand?" Justin knew these were high figures, but it was all part of his game. Mimi looked at Justin like he was crazy.

"You're working in the wrong house, little girlie!" Justin teased.

Justin pulled up to the Park Plaza Hotel on Park Avenue. The valet opened the door for Justin. He remembered Sally B was in the trunk and the room was in her name, but he did have a key.

"That's okay, I'll park it," Justin said.

"And the lady, sir?" the valet asked.

"She'll be waiting for me in the lounge," Justin said.

Mimi's door was whisked open by another valet after the first valet snapped his fingers.

"He'll show you where the lounge is," Justin said before he drove off and handed the valet a twenty dollar tip, something he didn't have to do, but he always felt for the hard-working minorities.

Justin drove to the second level underground parking and looked for space number nine nineteen. That was the suite that Sally B kept ready for special occasions.

Justin quickly got out of the car and opened the trunk. Sally B practically jumped out, gasping for air and sweating all over.

"Never again," Sally B said, aggravated.

She wiped her brow and lead the way to the elevators beyond the two glass doors.

"Took you long enough, Mr. Casanova," she said. "And why are you spending so much time with one kid? Goin' soft or what?"

"No, she's a challenge. We'll get her. I want you to go to the lounge and tell her which room to come up to. Be subtle."

"I know. I've been doing this a lot longer than you," Sally B said.

"Yeah, but I taught you everything you know," Justin said.

He entered the luxury suite. It wasn't half the size of his condo at Truman Towers, but it was large. He immediately closed the curtains, after turning on the light to find his way around. He hadn't been there in a while. He went about checking the two adjoining bedrooms to make sure everything was in place. He kept the lights dim and still had his sunglasses and baseball cap on.

Down in the lounge, Sally B initially sat at the bar and ordered a gin and tonic.

She studied Mimi, who was at the other end of the bar sipping a coke. Sally B noticed how clear she looked. Her hair shined in the light and her complexion was smooth and clear. She also had a mature look about her. Her nice leather jacket and fresh jeans enhanced her appearance. She looked very good for a kid who had probably been on the streets for ten days. After a few minutes, Sally B walked over to Mimi.

"Hi, I'm Sally B."

Mimi looked at Sally B in the mirror behind the bar. Sally B saw this and looked at Mimi through the mirror also.

"Who are you?" Mimi asked.

"I'm a friend of the guy who picked you up and brought you here this evening."

"So what are you here for?" Mimi asked.

"I'm gonna escort you upstairs in a few minutes. But first, we gotta make sure you qualify."

"Qualify for what?" Mimi asked.

"To have the privilege of being with this man. Are you from New York?" Sally B asked.

"No, Ohio."

"Any family here?"

"No, I just got here a few weeks ago."

"Kinda tough out here on the streets, huh?"

"How would you know?"

"Look, I've been where you think you want to go. Personally, I don't think you can handle it. You're too young and talk too much. You need to keep your mouth shut and maybe things will work out better for you. Ya know what I mean? How's ya pimp?"

"Who said I have one?" Mimi said, looking at Sally B.

"Everyone has one."

"Did you know him before you got here?"

"No, I met him at the bus station when I arrived."

"How's he treating you?"

"Look, what is this? Are we going up or what?"

Sally B pointed at her subtly with her index finger while she took a sip of her gin and tonic.

"See, that's what I'm talking about. You need to learn to listen more. Then you'll probably be paid better and treated better," Sally B said, quickly putting down her drink.

"I got a right to speak!" Mimi said.

"Yeah, but the real trick is to know how and when to, baby, that's how you get paid! Now, do you wanna get paid or do you wanna keep slingin' ya ass for nickels and dimes?" Sally B said, looking into Mimi's eyes sternly.

Mimi sipped the last of her coke and put her glass down.

"Paid!" Mimi said graciously.

"Let's go," Sally B said as she drank the last of her gin and tonic.

Sally B led the way to the elevator. Heads turned, eyeing Mimi's erect posture and sexy, slow glide as they walked through the semi-crowded foyer to the hallway elevator. Mimi got on with Sally B. Sally B put the suite card key in the slot for suites only. The elevator ascended.

"Be very nice to this guy and don't ask a lot of questions or give backtalk. He pays very well, and if you do him right, he may come back for more. He'll pay you so well you won't need to lay on your back for anyone else ever again. Understand?"

Mimi nodded as she looked Sally B right in the eye.

They reached the ninth floor. Mimi's glide kept her a half a step behind Sally B.

"How old are you?" Sally B asked.

"Thirteen."

Sally B scanned her mature proportions.

"Sure did grow up fast," Sally B said.

"My mama was a good cook. She used to dance in Vegas, but

she wouldn't let me explore. She kept tight reins on me. Never knew my father."

"I thought you were from Ohio." Sally B said.

"I am. My mom worked in Vegas."

"No brothers or sisters?" Sally B asked.

"Just me, as far as I know."

Sally B came to room 919. She slid the key card into the door lock and it opened. She put the key card back into her wallet, with the other one for Truman Towers. Mimi slowly walked, in definite awe of her surroundings, even though it was dimly lit.

"Never been in a room like this before," Mimi said.

"Have a seat. You drink?"

Mimi sat on the plush sofa near the bar Sally B went behind the bar and fixed a gin and tonic.

"Ah, no, I don't drink," Mimi said.

Sally B made a gin and tonic for Mimi and slid it on the bar toward her.

"Here, this is real smooth. I think you'll like it," Sally B said.

Mimi stood and got the drink. Sally B raised her drink for a toast with Mimi as she was about to take a sip.

"A toast first," Sally B said. "To the good life."

Sally B drank hers down. Mimi took a sip of the drink and frowned.

"You gotta drink it down straight." Mimi squinted her eyes and forced herself to drink the entire glass; then held her stomach.

"You'll be all right. First one is usually the hardest," Sally B said with a grin.

Sally B poured Mimi another one, but put water in her own glass, without Mimi knowing. Sally B came from behind the fully-stocked bar with the two glasses and handed Mimi the drink. They sat on the couch.

"My mom was always getting all of these men and they used to mistreat her and she'd still see them. I couldn't get away from it. We were so poor, they used to leave money on the kitchen table. They started to beat her. Then they started coming after me. They would take what they wanted and beat me sometimes. Then mom tried to keep tight reins on me. I got tired of it and ran away."

A tear ran down Mimi's cheek. Sally B wiped it away with her index finger.

"We'll help you now. Go talk to my friend in there."

Sally B motioned for Mimi to finish her drink. She did. Sally B walked Mimi to Justin's bedroom door. Sally B knocked one time and

Justin cracked the door. He still wore his shades, even though it was pitch dark in the room.

Sally B subtly nodded at Justin as he took Mimi's hand, escorting her into the room. Sally B closed the door behind him and went to the adjacent bedroom.

Justin escorted Mimi over to the bed. She sat down near the headboard and reached for the night light.

"Is it all right to turn the light on?" she asked.

"No! No need for that. Would you like another drink?"

"Yes."

Justin already had one ready from the bar in his room. He went behind the bar where there was a dimmer light than the rest of the suite. He turned the dimmer light on. It was enough light to see, but barely.

"You like the dark?"

"No, I like you," Justin said.

"But you can't even see me."

"Did Sally B talk to you about talking so much?"

"Yes."

Justin carried Mimi's drink to her. He stood in front of her and stirred her drink with his index finger He took that same finger and put it into her mouth.

"Good?" Justin asked.

"Yes."

"Good," Justin said and handed her the drink.

She drank the shot down, and became wobbly fast.

"Ya know I can help you live better."

"Will you, will you? I'm tired of living on the streets," Mimi pleaded.

"But you have to earn your keep. Are you as good as you look?" Justin asked.

"Better than I look."

Justin took the empty glass from her, put it on the night stand and placed a wad of cash in her hand.

"That's a grand," Justin said.

"Why?" Mimi asked, holding the money tight.

Justin took Mimi's hand and stood her up. She wobbled into his arms.

"Why? Because I can," Justin said.

Mimi began to kiss Justin on the lips. He returned the kiss to her forehead. She dropped the money on the bed and began to undress.

"That's not what this is really all about. It's bigger than this for you, Mimi. That is, if you act right."

"Anything."

"Now, what we don't want to happen is to misconstrue this for that four letter word called love. This is business. And that's all it will ever be. Understand?"

"Yes."

"Now we can do this. I gotta see what you're made of. Then we'll talk about what we're gonna do for you."

Justin wouldn't go through this process with the other girls. He mostly would let Sally B use her judgment. He felt it was too risky. He always thought that a woman would be his doom. That all great men were brought down by a woman. He believed that his existence was one of importance, no matter how much crime was involved. People would get hurt from time to time, but he felt it was either him or them. He always covered his tracks, but Sally B sometimes did not in her haste to move on to the next. Justin believed that if the current block wasn't on sold ground, the whole castle would come tumbling down. He repeatedly told this to Sally B, but she was beginning to slip up a bit.

CHAPTER NINETEEN

THERE WAS AN unmarked police car outside the Park Plaza, parked in a 'no standing' zone. They'd been watching Sally B for some time. Sally B was unaware of it.

These same two had been watching Sally B off and on for the past six months. The two detectives picked up the pace when they got word from a source in Albany that she'd been hanging around up there and that something might be going down. The cops couldn't arrest her because they didn't have a reason. All they knew was that her name was coming up in the upper echelon of the police department and they were told to tail her at random.

The two detectives were in their early fifties. They were referred to as Mutt and Jeff by their peers at the 3rd Precinct on the upper west side of Manhattan. Their real names were Jason Mutsby and Brian Jefferies. They were both Caucasian. With last names like that no one could resist calling them by their nicknames. Neither Mutt nor Jeff minded, as long as they got respect. Both were one year from retirement. They'd made the rounds in New York, so they knew everyone who needed to be known to make their job as easy as possible. They were parked in an old four-door black Chevy.

"I don't know why they got us on this girl. It's obvious she's got money," Mutt said. A few years earlier he'd had throat surgery, and it had left him with a raspy voice.

"Who cares, all we do is sit and wait till our shift is over. I'm not gonna get blown away because of some two-cent chick that nobody really cares about anyway," Jeff said in his nasal voice.

"What did the snitch have to say?" Mutt asked.

"He said Sally B walked in by herself, went upstairs, met somebody in the bar and brought her back up with her."

"She's probably some butch picking up women," Mutt said, jokingly.

"What do they have on her at the station?" Mutt asked.

"Nothin'. No home address, no relatives, just a name," Jeff said, not caring.

Mutt took a sip of his soda.

"I don't see the point," Mutt said.

"Look, it's just a cushy job. Relax."

Mutt slouched behind the steering wheel, leaned back and closed his eyes.

"Wake me in thirty" Mutt said.

"Gotcha."

Mutt turned his head towards Jeff and opened his eyes.

"Who's this in Albany watching her?" Mutt asked, then burped.

"Slob. I don't know. But they're on her," Jeff said while he waved away the funk the Mutt's burp had created.

CHAPTER TWENTY

"HOW'S YOUR EYE?" Randy asked. I sat in my eavesdropping chair in the basement.

"It's fine. It doesn't hurt as much."

"Tony, why don't you go upstairs for a minute," Randy said.

"No, you know it's late and Mom will send us to bed if I go up there," Tony said.

"Come on, just tip-toe to the bathroom, she won't hear you. I need to talk to Corey," Randy said politely.

Tony shook his head no.

"I wanna hear, too," Tony said.

Randy sighed and shook his head.

"So what did you and Uncle Henry talk about at the fishing pond, Corey?"

"Just things about us fighting. He said we should make friends and start acting like brothers."

"Did you tell him that I cut you on purpose?"

"No. I told him it was a mistake, but he figured it was a mistake made on purpose because of our fight. I know it was on purpose, but I forgive you."

I extended my hand for Randy to shake. Randy stared in my eyes for a few seconds, and gradually raised his hand to shake.

"I'm sorry I cut you, Corey," Randy said as he embraced me, lifting me up into his arms.

Tony smiled and was pleased that we were friends again. Randy put me down, and I peeked out the blinds of the window.

"Can you guys keep a secret?" I asked.

Randy and Tony said yeah.

"Not one of your wild stories again, Corey?" Randy said.

"No, it's true."

"What? Tell us," Tony said, excited.

"You guys can't tell anyone, okay?"

"What is it, Corey? Come on, tell us," Randy said.

"I think something is going on up in that apartment."

"What do you mean?" Randy asked.

"Because I saw this, or rather, I heard what sounded like a kid up in one of the rooms. It'd be better if we could just go into the apartment, then I could just show you. The police went up there, too."

"Why?" Randy asked.

"Well, somebody called them, I guess."

"Yeah, you probably called them, Corey," Tony said.

"Shut up, Tony," Randy said.

"So what did the police find up there, Corey?" Randy asked.

"Well, I really don't think they found anything because nobody was arrested."

"So you did call the cops, right, Corey?" Randy asked.

I paused for a second and looked Randy in the eyes.

"Yeah."

"Well, what made you want to do that if you weren't sure?" Randy asked.

"I felt sorry for the kid."

"But maybe the kid was sleep and woke up from a bad dream or something," Randy said.

"I don't think so, Randy. Why would an adult leave a kid alone at that time of the morning? Tied up? That's not right."

"Who knows?" Randy said.

"Does Mom and Dats know you were up there?" Tony asked.

"Shut up, Tony. I'm asking the questions," Randy said.

Tony rolled his eyes.

"So does Mom and Dats know you were up there snooping around?" Randy asked.

Tony smirked and nodded.

"Musta been a good question, huh?" Tony said.

"They kinda know."

"Whaddaya mean 'kinda'? That's a pussy answer. Either they know or they don't," Randy said.

"Well, I don't think they wanted to know that I had been up there, kinda like they were afraid or something."

Randy thought for a moment.

"What?" Tony asked.

Randy looked at me and Tony, then thought some more.

"Maybe we should go up there and have a look," Randy suggested.

"Do you really think he would leave any clues after the police paid him a visit?" I said.

"Well, you never know," Randy said.

"I think if I committed a crime and I got away with it and the police paid me a visit, I think I would clean up and not leave any clues," I said.

"You never know, Corey, maybe he made a mistake," Randy said.

"I don't know about that, Randy. Anyway, we couldn't get back in anyway. Dats has the keys and he's probably sleeping with them under his pillow at night to make sure nobody goes up there. He wasn't very happy about the police being here."

At the top of the basement stairs, we heard our Mom yelling down to us.

"All right, boys, it's time to go to bed. What're you doing down there anyway?"

"Just talking, Mom," I shouted back.

We heard footsteps coming down the basement stairs towards us. The stairs cracked as she walked. Mom yanked open the door to my room.

"You boys aren't fighting, are you?" Mom asked.

"No, Mom, we made friends," I said.

"You sure?" Mom asked.

"Yes, Mom, we hugged and shook on it," Randy answered.

I looked at the hole in Mom's silk nightgown just below her navel.

"Mom, you have a hole in your nighty," I said.

Mom quickly looked down and covered the hole with her hand.

"What could you boys possibly be talking about this late at night? Shouldn't you be doing something else--like sleeping? You do have school tomorrow, remember? Now go to bed," Mom said sternly.

"But I don't have school, Mom. My eye isn't ready for the public."

Mom frowned. "Boy, you'd better go to bed," she said.

She turned to leave the room. Then she returned and moved towards me. "Let me see your eye, Corey."

She removed my eye patch and gauze, and then examined my bad eye.

"No pus or anything. Tomorrow we'll put some medicine in it."

She put the gauze back over my eye, then the patch.

"You can finish what you were talking about, but make it snappy," she said before leaving.

Mom got to the foot of the stairs and took three steps back to the door of the room and opened it.

Me, Randy and Tony just looked at each other for a quick second.

"Just men talk. You know, like Dats and Uncle Henry do from time to time, Mom," I said.

"What kinda *men* talk?" Mom asked.

"Just about girls, Mom," Randy said as he ushered Mom by her hand out the door.

"Yeah, Mom, we have to catch up on what's going on at school!" I said.

"Sure," Mom said as she walked up the stairs.

After we were sure Mom wasn't on the stairs, Randy motioned for Tony to go check the stairs to make sure Mom wasn't eavesdropping. Tony ran back in and said, "no, she's gone."

"Corey, does the guy upstairs know that you were up there?" Randy asked.

"I don't think so."

"Are you sure, it's important!" Randy urged.

"Well, unless Mom and Dats told him. But why would they do that?" I asked.

"They wouldn't do that. But if he does know, and he is some kind of dangerous criminal, then that's not good for you. You understand what I mean?"

I looked at Randy, a bit scared.

"Yeah, I know what you mean."

"We gotta get up there just to have a look!" Randy said.

Tony and I looked at Randy like he was crazy. But deep down, I knew we had to find out what was going on up there, and if there was something wrong, then my life could be at stake.

Not only that, I had to find out if anyone upstairs was responsible for the painful mistreatment I had gone through. If Justin or his friend was responsible, who knows how many other kids were being mistreated or even killed. If I get my hands on my abuser, I'm going to cut off his ass piece by piece.

Sara got back into bed with Jim, who laid on his back with his hands behind his head, wide awake in the dark.

"So what's goin' on down there?" Jim asked.

Sara pulled the comforter over her legs to her waist.

"They were just making friends again and catching up on schoolgirls," Sara said.

"You think Corey told them he was upstairs?" Jim asked.

Sara was silent for a minute.

"I don't think so. Why would he?" Sara said.

"Think about it. Corey bites Randy in the neck. Randy stabs.

"No!" Sara said, interrupting.

"Let's just say for the sake of argument that he did stab him on purpose. Why else would Corey want to be in the same room with Randy and vice versa, unless some big news was being discussed? Think about it. If you were in Corey's shoes, Randy would be the last person you'd want to talk to unless you just had to get something off ya chest that you were either terrified by or excited by. Maybe in Corey's case it's both, knowing that kid."

There was a brief silence.

"Maybe you're right. What if he is telling them?" Sara said.

"All he can say is that maybe he heard something."

"No, we know he heard something. The question is, did he see something and maybe he's not saying?" Sara said.

"No, I think if he'd seen something, he would have told us. I'm still pissed at him that he went up there. It's my fault, though. That's what happens when I try to be sentimental. I always screw up. Should have never let him hold the keys while he was in here. Damn!"

Jim pounded on the side of the bed in anger. Sara slid close to

Jim and laid her head on his chest.

"Somebody's gonna have to die, Honey. If Justin finds out that Corey was up there, he's coming for him. We're gonna have to make a choice. Either we give Corey up or save him and run, and have Justin hunt us the rest of our lives. Or we kill Justin and save our family."

Sara began to cry silently as tears rolled from her cheeks to Jim's bare chest. He put his arms around her.

"I wish I never knew a Justin Lord," Sara said through her tears.

Jim felt the same way, but he had commitments. He had his mother's retirement bills, medical bills and he had to support his family. He held onto the prospect of one day scoring the big one with Justin, which would enable him to quit his piss-ass job as a mechanic at the bus company.

CHAPTER TWENTY-ONE

IT WAS 7:30 A.M. on Monday at the Park Plaza Hotel, room nine nineteen. Sally B was in the living room area of the suite, sitting on the couch reading the business section of *The New York Times* newspaper while sipping hot coffee. She was fully dressed and ready for the day. She knew it would be a long one.

Slowly, Justin's bedroom door opened. Sally B stopped reading for a moment, clearly interested in the night's outcome. Sally B knew if it wasn't to Justin's liking, he would kill Mimi—no stones left uncovered. Then Sally B would have to dump the body. For that matter, if at any time Mimi wasn't to Justin's liking, he would kill her immediately.

Justin came out of the bedroom first. He wore the same clothes that he'd worn the night before. He still had his dark sunglasses and baseball cap on. Justin walked in his usual swaying manner toward Sally B. Sally B stopped reading the Times, which was spread across the room service table. She looked at Justin in the eyes. Justin looked back toward his bedroom door slowly, then looked back at Sally B. He grinned and nodded approvingly. Sally B sighed and offered Justin a cup of coffee. Justin took a sip of Sally B's coffee. He grimaced as he swallowed the strong, sweet coffee.

"Sally B, I want you to take her to Saks today. Buy her a whole wardrobe, at least three of everything. The best. She's gonna make us a lot of money. Girl's got a golden backside. Damn near got you beat," Justin said as he playfully nudged Sally B, who frowned.

"But you know I might go with you on this little shopping spree. Kinda like that girl," Justin said.

"Musta pussy whipped you, for you wanting to go shopping with us," Sally B said.

"No, no, just like the way she makes me feel."

Justin rolled his shoulders back and started towards his bedroom, then stopped. He snapped his long, thick fingers.

"Go check on her: Size her up," Justin said as Sally B sat and stared at him.

"Come on now!" Justin said, yelling.

Sally B went into the bedroom, and came running out with a look of terror. Justin held his hand up to Sally B, stopping her in her tracks. Justin had made up the whole story about wanting to buy Mimi a new wardrobe. He was about to tell Sally B what really happened between him and Mimi in the bedroom behind closed doors.

Justin's face turned hard as stone as he began to speak, reflecting on the night's events.

It was almost dawn and Justin and Mimi had been in the bedroom all night. Justin was on top of Mimi on the king-sized bed. Her tanned skin was wet from sweating. She was exhausted from having sex all night.

"I'm tired. Can we rest?" Mimi asked in an agitated tone.

"Shut up, girl! This is nothing. I once fucked for two days straight!"

"Well, I'm not one of your two days, got it?" Mimi snapped.

This tone infuriated Justin. But he never let Mimi see him sweat.

Mimi looked at Justin's Mets baseball cap and dark sunglasses with disdain as she laid on her back, and he continued to have his way with her. She was almost motionless, not giving him feeling in return.

"And you need to take off those damn sunglasses and stupid baseball cap. It's distracting with you naked."

Thoughts ran through Justin's mind. He was actually wearing the baseball cap and sunglasses to protect Mimi so as to not reveal his identity; that way she might live a little longer. The second reason was he liked the Mets.

By then, Justin had grown tired of Mimi's smart mouth.

"Distracting? I like the Mets."

He turned the cap backwards on his head. This was his way of giving in to her request, because he truly liked her. He kept the shades on. Even though he felt for her, his patience declined because of her arrogance throughout the night.

"You need to get a grip, Justin," she yelled.

This unnerved him. He gradually sat up, straddling her.

"So you want to see me, huh?"

Then there was disdain in his voice.

"Yeah! I've had enough of you anyway! Go away!"

"Go away, huh?" Justin repeated.

Still, Justin didn't let her see him sweat. He scanned the room. His eyes stopped at the dresser drawer, then they shifted back on Mimi.

"Okay, but you'll be remembering this face for the rest of your life."

Justin leaned over and turned up the light on the night stand to its brightest. He took off his baseball cap, then his sunglasses.

"That's better. You're handsome," Mimi said.

"Let me give you a massage, girl. You need to relax. Turn over."

Mimi turned over and laid down on the bed.

"No, sit up with ya back to me. I'm gonna give you the special treatment."

Mimi sat up in the middle of the bed with her back to Justin.

"How's this?" Mimi asked.

"Perfect. So did you get a good look at my face, Mimi?" Justin asked sarcastically.

"Yep, a real good look."

"Ya know, you talk an awful lot to be in the business that you're in. Didn't anybody ever tell you the best way to move up is to have a strong back and a closed mouth?"

Justin reached in the night stand drawer and took out a black leather belt. He dropped it near Mimi.

"Hey, this is a free country and I can say whatever I want to you or anyone else," Mimi fired back.

Justin grinned.

"But you'll never get ahead, Mimi," Justin said, smiling.

"Yes, I will too!"

"You sure will," Justin said, picking up the belt with his left hand while still massaging Mimi's right shoulder with his right hand, and quickly wrapped the belt around Mimi's neck, choking her. Mimi tried to fight back. Justin pushed her face down on the bed into a pillow and put his knee on her back.

"Hope you remember my face when you get to hell," he said as she took her last breath of air.

"How'd you like that story?"

Sally B had a blank look.

"Now do you see why I killed her, Sally B? She just talked too much."

"And what am I supposed to do with the body, Justin? Just walk outta here with it over my shoulder?"

Justin smiled and said, "Hey, that's a good idea."

Justin went to sit on the couch, and he drank more of Sally B's coffee. Sally B stood there stunned momentarily, then exasperatedly walked over to Justin and stood in front of him.

"Now, Justin, how am I supposed to move the body?"

"I don't know, that's what I'm paying you for. And make sure you wipe her down good. You dump her in the river."

Justin picked up the Times newspaper, leaned back on the couch and flipped to the business section.

"Dump her in the river. We'll do it tonight, I guess, when we go out again. This time we're gonna find us a nice young boy. That's what I need, a nice young boy. Then we'll get back to Albany, maybe. So I can train him to my liking," Justin said calmly.

CHAPTER TWENTY-TWO

IT WAS APPROXIMATELY 8:00 A.M. Jim stood at the garage door of the Capital District Transportation Authority when Henry raced in driving his pickup truck, blowing his horn several times. Jim was surprised to see Henry. Henry pulled in front of the garage door near Jim. The night shift was about to end and the day shift would begin. Workers were milling about, waiting for the clock to strike eight.

"Henry what are you doing here? You don't gotta work today?" Jim said as he walked over to Henry's window.

"Came to say good morning to you, Jim," Henry said with a big smile.

"For what? What is it now, Henry?"

"That's right, ol' buddy."

"Come on, Henry what's up? I gotta get ready to do my slave time."

"Well, I was on my way to work maybe. Anyway I wanted to find out how Corey's eye was doing."

"You coulda called for that, Henry."

"I know, but I stayed at this chick's house last night. Wow, it was good, too. But anyway, she doesn't stay far from here, so I thought

I'd catch you."

"Well, he's doin' okay. He didn't sleep much last night, according to Sara. She said he and the boys were up late talking."

"Talking?"

"Yeah. She said they were getting caught up about the latest at school and girls. Who knows," Jim said as he glanced at his wristwatch.

"Oops, time for you to punch in, huh?" Henry said.

Jim began to walk away.

"Oh, Jim, when's the last time you talked to Corey?"

"I talk to him every day, Henry"

"No, I mean talk, talk, Jim."

Jim walked back to Henry's car, sighing.

"Come on, Henry, what are you getting at?"

Henry's smile faded.

"Jim, I think you need to have a serious man-to-man talk with him. He's got a lot of things on his mind."

Henry began to drive off. But before he got out of Jim's' earshot, he said, "He needs you, Jim. Talk to him."

Jim acted bewildered, but he knew what Henry was talking about. Henry waved at Jim as he left the gate leading to the garage area. Jim gradually raised his hand, giving Henry a half wave.

Back at the Harris house, Randy and Tony were readying themselves for school. Sara had just finished cooking them the usual: scrambled eggs, grits and toast. She hurriedly sat three plates on the table.

"Come on, boys, it's almost eight-fifteen. You're gonna be late and your food's gonna be cold."

Sara was about to dish eggs and bacon on the third plate, and then didn't, remembering that Corey was not going to school. She put the pots on the stove and quickly walked to Randy's bedroom. She stuck her head in.

"Boys, your food is on the table and you're not leaving until you eat, and brush your teeth when you finish."

"Yes, Mom," was said by Randy and Tony. Randy was fixing Tony's tie.

"Tony, was Corey awake when you came up?" Sara asked.

Tony shrugged his shoulders. Sara went to the top of the basement stairs and yelled to me.

"Corey, do you want to eat now or later?"

After a few seconds, I strolled out of the basement to the foot of the stairs, rubbing the sleep from my one unpatched eye.

"Ummm. Mom, is Randy and Tony still here?"

"Yes, they are, Corey," Mom said impatiently.

"They're not going to school?"

"Yes, they are, Corey. They're running late because of your little pow-wow last night. Well, are you eating now or later? I gotta get to work, Corey."

"Okay, I'll eat now."

I walked to the top of the stairs with my boxer shorts, T-shirt and bare feet. Mom went back into the kitchen and fixed my plate. Randy and Tony darted by me into the kitchen. They took their seats. Randy always took Dats' place whenever he wasn't there, and Tony would sit anywhere he could. I was about to enter the kitchen to take a seat at the opposite end of Randy when Mom warned me.

"Corey, don't dare come to my table without washing up. You know better."

I turned and went to the bathroom. The light was already on. I looked in the mirror above the sink. I touched the eye patch a couple of times, then talked to Mom.

"Mom, when do I get this patch off?"

"Soon, hopefully. I need to call Dr. Bill. As a matter of fact, I need to put some medicine on it." Mom got up from her chair, went into her bedroom and grabbed my eye medicine. She came into the bathroom and turned me toward her. She was gentle in taking off my eye patch and gauze. She squeezed some eyedrops from the rubber container into my eye. I squenched a little.

"Thanks, Mom."

"You're welcome."

She closed the medicine top and put it into the medicine cabinet. Then she returned to her kitchen seat. I went back to washing my face.

Mom looked at Randy and Tony, who were eating slow.

"Hurry up, boys, it's almost eight-thirty."

Tony was eating very slowly. Slower than Randy was.

"Mom, we have this every day. I can't eat any more," Tony said wimpishly.

Mom bolted up from her chair, stomped her way into the bedroom and came out with Dats' two-inch thick, black leather belt and stood over Tony.

"Now, you think you can't finish that food, huh? Maybe this rawhide will give you some inspiration," she said.

Tony looked out of the corner of his eye at Mom and saw the thick silver belt buckle in his face. His plate was half empty of the small amount of food he had.

"And I mean it better all be gone before eight-thirty," Mom said with anger.

Tony looked behind him, above Mom, at the clock on the refrigerator.

"People starving in Africa and you're complaining!" Mom said.

"Well, give it to them," Tony said.

"What?"

Mom grabbed Tony by the collar with his mouth full of food. He had pushed the wrong button. Even I had to laugh at Tony's last remark. Then Randy joined in on the laughter. Tony swallowed his food and he laughed. Then Mom couldn't help but laugh.

"Oh, you think it's funny, huh?"

Mom dragged Tony toward Randy's bedroom. Randy and I were still laughing.

"Now you just laughed your way to a good ass whippin'!" Mom said.

She began to laugh sarcastically, while dragging Tony into Randy's bedroom.

"No, Mommy, it's not funny," Tony pleaded.

"Swallow that food, boy. Don't want you to choke to death. I'll go to jail for murder."

Tony, with one big swallow, downed what started this in the first place. She began to beat Tony with the belt as he stayed on the ground maneuvering, trying to get out of the way of each lash, while hollering and crying. Randy and I watched at the doorway. We both had little smiles. Mom looked at me and Randy with a half grin.

"You two think it's funny? I'll give you some, too."

As Mom started out of the room, Randy and I ran. Randy got out of the house and I ran downstairs.

"Mom, I'll be back to eat my food in a minute," I said.

"You better. And not one drop better go to waste. You kids think money grows on trees, don'tcha," Mom said as she made her way back to the kitchen and into the bedroom.

Mom closed the door behind her.

I had made my way back upstairs. I went into Randy's room to help Tony fix himself for school.

"You shouldn't have said that, Tony," I said.

"It didn't hurt anyway," he said defiantly.

"You better get outta here before Mom comes back."

I stuck my head out the door and then back into the room.

"Here she comes."

Tony quickly grabbed his school backpack and ran out of his room toward the front door. He looked over his shoulder and saw that Mom wasn't coming.

"Liar," Tony said to me as he slowed down and opened the front door.

"I thought it didn't hurt?" I teased.

Tony flipped me the finger and left. The door slammed. I went to close the hallway dining room door I heard faint crying from Mom's bedroom. I gradually walked to her bedroom door and listened momentarily. I was surprised because Mom had never cried after she gave us a whipping before. I gently pushed open her door. She didn't hear the door open because she was crying so loud. I watched her sob for a minute, then I inched towards her. She still didn't realize I was in her room.

"Mom!" I said softly.

Mom slowly turned her head towards me and just stared at me while she cried. She reached out to me with both of her hands, and I took hold of them and sat on the foot of the bed with her. We embraced, and she cried.

"I'm sorry, Corey. I'm sorry, Honey," she said.

"Mom, what's wrong?"

I gently pulled away from Mom's embrace. I went to get some tissue from the dresser. I grabbed a handful. Mom was still crying. I sat back down next to Mom, and she leaned her head in my chest. I wiped her face as best as I could in that position.

"Mom, what is it?"

"Nothing, Honey, just pressure," she said.

"But, Mom, I've never seen you cry like this before, even after you and Dats had a fight."

I sat down next to Mom and just stared out.

"Is there anything I can help you with, Mom?"

Mom patted my knee as she wiped her eyes with her free hand. I looked at the locked cabinet in the corner, wondering if that had anything to do with Mom's grief. Then I thought maybe it did. Did it connect with me being molested? Then I looked at her keys to the upstairs apartment on the dresser I remembered how still she was when Justin got on the elevator at the hospital, like she didn't even know him. For somebody who had rented from Mom and Dats for the past four years, as far as I knew, it seemed like they would know each other better. I wondered if it was Justin who raped me. I had to find out.

No matter how difficult it would be to unmask my attacker, it would be nothing compared to the pain inflicted upon me each time I had been taken advantage of. My goal was to find my abuser. I hated who I was. No telling how many other kids were being made to feel this way by the mysterious culprit. I swore I would do all that I could to stop this maniac. My insides felt like an open space to the depths of whom I was, torn away and it made me hate. I had to stop it!

CHAPTER TWENTY-THREE

SALLY B STOOD AT THE DOOR, preparing to leave the Park Plaza Hotel suite. Justin sat on the sofa with an IBM personal computer, computing the night's earnings. Normally Justin and Sally B would do it together if they were in the same city. But Sally B had more pressing matters to attend to, like getting rid of Mimi's corpse that was still sprawled out on Justin's bed, getting colder with every minute.

Sally B had a disgusted look about her as she turned the doorknob and spoke to Justin.

"I'll be back in a couple of hours."

She grabbed the plastic sign from the knob. Justin kept at work on his computer. Sally B grew more agitated as Justin was nonchalant about the situation at hand. She sighed in disgust.

"I'm putting the 'do not disturb' sign on," she said.

"Rigor mortis sets in it's gonna be difficult," Justin said calmly, without taking his eyes off of his computer console.

Sally B rolled her eyes and left. She hung the "do not disturb" sign on the door. She looked both ways in the hallway and saw the cleaning lady two doors down toward the elevator. It was around 10:00 a.m., so it was normal for cleaning to start. A few of the other doorknobs had "do not disturb" signs on them.

When the maid saw Sally B put hers on, a look of frustration squeezed through her smile as Sally B approached her. The maid knew this would mean possible overtime.

As Sally B passed by the maid, she spoke to her.

"Hi. It's clean," Sally B said with a half smile.

"I'll clean," the maid said.

The maid was in her mid-forties and a bit overweight. She spoke clearly, but had a difficult time hearing.

Sally B looked back and smiled. Sally B entered the elevator and immediately began looking at herself in the mirrors that were on the three sides of the walls. She patted her hair, then put more lipstick on. Her loose, white blouse draped nicely over her medium-sized breasts. Her fashionable blue jeans fell over her medium-sized curvy hips. She was definitely a looker to any man, no matter how she dressed. She often times would downplay her clothing to defray attention toward her, unless the situation called for it. She'd taken the elevator down to the garage, but decided against driving. She reinserted her key card and pressed the lobby button. She walked through the lobby and drew stares from a few people milling about and two bellboys who were waiting at their station.

Sally B left the Park Plaza front entrance as one of the bellboys raced to open the door for her. He smiled, and she forced a smile in return. Her mind was on getting the body out of the hotel. She'd been in sticky situations before, but none this dangerous. Nobody would miss Mimi because she was probably written off for dead already by the police. Sally B thought she'd probably been on the streets longer than she said, judging by her aggressive style with Justin. This girl knew her way around too well to only have been on the streets two months. And if she had been there longer she'd have been more familiar with the number one rule: Whatever the customer wants, he gets, and no back talk. At any rate, Sally B needed to dispose of the body and she knew she had to work fast. She knew Justin wouldn't be of any help to her.

She stood outside the Park Plaza for a few minutes, looking at the sun that was up but not hot.

Mutt and Jeff, the two detectives, were still in their car across the street from the hotel.

Mutt, who was still behind the steering wheel, was half asleep. Jeff, in the passenger seat, read *The New York Post*, page six, the gossip section.

Sally B had started walking up Park Avenue, toward 57th Street. Mutt and Jeff were parked toward the middle of the street. Jeff glanced up and spotted Sally B at the corner, waiting to cross the street headed west toward Fifth Avenue.

Jeff nudged Mutt and he awakened.

"What, what is it?" Mutt said groggily.

"Look who's walking," Jeff said, nodding to Sally B as she crossed the street about three car lengths in front of them.

Mutt started the engine and pulled out of his parking space. 57th Street was a one-way in the opposite direction. "Shit, we're gonna lose her!" he said with an extended look to Jeff that meant 'get out and follow her on foot.'

Jeff glanced at his watch, then lifted his wrist up to Mutt's face, showing him the time.

"It's almost ten-fifteen. We're off duty now," Jeff said to Mutt. Mutt frowned. "Why don't you follow her?" Jeff said.

"Come on, add some excitement to your boring life. Just follow her a few blocks. I'll circle the corner and meet you at 5th and 59th," Mutt said. "Besides, you need to exercise those old legs," Mutt said with a big smile.

"Exercise? The only exercise these legs need is the walk from my front door to the mailbox to pick up my pension check." They both chuckled. "And anyway, suppose she goes into a building," Jeff said, searching for an excuse not to walk.

Mutt opened the glove compartment, exposing two walkie-talkies.

"Ta da!" Mutt exclaimed.

"Shit. I'm months away from retirement and you got me following some bimbo who's probably doing nothing wrong," Jeff said as he grabbed a walkie-talkie and begrudgingly got out of the car. Horns began to blow as one car just missed hitting Jeff before he ran across the street.

Jeff was about a half a block behind Sally B as she approached 5th Avenue. He walked with his chest poked out and on his toes. She crossed the street and headed toward uptown.

The crossing light caught Jeff, but he darted across behind Sally B anyway.

Jeff was really closer than he wanted to be as they both walked up 5th Avenue.

Sally B looked back over her right shoulder quickly. Jeff looked directly at Sally B, then looked past her up the street. He was very experienced and didn't panic at Sally B's abrupt look back at him. He muttered to himself.

"She's looking back at someone else."

Jeff had done surveillance work before and knew how to handle unexpected situations. Sally B picked up her pace, not because of Jeff following her, but just because of Mimi's body laying on the bed in the suite.

Justin was in Sally B's bathroom. He had her radio blasting on KISS. Uptempo music blared out.

The maid ignored the "do not disturb" sign on the door, having thought Sally B had said "clean" instead of "it's clean". The maid lightly knocked on the door and listened for an answer. She opened the door and peeked inside. Seeing no one, she frowned at how everything was out of place, then went inside, and closed the door behind her. Justin couldn't hear the front door close because he had the music up.

The maid walked back out of the suite to get her cleaning cart, directly outside the door.

She easily pulled the cart into the suite with one hand, while holding the door open with the other.

Justin was still in the bathroom. He sat on the toilet reading *Time* magazine as the music continued to blare. The maid began to fluff the pillows on the sofa. She wiped down the coffee table with a damp cloth. She dumped the ashes from the ashtray into her trash can. She gently put the glass ashtray back on the marble coffee table. She stopped and looked around, seeing what needed to be attended to next. Her eyes stopped scanning at the ceiling to floor curtains that covered the balcony windows. She wanted more light. She made her way to the curtain's drawstring, which was near the entrance of Sally B's bedroom. Inside this bedroom, near the entrance, was where Justin was.

The maid opened the curtains and the sun shined brightly into the suite. Next, the maid moved toward Sally B's bedroom door and opened it, looking in at the unmade bed.

From all his years of crime and sleeping with one eye and ear open, Justin could definitely hear the door being opened and was startled to his feet. He quickly cleaned himself.

The maid walked to her cart and started to roll it towards Sally B's bedroom, then abruptly stopped when she looked at Justin's bedroom door, saw that it was closed and decided to walk to it and see what mess was ahead.

Justin emerged from the bathroom, cautiously opening the door, then he tiptoed to Sally B's bedroom door. He looked into the kitchen area, then into the living room area, not seeing anything but the maid's cart. He walked towards the cart, and then he saw her about to enter his bedroom.

Justin said, "Hello."

The maid didn't hear him, she slowly began to open the bedroom door.

Justin ran towards the maid as she was about to walk in the room. He grabbed the door handle, gently pushed the maid out of the way and closed the door.

"We don't need service right now," Justin said as he escorted the maid to her cleaning cart, then to the front door.

Justin opened the door and saw the "do not disturb" sign and pointed it out to the maid.

"Can't you read, lady?"

The maid only smiled and began to back away.

"Sorry, sorry, sir. I thought the lady said to clean," the maid said.

"Your name is Simmons, huh?" Justin said as he looked at her name tag.

Mrs. Simmons pointed at her name tag and nodded.

"Yes, that's my name. I'm sorry I guess I didn't hear the lady clearly. I can't hear so good. Please forgive me."

Justin wasn't happy with the maid seeing him. She is the only person in New York who had ever seen him with Sally B. And the only person who could ever make any kind of connection. He knew he should have disposed of her, but couldn't because he knew that Mrs. Simmons had made an honest mistake.

Justin closed the door and went back inside, hoping this wouldn't come back to haunt him.

Sally B entered Saks Fifth Avenue department store. It was only about 11:00 a.m., so the store was relatively empty. There were sales people milling about as Sally B walked through the cosmetics section of the store on the first floor. Jeff was over across from Sally B about five rows, glancing at the men's leather bags and briefcases. He peeked at Sally B as she made her way toward the elevator at the rear of the store. He cautiously followed her because she had already spotted him once in the street and he didn't want her to see him again. Since he sensed that she was on her way to the elevator, he moved swiftly towards it himself, hoping to beat her to it and keep her from thinking that he was following her.

Jeff moved through the women's cosmetics section and down the aisle toward the elevator. He had caught up to Sally B, who was directly across in the opposite aisle. He wanted to make sure she was getting on the elevator because she paused for a second and glanced at lipstick. He didn't want to get on the elevator without her directly behind him. He stopped for a second to look at lingerie, even though he really wasn't interested in it. Then a salesgirl came to him.

"Something for your wife or girlfriend, sir?" the salesgirl asked.

Jeff's attention was divided as he turned toward Sally B, who was still in the aisle behind him. The salesgirl noticed this and smiled at him. "Secret admirer, sir?" she whispered as she nodded toward Sally B.

Jeff forced a smile and shook his head no. Jeff knew he was being too obvious to the salesgirl, and walked toward the elevator nearby. He pushed the "up" button. He was nervous because he knew that he could lose Sally B if he got on the elevator and she didn't. The whole idea of him and his partner being called Mutt and Jeff would resurface again for fouling up a situation. They fouled up a couple of times before and had been temporarily demoted to walking the street beat. They'd always made their way back to their suits by stumbling onto a bust.

Jeff was still waiting for the elevator to arrive, and as it did, so did Sally B, directly behind him. He sensed what he hoped was her presence. He walked on the elevator and she followed him. They both turned and faced the door, waiting for it to close. They heard the 'bing' and the door slowly began to close. Jeff took an extra long time to turn around, to give whomever it was time to press the floor number they were going to before he pressed his floor. Sally B stood on his right side in front of him, with her back leaning against the shiny wooden elevator wall. The elevator door was closing, but not before someone else ran on, causing the door to open again.

Sally B was always extra cautious. She made sure she was never followed, and if she was, to give a little diversion to shake any unknown followers off and leave them in the dust. Just as the last person, a young white woman, rushed to get on the elevator, the doors almost closed. The doors opened wide as the woman touched the inner door. Sally B rushed off the elevator, leaving Jeff behind. This way she would definitely know if she was being followed, and Jeff knew exactly what she was doing. It was a mind game and Sally B had beat Jeff. He knew his cover would be blown if he suddenly got off that elevator, or even so much as peeked out to see where she was heading, because she was back at the cosmetics stand watching the door of the elevator. When Sally B saw the elevator go up, she sighed in relief and walked toward the stairs that were to the right of the elevator. She walked up to the fifth floor, where the women's department was located.

On the elevator, Jeff had a frustrated look as he got off at the second floor. He decided to take his frustration out on himself by walking back down to the first level. He began to walk down the wide spiral staircase, and as he got on, he walked past Sally B who was on her way up toward the third floor. He knew it was too risky to try to follow her anymore because she'd seen him twice, and he knew a third time would be a strike out.

Jeff kept going down the stairs and decided to go to the men's room, which was to the right of the staircase on the first level in the door marked 'employees only'. As he walked in, he was stopped by a Caucasian man in his early forties.

"Excuse me, sir. Back here is for employees only, and since I'm the supervisor, I know you're not an employee," the supervisor said as he looked Jeff up and down, frowning at his unmatched attire.

Jeff rolled his eyes and went to reach for his badge in his blazer chest pocket beneath his raincoat. The supervisor jumped back in fear.

"Don't shoot!" the supervisor cried out.

Jeff shook his head and took out his badge, flipping it in the supervisor's face.

"Police."

The supervisor waved Jeff on inside.

"Where's the men's room?" Jeff asked.

"In the rear. Keep straight back, you'll find it," the supervisor said as he exited.

Jeff walked the twenty feet to the bathroom and entered the small, one toilet room that was relatively clean. He immediately took out his walkie-talkie and called Mutt.

"Mutt, you there?" Jeff said in a low tone.

There was some static at first, then Mutt answered back.

"Go ahead. Where are you?"

"I'm at Saks in the first level bathroom. Oh, she's a smarty. She knows how to check to make sure she's not being followed."

"Huh?" Mutt replied.

"Oh, nothing. Just get over here and park across the street from the entrance, but get close to the corner of 48th just in case she leaves out the side door," Jeff said.

"Yeah, yeah, I'll be right there. I'm at 46th and Madison," Mutt said.

"What! What took you so long? I thought you were following me?" Jeff said.

"Hey, this is your first time radioing me back," Mutt said.

"I'll be out front. Hurry up! She could come out at any time," Jeff said as he clicked off the walkie-talkie. He sighed and hit the door in frustration and said, "I'll be glad when I retire."

Sally B was in the women's coat section. A salesgirl was with her. Sally B picked out a full-length leather coat and the salesgirl took it off of the rack for her and helped her try it on. She walked over to the mirror, stared at her reflection, then reflected, "I think I want something a little bulkier. Maybe a mink."

The salesgirl helped Sally B out of the leather coat and followed her over to the mink coat section. The salesgirl laid the leather coat over a chair next to a rack full of full-length mink coats.

"These should be on sale right now," Sally B said to the salesgirl.

"Yes. Would you like to try one on?" the salesgirl asked.

Sally B pointed to a long, black mink coat.

"This one, please," Sally B said.

The salesgirl took out her key ring and unlocked the coat from the wire link that surrounded all of the coats on this rack.The salesgirl looked at Sally B's size, then looked at a couple of the collar sizes of the coats.

"Here, this one should fit you," the salesgirl said.

"That looks great," Sally B said.

The salesgirl helped her put it on, and Sally B smiled as she looked at herself in the full-length mirror nearby. She walked back to the salesgirl.

"I'll take it."

"Yes, ma'am," the salesgirl said excitedly.

The salesgirl would clear a nice commission on a ten thousand dollar mink coat. She moved with subtle quickness toward the cash register.

"Would you like to take this with you now or have it picked up later?" the salesgirl asked.

"Now," Sally B said as she looked over both her shoulders.

"Cash or charge?" the salesgirl asked.

"Charge."

Sally B took out her gold American Express credit card from her purse and handed it to the salesgirl.

Jeff was in the car with Mutt, parked on the corner of 48th Street and 5th Avenue, waiting for Sally B to exit Saks.

"What's taking so long?" Jeff asked.

"You know women, try to buy the store with a dollar," Mutt replied.

"I got a funny feeling she's got more than a dollar," Jeff said.

Jeff watched the front door of Saks, and finally he saw Sally B come out.

"There she is," Jeff said.

Mutt turned to the direction of the store. He immediately started up the car and drove up 5th Avenue. Sally B began to walk east on 48th Street.

"Looks like she bought a coat," Mutt said.

"That's good, Sally B, keep right on using that credit card.

We'll keep good track of you," Mutt said sarcastically. "She probably caught a sale she.couldn't pass up."

"Whatever. Just get around the block," Jeff said.

Mutt instantly sped up 5th Avenue, cutting off a couple of cars
as he made his way toward 49th Street to make a right turn. The light
at the corner turned red, and he paused to see if any cars were coming. Then he turned right, heading east on 49th Street.

"She's probably going back to the hotel."

Mutt sped down 49th Street.

Sally B flagged down a cab. One stopped and she opened the
back passenger door opposite the driver. Then she gave him a one
dollar tip.

"Park Plaza Hotel," Sally B said.

Mutt and Jeff were at 46th and Lexington. It took them longer
than anticipated.

Sally B's cab pulled up to the front of the Park Plaza. She paid
the driver seven dollars.

"Receipt, please," Sally B asked.

The driver gavè her a receipt, and Sally B took her extra large
black garment bag off of the car seat as she got out of the cab.

"Need some help?" the cab driver asked. He smiled as he
admired Sally B's shape.

"Thanks, but I got it."

The cab sped off. A bellboy automatically approached Sally
B. "Can I help you with that, ma'am?" the bellboy offered.

"No, thanks, I can handle it."

She grimaced as she struggled with the bag, even more so
than she did while she carried the full-length mink from 5th Avenue to
Madison, which was a block apart. She acted as thought it was twice
as heavy. She had her reason.

"You sure you don't want me to help you?" the bellboy pleaded
as Sally B entered the hotel entryway.

Sally B entered the hotel, struggling, and slung the thick black
garment bag over her shoulder and walked to the elevator. She looked
back at the bellboy.

Mutt and Jeff pulled up in front of the hotel as Sally B entered
the elevator. Mutt stopped the car and Jeff looked over both of his
shoulders.

"I wonder if we missed her," Jeff said.

"Why don't you ask the bellboy?" Mutt queried.

"Yeah, and blow our cover? Right," Jeff replied. "We couldn't
have missed her by more than a few seconds if she did go in already."

Jeff rolled down his passenger window facing the hotel.

"Hey, bellman!" Jeff called as he waved the bellboy to come to him.

The bellboy looked around hesitantly, then went to the car

"Yes, what can I do for you, sir?" the bellboy said with a smile.

"Me and my friend have a bet going on," Jeff said.

"Uh huh. What is it?" the bellboy replied, with an inquisitive look.

"Well, we wanted to know if the person that just walked in with the large, black garment bag was a man or a woman?" Jeff asked.

"She's most definitely a woman. One of the prettier ladies who've stayed here," the bellboy said.

"Gotcha," Jeff said as he pointed to Mutt while he slowly drove off.

Jeff left the bellboy standing, then the car stopped abruptly Jeff waved the bellboy to him again. Jeff reached his hand out of the window to shake his hand and slipped him a dollar while they shook.

"Thanks," the bellboy said as Mutt drove off.

Mutt took a right at the corner and stopped.

"Well, she's in there!" Jeff said.

"That was a pretty good story you came up with back there," Mutt said.

"Well, what did you expect, for me to come right out and ask him?" Jeff said. "Come on, let's get to the front."

Sally B was in the suite. Justin sat on the couch reading his computer printouts.

"You're back," Justin said.

Sally B rolled her eyes and threw her leather Gucci purse on the sofa, near Justin.

"So, what did you buy?" Justin asked.

"A bag," Sally B replied.

"A bag for what?" Justin asked.

"How'd you think I was getting rid of the mess," Sally B said, annoyed.

Sally B took the mink coat and threw it on the sofa. Justin looked at the coat and frowned.

"Expensive bag, wouldn't you say?" Justin asked.

"Yeah, well, I had to get one big enough," Sally B said.

"I see. You're gonna carry her out in broad daylight, like

nothing ever happened. Clever. Now I see why I hired you. You know exactly how I like to work. But since I can't do it, you carry out what I would do very well. See, deep down, you and I think alike," Justin said.

"Yeah, right!" Sally B snapped.

On that, Justin sprang to his feet, darted over to Sally B and grabbed her deep in her collar.

"Now wouldn't you have done the same thing if you had no more use for someone and they were a threat to you and everything you ever worked hard for?"

Justin pulled her collar hard and tight.

"Would you?" he shouted.

"Come on, Justin, this doesn't tickle."

He rammed his hand up her vagina and she cried out.

"Does that tickle?" he said as he pushed harder.

"Yes — I mean, no, it doesn't tickle. And yes, I woulda done the same," Sally B said, in pain.

Justin pushed her away.

"Now go take care of that trash in the bedroom," he said as he brought his pants and shirt back to neatness.

Sally B grabbed the garment bag and headed to the bedroom.

"We're going to Bangkok, after we go back to Albany next week."

Sally B angrily pushed open the bedroom door where Mimi's dead body lay.

"I gotta go do something. I'll be right back," Justin said.

Sally B knew this was out of the ordinary for Justin to go out to do something without asking for her help.

"Where are you going?" Sally B asked.

Justin was about to open the suite front door, then looked back with a smile.

"Oh, so you do still love me, don't you?" Justin said.

"Look, I work for you and I'm in this. If you're caught, I'm caught. Where are you going?" Sally B asked, irritated.

"Never mind. We had a visitor earlier. She may come back."

Sally B ambled from the bedroom to the door of the bedroom.

"Who was it?"

"It was the maid."

Justin took the 'do not disturb' tag from the outside of the doorknob.

"Did you tell the maid to ignore this?" Justin asked as he held the sign up to show Sally B.

"No, I told her not to go in, that it was already clean."

"Well, she came in while I was in the bathroom. I don't think she saw anything. She was standing by my bedroom door about to enter when I came from the bathroom. It was probably just an honest mistake on her part."

Sally B shrugged her shoulders and headed back to Mimi's dead body. Justin began doing push-ups.

"Yeah, probably was," she mumbled. He stopped his push ups.

"I'll be back in a few minutes. Wait 'til I return before you leave," Justin said.

"Yeah, sure."

Justin put his Mets baseball cap on and pulled it low down on his forehead. Then he put his dark sunglasses on. He walked back to his room where Sally B was. Sally B stood and looked at Justin blankly. He walked to Sally B and kissed her lightly on the forehead. Then he left the bedroom and went out the suite door.

Sally B blew air, sighing as Justin walked away.

There was no blood involved in Mimi's death. Even so, Sally B would put on her gloves before she would touch anything in the room. She went into the living room area and got her big traveling bag. Out of the side zipper pocket, she took two plastic surgical gloves and put them on. Luckily Mimi only weighed a hundred pounds, making her a little easier for Sally B to handle since she was in decent physical shape.

Sally B went into the bedroom and turned Mimi's body over into the unzipped garment bag. She closed Mimi's eyes and began to fit the remainder of her body into the garment bag, wrapping it in the mink coat.

Justin had taken the elevator to the basement. He got off and walked toward the housekeeping section. He looked into the house-keeping supervisor's office, and it was empty. Then he went to the laundry section. One lady was exiting as Justin headed that way. When he saw an employee leaving, he intentionally dropped his key card on the ground as the woman passed so that she couldn't see his face as she passed by. It was still early, but late enough for the maids to have returned with their baskets full, ready to dump the dirty linen into the wash. That was what Justin was banking on. It would only be luck and fate that he'd find Mrs. Simmons in the basement emptying her cart and preparing to go to clean her next floor full of rooms.

Justin quickly looked in the laundry room and saw two older blonde women intalking. He was looking for a brunette.

Justin had missed her and he was pissed. He headed back toward the elevator when he heard one of the women that was in the laundry room drop her keys as she left the room. Then he heard a third voice. He was sure it was Mrs. Simmons. He remembered she spoke very loud because she had a hearing deficiency.

Justin got to the entrance of the laundry room and looked down both ends of the empty hallway before he entered. Mrs. Simmons was emptying dirty sheets into the washer, then she turned and saw Justin and was startled.

"Oh, it's you. You have dirty sheets or something?" Mrs. Simmons asked.

Justin took his hands out of his pockets. They were gloved with the surgical plastics. In the blink of an eye, he had the door closed and was on Mrs. Simmons, his hands squeezing her throat with practiced skill. He was quick with his killing.

He ran to the door, opened it and looked at both ends of the hallway. He placed his hands back into his pockets and swiftly headed toward the elevator without anyone seeing him.

At the opposite end of the hallway another maid came from a supply room carrying clean sheets. By then Justin was on the elevator as the maid passed by the laundry room and noticed that the door was closed.

She opened the door, and upon seeing Mrs. Simmons' dead body, she began to scream loud. Loud enough for Justin to hear as the elevator began its ascent.

Justin was clever. He knew that whenever a suite key was used, it was recorded by computer that someone was headed to the suite. But it didn't record who was headed to a suite. So to keep him and Sally B clear of problems, he got off on the first floor and casually left the hotel through the front door, like nothing ever happened.

Mutt and Jeff were in their car across the street, down from the hotel, reading the paper. Justin went to a phone booth around the corner on 45th Street and called up Sally B's room.

"You have to get out of there now. With everything! You got that, Sally B? Hurry up."

"What's goin' on?" Sally B asked.

"Don't ask questions, just get movin'. I'll meet you at the corner of Lexington and 43rd. Got it?"

"Yeah," Sally B replied and slammed the receiver down.

"Shit!" Sally B said as she scurried around, throwing her belongings in her purse and then snatching the disc from the computer. She picked up the bag by its shoulder strap and put it over her shoulder. She ran to Justin's bedroom, kicked the door wide open, took the plastic gloves off and threw them in a side pocket of her shoulder bag. Mimi's body was in the garment bag wrapped and ready to go. All Sally B had to do was get to the elevator without anyone seeing her carrying a garment bag thrown over her shoulder like a sack of potatoes.

Down in the basement was chaos. A group of co-workers stood over Mrs. Simmons' body crying. The supervisor was urging them to move back.

"Come now, move back and don't touch anything," the supervisor said.

Co-workers shouted, asking questions in rapid fire.

"Did she have a heart attack?"

"Is she dead?"

"Someone call a doctor!"

"Did someone kill her?"

"Please calm down, everyone, the paramedics are on their way," the supervisor said.

The supervisor, a white female in her early thirties, knelt down to the motionless Mrs. Simmons and checked her wrist for a pulse. There wasn't any, but the supervisor kept it to herself.

Sally B was at the elevator. She struggled to hold Mimi's body on her right shoulder. Hopefully the bellboys wouldn't think anything of seeing her carrying the heavy garment bag out the door, the same way they believed it when she carried the bag in the building. She was sweating. She'd already put her card key in to call for the elevator, but it was taking longer than usual. She heard a door slam at the same end her suite was on, but further down where she couldn't see. Someone was coming, and so was the elevator, finally. Sally B kept looking down the hallway and whispering to herself.

"Come on! Come on! Come on!"

Just as the elevator door opened, the person could be seen coming from the direction of Sally B's suite. Sally B hurried onto the elevator, and the door closed as the man's voice echoed off the walls saying, "Hold the door."

Sally B wasn't about to. She sighed as the elevator whisked her down. To her it seemed like forever. She knew she could still be caught getting off.

The paramedics arrived in front of the hotel with their siren blaring. Mutt and Jeff looked at each other. They decided they would check with the bellboy to see what was going on.

"Let's check it out," Jeff said.

Mutt and Jeff got out of their car and hurriedly entered the hotel behind the paramedics.

"What's goin' on?" Mutt asked anyone.

"Heart attack," one of the paramedics said as they rushed to the service elevator.

The service elevator was at the opposite end of the basement, near the suite elevator that was bringing Sally B down. Sally B's elevator door opened to the basement floor, where all the chaos was happening. She had accidentally pushed the wrong button. She saw hotel workers darting by. She knew there'd be trouble for her even if she stuck her head out to ask what had happened. She mashed the button for parking level one. The door closed, and she sighed.

A bellboy led Mutt and Jeff, followed by the paramedics, into the service elevator. It promptly stopped at the housecleaning level in the basement. They all ran out. The workers were signaling for them to come in the laundry room.

The paramedics attempted to revive Mrs. Simmons, while Jeff, who had experience working with homicides, searched for any clues that might reveal foul play.

"She's gone!" one of the attending paramedics said, after several attempts to revive her.

Then Jeff went to look at Mrs. Simmons, while Mutt looked around. Jeff knelt down to her and opened an eyelid, using his Bic pen top. Even with his lightest touch, Mrs. Simmons' head limped to the left.

"Her neck's broken," Jeff said.

There were sounds of disbelief from Mrs. Simmons' co-workers with this revelation.

"Don't anyone touch anything. Everyone please move out. We have to tape this area off," Mutt commanded.

Sally B's elevator stopped at the first level parking area. To not be over suspicious, she didn't even bother to check to see if anyone was coming before she walked off the elevator. She simply threw Mimi's body over her shoulder again and strode to her rented car. She had her own car, but it was parked at their Truman Tower penthouse garage, miles away. She was sweating, which was unusual for her because she was mostly cool under fire, but this was too close for comfort. By the time she reached her car, she was pouring with sweat and her energy was spent. She couldn't drop Mimi's body on the car or ground because she knew if she did, she wouldn't be able to pick the dead weight up again. The car key was in her purse, which was in her black shoulder bag. She went to the driver's side of the car and leaned against the rear door while fishing through her shoulder bag, searching for her purse. She sighed and tried again. Mimi's body almost fell from her shoulder, but she managed to catch the black bag between her body and the car. She finally managed to hold on to Mimi's body and began fishing through her shoulder bag for her purse; that time she found it. She flipped her key chain to the trunk key, got a tight secure hold of the garment bag and stumbled a bit as she walked to the trunk. She heard two male voices coming from the elevator. She was parked a short distance from the elevator door, but there were concrete partitions separating each space. She paused until she heard the voices fade and the elevator door close. Then she hurried, finally got the key into the trunk lock, opened it and threw the body in. She slammed the trunk shut and ran to the driver's door. She fumbled with the keys in her slight panic from hearing the sound of sirens coming in from the garage entrance. She located the key and unlocked her door as her breathing rate increased. She practically jumped behind the wheel, paused for a few seconds to get her bearings straight, put the key into the ignition, started the car and calmly drove out of the garage. Upon reaching the exit, she could see the paramedic's truck, a black and white police car and a fire truck. She only glanced to her left as she passed by.

Mutt and Jeff watched as the paramedics wheeled the dead body of Mrs. Simmons out on a stretcher, covered with a white sheet from head to toe.

Sally B knew that Justin was involved in some way, but turned right onto Park Avenue and never looked back. She was very nervous, frequently checking the rearview mirror, making certain she wasn't being followed and making sure she looked good. The last thing she wanted was to look like she had panicked in front of Justin. This might give him reason to want to get rid of her. She headed south on Lexington. In the middle of the block she could see Justin leaning against a light pole. She showed the first sign of relaxation. She couldn't help but grin at Justin with his baseball cap yanked on his head and sunglasses covering his eyes.

Justin spotted Sally B approaching and walked off the curb, then into the street to where she could pull right up to him. A poker face replaced Sally B's smile as she stopped. Justin smiled through the passenger window, opened the door and got in. Sally B sped off.

"What did you do back there?" Sally B asked.

"Took care of my binness."

"You almost got me caught while you were taking care of your binness. Binness, huh?" Sally B said with anger and sarcasm.

"You know, your mouth is beginning to precede you," Justin said.

"No, I'm just trying to help."

"Well, I don't need that help. I've become a wealthy man with bin-ness. Now drive," Justin said.

"Should I take you with me while I dispose of the body?" Sally B asked.

Justin first looked at her by turning his head slightly to the left, then looked at his watch.

"Yeah, but I was never in this car, got that?"

"Yeah, I got it," Sally B said.

There was a silence as she continued to drive. She took a left on to 39th Street on her way to Second Avenue and drove taster. It was really too early to dump the body, but if she didn't, it would start to smell, and that could get her caught back at Truman Towers. So it had to be done, and hopefully no one would see her.

Sally B had decided to wait until dark to dump the body. It was late and there was still traffic on Franklin Delano Roosevelt Drive. They drove along the East River on the FDR. Sally B took the next exit and soon she was close to the banks of the river. She pulled over and got out. She hurried to the trunk and took Mini's body out of the garment bag. She looked around at Justin who sat in the front passenger seat, watching her. She frowned at him, irked because he wouldn't help her. But then he never had. But he was never actually at the dumping area.

For him, it was a matter of not getting his hands dirty. Sally B put Mimi's body over her shoulder and carried it to the edge above the East River. She threw the body in without anything weighing it down. She knew it would probably be found, but as long as the body couldn't be linked to her, she was cool.

Bad dreams would follow during the next couple of days, but she would survive. She had learned to over the years. This was the part of the business she hated most. She hated Justin during this time also, because nothing was ever on him. She always carried the full blame.

CHAPTER TWENTY-FOUR

IT WAS LATE AND MOM was asleep. Dats was called in to work unexpectedly at CDTA. Apparently too many people were out sick and they needed the help.

Me, Randy and Tony were in the basement sitting up talking, waiting for the night to come further into the morning. We were fully clothed.

"Did you get Mom's keys, Corey?" Randy asked.

I went to my bed, reached under my pillow and pulled out the keys.

"Are you guys sure you want to do this? We could get in a lot of trouble if we get caught," Tony said.

"Shut up, you wimp, and stop talkin' about gettin' caught. That's all we need is somebody thinking negative," Randy said.

"Tony, we gotta go up there. I know nobody's home because I watched all day out the front window and nobody came in or out. If you're scared, you stay down here," I said.

"But maybe you should get Uncle Henry to go upstairs since he's bigger. At least if he gets caught up there, Mom and Dats won't beat him," Tony said.

"Tony, look, tonight is the night," I said.

"But, Corey, I don't understand why this is so important to you. Can't you just tell Mom and Dats?" Tony pleaded.

"I've already tried that."

"But what's the big deal, Corey? You're not a cop." Tony said.

I was starting to become irritated. Tony was chicken shit.

"Why should we risk getting into trouble for something you aren't even sure about? Just because I'm the youngest doesn't mean I'm stupid. And Randy, you can slap me around if you want to, but I don't think we should go up there."

I was even more irritated because time was being wasted, but Randy knew Tony was right. I had to give him more of a reason why I knew that may be the only way to keep Tony from waking Mom and telling her what we were gonna do. I didn't realize how much I had scared Tony by telling him what happened when I snuck up there.

Randy was fed up and charged after Tony and grabbed him by the neck.

"Boy, you're gonna go up there with us!" Randy said.

I went to Randy and took his hands from Tony's neck.

"Randy, Randy, let'em go, let'em go! I just need to talk to

him. Actually, I need to talk to both of you."

I slowly helped take Randy's hands from around Tony's neck. We looked each other eye to eye. Randy knew something was up, and for the first time in his life, he obeyed me, reluctantly of course.

"I think after I tell you this, you'll probably want to help me even more."

CHAPTER TWENTY-FIVE

AT THE LAVISH CONDO, number ten-sixteen in Truman Towers, Justin was vigorously riding his stationary bike in the hallway near the living room. He had worked up a good sweat. He wore a grey T-shirt, black silk boxer shorts and black, low-cut suede Puma sneakers with no socks.

"Sally B, you oughtta try this. It's great for your heart," he said with a big smile. Sally B wore a black cat suit as she stood with her arms folded, looking at traffic out of the window. She slowly turned her head toward Justin, then answered, I didn't know you had a heart," she said with a smug look.

Justin smiled, then began to slow his pace. After a few minutes, he climbed off of the bike, anxious to get back to work. He took the towel from the nearby table and wiped himself off. He drank a tall glass of ice water that Sally B had brought for him.

He made his way toward the fax machine in the corner of the living room, next to the sofa. He kept it there for convenience, since it was his most used possession. Justin faxed information to Bangkok regarding his next sale of human flesh. Whenever Justin sent a fax to one of his business partners across the globe, he always spoke in code. Most often the terminology was in fishing terms. To go fishing was to go out and find a potential teenager, capture him or her, train them, then ship them off to Bangkok, Italy, India or anywhere a client of Justin's might be.

To send a 'sonny' was to send a ten year old, small in size. if it was a boy, Justin would simply say 'sonny' for male and 'she' for female.

If it were a teenager thirteen or older, the child was referred to as a 'bass'. If it was a large or small person, Justin would say a 'big' or 'squeak' bass. If the catch was a beauty, Justin would refer to the bass as a 'beautiful, big bass'. The fax read:

Dear Partner:

Due to extenuating circumstances, there will be a delay in the delivery of the original. Our fish was a little too mouthy and we had to throw it back in the sea. However, we will go deep-sea fishing in the next few hours and I can assure you we'll get a great catch. Don't worry about your deposit. It has been well spent and the balance due me will be rushed here when you receive this whale of a catch.

P.S. Stanley, you never told me how the last one was that I sent you.
Your friend, "L"

Justin hit 'enter' on his computer, and the fax was sent. His business partner, Stanley Means in Bangkok, would be happy to receive this letter.

Next, Justin would fax a letter to his business partner in Italy. But before he could get started, a fax was coming to him on his computer. It read:

Dear "L"

Received your fax, but the last bass you sent me jumped to its death. However, I must admit the short time it worked I made much by way of dollars.
Yours, Bang, Bang

They could be dealt with easier.

Sometimes it was hard for Justin to do business in foreign countries because of the language barrier of the kids. Justin had no problem with the different languages because he'd spent time wherever he did business. He knew enough to get by. What he didn't know, he found out. He was not to be denied. Even so, some of the people he dealt with liked it better that way, because the kids were easier to control if they didn't know the language. They were more apt to do what they were told, and by doing so would live longer.

Sally B was in her bedroom getting some of her things together, in case they had to leave New York fast. Most of the time they would leave in a hurry, not because they were being chased but because Justin liked the hectic pace. It made him feel more in charge.

It was getting late and Justin's patience was beginning to wear thin.

"Are you almost ready in there, Honey?" Justin asked.

Sally B sighed, shook her head and smiled. She really hated being rushed, but she put up with it because it was Justin. She liked when he called her 'Honey'. Even though she worked for him, she felt an undeniable attachment to him. This was what really kept her around.

She walked to the bedroom entryway.

"You know, you can be very sweet at times. This is the you that I like. The you that really makes you. If it wasn't for that sweet part of you, I woulda been gone a long time ago."

She began to walk toward Justin as he just stared at her, hypnotically seducing her.

"You! You are what make me tick. I've had many a sexual pleasure but you bring me more than just flesh. You're a challenge, a reservoir full of power and passion for people that I could never possess. Come here, Sally B, let me hold you."

She gently accepted his open arms as she sat on his lap. She kissed him softly on the forehead and he rubbed his face on her soft, protruding nipples. She worked her kisses down to the bridge of this nose, then to the top of his lips, licking his lips lightly.

"Please, Justin, please."

They sank down on the sofa. She was on top of him as they wrestled their clothes off each other.

CHAPTER TWENTY-SIX

ME, RANDY AND TONY sat in silence. They were stunned. They couldn't believe what I'd just told them.

"In the booty, Corey? In the booty?" Randy said.

Tony could only be afraid at how I described this attacker. He really knew nothing about sex, only what he'd seen on TV or heard Randy or others talk about. He really understood the pain though, because once he had to be examined rectally for hemorrhoids, and that was painful.

I lounged at the foot of Tony's bed, and Randy came and sat with me, putting his arm around me.

"Why didn't you tell Mom and Dats?" Randy asked.

I looked at Randy in his eyes, then he sadly turned his head toward Tony, remembering the day I got pushed by them into Mom and Dats' bedroom.

Then I thought, I shouldn't be telling Randy this because he could be my attacker. At that point, deep down, I didn't quite believe he was my attacker. If he was, our day would come to settle our score.

"I wanted to but couldn't after I seen Mom and Dats in the bed." I paused, reflecting back. "Dats was face down on the bed and Mom was on top of him and they were doing it. It made me sick. Then I realized something was wrong. But I never said a thing to them about it. Then I saw that Justin at the hospital."

"He was at the hospital?" Tony asked excitedly wanting to know more.

"Shhh, go on," Randy said.

"Then I saw Justin and that woman carrying that bag upstairs. I know there was a body in the bag. But where could they have hidden it that fast? Then Mom and Dats acted so strange when Justin was on the elevator with us at the hospital. I just think that if I was renting an apartment to someone for a few years and they don't speak or act like they're scared to speak, and then Mom and Dats didn't say much about the cops being up there, something's not right, and I know it. We gotta go up there. If nothing else, just to see how this guy lives. Who knows, he could be some killer."

"Are you gonna ever tell Mom and Dats what happened to you, Corey?" Tony asked.

Randy and I looked at each other. I was thinking that Justin, Uncle Henry, Mom and Dats, or even Randy could have molested me. I didn't want to believe it was Randy. I was confused.

"No, I haven't, but I will. And you can't ever say a word to them. At least until I approach them first. You gotta promise me that, Tony."

I leaned into Tony's face. He laid with his head at the foot of his bed.

"And if you ever tell Mom, Dats or anyone, I'll cut your tongue out, just like I cut Billy's finger off."

Tony was scared and nervously asked, "Who's that?"

"Just someone who didn't listen to what I told them."

"Randy, is that true?"

"Yeah, you saw how he almost bit my neck off."

"Well, what about Uncle Henry? You could tell him," Tony said sadly.

"Tony, this is some heavy shit to be accusing somebody of. If the wrong person hears it, there could be trouble," Randy said.

Randy and I knew we were going to have to have Tony in on our search upstairs. But we were going to have to trick Tony into doing it, because if he wasn't in on it, he'd probably tell like he always did.

If we asked him straight out to come with us, he might think that we wanted him to get in trouble with us if we were caught.

"Corey, since Tony doesn't want to go, we can't do it because we're gonna need somebody to be the lookout while we search the place," Randy said.

"Well, why do I always have to be the lookout? Why can't I go inside the apartment, too?" Tony said.

The plan worked. Randy and I had done this many times before when Tony was really afraid to do something, but we never told how we got him to do things, because if we did, he would never fall for it again.

"Okay, you can come into the apartment with us, but you gotta be careful not to touch anything or make any noise," I said.

Tony stood and put his old dirty sneakers on with his pajama bottoms, like he was going to battle.

"Okay, when we go . . . sir?"

He even saluted toward Randy and I. Me and Randy smiled, then tackled Tony onto the bed, playfully. We suddenly stopped rolling on my bed and seriously looked Tony in the eyes and said, "It's time."

We all got up and went to the foot of the basement stairs. Randy slowly made it up the first couple of stairs in the dark. He reached the middle of the twenty stairs, and they began to crack as he crept up the remaining ten stairs. The cracking didn't seem that loud while the rest of the world was awake, but it was 2:00 a.m. and you could hear everything throughout the house.

Randy heard a "shhh" from me at the foot of the stairs. He grimaced with each crackling of the stairs as he made it to the top. He waited for me and Tony to come up.

Mom was in bed tossing and turning. Because of her light sleep that night, she could be awakened by noise from the cracking steps. I made it up fairly quickly after Randy. Me and Randy knelt at the top of the stairs at the end of the dining room table.

"C'mon, Tony," I said in a strained whisper.

Tony began his ascent up the dark staircase. He was nervous, and still unsure about the whole escapade.

He lightly stepped on the first step, and it crackled loud. He stopped and put his hand on his heart to check his rate. It was running at rapid fire. He sighed, then took the next few steps rapidly. Confidence took over and his pace quickened. Then he became overconfident and slipped and fell at the top step. His fall made some noise.

"Stay there," I whispered angrily.

Mom tossed and turned in her bed. But the question was: Did Tony's fall wake her up? We weren't sure, so we all stayed on the floor for a few more minutes. It was very quiet, so we figured it was clear to head upstairs. I patted Tony lightly on his back.

"Go ahead!" I said, whispering.

Tony began to slowly crawl to the dining room door. Me and Randy followed, being very careful. Tony was finally at the door, and he reached up and gradually turned the knob. I grabbed Tony's hand as he turned the knob, to help keep the noise down from the latch. Once the door latch was unlatched, I took Tony's hand down and pushed the door open, enough for the three of us to get in one by one. We crawled through the hallway to the foot of the stairs and stopped.

"I think we should crawl up the stairs also," I said.

As I began to crawl up, Tony followed, then Randy.

"If you start to hear the slightest crackle, stop," I whispered.

We made it up to the apartment without incident. I used the key to open the door. I went to the refrigerator and opened the door, using the light so we could see our way around. Tony and Randy just stood in the kitchen, which was a foot away from the front door. For what Randy and Tony could see, there was nothing unusual about the kitchen, except it was cleaner than ours.

We tiptoed to the living room area towards the front of the house.

"But we can't see anything," Tony said.

"Shhh," I said. "Just keep going. There should be a light somewhere up front."

We walked to the front.

"Corey, we came up here but we can't see anything to find out if something is going on. I'm turning the light on."

Randy walked to the end table lamp and turned it on.

"Nooo!" I said before I could stop Randy.

The light popped on, and we saw a normal looking living room.

"Everything looks normal, Corey," Randy said.

I went into the room where I heard the child's voice, which was off the living room in front.

"But this is where I heard that kid talking, or whatever he or she was doing."

Randy and Tony followed me into the bedroom. "It's only a bed, Corey," Randy said.

"He had that kid's arms and legs tied to those bed posts."

"It's just his guest room," Randy said.

Tony looked around at the bare dresser that was near the head of the bed. I looked under the bed, finding nothing. Randy looked at the bare-walled room, then at the ceiling paint cracking over the head of the bed. Next he scanned the area near the foot of the twin bed. Then he looked directly above himself, near the bedroom door.

"Look, what's that?" Randy asked.

I got up from the floor, and Tony stopped looking through the four dresser drawers. We all looked up at the ceiling door. Then we looked at each other, wondering.

"I don't know. I don't remember seeing it the night I snuck up here," I said.

"It's probably a door to the roof, that's all," Randy said.

I looked in the corner behind the door and saw a stepping stool.

"No, wait, let's take a look up there," I said.

"C'mon, let's get outta here. Nothing's going on," Tony said.

I grabbed the step ladder and stepped on it, but couldn't reach the ceiling door latch.

"C'mon, Corey, it's probably just to a crawl space. Let's go!" Tony said.

"Well, we're gonna crawl to see."

"Are you gonna help me get up here, Randy?" I asked as I stood up on the step ladder, waiting for Randy to give me a boost up.

Randy was indifferent. He looked at me, then at Tony who had a pleading look, urging us not to go up.

"If you help him up there, I'm going!" Tony threatened.

I hastily but quietly climbed down from the stool and grabbed Tony by his collar.

"You look, I'm sick of you! Now, you wanted to come with us and we let you. If you so much as take one step toward that door, it will be your last," I snapped with conviction.

All Tony could do was look into my eyes with fear. Tony remembered what Randy had secretly told him about how I had cut a guy's finger off because he was trying to take my pennies.

I let go of Tony's collar and lovingly patted him on his head. He was frozen still. All he could and would do was watch me climb back onto the top step of the ladder. Then I stepped onto Randy's shoulder and held on to the wall for balance as I jimmied the latch to the ceiling door open. I finally got the door open. The door opened inward, and I pulled myself up through the small doorway of the attic.

I laid down on my stomach and looked back through the ceiling door at Randy and Tony.

"Corey, what is it?" Tony asked.

"It's more than just a crawl space!" I said.

Tony and Randy looked at each other curiously.

"I'm coming up," Randy said.

Randy got up on the stool. I reached down for him and helped him up.

"I wanna come up, too," Tony said.

Me and Randy looked down at Tony, then at each other. Tony climbed up on the step stool and reached for me and Randy's outstretched hands. He could barely reach us, but he stood on his tippy toes and jumped for our hands, grabbing them as the ladder tipped over.

"There goes the ladder," I said.

"How are we gonna get down?" Tony asked.

"Don't worry about that," I said.

We easily pulled Tony up into the attic. It was dark and cluttered a bit.

"Where's the light?" Tony asked.

There wasn't one. We cautiously walked around, feeling our way in the dark. I walked to the wall, feeling around for a light switch. Tony stood by the exit and Randy walked forward, unsure of his next step.

I found a light switch near the back door and I flipped it on. We all sighed in relief. The area was cluttered and dusty.

"Let's go now," Tony begged.

I walked toward the exit, but Randy went to the back wall, which really wasn't a wall. It was only a folding door that was locked.

"Hey, wait, it's a door," Randy said.

Randy tried to force it open. I went to help him, trying to jimmy the lock, but it was bolted from the other side of the door.

"Why would it be bolted from the other side if nothing was over there," I said.

"But how did they bolt it if this is the only way in?" Tony asked.

"Hey, that's smart, Tony. Now you're helping," Randy said, condescendingly.

"Shut up, I'm no dummy," Tony shot back.

"There must be another way back there," I said.

"But where?" Randy asked.

"Somewhere in the back. It has to be," I said, while trying to peek through the small opening that was available from me jimmying the original door lock.

"But why is there light back there?" I said.

"What kinda light?" Randy asked.

"It looks green," I answered.

Tony pushed his way to me and looked in the crack. "It's computer light. There's a computer back there. Listen, you can hear it running a little. Somebody left a computer on," Tony said.

"Of course, that's it. You are good for something, aren't you?" Randy said.

Tony was proud of himself as he smiled and blew his fingertips, then rubbed them on his chest.

"Okay, that's enough. We gotta come back another day. Sometime when Mom and Dats aren't home. Maybe we can climb on the roof to get in," I said.

Sara was restless and woke from a bad dream. She'd gotten up. She opened the refrigerator and took out the milk. She got a glass from the sink rack and poured herself a full glass. She went back into her bedroom. The fridge door slowly closed by itself.

Randy was the first to jump down through the small, two foot by two foot ceiling door. He made a noise.

Sara had her light off in her bedroom, but turned it on when she heard the thump from upstairs. She glanced at her clock at the head of the bed sitting on the night stand. It read 3:00 a.m.

Randy pulled the ladder over and made another thumping sound.

"Shhh," I said, agitated.

"C'mon, hurry," Randy said.

Sara finished her milk. She turned the light off, then laid in the bed on top of the lightly quilted covers.

Randy had helped me down. Tony was the last to come out. Before he grabbed for Randy's outstretched hand, he decided he wanted one last look at the green light coming from the room. On his way back to the back door, he bumped a table and a light fell and broke.

"What's that?" Randy said in a strained whisper.

Tony hurried back to the exit and reached for Randy's outstretched hands.

"C'mon," Randy said.

Sara heard something fall, but couldn't figure it out. That's three noises, she thought. But she was hesitant about anything she thought Justin was doing. She wanted to keep away, so she just laid there.

Randy had Tony in his large arms. He stepped down onto the last step of the step stool. I was at the apartment front door, about to make my way back downstairs.

Randy and Tony immediately ran out of the room. They were at the front door of the apartment with me.

"Did you put the ladder back?" I asked.

Randy thought for a second. "No," he said.

He turned to his younger brother, "Go put it back, Tony."

"No, it's too dark. Why do I have to do the dirty work?" Tony said.

"I'll do it myself," I said.

I lightly ran back to the room and darted back to the front door. By then I knew my way around pretty good, even in the dark.

"Let's get back," I said.

We slowly started down the stairs, one by one behind each other. The stairs cracked loud as we walked.

Sara sat up in bed when she heard the crackle on the stairs.

We all were at the bottom of the stairs on our way back into the house.

"Randy, is that you?" Mom called out from her bedroom.

"Oh, shit," Tony said to himself.

Mom got up from her bed and began to walk out of her room. We would surely be caught, we thought.

The phone rang. The ring seemed like it was twice as loud as normal since it was so quiet and it startled everyone.

Mom never made it out of her room. She instead went back to her side of the bed, closest to the locked cabinet, to answer the phone.

"Hello?" Mom said.

On 'hello' we scattered. Randy went to his room and jumped under the covers. Me and Tony quickly but quietly went downstairs into the basement and got into bed.

Mom was still on the phone.

"I'm on my way home, Honey," Jim said on the phone.

"I thought you had to work all night?"

"We got the emergency taken care of so they are letting us go. How are the boys?"

"They're fine. Justin is making a lot of noise up there tonight."

"Justin? Justin's in New York, Honey."

"Oh my God, I'll call you back," Mom said, dropping the phone and running towards the front and out the door. She ran upstairs.

I quietly ran up the basement stairs once I heard Mom running upstairs to Justin's apartment. She went to open Justin's door, but realized she didn't have her keys.

I was on my way to Mom's bedroom with her keys, but heard her footsteps coming back down the stairs from Justin's apartment. I gently laid the keys on the dining room table. Mom was at the middle of the stairs. There was no time for me to make it back down to the basement. Mom came through the dining room door and dashed to her bedroom, turning on her wall light that lit the entire bedroom. She looked on her dresser for her keys. It was cluttered, but she always knew where her keys were. She began to fumble through everything, looking for her keys in a panic.

I had ducked behind the dining room table. She went to her closet and checked her pants that were hanging on a nail behind the door. She checked her pockets. Still no keys. She was angry and scared. She thought, what if the boys had the keys and were in Justin's apartment? She ran into Randy's room and woke him up.

"Randy, wake up." She turned on his bedroom wall light. It lit the entire room brightly. She went and shook him as he faked sleep under the covers.

"Randy, wake up."

Randy hesitantly brought his head from under the covers, faking like he'd been asleep for hours. He squinted his eyes.

"Mom, the light."

"Damn the light. Have you seen my keys?"

"No, Mom, I'm asleep."

"My keys, I had them in my room on the dresser. I know it."

"What about your purse, Mom?"

Randy glanced at his watch on his arm. "Mom, it's three in the morning. Why do you need the keys?"

"I just need them. I heard noises upstairs and Justin isn't home. I think somebody broke in or is up there."

"Mom, check your purse."

She ran back to her bedroom. I crawled under the dining room table, hoping she wouldn't look down or drop anything from her purse. As she darted back to the dining room area and turned on the light, she dumped the contents of her purse on the dining room table, and some lipstick fell on the floor in front of me. I froze, even stopped breathing momentarily. She glanced at the lipstick, but did not pick it up.

"Here they are, right here on the damn table," Mom said.

After she grabbed the keys, Randy got up and went to the hallway. I was still under the table. Mom ran upstairs with the keys.

"Mom, why don't you call the cops?" Randy asked.

Randy looked back and saw me under the table and motioned for me to get downstairs. I crawled from under the table and ran downstairs, not caring how much noise the steps made as I ran. I thought since Mom was in a panic, she would never notice the noise.

Sara opened Justin's door and slowly walked inside. She flicked on the wall light switch. She saw and heard nothing but the water dripping from the faucet. She moved with caution about the apartment into each room leading up to the living room. She turned on the light and saw the door to the living room bedroom open. She went to the room and went inside. She looked up, and the ceiling door latch was unlocked. Randy and Tony forgot to lock it. Randy came upstairs and called out, "Mom."

"In here," she said, agitated.

Randy went into the room where he knew Mom was.

"Mom, what is it?"

"The latch. You know what it is!"

"Mom, what are you talking about?"

"You were all up here, weren't you?"

"No, Mom."

She looked at the way Randy was fully dressed.

"Why are you still dressed in bed?"

"I fell asleep. I was reading a comic book."

"Since when do you fall asleep in your *precious* clothes?"

I just did."

"Yeah, sure."

She grabbed the ladder and slammed it down directly under the ceiling door.

"Climb up there and lock that latch. If Justin comes home and finds that unlocked, he'll have a fit."

Randy climbed up on the short step ladder and locked the latch.

"And I'm gonna deal with somebody later," she said as she looked at her keys, almost sure how they got on the dining room table.

Randy hopped down from the top of the step ladder.

"All right, let's go," she said.

"Mom, can I go back to bed now?" Randy asked.

She didn't answer. She closed Justin's door.

"You boys are gonna have to deal with your father, if I decide to tell him."

She heard keys opening the front door. Jim entered, out of breath.

"I hurried after you dropped the phone," Jim said.

"It's nothing," she said.

"Why are you coming from up there with Randy? You know Justin doesn't like the kids up there," Jim said as they all entered the dining area of their apartment.

"Corey put you up to this, didn't he, Randy?" Jim said, snatching Randy's arm.

"Put me up to nothing. We didn't do anything!" Randy said.

"I'm settling this right now," Jim said as he ran down the basement stairs.

He yanked open the basement door to my and Tony's bedroom.

"Corey, get up!" Dats shouted, waking up Tony, too.

"You too, Tony, get up. Now!"

Tony and I slowly rolled out of our twin beds.

"Yes, Dats!" I said.

"Don't 'yes' me. Get upstairs."

I got out of bed and Dats grabbed me by the back of my pajama collar, dragging me upstairs. We both stumbled up the stairs, me feeling the brunt of the pain from bumping into the wooden handrail and concrete wall. Tony slowly followed from behind. We reached the top of the stairs into the dining room area where Mom and Randy were waiting. Dats pushed me over near the entryway of Randy's bedroom. Randy stood near Mom, who stood near the head of the table, closest to the kitchen.

"Now, I need to know who was upstairs," Dats shouted.

Me and Randy looked at each other, wondering who would tell. Dats walked over to Randy and got in his face.

"Corey put you up to this, didn't he?" Dats said calmly.

Randy couldn't look Dats in the eye. He only stared out towards him, not making a connection. Then there was silence. Then whack! Dats slapped Randy in his face.

"I asked you a question, boy!"

Randy's eyes were filling up with water.

"Tony!" Dats said, yelling.

Dats didn't know it, but Tony was at the top of the stairs, listening.

"Yes, Dats," Tony said, barely audible.

"Who's idea was it to go upstairs?" Dats asked, while still staring in Randy's eyes.

"Well," Tony said, all choked up.

"What, what!" Dats yelled as he moved from Randy towards me.

I was scared. Randy was his prized son, and I knew if he'd slap him, then my punishment would be much more harsh.

"You should know better, Randy. You're the oldest," Dats said as he stood directly in front of me.

"Now, how did or who took the keys from your Mom's dresser? Who stole?" Dats said as he left me and went to Tony.

Dats picked Tony up and banged his back against the wall, one time very hard.

"You wanna tell me who took the key?"

Me, not being able to stand it anymore, yelled out.

"I took it. It was my idea. Now put him down."

Dats put Tony down. He slowly began to roll up his sleeves.

"Boy, do you realize what kind of trouble you can get in for stealing and breaking and entering?"

"I didn't break anything," I shot back.

"And you didn't disobey or talk back either, right?" Dats said as he bent down to look into my face.

"No, I didn't do anything. What about you?"

Dats was shocked at my insubordinance as a hard smile inched across his face, while looking at Mom, who began to cry.

"Ya hear that, Honey? That's a bastard child for you," Dats said, calmly, yet laced with anger.

Mom's tears ran down her face as Dats punched me in the face with a full blow. I was knocked to the ground.

"That's what happens when you talk shit like a man to a man, but you don't have the ass to back it up. You wind up on ya ass."

Even though I was obviously hurt by the blow, I immediately rushed to my feet, still displaying defiance. This angered Dats even more. He belted me with another punch. Again, I was hurt but rushed to my feet in defiance. Being molested hurt ten times more, I thought. That time Dats angrily got in my face.

"You don't have any idea of what you have done, boy. I'd suggest you make me your best friend because that clown upstairs isn't. And if he finds out you've been up there, all hell will break loose," Dats yelled.

I began to stare Dats 'down', thus adding insult to injury Dats grabbed me by my pajama collar, backed me into the wall near the dining room door and raised his fist to strike me when Mom stopped him by holding his arm back.

"Enough," is all Mom had to say, and Dats backed off.

He pushed me away, then walked toward his bedroom.

"Go to bed," Mom said softly to us as she followed Dats to the room. She picked up her lipstick on the way to her bedroom. Mom and Dats went into their bedroom. We just stood there and looked at each other for a moment. I slid to the floor from where I stood and put my head down. Randy came and sat next to me, and Tony followed. We sat there the remainder of the night. We were all convinced that something was grossly wrong.

My first thought concerned Mom and Dats' problem; was it connected to me being molested? If it was that meant there would be more people to punish for mental anguish. I felt that I could keep from exploding and going on a rampage for a little while longer. My patience grew thinner by the moment as long as I knew a child molester ran loose. I didn't want to have to kill my parents. I had to be sure. I had to find out who was responsible.

CHAPTER TWENTY-SEVEN

SALLY B AND JUSTIN sat in the living room of their condo in Truman Towers. Sally B was keying information in on Justin's IBM personal computer.

Justin was about to use the telephone.

"Hey, what's going on, my friend?" Justin said.

"Nothing much, just working hard, trying to get through this night," Captain Lee said, drearily.

"You got any info for me on that 911?" Justin asked.

"Oh, yeah, it was a kid's voice and it was called in from 139 Grand Street. I looked it up and it's a house on the corner of Myrtle Avenue and Grand Street."

There was a brief pause.

"Hey, wait, don't you live there?" Lee asked.

"Yeah, I live upstairs, though. It's a two-family house. It was probably some kid playing around."

"What did you do, make one of the kids on the first floor mad or something? You know how kids play games. Hey, I was just gonna let it fly, but if you want me to call the kids' parents, I will, Justin."

"No, no. That's okay. There was no harm done. I can take a joke."

"Okay. I gotta get back to this stack of papers. Talk to ya, buddy. Bye." Captain Lee hung up.

Justin was silent as he put the receiver down. Sally B was still keying information into the computer.

"It was the kid who called the cops. He's seen something. I know he's been up there. We gotta take care of this as soon as we get back," Justin said.

"Maybe the boy was upstairs. And maybe he did make the call. That doesn't mean he knows what's going on," Sally B said with concern.

"Look, we didn't get to where we are by taking chances. The

boy had to see something. Plus, that kid that we got rid of said he heard someone in the house that night. Then we get a visit from the police the next day. No, this is not a coincidence. We'll do what we have to do. Now, are you with me, Sally B?"

There was a pause as they both looked into each others eyes. Sally B blinked occasionally but Justin, waited for an answer, never blinked.

After a few seconds of this eye contact, Sally B shifted her eyes, looking from side to side at her surroundings, then she answered.

"I'm with you."

"Good. Now let's get back to work," Justin said, as if never skipping a beat.

"We're gonna get us a kid, bring him or her back to Albany, train it, then sell it. Profit being somewhere around twenty G's."

Sally B was there physically and hearing the words Justin said, but she wasn't really listening him. Her mind was elsewhere.

She thought about the child she never had.

It was 4:00 a.m. and Sally B was more tired than usual, what with the events of the day. They still needed to go out and recruit a new kid, so arguing about Corey was out of the question.

"Sally B, I need you to call Jim and Sara," Justin said.

She turned from the computer and began dialing Jim's phone number. Justin was in deep thought as she was about to dial the last digit. Then he reconsidered.

"Never mind, Sally B. I don't want to alarm them. We'll wait until we get there."

Relieved, Sally B sighed as she patiently hung up the phone.

CHAPTER TWENTY-EIGHT

JIM SAT UP IN BED, unable to go to sleep. Sara, too, was unable to go back to sleep. Jim picked up the telephone and squinted his eyes to see the number panel so that he could continue to dial. He got out of bed. He never took his clothes or shoes off. He grabbed his keys from the dresser near the bed.

"Where are you going, Jim?"

Jim was silent. Sara got out of bed and followed Jim to the kitchen back door.

"You think you wanna come, huh?" Jim said as he stood outside in the back, holding the screen door open.

Sara couldn't quite figure him out.

"Ya know what, that might not be a bad idea. Then we can settle this discrepancy once and for all."

Jim took Sara's hand and went back inside the kitchen. Then he led her out of the kitchen back door, with only her nightgown on. Once she realized where he was taking her, she yanked her hand from him and ran back in the house. He went in after her.

"Don't do this, Jim. We know whose child this is. Why must you carry on like this? We have enough problems. Now stop!"

"You're goin' with me, woman," Jim said as he turned to take Sara's hand. She snatched her hand away.

"I'm not going anywhere, Jim. You start this whenever you think things aren't going right for you. Now stop," Sara pleaded.

"You're not goin', huh? You don't wanna support me, my efforts, my husband ways," Jim said with vengeance.

"No, I am not going out there to make a fool of myself."

Whack! Jim slapped Sara hard across her face with his open hand. She attempted to retaliate, but stopped on a dime just as he was about to deliver a crushing blow to her face. Both stopped simultaneously. Sara looked at Jim's fist, and Jim looked at Sara's eyes filled with rage. He slowly put down his fist and walked out the back door.

"I don't need you anyway. I can do this myself," he said with a venomous calm as he ran to the garage and got in his car.

He used the remote control to open the door. His wheels screeched as he backed out, almost ripping off the driver's side exterior mirror. He sped up Myrtle Avenue. While doing so, he opened his glove compartment and took out his .38 pistol, checking to make sure it was loaded.

Sara immediately went to her bedroom phone and dialed a number.

The phone rang one time before Henry's loud voice answered.

"Yeah, it's me."

"Henry, it's me, Sara."

Henry sat up in his bed once he detected panic in her voice. "Hey, what's the matter, sis?"

"Well, I'm not sure, but I think Jim is going up to Tibby's to start some trouble."

"What? How do you know?"

"Well, we were arguing about Corey again, but more than that—"

"Never mind, I'm on my way to Tibby's as we speak. You stay there. I'll take care of this," Henry interrupted. He jumped out of bed in his red polka dot shorts and put on his pants and shirt.

Tibby was just getting ready to close up. It was about 4:30 a.m. There were a few regulars sitting at the bar. Music was playing at a lover's pace. The DJ had slowly got into a romantic mood, more for himself than anyone else. A woman he didn't know danced near his turntable. He hoped that the romantic sound would help him bring her home for a one-nighter.

"Okay, you guys, you know the rule, away from the bar!" Tibby said as he wiped down the bar with his white towel. Tammy was at the cash register, like a good little wife, ringing up the night's receipts.

The DJ moved closer to the woman he was trying to lure to his apartment.

All the people at the bar moved to the tables that were near the bar. The only light in the place was the one behind the bar used by Tibby and Tammy to see when they poured drinks.

Like a tornado, Jim flung open Tibby's front door in a rage. He stood in front of the door as it closed. Everyone in the bar stopped simultaneously. They all stared at Jim as he stood and eyed everyone in the joint, stopping and meeting Tibby eye to eye.

"Jim!" Tibby said, speaking in a cautious manner.

Jim looked at Tibby hard, then cut his eyes toward Tammy, who was unaware of the feud that was going on between Tibby and Jim.

Jim walked to the bar where Tibby stood. Underneath the bar where he stood was a .38 pistol.

The patrons went back to their conversations, including the DJ.

"I need to know, Tibby," Jim said angrily.

"Need to know what, Jim? Here, have a drink." Tibby poured Jim a coke and put it on the bar. Jim knocked the drink to the ground.

Tammy was alarmed by the glass crashing to the floor, and quickly closed the computerized cash register drawer and walked over to Tibby. A few patrons looked on.

"Honey, what is it?" Tammy said, concerned.

"It's nothing, Honey. Jim's just had a little too much to drink. Why don't you go to the back room and get our things together so we can get outta here. We'll cash out later when we come back this afternoon," Tibby said.

"What's the matter, Tibby, you never told the little lady here the real story?" Jim said.

Tibby looked to his other patrons and said, "Okay, everyone, time to go home. Let's go." The patrons sat and just looked at Tibby, interested in what was about to transpire.

"Look, I said go home!" Tibby yelled.

The patrons still just looked at Tibby, no one moving a hair. Tammy stood nearby. Tibby reached under the bar and took out his baseball bat. The patrons began to leave.

"What're you gonna do, beat everyone in here because you can't control them the way you controlled my wife?" Tammy gasped and looked at Tibby.

"Sure! He didn't tell you, did he? That's right, my ten-year-old son is his and he knows it . . ."

Tibby turned to escort Tammy to the back room. But Tammy wouldn't let him lead her away.

"C'mon, Tammy, he's drunk," Tibby insisted.

"He hasn't told you the half of it, has he, Tammy?" Jim yelled as he slammed his hand on the top of the bar. Tibby began to forcefully lead Tammy to the back room. Jim couldn't stand to be ignored, so he followed them, walking on the opposite side of the bar.

"You don't want to hear this, do you?" Jim said. Tibby, without looking over at Jim, waved him off.

"Don't ignore me, you son of a bitch," Jim warned.

Tibby continued to walk, and this infuriated Jim. He picked up a shot glass and threw it against the wall mirror behind the bar, splattering glass everywhere.

Tibby lunged toward Jim, and in a second, Jim whipped out his .38 caliber pistol, cocked the hammer and pointed it an inch away from Tibby's forehead. Tibby stopped in his tracks. Fear engulfed his face. He was powerless. All he could do was stand there. The few patrons scattered out the front door just as Henry entered through it.

"Jim!" Henry yelled as he cautiously walked towards Jim with outstretched hands.

The DJ started towards Jim, but Jim quickly warned him off by swiftly swinging the pistol in his direction, then back at Tibby.

"Gimme the gun, Jim!" Henry said.

"Shut up, Henry. You got nothin' to do with this," Jim yelled.

"Jim, it's not worth it. You're gonna go to jail," Henry pleaded.

"Shut up, Henry. This is my fight."

"You're gonna shoot 'em, over what? Some shit you think is happening because somebody else said it's happening? Man, you're crazy" Henry said as he continued to walk toward Jim.

"You make me sick every time I think about you, every time I look at my Corey I wonder, every time I make love to my wife I think about you, and I'm tired of it."

"Jim, save yourself. You've got a family. You don't need this," Henry said, pleading as he reached for Jim's gun.

Soon Henry had his hand around the barrel of the pistol. He slowly moved the gun from in front of Tibby's face. Henry gradually took the gun away from Jim.

Tammy tugged on Tibby's arm for him to come with her. He slowly moved back from Jim. Henry put his arm over Jim's shoulder, and they gradually walked toward the front door. Jim and Henry were standing in front of the bar.

"Look, man, whatever's bothering you, this ain't gonna solve anything."

Henry held up Jim's .38. Jim cut his eyes slightly at Henry, knowing he was right. "You need a bigger gun," Henry said jokingly.

"Yeah," Jim replied, barely audible and just a tad embarrassed.

"Yeah, you're right. I shoulda slit his throat long time ago," Jim said, nonchalantly.

Henry patted Jim's forehead and replied, "Oh, brother." Henry led Jim to his car and opened the door for him. Jim got in, slouched down a bit and started it up. Henry leaned over to Jim's driver's side window.

"Ya know, if there's something bothering you, you should tell me. Maybe I can help," Henry said, father-like.

"Yes, daddy," Jim said with a hint of sarcasm. Henry checked his watch.

"Well, I guess I'll go and get ready to punch that clock. Tell Sara I'll talk to her tomorrow. N'you go home and get some sleep. You look terrible." Jim drove off, screeching his wheels. Henry waved his hand at him, smiling with a hint of sympathy behind it.

Tammy sat on the small, black leather sofa in the back office of the bar. Tibby gathered some papers from his desk drawer and stuffed them, irritatingly. Tammy waited for an explanation, with her arms folded. "So what's this feud between you and Jim Harris all about?" Tammy asked, with her leg swinging back and forth from nervousness as she sat.

"It's nothing, Honey."

"Apparently Jim thinks so. Now, what is it? Don't lie to me."

Tibby paused and sat in his leather chair.

"Look, ten years ago Sara and I had an affair. We were young and foolish. This was way before you came into the picture."

"Yeah, but while her husband was deep into the picture, right?"

Tibby paused for a few minutes, and carefully contemplated

his next response.

"Look, it was wrong and I admit that. But it just happened. I won't make any . . ."

"Is it your . . ." Tammy said, almost in a whisper, both afraid and angry.

"What?" Tibby interrupted. Tammy summoned up the courage and energy to ask the question she really didn't want to hear the answer to, but felt it was her duty to do so or she'd be kept in the dark for the rest of her marriage.

"Is Corey your son? And why didn't you tell me about this before we were married?" Tibby was nervous and very vulnerable. He knew that Tammy wasn't afraid to leave him, and this was the last thing he wanted or needed.

"Is Corey your son, Tibby?" Tammy shouted, almost in tears.

"We did have a son," Tibby yelled out, painstakingly.

Tibby was choked up and went to Tammy on one bended knee. "But I love you, Honey, it was a mistake. I'd never do it to you. I'd never do it again. Please don't leave," Tibby begged as he put his head on her crossed leg, stopping her from shaking.

Tibby began to weep. Tammy just watched as tears rolled down her cheeks. She hesitantly reached over Tibby's head and began to rub it.

"You're not still seeing her, are you?" Tammy asked, preparing for the worst.

Tibby hesitated, then slowly turned his head toward Tammy, embarrassed at the situation, and delaying to answer.

"You aren't, are you?" Tammy asked again, somewhat impatient for an answer.

Tibby could only close his eyes and bury his face in his hands.

CHAPTER TWENTY-NINE

IT WAS 7:00 A.M. This was the first morning in a while that everyone was at the breakfast table eating on a weekday. Usually, Dats would either be at work or still asleep. Mom would be running around, getting everyone together for school. But that morning, all was calm. I had gotten up extra early to prepare breakfast for everyone.

I liked to cook, but didn't particularly care for getting up early to do so. That day was different. I had a lot on my mind. Mom and Dats knew we were all upstairs, and that was not good. I knew it would be twice as hard to get back up there again. With Mom and

Dats keeping a watchful eye and Justin coming home soon, it would be almost impossible to get up there to check the other side of the attic. To compound the situation, my eye was getting better and it would be time for me to return to school any day. I wasn't ready to return to school yet.

All you could hear were forks banging into plates as everyone ate.

Dats sat in his usual place at the head of the kitchen table, closest to the entrance, heading toward the dining room area. Mom sat on the corner, near Dats. Tony and Randy sat in the two chairs closest to the refrigerator. I sat at the opposite end of the table facing Dats. I occasionally looked up at Mom, then at Dats. Mom glanced back at me, but not before taking a sip of her black coffee. She'd had a long night, so she needed her coffee black. My eyes caught Mom's eyes looking at Dats, and we both glanced at him momentarily. Tony looked at me as he hesitated eating his eggs. Almost in slow motion, the mood of tension began to swell. Randy kept cool. He knew there was a problem, but always tried to keep cool. I knew he'd be the one to break the ice.

"Mom, can I go to school today?" I asked. But I really didn't want to.

"How does your eye feel?" Mom asked, while cutting her eyes quickly at Dats.

"Kinda in between," I said, looking at Dats, then at Randy and Tony. Tony was scared. He didn't want his father going off on him, or neither of us for that matter.

"You're goin' to school, boy," Dats said under his breath as he swallowed a fork full of grits.

I was silent. I knew not to question Dats' command at all. My silence was a 'yes, sir' and Dats didn't want to hear anything. Tony accidentally bumped Randy's elbow and dropped his fork on the floor. It was so quiet, you could hear it throughout the house. This was the quietest the Harris house had been during the morning since before any of us were born.

The doorbell rang. Everyone looked up simultaneously at each other, except for Dats. He slowly turned his head, rolling his heated eyes toward the front door, then looked back at everyone at the table, which meant for us to sit and wait.

It was almost as if no one wanted to find out who was on the other side of the door ringing the bell. If it were Justin, Mom and Dats knew they would be in trouble. For the first time, they really felt their children's lives were in danger. Little did they know, we had seen nothing that gave us a hint at what Justin was into. Mom and Dats couldn't ask us either, because we would then know for sure something was wrong. As far as I was concerned, there was something going on, and I was determined to find out. The front door bell rang repeatedly. I gently put my fork on my plate and stood.

"I'll get it?" I said in a questioning tone.

"Finish your breakfast, Corey, I'll get it," Mom said.

Tony and Randy only watched as Dats looked at them with caring eyes, and gave a cold look to me. I felt the wrath of Dats' intense glare, and nervously sat back down.

Mom made her way to the front door in a not-too-jolly mood. Upon reaching the dining room door, she saw a large silhouette shadowing through the front door curtain. It could be only one person. Mom got to the door and peeked through the white curtains that came a few inches from the top of the door to just below the doorknob.

The curtains weren't very thick. Uncle Henry smiled and waved at stoical Mom as she peeked through.

"Not in a cheery mood, I see," Uncle Henry muttered to himself.

"Hi," Mom said as she opened the door, then turned and headed for the kitchen.

Uncle Henry hurried in and gently closed the door, then quietly hurried to Mom. He tapped her on her shoulder and motioned for her to move over to the corner of the dining room where no one could hear them. Mom wasn't in the mood to be questioned, and showed it with each tug that Uncle Henry made as he guided her away from the ears of the rest of us.

Randy and Tony both glanced toward the living room and saw Mom being tugged into the corner. Their curiosity showed, causing me to mouth the word "what?" towards them.

Randy and Tony just looked down at their plates, continuing to eat.

"So what's going on, Sara?" Uncle Henry asked.

Mom just looked at Uncle Henry with the strangest look, a look like he knew there was more than she could ever tell him. Uncle Henry let Mom go into the kitchen. Uncle Henry followed.

"Good morning," Uncle Henry said with his usual enthusiasm.

"Hi, Uncle Henry," I said, but not with my usual zest. Randy and Tony both said hello.

Mom went into her bedroom and closed her door.

"Hey, Jim, what's up? Everything okay?" Uncle Henry asked.

"Aren't you going to work today?" Dats asked in a low tone.

"Mom, I'm almost ready," I said.

"Well, I decided I'd take the day off. Maybe do some fishing," Uncle Henry said, darting his eyes to me.

"Mom, I'm still feeling some pain in my head. Maybe I should stay out one more day," I suggested.

"You'll go to school, Corey," Dats said. " 'Cause if you're around here today, you're liable to get kilt," Dats said.

"What's that supposed to mean, Jim?" Uncle Henry asked.

Dats just glared at Uncle Henry, then back at me standing with my back toward him. I began to organize the dirty dishes in the sink.

Randy and Tony were finished eating. They both got up. Tony gulped down the remainder of his Nestles chocolate milk while Randy left the kitchen. Uncle Henry patted Randy on his back as he walked by.

"See ya, Uncle Henry," Randy said, without looking back at him. Then Tony put the empty glass down hard, almost breaking it. Dats shifted his cold eyes to the glass, checking to see if it had a crack. Dats then fixed his eyes on Tony for a few seconds as Tony went past Uncle Henry

"You're going to school, Corey, and I mean it!" Dats said.

"But Dats, my eye hurts."

"What did I say, Corey?" Dats shouted.

Uncle Henry, without letting Dats see him, motioned for me to leave the kitchen. I obliged and got out, going to Randy's bedroom.

"Jim, I know you raise your kids the way you want, but this is a serious injury Corey has. If he gets it infected, it could blind him," Uncle Henry pleaded.

"Henry, I didn't ask you!" Dats said.

"Well, why don't you just pluck his other one out then. Maybe you'll be happy when he's completely destroyed. You think you're the only one wronged in this world. Well, you're not. Those kids need you. And not like this. You gotta help them see things the way they're supposed to be and not take things out on them," Uncle Henry said.

Dats burst from his seat and got in Uncle Henry's face. "Whaddaya know about kids? About raising a family? You never had any kids. For that matter, you never had any one main girl. You ever raised a family? No! This is my family, not yours."

Uncle Henry was not prepared for this outburst from Dats. "Are you crazy, Jim? You need to calm down. You're attacking everyone. You beat your kids for nothing last night, didn't ya, *Jim*?"

Dats didn't answer as he just stared at Uncle Henry. "You wanna know why I hit Corey? Why I went up there to get myself in trouble? Because I wanted to. It's as simple as that. And if they ever step foot in that apartment upstairs, it will be their last time!" Dats said as he sat back down. He knew that Justin would find out and that someone would die. The question was: Would Dats stand by and watch Justin kill me off?

Mom came out of the room and walked past Dats and Uncle Henry. She came into Randy's room, taking me by the hand and into the living room.

"Corey, now if you're in pain, I'll ask your father to let you stay out another day," Mom said.

"It really does hurt, Mom," I replied. I could lie well.

"All right," Mom said. She cautiously walked back toward the kitchen.

"Jim, Corey needs to stay out one more day. I don't wanna chance his eye getting infected."

Dats looked straight ahead in a daze in his chair at the table and mumbled, "Yeah, sure."

Dats got up from his seat and slowly went into his bedroom, closing the door behind him. He went to Mom's side of the bed near the locked cabinet and stared at himself in the mirror on the door.

"Sara, come here," Dats said softly. "Sara," he said a little louder: "Sara," Dats said even louder. Then Dats shouted it out, "Sara, get in here now!"

Mom burst open the bedroom door.

"What do you want?" Mom asked.

"Get me the key," Dats said.

"No, not now, Jim, Henry's here," Mom said pleadingly.

"Tell'em to get out and you get in here," Dats commanded.

Uncle Henry couldn't help but hear this.

"Jim, I'm not leaving right now. I'm not gonna let you hurt my sister." Dats stood up and turned toward Uncle Henry; Mom turned toward Uncle Henry.

"Just go, Henry I'll be all right."

"I'm not going. He needs to calm down. He's taking his frustrations out on everyone."

"He won't hit me," Mom said. Uncle Henry gave her a strange look.

"Well, what else could he do to hurt you?" Uncle Henry asked.

"Nothing."

"Tell me, Sara, spit it out."

"Nothing."

Dats sat back on the bed and turned toward the mirror, fuming.

"You tell me if he lays one finger on you, Sara, and I mean it," Henry said. Then Uncle Henry turned to leave, and out of nowhere Dats pushed Mom out of the way and jumped on Uncle Henry's back. In one sweeping old Army self-defense move, Uncle Henry had Dats off of his back and was on top of him, preparing to pounce on him. Me, Randy and Tony were all within view of this. Mom was crying.

"No, Uncle Henry, don't," I said. Uncle Henry got up, and Dats just laid there, unpunched and unharmed. Mom slid down to the floor out of sympathy for Dats. Uncle Henry took the three of us and walked toward the front door.

"I'm walking the boys to school," Uncle Henry said as he left.

Just as we were about to step down on our last step to the concrete, a black Taurus with tinted windows pulled up. Uncle Henry looked inside at the driver, and it was Sally B. Unbeknowst to him, Justin sat in the back seat with a young girl.

Uncle Henry was surprised to see Sally B, but kept walking with us. I remembered Sally B and was anxious to talk to Uncle Henry about her. Uncle Henry and us boys were headed up the hill.

Justin got out of the back seat with the twelve-year-old girl. I looked back down the hill and saw Justin. Our eyes met. Justin smiled, moved the girl over toward Sally B and then pointed his hand towards me like he was holding a gun.

I knew I had to tell Uncle Henry what I knew. But I wasn't sure if I would be believed.

"What is it, Corey?" Uncle Henry asked.

"Nothing."

"Well, let's go. Ya brothers are gonna be late for school if you keep dallying along." I caught up with them as they walked up Myrtle Avenue.

In the kitchen, Sara and Jim were still sitting on the floor.

"What're we gonna do, Jim?" Sara asked.

Jim looked over at Sara. Silence followed.

"I want the truth, Sara," Jim demanded in a low tone, "or it will never stop. It'll always be this way," he said.

They heard the front door open, then close. They heard footsteps going upstairs.

"Now we have to deal with him," Sara said.

"I need to know, Sara. Is Corey my son or not?" Loud bangs

came from the dining room door.

"I'm not answering. What are you gonna do, kill Corey if he isn't." Sara asked.

The banging on the door stopped. Sara and Jim heard footsteps going up the stairs.

"Or are you gonna let Justin do it?"

"I have this scary feeling that he knows, Jim. I know it was Corey who called the police that day they were up there. Corey was the only one who would do something like that."

"I won't let him hurt my son, Jim. We gotta do something about this."

Jim cuddled with Sara. He had a glazed look in his eyes. Millions of thoughts ran through his head. He was sad and hurt. His mind was confused but his heart loved his family.

"Jim, you've got to protect us. The money's not that important."

"I'll protect you, Sara," Jim said as he hugged her tighter.

CHAPTER THIRTY

UNCLE HENRY AND TONY walked ahead. Randy waited for me to catch up with them. Randy had seen Justin walk away towards the front of the house at the bottom of the hill.

"Did ya see him, Randy?" I asked, suspiciously.

"I saw some guy, yeah. Is that who we were spying on?" Randy asked.

"Yeah, couldn't you see? He's always wearing black," I said. Uncle Henry and Tony were at the corner of Myrtle Avenue and Philip Street, which was one block from the school at the top of the hill. The remaining block to school was about fifty yards long. Mann's Corner Store was on the corner of Myrtle and Philip.

"Will you guys come on," Uncle Henry shouted down to me and Randy. We were about forty feet down on Myrtle Avenue. Me and Randy simultaneously looked up at Uncle Henry and Tony. They were waiting for us at the top of the hill.

"Race you," I said to Randy quickly, then I said, "Go." I took off up the hill. Randy smiled, knowing he was still within striking distance. He darted up the hill. Uncle Henry saw the race coming to him and opened his arms wide with his palms open, signaling to me and Randy that the first one to touch his palms was the winner.

Breathing heavily, I was about five feet ahead of Randy, who had barely broke a sweat. Then we were neck and neck. This was my chance to beat Randy. Even though I jumped the gun in the race, I felt things were even, given Randy was three years older with the strength of an adult. Randy definitely had gained some of Uncle Henry's strength through Mom.

My eyes were fixed on Uncle Henry's right palm, the finish line. Randy looked over at me. We were about twenty feet from the finish line and he said, "You think you can pull it off? I don't. We're not in the kitchen."

Randy blazed by me and touched Uncle Henry's left palm, winning by almost ten feet.

"I'll outcook you any day, though," I said confidently, breathing heavily.

Randy smiled and looked at me.

"Musta been that cat I fed you," I said with a smile.

Randy had a curious look about him, knowing full well that I probably did feed him some cat.

"Ah, that's all right, Corey You'll get'em the next time," Uncle Henry said with a smile.

Uncle Henry draped his long, large arms over me and Tony's shoulders as we continued to walk up Myrtle Avenue toward school.

"Uncle Henry, why is Dats so angry with everyone lately?" Tony asked.

Uncle Henry shrugged his shoulders, knowing he could give a better answer.

"He really snapped when he found out we were upstairs," Tony said.

Uncle Henry had a surprised look. Tony's line of blabbering didn't sit well with Randy, who gave a sour look to him. I didn't like it either, but I wasn't as pissed off as Randy. I realized it would make it easier for me to talk to Uncle Henry later when we were alone.

"All parents have problems, Tony. It's just a way of life," Uncle Henry said.

"How come you never got married, Uncle Henry?" Tony asked.

"Well, I never found 'Miss Right'."

"You think you'll ever get married?" Tony asked.

"Who knows, partner, who knows. I've seen enough marriages go to pot so I might just leave well enough alone."

Tony said, not really knowing what 'well enough' was.

"Anyway, what were you guys doing upstairs last night? That's breaking and entering. You boys could go to jail or be sent to a home for bad kids," Uncle Henry said.

"But we didn't break in, Uncle Henry," I said.

"With or without the key, you were somewhere where you weren't supposed to be. It's somebody else's property," Uncle Henry reiterated.

"What is it with that guy up there anyway, Uncle Henry?" Randy asked, almost fed up.

"I don't know much about him and I don't want or care to know. He seems kinda strange. I only see him once in a while."

We were approaching the corner of Myrtle Avenue and Eagle Street. Myrtle Avenue ended there and began again about a mile up behind the governor's mansion and the Empire State Plaza.

Cathedral Academy was separated from the governor's mansion by a twenty-foot high brick wall that was actually on the side of the mansion and the back of the school. Two moon-shaped basketball hoops were in the backyard of the school.

Kids scuffled around on the sidewalk and in the backyard.

Randy and Tony were crossing from the corner of Myrtle Avenue and Eagle Street going to school. Me and Uncle Henry waved goodbye to them from the corner of Myrtle Avenue. Tony saw some of his school friends and ran towards them. Randy went to talk to a pretty girl, who was leaning on the light silver rail that surrounded the entire school from the Eagle Street side to the front of the school, which was on Park Avenue. Mind you, this is the Park Avenue in Albany, not New York City.

Me and Uncle Henry turned around and began the short walk back home.

"Uncle Henry, do you think Mom and Dats are gonna be okay?"

"Sure. What they're goin' through is only temporary."

"Uncle Henry, I've got something to tell you but I don't quite know how."

CHAPTER THIRTY-ONE

JUSTIN HAD GONE to the living room of his apartment with Sally B and the new kid. The kid was thirteen years old. She was a brunette and very attractive for her age. She sat with Sally B on the sofa. Justin stood in the entryway, staring stoically straight ahead. The kid, Angie, was nervous.

"Please, I want you to relax, Angie. I'm not gonna hurt you."

Angie took a deep breath.

"Is your name really Angie?"

"Yes."

"Why are you on the streets?"

"I ran away from home."

"Something goin on you didn't like?"

"My parents beat me."

"I understand. My parents did weird thing to me, too. Like lock me in a small closet."

"Really?"

"You have brothers and sisters?"

"No. . . .I mean yes."

"Which is it?"

"Well - my sister died a short while ago."

"Why'd you run?"

"I wanted out. And I wasn't takin' any more abuse!"

"Well, you don't have to worry about any more abuse. I just want to make you comfortable. OK?"

"OK."

"You ever been outside of New York City?" Justin asked.

"No," Angie said.

"How long have you been on your own?" Justin asked.

"About one month," Angie said.

"When's the last time you talked to your parents?" Justin asked.

"Three months," Angie said. She knew she sounded confused.

"I thought you've only been gone for one month?" Justin said.

"Yeah, but I was staying with my friend for a month before I dropped out of sight!" she said reassuringly.

"Uh-hmm," Justin replied.

Sally B looked at Justin because she knew he was contemplating killing Angie because he might think she just lied to him. Justin silently, with a slight tilt of his head, motioned for Sally B to come back to the kitchen with him. Sally B patted Angie on her hand and followed him into the kitchen, leaving Angie on the sofa.

Justin and Sally B walked slowly to the kitchen, headed for the back porch. As they opened the kitchen back door to the porch, Justin closed the white wooden door gently. He looked back toward the living room through the wide window on the upper part of the door. He wondered about Angie, his new child project. Justin then closed the screen door behind him, and with his eyes fixed on the brown wooden porch floor, he walked over to the ledge that surrounded the porch. It was located directly above Sara and Jim's kitchen. Justin slid his feet as he walked on the thick black rubber covering on the porch floor. Sally B's eyes shifted in thought from the portable barbecue pit standing in the corner opposite Myrtle Avenue to a raggedy old mop and green pail in another corner near a small ladder. The tension was thick enough to cut the thin white clothes line that hung from one end of the porch ceiling to the other. Justin walked to the railing opposite Myrtle Avenue and looked at the steel fire escape steps that were attached to the house. They went from as high as Justin's porch to the ground in our neighbor's back yard.

Sally B leaned against the wall just to the right of where the bathroom window was. She was thinking. Then Justin made his way over to the Myrtle Avenue side of the porch railing, resting both of his hands on the wooden railing and staring up Myrtle Avenue.

Justin being out on the porch in broad daylight was a sign of uncertainty and nervousness. He knew he was taking a big chance with Angie. Even though she was vulnerable at this time in her life, this didn't guarantee that she would want to do what would be required of her. He always thought kids would bolt back to their parents while out on one of their jobs, and then identify him. Maybe it would be better to send Angie out of the country.

Uncle Henry and I were walking down Myrtle Avenue. I caught Justin looking at me, and I started staring at him. Justin didn't move.

"There he is, Uncle Henry," I said, gritting my teeth. I strained not to look up again.

"Where, what?" Uncle Henry said, looking around.

"Up, up," I said, not wanting to be so obvious. Then Uncle Henry looked up toward Justin's porch. Justin smiled and nodded his head. I looked at the fence that separated the neighbors' yard and a large tree that was in that yard. My eyes slowly designed a trail up the back to Justin's apartment. We finally passed the back of the house and were almost at the front. I thought, it had to be him. My gut feeling kept telling me he was my abuser and I'm gonna bust him some how.

"That's only the second time I've seen him out during the day. He never comes out," I said firmly.

"Oh, yeah, what is he, a vampire or something?" Uncle Henry said sarcastically.

"What if he is, really, Uncle Henry?"

I was at that moment wishing it all was just a joke and that I could just brush it off.

"Yeah, right," Uncle Henry said, totally dismissing the thought.

Justin turned toward Sally B with a look of sincerity.

"I believe it's time we had a conversation with the Harris'. But first we gotta take care of this Angie situation." Justin coolly entered the kitchen from the back porch, followed by Sally B. They both headed toward the living room.

Upon entering the living room where Angie sat on the sofa erect and straightfaced, Justin wasted no time with his line of questioning. Angie jerked her head toward Justin in rapid fire. Questions ripped from Justin's lips so fast, Angie only had a chance to quickly nod yes to each answer.

"You did realize we did you a big favor by taking you from New York, right, Angie?" Justin said.

She quickly nodded yes.

"You like yourself, Angie?" Justin asked.

She nodded yes.

"Why?" Justin asked, not giving her a chance to answer.

"I . . ." Angie was cut off by Justin as he doubled his questions in rapid fire.

"Why? . . You owe us, right, Angie?" Justin got so close in her face that she couldn't even nod yes.

"Are you good, Angie?" Justin asked in a whisper. "You are good, right?"

"Yes," she quickly whispered.

"Are you good, Angie?"

"You believe in God, Angie?"

"You believe in God? You believe in me when you think 'bout praying? You think about me? 'Cause I'm gonna answer your prayers, Angie. Me! I'm here to help you, not hurt you. You wanna work, you can work. You stick in there 'til the end, Angie, the very end, Angie."

By then Justin and Angie were nose to nose, sitting on the

couch. Trickles of sweat were bubbling up on Angie's forehead.

"We gonna get along, right, Angie?" Justin said, asking his final question.

"Yes," she said, as if frozen in a hypnotic stare.

They sat and stared at each other momentarily. Angie was breathing much heavier than Justin. In fact, Justin's heart rate and breathing were normal.

"Good!" Justin said with a small smile.

Justin got up from the sofa. He went to whisper something in Sally B's ear. As he began to whisper in Sally B's ear, he angled himself so that he could get a good look at Angie as she sat on the sofa.

He whispered, "Just go along with me, I wanna see if Angie is gonna be nosey and try to read my lips. If she stares at us, we won't want to keep her."

To Justin's liking and calming to Sally B's nerves, Angie paid no attention to Justin. He smiled and walked away from Sally B, toward Angie.

"You know, Angie, you're one of the few who's actually had the pleasure of being in my company here in Albany. Normally I don't even know who's out there working for me because I trust Sally B's judgement. Sally B usually does all of the recruiting, unless I need someone special, someone that has to go to another country for awhile and work."

Angie did not move her head or eyes as Justin slowly paced back and forth in front of her while she sat on the couch.

"Do you follow what I'm saying, Angie?" he asked as he stopped directly in front of her.

Angie remained quiet. Sally B became nervous again because she was afraid Justin might take this as an act of defiance. For this, Justin would surely dispose of her.

Angie's eyes were transfixed straight ahead, almost hypnotic-like. Sally B looked deep into her eyes from her love seat.

"Angie, it's okay for you to talk now," Sally B said, trying to help her.

Angie took her black purse from the floor and put it in her lap. Justin looked over at Sally B, then down at the top of Angie's silky hair. He rubbed his fingers through her hair.

"Again, Angie, do you follow what I mean?" he asked again.

"Yes," she said, hardly audible.

"What's that?" Justin asked as he grew impatient. "I can't hear you, speak up!" he said as he walked away from her. He turned his back to her to look out the window. He saw two teenage girls fighting across the street.

"Come here, Sally B, look at this witch fight!" Justin said.

Sally B went over to the window in front of Angie and looked out. They watched the two teen girls pulling each other's hair out. Angie, still in a hypnotic stare, eased her right hand in her black leather purse. It was medium-sized and could be carried over her shoulder.

"That's what happens with bad upbringing," Justin said.

"Oh, yeah, what's your excuse then?" Angie said with venom.

This brought shock to Justin and Sally B.

"And this is for my sister!" Angie said.

In an instant, she brandished a six-inch switchblade knife. Angie was obviously an amateur at this sort of thing. Justin immediately dismantled her and threw her to the ground, making a loud thug.

Downstairs in Mom and Dats' apartment, me and Uncle Henry heard a loud thug.

"What the hell was that?" Uncle Henry asked as he stood.

Mom and Dats both quickly came into the living room.

"What was that noise?" Mom asked.

"It sounded like somebody fell, Mom. You want me to go see?" I said as I stood up.

"Corey!" Mom and Dats shouted.

I sat back down, dejected.

Back upstairs in Justin's living room where he had Angie pinned on the floor with his knee in her back, Justin had taken his black leather belt and hog-tied her. He grabbed her hair with a firm grip, and the six-inch blade was inches away from Angie's throat.

"Who sent you, Angie?" Justin asked.

"Fuck you!" Angie said.

Justin yanked Angie's head back harder, and the blade was cutting her throat slowly.

"Who sent you, Angie? I'm trying to make this as easy as possible for you."

"Get the masking tape from the kitchen, Sally B," Justin ordered, smiling at Sally B psychotically calm.

Sally B hesitated for a second.

"Now!" he said, a little louder but still calm.

Sally B dashed into the kitchen.

In the Harris' living room, everyone listened as Sally B's footsteps were hard racing toward the back of the house to the kitchen. A muffled scream was heard. Sally B's footsteps were heard running back toward the front of the house into the living room. Then there was no scream heard. Mom and Dats stared at each other. Uncle Henry and I stared at the ceiling, waiting for the next noise.

Sally B had put a large piece of grey masking tape that went from ear to ear over Angie's mouth.

"Now, I'll take that tape off and I won't cut you if you tell me who sent you, Angie. If you want to give me an answer, just nod yes and I'll take the tape off," Justin said, smiling.

Justin was in front of Angie. She was still hog-tied on the floor.

Angie nodded yes.

"Go make sure the door is bolted, Sally B," Justin commanded as he pointed toward the kitchen.

"And walk lightly this time," Justin said.

Sally B calmly got up and walked to the door of the apartment and double-bolted the locks, then walked back into the living room.

"They're still downstairs, right?" Justin asked.

"I believe so. I couldn't hear anyone when I went to lock the door."

"They could be listening," Justin said.

"Could be," Sally B said.

"She wants to talk, Sally B. She wants to tell us who sent her," Justin said comically.

"I don't think we should take the chance of taking the tape from her mouth. What if she screams and somebody downstairs hears her?" Sally B said as she stood shocked at the turn of events.

"We should take her upstairs," Sally B suggested.

Justin smiled approvingly.

"What's goin' on up there?" Uncle Henry asked as he began to pace.

"Somebody probably just fell," Dats said.

"I'm turning on the TV. Jim's probably right. No need for us to stick our nose in somebody else's business," Mom said as she turned the TV on and increased the volume.

Mom got the remote and changed the station from CNN News to MTV. There was a rock song playing loud. Uncle Henry looked at Mom strangely. She just looked away.

"Sara, what's goin' on up there?" Uncle Henry asked.

"Look, Henry, we don't pry into his business upstairs, and it's not time to start now," Dats said.

"But you heard that noise. And it sounded almost like a scream a little while after that," Uncle Henry said.

"Maybe I should go up and have a look," Uncle Henry said as he started toward the living room exit, but not before Dats got in his way, stopping him.

"Mind your own business, Henry. We've done it for the six years he's been up there, and everything's been fine," Dats ordered.

"Well, how do you explain the cops being here the other day?" Uncle Henry pleaded.

"A prank, that's all," Dats said.

"Sure it was," Uncle Henry said as he went back and sat next to me, near the window on the love seat. He didn't want another physical confrontation with Dats.

Sally B went to the back porch and brought back in the six-foot wooden ladder that had old paint splattered on it. She carried it with ease throughout the house into the spare bedroom, off the living room. She opened it up and positioned it directly under the ceiling door.

"Sounds like they're moving something into another room."

Uncle Henry looked at Jim and asked, "Is there another room up there?"

"Mind your own business, Henry," Jim said.

"Something could be wrong up there," Uncle Henry said.

"Well, if it is, he'll let us know," Jim replied.

Justin went over to Angie, who was still hog-tied. He yanked at the belt, and this caused her great pain. Angie grimaced, but she didn't cry out. Even if she wanted to, she wouldn't be heard.

Justin picked Angie up by the belt and began walking up the ladder. This took great strength on Justin's part because Angie weighed at least one hundred and ten pounds. Angie was experiencing greater pain in her shoulders. Her breathing wasn't good either.

Sally B followed behind Justin and Angie. She saw the pain on Angie's face as Justin lifted her up.

Sally B tried to push Angie up by her knees to relieve some of the pressure on her shoulder joint that was causing her pain.

"Don't push. I want her to hurt," Justin said, calmly.

Sally B reluctantly stopped helping Justin. Justin reached the top and harshly pulled Angie through the small ceiling door, bumping her face, shoulders and legs on the edge of the entryway. He pulled her away from the entrance so that Sally B could get in. Sally B climbed in and closed the ceiling door. Justin turned the light switch on. Sally B sat on the edge of a small chair that was among the junk in this small attic room. Justin looked over to the sliding door that lead to the back of the attic where his computers were located. He saw that even though the door was still locked, it was slightly ajar to where one could peek inside.

"Somebody's been up here," Justin said as he went to the sliding door's small opening and peeked in, looking at the back area. Then Justin looked around and saw the broken light that Tony had knocked to the ground. He pointed to it on the floor.

"Look at this! Who did it? I know I didn't, and I know you didn't, so somebody musta been up here!"

Sally B was lost for words as she thought quickly. She knew Justin was right, but didn't want to feed his frenzy.

"I don't know, maybe it fell."

"Never mind, we'll deal with it later."

Justin went back to where he laid Angie.

"You ready to talk? Nobody can hear you if you scream. And if you do scream, I'll kill you. Understand?" Justin said.

Angie nodded yes.

Justin ripped the grey masking tape from Angie's mouth, causing her pain again. But Angie would not cry out. Not for fear of Justin, but out of pride. She knew this would probably be the end of the road for her.

"Now talk!" Justin demanded.

"Nobody sent me, you scumbag. I've been on the streets for a year. I didn't realize who you were until I was sitting in here waiting for you. You killed my sister you piece a shit! Now do what'cha gotta do!"

"Who knows you're here?" Justin said, with a tad of anger.

She spit in his face.

"You spit, you like to spit, huh? That's very rude of you, Angie," Justin said as he climbed in back of her. He smiled, then licked some of the spit from around his mouth. Then he wiped the remainder off with his hand. He yanked her by her hair.

"You sure you won't tell me who sent you?" Justin asked.

"Fuck you! Nobody sent me. All those bullshit plaques from Fordham on your wall. What'd you buy them? You're not smart. I'll see you in hell."

Justin had heard enough. Without blinking an eye, he raised Angie's head, looked in her eyes from behind her and said, "But you won't be the one to bring it down."

Justin looked to Sally B.

"Tape, please."

Sally B methodically walked toward Angie with the grey masking tape and covered her mouth.

"Goodbye, Angie."

Justin calmly raked the dull switchblade across the front of Angie's throat, killing her instantly.

Angie's head was limp in Justin's hand. He gently laid her down.

"It got awful quiet up there. I wonder where they went?" Uncle Henry asked.

"Henry, you need to leave that alone. It's none of your business. I wish you would just go. Don't you have to work today?" Dats said.

"Nope, not if I don't want to."

"Well, get out of here. Go somewhere."

He was no longer as angry as he was a few hours ago.

"Well, maybe I will go mind my business and just go fishing," Uncle Henry said as he put his arm around me.

"Maybe I'll take Corey with me."

My eyes got wider and my grin matched Uncle Henry's. Dats' half-straight face was taken over by a slight sour smirk. He thought I was spending and enjoying a little too much time with Uncle Henry. But he also thought it would be good for Uncle Henry to take me away from the house. That way, if something was going wrong with Justin upstairs, I wouldn't see it or even think about it.

"All right, you can go this time, Corey, but tomorrow you're going back to school, eye or no eye," Dats warned.

"Well, let's go, kiddo," Uncle Henry said enthusiastically as he stood with me.

"Be careful with your eye, Corey," Mom said. She really didn't know what to say because she was afraid, knowing that something was wrong upstairs. And Uncle Henry suspected something. Mom knew that, if only to protect her and the family, Uncle Henry might start to ask questions about Justin, and maybe even try to take a look upstairs. She knew this would be trouble for everyone. Really, all that I wanted was to catch the bastard who continued to violate me. I often wondered how it would if I just massacred everyone in the house. Then I would not have to suspect anyone.

* * * * * *

Sally B sat on one of the old dusty chairs located in the small attic where Justin had just sliced Angie. She stared at Angie's limp body, blood dripped from her neck. Justin stood over Angie's body, smiling.

"Next we'll deal with the Harris family. We've been getting too sloppy, Sally B. This girl wasn't checked out properly," Justin said angrily.

"You wanted to bring her here. I suggested you let me keep her in New York for a couple of weeks to school her. But you said she was special and you wanted to prepare her to go overseas," Sally B said defensively. "You're starting to butt-in on my job too much, Justin. Let me do my thing. Or what is it, are you getting bored up here in Albany? You need to conquer new things, or what?"

Sally B went to Justin in a pleading voice.

"Please, Justin, you can't blame me for this. I didn't want this. My gut feeling is usually right. But you wouldn't listen to me," Sally B said.

Justin could only stare at Sally B. This silent stare alone was Justin's way of admitting that she was right. He was getting bored and wanted more hands-on. And maybe he was losing his touch at examining people. Justin moved from over Angie's body and walked toward the back door of the attic. He looked down and made sure there was no blood on his shiny black cowboy boots.

"We gotta get this situation straightened out downstairs. I'm getting sloppy and I gotta clean that up. And clean that mess up. Make sure all the blood is up. Check the wood, make sure none of the blood soaked in. Get some caustic acid; it'll burn up all the blood." Sally B took off both of her brown shoe boots and checked to make sure they didn't have blood on them.

Justin took the keys from his pocket, then unlocked the door leading to his computer room in the rear of the attic. Sally B thought to herself, wishing he would just stay back there like he used to do and leave the outside world to her,

"Where am I gonna dump this one, Justin?" Sally B asked, not necessarily wanting or expecting an answer, but more to show Justin her aggravation with him.

Justin didn't respond to her question. He only looked back towards her. She knew he wouldn't be responding too much more to anything except for the matters at hand, and a possible move from this house.

His reason for being in this town and in this house was because the whole six years he'd been there, nobody paid any real attention to him. Attention was blossoming and he was getting sucked into it, and his stone cold heart wanted and needed more warmth, but his mind would take over and never allow this to happen because whenever it did, there was trouble. He liked Angie, this being his reason for bringing her back. He was actually upset that he had to kill her, but defiance and treason were cause for extermination.

Before he moved to Albany, Justin got involved with one of his tricks, and there were problems. He had to eliminate four people to make sure there were no tracks. It looked like he would have to do the same with the Harris family. Sally B dreaded the thought that innocent people might die because an intelligent man had turned psycho killer and once again reached his boiling point.

* * * * * *

"C'mon, Corey, let's go catch some fish before ya father changes his mind," Uncle Henry declared, putting his large arm on my shoulder, leading me out of the living room.

Mom and Dats glanced toward each other, indicating that they knew something was wrong. They weren't sure what, but they had the feeling they'd be hearing from Justin very shortly.

I ran downstairs to grab my jacket. Uncle Henry went back into the living room.

I decided to check to see if Mom and Dats were talking about Justin. I got the long pipe from behind the radiator that was near the front window of the basement. Then I climbed up on the eavesdropping chair and removed the piece of wood covering the hole where I would stick the pipe to hear. I stepped off of the chair and sat in it, then placed the pipe to my ear and listened.

In the living room, Mom was petrified.

"Do you realize the mess we would be in if they had gone upstairs and saw something happening? Jim, we've got to get outta here. I know there's gonna be trouble," Mom said. I could hear her pacing. She was nervous.

I was shocked to hear my mother speak that way. I had always known her to be strong and to carry the family, not weak and cracking. I listened some more. Their words were muffled a bit coming through the pipe, but everything could be understood.

"Sara, what's going on with this guy upstairs? Do you guys owe him some money or something? Because it sure does seem like you're trying to protect him. And if you are, then you did a poor job a few minutes ago in front of Corey. He's a smart boy and it doesn't take long for him to figure things out. Now if you need some money to pay back to this guy, I can spare a few dollars if it means less headaches for the both of you. You two look like shit. Now come on, tell me," Uncle Henry said with a pleading look.

For a moment, I couldn't hear anything as a truck passed by outside in front of the house. Once the truck passed, I still couldn't hear anything. I thought maybe Mom and Dats were thinking about whether or not to say anything to Uncle Henry out of fear for themselves and him. My heart rate picked up with each second of silence. Not because I was afraid, but because I was excited. Excited that I finally might get some insight as to what was going on upstairs, and maybe a lead to solve my own questions about my molestation.

I listened intently as Mom and Dats started talking to Uncle Henry again.

"Well, we do owe him some money," Dats said as he glanced at Mom. Figuratively speaking, he did owe Justin money. She knew it was a lie about them owing Justin money, but she went along with it because she didn't want Henry involved.

"How much do you owe him?" Uncle Henry asked.

Again Dats glanced at Mom before he could answer.

"C'mon, what is all this eye movement between you and Sara?" Uncle Henry said, moving face to face with Mom.

"Sara, how much?" Uncle Henry sweetly demanded.

"Thousand. It's a thousand dollars, Henry," Dats said as he got up from the love seat near the living room window "You satisfied now? And no, we don't want your money. We'll get outta this bind ourselves," Dats stated with pride.

"Sara, is that the way you feel, too?" Uncle Henry asked, still in her face.

Mom, frustrated, snapped, "Oh, Henry, leave it alone, please."

She walked from in front of Henry and took a seat on the sofa near the wall. She fixed her eyes on the television, not really watching anything, just avoiding Henry's eyes. Sara knew that the more eye contact she made with Henry, the more she wanted to tell the truth about Justin.

"Sara, you can't even face me. Look at the both of you. It's more than the grand, isn't it?" Uncle Henry asked, getting down on one knee in front of her, pleading. "Sara, you gotta tell me."

"Oh, Henry, it's nothing else!" she shouted. "Now why don't you just take Corey and go fishing? It's nothing else, dammit!" Mom shouted, while looking at the television.

"Okay, I give. I'll leave you two to yourselves. It's your business," Uncle Henry said as he stood up and shrugged his shoulders.

"Corey!" Uncle Henry called out as he left the living room, leaving Mom and Dats sitting silently.

Back in the basement, I was putting the pipe back behind the radiator. I covered the hole up. Then I dashed out the door.

"Here I come," I said as I ran up the basement stairs.

Uncle Henry looked down the stairs as I raced to the top. He walked out of the dining room door that led to the hallway, and then to the front door, with me close behind. I got to the front door and turned my head to look up toward Justin's apartment. I paused, then went down the front steps.

Justin's door opened and out came Sally B. Her face was clear and calm, covering up her true feelings. She raced down the steps. She knew this next job would be her toughest because she knew someone had been upstairs and that they might come up again. She had to hurry She got to the bottom of the steps and paused.

Inside in the living room, Sara and Jim heard the footsteps pause at the bottom of the stairs. They were both wondering if the next footstep would be headed out the front door or toward their door.

Sally B opened the front door and walked out onto the top step. Both me and Uncle Henry heard the front door close, just as we were about to walk across the street to Uncle Henry's truck.

Uncle Henry was the last person Sally B wanted to see, even though this was the best person for her to see if she was ready to spill her guts as to what was happening. If Uncle Henry pushed the right buttons, she would vomit the ugly truth all over him.

"Hey, Sally B," Uncle Henry said in his usual loud, happy-go-lucky tone as he made his way back toward the steps. Even Mom and Dats heard Uncle Henry speaking to Sally B, causing both of them to peek through the blinds at me and Uncle Henry while they spoke.

"I didn't know you were up there," Uncle Henry said.

"But how would you?" Sally B said as she cautiously made her way down the angled front porch steps.

"How ya been, Sally B? I haven't seen you since that day in Banes' restaurant."

"I've been out of town."

Sally B finally reached the last step and just stood there, because Uncle Henry was blocking her path. Sally B looked at me, and glanced up and down.

"Oh, this is my nephew, Corey. He lives on the first floor. He didn't even know who was living up there until recently," Uncle Henry said. Sally B knew he was searching for answers.

"Nice to meet you, Corey, " Sally B said as she extended her hand to shake. I shook her trembling hand.

"Nice to meet you, Ms. Sally," I said politely as I let her hand go.

"Well, I gotta go, Henry I'll see you around," Sally B said as she made her way around me and Uncle Henry.

Uncle Henry couldn't just let her go, so he gently grabbed her arm.

"Everything okay, Sally, you look a little flushed?" Uncle Henry asked softly.

Sally B forced a smile, and with all her might and determination not to break down and spill her guts she said, "Everything's just great."

"Okay. See ya later then," Uncle Henry said as he released her arm.

Sally B got into the car and drove off. Uncle Henry looked at the first floor window and saw the blinds close. He knew Mom and Dats were watching. Then he turned and watched Sally B drive down the street.

"Sally B's never said 'great' to me in her life?" Uncle Henry said to me. "I wonder what's bugging her. Well, c'mon, Corey, let's go catch some fish," Uncle Henry said as he led me across the street to his truck.

I thought about how Sally B's hand trembled when we shook. I couldn't help wonder if she was nervous because she knew she was responsible for raping me, then became shocked and surprised when she met me unexpectedly.

This made me want to get back with her again. I wasn't sure how I could but, I had to.

I should have crushed her hand while I had the chance. I'm going to stop this crap!

CHAPTER THIRTY-TWO

JUSTIN SAT IN THE COMPUTER ROOM near a portable cellular phone. His computer was on, but he wasn't entering information. He smiled a bit, then picked up the small black telephone. He keyed in seven digits. The phone rang several times before it was picked up. His smile evaporated.

"Are you alone?" Justin asked.

There was a long silence, not quite veiling the fear that Justin sensed from the other end.

"Yes," the voice said softly.

"We have to talk in private. I have some serious issues that need immediate attention. Is it okay to come by or do we need to meet elsewhere? Mind you, we need to move fast," Justin said.

"It's safe to come here," the voice said sadly. The caller didn't really want Justin around.

"You sound awful." Justin said.

"Yes. We were just in the middle of an argument."

"I'll be there shortly," Justin said.

Justin listened for the phone to hang up and then he followed suit. He methodically got up from his chair. He looked around, checked the order of his domain, then turned off the computer from the back switch. Almost in a marching pace, he moved toward the sliding door. He took his keys from his pocket to lock up after leaving.

Justin locked the door and crept toward the ceiling door. It was like Angie's body wasn't present and it was business as usual. He made sure not to step in the blood that was in the area near Angie's throat. He climbed onto the ladder and made his way down into the bedroom off the living room. Upon reaching the last step of the ladder, he stood there and just looked. Again, he checked his domain, making sure everything was in order. Each second he stood, he not only looked to see if all was to his liking, but he also listened and enjoyed the serenity that the silence brought him. He longed for this serenity more than ever. If there was something disrupting this peacefulness, then he would permanently eliminate the cause. He knew the first step toward that direction was to dispose of Corey, no matter what it took. He separated two blinds and glanced out the bedroom window. He saw two boys who looked to be Corey's age. They were playing on the steps across the street. This caused Justin's right eye to squint. He then looked at his shoes and, for a moment, he thought back to his childhood. He saw his life regimented and very much in order, up until he went out on his own at sixteen.

He saw himself at ten years old. He was in his bedroom with his Boys Academy uniform on. Boys Academy was an all boys military school known across the country for having exceptional students and strict discipline. Young Justin had fallen asleep while studying for a test he had the next morning.

Then, the man responsible for raising Justin walked in and caught him sleeping. Justin called him Pop. Pop was in his late forties, robust, married, and very strict. His eyes always had a cold, hard glare about them. But Justin never believed Pop was any kind of father to him because of the way he was treated by him. Pop entered his dimly lit bedroom. Young Justin was fast asleep with his head on his desk. This angered Pop.

"What is this? You don't have time to sleep!" Pop shouted, waking young Justin by roughly shaking his shoulder. Justin opened his eyes, startled, and jumped up. Pop and his wife devoted their life to making a better way for young Justin. They worked hard to pay for his education. They sacrificed by living in a lower-class section of Brooklyn to make sure he had the best. He grabbed young Justin by the back of his uniform collar. He dragged him over to the bedroom window. They saw kids young Justin's age hanging out on the corner, drinking and selling drugs.

"Is that what you want to be like, huh? Is it? We slave to bus you all the way across town to send you to the best school in the country. Those kids will never even think about attending your school and you show your appreciation by sleeping when you're supposed to be studying? In order to be the best in this world, there's no time for sleep," Pop shouted.

Pop's wife, Emily, entered. Emily was in her early forties, and looked every bit of it. She was also overweight. She was a small lady, and did whatever Pop said or suggested.

"I caught him sleeping again," Pop said.

"He must be punished," Emily said with a mean smile.

"We should have left you where we got you from," Pop said as he tossed young Justin in the closet and locked the door. His eyes were wide open in the dark closet. He could hear his father yelling, "and I told you about these wrinkles in the bed covers. You're in the hole for two days."

Young Justin listened with a smile in the pitch dark closet. His father's yelling faded as he drifted off to sleep, cool as a kitten.

Justin's thoughts switched back to looking at the boys playing across the street, and he again checked the bedroom, making sure everything was in perfect order. His thoughts of his early childhood kept him on edge those days. He left the small room near the living room and headed to his own bedroom.

CHAPTER THIRTY-THREE

UNCLE HENRY AND I were parked outside Hampton's Hardware store, located on Pearl Street just about five minutes away from our house.

We sat in the truck and waited for Sally B to come out. We were definitely parked far enough down the block for her not to see us. She'd already been in there for fifteen minutes.

"What could she be doing in there?" I asked as I began to grow impatient.

"That's a good question."

Sally B came out carrying a large brown bag with 'Hampton's Hardware' advertised on it in large green letters. Mr. Hampton, a balding Caucasian man in his mid-fifties, came out behind Sally B.

We watched Sally B as she shook Mr. Hampton's hand, smiled, and walked towards her car.

Sally B went to the driver's side of her car and looked down the street, then up the street in the direction of me and Uncle Henry. We froze in our seats as Sally B looked a few seconds longer in our direction. Both Uncle Henry and I thought we'd been spotted. We thought being six cars away was far enough.

"Don't move!" Uncle Henry said, barely moving his lips.

Both of us looked directly at Sally B. She hesitated opening her car door handle.

"She's seen us," I said convincingly.

"Not quite," Uncle Henry said.

Sally B glanced at her watch, then walked toward the rear of her car and then to the sidewalk.

"Oh, no, she's headed our way. She's seen us, I know she has," I said, stone faced.

Uncle Henry turned his head slightly to the right, and at the north end of the street behind us he saw the front of the bank. It was located on the corner of Madison Avenue and Pearl Street, not far from the hardware store on the same side of the street. "She's going to the bank. I know she hasn't seen us," he said, talking faster now.

"But what if she did?"

Sally B was three cars away.

"Be still," Uncle Henry whispered as Sally B walked by. "Don't move."

Uncle Henry reached to adjust his rear-view mirror and didn't see Sally B walking toward the bank. Then he turned his head around fully to look through the window in the back part of the cab of the truck.

"Where'd she go?" Uncle Henry asked, bewildered.

"Looking for me?" Sally B said.

Sally B's voice startled Uncle Henry as he turned toward his driver's side door, which was nearest the street.

"Oh," Uncle Henry said, very surprised.

"How'd you get over there so fast?" Uncle Henry asked.

"Walked," Sally B said calmly as she leaned with her right shoulder resting on Uncle Henry's door, with her arms folded across her chest while looking in the side mirror. She smiled a small grin.

"If you're gonna do police work, you'd better learn better tactics." She paused as Uncle Henry recovered from the embarrassment of being outsmarted.

"Well actually, Sally B, we weren't doing police work. We were just kinda driving down the street, stopped and saw you," Uncle Henry said.

Sally B turned to face Uncle Henry, then looked at me.

"Is that true, Corey?" she asked.

I knew that Sally B knew, so I wasn't going to be the one to keep a lie going not caught red-handed at least. Then thoughts swirled through my mind.

I thought back for an instant, remembering how in the movie, Godfather II, Michael lied to his wife right to the end about the killing of the five heads of families. Michael's wife knew the truth, but he still lied.

Then one time I was in the car with Mom and we saw Dats with another woman, and both of them looked at each other from a distance. Dats always denied it was him.

"No, we weren't following you," I answered sheepishly.

I tried to play the naive kid role, but she knew better than to fall for it.

Sally B smiled, and as she walked away she said, "You're a good kid." She walked toward her car and got in. Sally B thought about what had just happened. She knew it wasn't a coincidence.

Uncle Henry looked at me and sighed.

"Good goin', kid. Where'd you learn to lie like that?"

"Dats."

To Uncle Henry, my answer had two meanings: One, that I was a good liar; and two, he suddenly realized that Dats was a great liar and that he may have been lying about the thousand they owed Justin.

Uncle Henry chuckled and turned, facing forward to start up his truck.

Sally B had made a U-turn headed north, and blew her horn as she passed by us. Uncle Henry pulled out of his parking space, heading in the opposite direction.

Uncle Henry watched Sally B stop at the red light. He was tempted to turn back around and follow her.

"Don't do it," I said with an embarrassed look for Uncle Henry.

"Well, could you have done any better, smart mouth?" Uncle Henry asked in a playful, defensive manner.

I didn't want to hurt his feelings with my next statement.

"But I woulda parked on that street that was opposite the hardware store. And then three cars behind the closest car. That's how the plain clothes cops do it up by our school. They're up there watching who comes out of this house on Park Avenue, down the street from school. Randy said crack heads live in the house."

"Oh, yeah, what're you doing watching?"

"Well, we can't help but notice them. They always offer us some of their doughnuts."

Uncle Henry chuckled.

"Well, we'd better get to the lake while the fish are still biting," Uncle Henry said. I would never say this to him, but Uncle Henry sure can be a jerk sometimes. He messed it up. Sally B may have given me some small clue that would help lead me to my abuser. I don't give a shit about anything else. I could've smacked him upside his egg head for getting us exposed.

CHAPTER THIRTY-FOUR

JUSTIN HAD SURVEYED the entire house. He knew the attic would be taken care of by Sally B. He glanced around his kitchen once more, and then headed downstairs, slowly.

He reached the foot of the stairs and walked toward the front door and peeked out. Then after seeing no one, he headed toward Sara and Jim's door. He paused for a second, then knocked.

Sara and Jim were inside, still sitting in the living room, blank-faced. Jim sighed and went to the door. Sara reluctantly followed. They knew who it was because they didn't hear the front door that led to the front porch steps slam.

Justin lightly knocked on the door two times, almost as if it were a code. Jim took a silent, deep breath, then looked at Sara, who stood near the entrance to Randy's bedroom. Jim opened the door slowly.

Justin moved back a few steps to let the wooden door swing out towards him.

"Justin, how are you?" Jim said, trying desperately to hide his nervousness. Justin rarely made an appearance to Jim's front door, or back door for that matter. When he did, Jim knew there was a problem.

Sara stood smiling, sadly.

"Hello, Jim," Justin said as he looked over Jim's shoulder at Sara.

"Sara. How are you?"

"Fine, Justin. Please, come in," Sara said politely with a slight tremor in her voice.

Justin walked in as Jim moved aside.

"You feeling okay, Sara? You look a little peaked," Justin said as he stood in front of Sara, as if he were examining her.

"No, I'm fine," she replied, nervously looking for somewhere to put her hands.

She abruptly extended her hand, ushering Justin to the living room.

"Come have a seat," Sara said.

Justin turned toward the living room and glanced at Jim, who was half smiling. Justin walked to the living room and sat in the love seat that was close to the front window. That way he could see who was coming and going.

Sara and Jim sat on the sofa, close to each other. The television was on, but the volume was muted. Justin glanced at the rock music video that played on MTV. Then he looked out the window, then back at Sara and Jim.

"There are some matters I wanted to take up before I leave town for a while," Justin said.

"Yes," Jim said.

"My next payments to you might be a little delayed because of my absence. I will pay extra to cover for the delay. Is that okay?"

Jim shook his head 'yes'.

"You know, I pay you two very well to keep my place in order and discrete. You've given me very good coverage when I'm not here."

Justin knew that they knew what this conversation was going to come down to. Sara and Jim knew that Justin was toying with them. They wanted him to get to the point.

"Your jobs are very simple. Granted, Jim, you have extended me some people from your old Brooklyn stomping grounds who've done well in my organization. However, there has been a leak."

Justin heard tiny footsteps running up the stairs. He glanced out the blinds and stood. It was Corey. Justin smiled and looked at Sara and Jim as he was on his way towards the dining room door. Sara and Jim quickly looked out the window and could see Henry's truck. Sara was shocked that they had returned so soon. She thought they couldn't have gone fishing and that maybe they forgot something.

I was in the hallway and turning the dining room doorknob, and so was Justin. I felt someone else turning the knob, and let go.

"Mom, it's me," I said, laughing as the door opened. My smile quickly vanished upon seeing Justin. Justin's smile was bigger than ever.

"Oh, hi," I said.

I was more surprised than afraid. Justin extended his hand toward me, and I reluctantly shook it. I actually thought it would be good for Mom and Dats if I shook Justin's hand and acted like nothing was wrong. Mom and Dats had these fake smiles that said trouble all over them, but I played it off. As I let go of Justin's hand, my middle finger rubbed over a bump in the center of his palm. This bump was familiar to me. My forehead wrinkled a bit as I thought, but then I was distracted by Justin.

"So how is your eye, Corey?" Justin asked.

"It's getting better," I answered, straight-faced.

"Good. Glad to hear that. Nice patch!" Justin said as he looked to see who was coming in the front door as it opened.

The shadow on the door curtain was large.

"Hey . . ." Uncle Henry said, smiling as he entered.

He saw Justin with his family, and his smile disappeared quicker than mine did when I initially entered.

"Justin," Uncle Henry said, cordially.

"Henry, how are you?" Justin asked.

"I'm fine!" Uncle Henry replied as he walked past Justin with a cautious look.

Justin moved past me and started walking toward the stairs to his apartment.

"Take care, everyone!" Justin said as he walked up the stairs to his apartment.

Everyone watched him with serious eyes. Feeling their eyes on him, Justin bent over the wooden railing and looked at everyone.

"Cheer up. It's not that serious--not yet anyway," Justin said, laughing.

"What?" Uncle Henry said while moving closer to the stairs and looking up toward the top of the railing, seeing no one as Justin closed the door to his apartment. Uncle Henry walked back into our place.

"What did he mean by that, Jim?"

"Oh, nothing, Henry. He's just strange like that at times."

Mom went towards the kitchen, hoping Henry would just take me and go fishing.

"What did you come back for, Henry?" Mom yelled, with no bad intentions.

"Corey wanted to get his Walkman, is that okay? Go get your radio, Corey," Uncle Henry said, nudging me along.

I went downstairs. Dats looked at Uncle Henry.

"I smell him, Jim, and it don't smell clean."

Henry got in Jim's face.

"You need to tell me before somebody gets hurt. I get the feeling that under all Justin's little niceties, he can be very nasty."

Jim nonchalantly answered.

"You're barking up the wrong tree. Just go fishing and stop thinking about it."

I ran back upstairs with my Sony Walkman in hand. The doorbell rang for up stairs. The buzzer went off, opening the front door. It was Sally B. She paused in her stride when she saw Uncle Henry, and forced a smile. Then she continued upstairs, carrying her medium-sized brown bag.

Uncle Henry's eyes followed her upstairs until she walked into Justin's apartment. Justin closed the door and bolted it behind Sally B. She put the brown bag on the kitchen table and sat in the chair.

"What is it?" Sally B asked.

"I think Jim and Sara know that I know about the 911 call that Corey made."

"So what are you gonna do?"

"No, it's what you have to do, Sally B."

Sally B knew what this meant. For the first time, Justin was asking her to kill. Justin moved behind Sally B and massaged her shoulders.

"I've always taken care of these things myself, Sally B. As a matter of fact, I take great joy in doing so, but I think you have a better shot at them now."

"You mean, kill the boy?"

"No, I mean the entire family."

"But Justin, I'm not a killer. I run your business for you. Why are you asking me to do this?"

"Are you saying you won't do this for me?"

"No, I'm saying I don't think I have the nerve to do it."

Justin stopped massaging her shoulders and began to slowly pace about the kitchen.

"Oh, so it's not a matter that you don't want to do it?"

"No, it's not," Sally B said. "I don't have the nerve to do it."

"Nerve, Sally B. That's what it is! You see, I never really want to harm anyone, especially on purpose, unless I'm pushed. Sally B, it's not like you or anyone else wants to kill. It's only for a split second that we want to kill when the nerve is there. Then it's gone . . . except for people like me. See, I'm constantly pushed, and when I'm pushed over that line, that's when the nerve comes. For some, their line isn't that far from nerve. For others like yourself, that line is a long ways away from the nerve. You just need to be pushed. You know who pushed me all my life, Sally B?"

Justin bent down and got in her frightened face. She shook her head no. Justin went back to pacing and talking.

"My parents. Those fake parents of mine pushed me enough to kill for a lifetime, Sally B." A painful expression etched across his face. "They locked me in closets, beat me, violated me, whatever you could imagine destructible, they did it. On top of that, they did everything to make me their 'boy wonder', even sent me to the best schools--that is, until I quit and ran, ran as far as I could, yet I was right up under their nose." A small, hard smile worked its way through his pain. "Then I really learned survival on the streets. That's being pushed." He got in Sally B's face. Anger swelled in his eyes. "So you see, I'm pushed. No, you don't have to do it, Sally B, I'll do it!"

Justin leaned on the front door leading to the stairs and calmed himself.

"But I'm gonna wait, Sally B, because I've been to war many, many times and I know tactics. See, right now, they're waiting for me to come get 'em." He paused momentarily, then began walking slowly again. "No, I'm gonna wait. It's that element of surprise that gets 'em every time. Now, do you have the acid to take care of Angie?"

"Yes."

"Well, take care of it. Soon her body will start to smell. Don't leave any trace of who she is. That housekeeper in New York was a little too close for me."

Justin started toward his bedroom.

"Suppose they come after you?" Sally B said.

This statement stopped Justin in his tracks. His back was toward her.

"Nobody's ever come after you before, Justin."

Justin slowly turned toward her.

"Let the games begin, but I'll surely win," Justin said with a smile, then headed into his bedroom and closed the door behind him. Then he stuck his head out of the door, catching Sally B as she walked toward the front.

"Did you like that rhyme, Sally B?"

Justin went back into his bedroom, laughing hysterically. Sally B went to the room off the living room, carrying the brown bag. She shook her head and mumbled, "Unbelievable." She put down the bag and went to the kitchen to get a thick green plastic bag from a drawer that was behind the front door area. It was a large cabinet with eight drawers, built directly into the wall of the house. The cabinet was atop the drawers, with a shelf area between the two, separating them.

Sally B quickly went into the attic. She brought the brown bag up with her. She took the contents out of the bag. It was caustic acid. She opened the container and knelt down toward Angie's face.

Sally B opened Angie's mouth and began to pour the acid on her teeth. Once Sally B was satisfied, making sure she poured enough to corrode her teeth, she began pouring it on her face. The acid immediately began to eat her skin. She made sure not to get any of the acid on the floor

Then Sally B opened Angie's hands and poured acid on her palms and fingertips. After completing both hands, she did the same to her feet. This process would leave no clue as to who Angie was. After this incident, Justin didn't want this to happen again. Sally B never had to be told this by Justin. She just knew never to let it happen again where anyone could be traced to him.

Sally B always pushed the right buttons for Justin. This was what had kept her around for ten years, the longest of any of his associates. Justin admired this form of thinking in Sally B. He felt like she was a part of him. Sally B sensed that he felt like this about her, but she never let her guard down, nor became comfortable. Corey was a different story for her. She couldn't find it in her to do harm to Corey or his family, no matter what Justin said. She knew, if anything, this would be their reason for parting. And Justin wasn't about to let Sally B just walk away from him. She knew he'd rather kill her than take the chance of her handing him over to the police.

As for my brief encounter with Justin, I didn't like him. It was my gut feeling and everything else that I had seen. Sally B, I couldn't figure. Why was she with this man? I wouldn't doubt if both of them were the cause of my being mistreated. If they were, I hope they both go to hell after I scald them in boiling water.

* * * * * *

Me and Uncle Henry were in his truck, stopped at a stoplight on the corner of Grand Street and Warren Avenue. This was two blocks south of our house. Uncle Henry's right signal light flashed, preparing to go right.

"Uncle Henry, it's right on red. C'mon, let's go. By the time we get to the lake, the fish will stop biting."

It was obvious Uncle Henry's mind was somewhere else. The light turned green. Instead, Uncle Henry hastily changed his signal to go left and let the oncoming cars go by, then he screeched his wheels making a left turn.

"Uncle Henry, where are you going?"

"To the police station."

"But why?"

"I'm gonna find out about this guy."

"But why would they know something? Why would they even tell you if they do know something about him?"

"The same reason you made that 911 call on him."

I went dead silent.

"Yep, I know it was you who called them. Only you would have enough nerve to pull such a gag."

"But I thought he was doing something to a kid up there."

"Don't you still think he was?"

"Well, kinda, but I'm not sure."

"Well, you're my family and I got a sister and brother-in-law back there that I care about as well as your brothers, and you guys are all I've got, and I'm gonna always make sure you're safe."

Uncle Henry stopped on Warren Avenue and parked behind five black and white squad cars. It was a five-minute walk from our house.

Uncle Henry got out of the truck. I sat. I thought he was wasting time.

"Well, are you coming, Corey?"

I frowned.

"We're wasting our time, Uncle Henry."

"No, we're not."

"Even if he is doing something, think about it. What good will it do? He's been living right over our heads for six years and I never knew who he was. They guy only came out at night. He's got an attic where one part is locked off . . ."

I realized I had said too much. Uncle Henry gave me a strange look.

"How do you know he's got an attic?"

"Well . . ."

"Corey, have you been sneaking around up there?" Uncle Henry asked, with a mischievous smile.

"Well, I kinda got lost. Well, me and Randy and Tony, we wanted to check out the place, that's all. We never knew the house had an attic. We wanted to check it out."

"Is that what you've been trying to tell me?"

"Well, partly, but we never got around to going fishing again until today."

Uncle Henry ran back to the driver's side of his truck and got in. He started it up.

"Well, let's go fish," Uncle Henry said.

Then Uncle Henry had a more serious face.

"And I want to know everything! And you can start with this attic."

I knew Uncle Henry meant business and would not let the subject die. I did want to know myself, but I wasn't sure if I should tell him about the molesting part. This was what bugged me the most, and was the only reason I went to help the boy upstairs that night, because I knew what pain was all about.

Anybody who does weird things to kids, or to anyone for that matter, should be put to death.

CHAPTER THIRTY-FIVE

DATS LEFT THE HOUSE and turned the corner as Tammy drove up. Tammy, Tibby's wife, pulled in front of our house.

She got out of the car. She had definitely been crying. She ran up the stairs and rang our doorbell several times. Sara peeked out of her front door curtain and asked, "Who are you?"

Tammy began to cry. Sara was reluctant to open her door, but did so after a moment.

"Yes?" Sara said.

"I'm Tammy. Can I speak to you a minute, please?"

"What is this about?"

Tammy started to weep hysterically, but still managed to answer.

"I'm Tibby's wife."

Sara opened her door wide and allowed Tammy to come in. Tammy immediately put her head on Sara's shoulder and continued to cry. Sara was unsure, but put her arms around Tammy's shoulder and led her into the house toward the kitchen. She ushered Tammy to the seat closest to the wall at the head of the table. Sara went to the refrigerator and took out a glass jug of ice water. She grabbed a glass from the cabinet that was in the corner near the sink, poured the water and handed the glass to Tammy. Sara checked her kettle to see if it had enough water for coffee.

"Coffee?"

Tammy shook her head 'no' while she drank her water, her face wet with tears. Sara handed Tammy a napkin from the pile that was on the shelf. Sara put more water in the kettle, just in case Tammy changed her mind. She put a large jar of Maxwell House Instant Coffee on the kitchen table, then turned the flame on under the coffee pot and sat in the chair next to Tammy, at the corner of the table.

"Now, what seems to be your problem?"

"Well, I've been married to Tibby for only a little over a year and we have one son. I knew he was married before and I know about his other two children. Now, I just want you to know that I'm not here to start trouble. I love Tibby very much and I love my son and I wouldn't do anything to disrupt that, just as I wouldn't want to do it to anyone else's family. All I want to know is the truth."

"Well, hasn't Tibby told you the truth?"

"Sort of, but I don't know what to believe. I'm not sure anymore. That's why I came to you. I'm glad Jim isn't here because I know he is angry with Tibby and I wouldn't want to get him started all over again."

Sara sighed and stood. She turned off the flame from under the boiling kettle. She got her favorite black cup from the dish rack that sat on the side of the sink.

She poured her water into the cup. She made her coffee. She stirred it several times, and began telling her story.

"I used to date your husband long before you came along. We were in love for a short time, then realized it was only for a fleeting moment. That fleeting moment produced a child."

Tammy positioned herself erect, waiting for the moment of truth.

"That son is no longer with us."

"But Jim . . ."

"Never mind."

"But what about the son that you and Tibby had?"

"What about him, he's dead!" Sara said sternly. She had lied to Tammy.

Tammy knew to back off. And that's exactly what she did.

"I'm sorry to have bothered you."

Sara's hard look had transformed to a hurt look, almost like she had lost someone special to her. Tammy touched her hand gently, with caution.

"Is there something you want to talk about?" Tammy asked timidly.

"You can't tell Jim about this conversation. And stop bugging Tibby. He's a good man. He'll take care of you. As for me, I can handle things here."

"Well, I guess I should give you your house back, Sara. I've already overstayed my welcome."

Tammy rose from her seat with a soft smile.

"Thanks for everything."

Sara stood, forcing a small smile. Tammy had rekindled memories in Sara that she'd rather not think about.

Sara looked at the clock atop the refrigerator. It was 1:00 p.m. Tammy began walking toward the front door. She felt she had to say something nice since Sara had relieved her of her worries. Tammy turned slightly in her stride and looked back at Sara, whose mind was obviously somewhere else.

"If you ever have some time and you want to go for coffee or something, just call me."

"Huh? Oh, sure!" Sara said, her attention divided.

They were at the front door, and Tammy turned to face Sara.

"Again, it was nice meeting you, and thanks," Tammy said, extending her hand to Sara to shake.

Sara shook her hand and said, "Take care."

Sara opened the door for Tammy. Tammy gently opened the screen door, and Justin's door opened. Sara and Tammy looked up. Sally B came walking down the stairs, fast paced. Before Tammy hit the second step, Sally B was at the front door.

"Hi, Sara," Sally B said kindly.

Sally B just stood there a second, then glanced at Tammy, who watched them.

"Oh, Sally B, this is Tammy."

"Hi, Tammy"

There was a certain eeriness that Tammy noticed between Sally B and Sara. Sally B walked past Tammy.

"Well, I guess I'll be going, too," Tammy said.

Sally B jumped in her car and drove away. Tammy walked to her brand new polished red Cadillac Seville, got in and drove off. Sara walked back inside the house and immediately went to the wall telephone near the kitchen entryway. She dialed a number and waited for someone to pick up the phone.

"Tibby, your wife was just here."

"What did she want?"

"I can't talk about it here. Jim might walk in any minute. Can you meet me in the lot behind the McGin football field?"

Tibby hemmed and hawed for a second.

"Aw . . . sure, I'll be there in twenty minutes. I just gotta lock up."

"Okay, thanks," Sara said.

Tibby hung up, and Sara did, too; then changed into her exercise gear and automatically snatched her keys from the dresser. She closed her bedroom door and put the padlock on. She grabbed her sunglasses from atop the refrigerator near the radio. She rushed from the kitchen through the back door and locked it.

Sara made her way to her white Mazda 626. The car was one of the perks they were able to enjoy as a result of Justin's money. She pressed the automatic, garage door opener. The wooden door opened with ease. Sara drove out in a hurry, hoping she wouldn't run into Jim along the way.

She pulled the baseball cap low on her forehead to shield part of her face, hoping no one would recognize her.

From the house, the drive wasn't far. Sara was both happy and sad to be going to meet Tibby. She had fond memories of their times together. The only bad memory was that of their unplanned child. With Jim constantly badgering her for explanations, and then Tammy showing up, thoughts of Sara's teenage years with Tibby were rekindled. She needed to talk things over.

Sally B pulled up in front of Tibby's bar, just as Tibby was getting into his car. She slammed on her brakes and waved Tibby over to her.

"Hey, Sally B, what's up?" Tibby said as he stuck his head through her driver's side window.

"Get in!" she said sternly.

"But I gotta meeting in ten minutes," Tibby said, looking at his watch.

"It can wait!"

Tibby sighed and got into her car. She drove off around the corner and parked on Third Street, about a block from Tibby's bar.

"I may need your help tonight."

"Okay."

"Where can I dump a bag without being seen around here?"

"Well . . ."

"And I don't want the package recovered."

"You could go to the dump, but that might not work. What is it anyway that you gotta dump?"

"Never mind."

"I guess the best place would be the Hudson River. Sally B, what is it? You're acting awful strange. Is everything okay?"

"Everything is fine, I'm just in a hurry and I gotta take care of a few things before it gets outta hand."

"It's not Justin, is it?"

"When isn't it?"

Sally B started up the car and drove back around the block towards Tibby's bar. From the bar you had a clear view to Central Avenue. Central Avenue was the main street in Albany. At the intersection where Tibby's bar was, on the corner of Third Street and a block away from Central Avenue, you could see who was at the stoplight on Central. Tammy waited to make a left, heading towards the bar.

"Shit, there's Tammy!" Tibby said nervously.

He would surely be caught by Tammy. Tibby couldn't get out of Sally B's car, because Tammy would spot him.

The red light turned green for Tammy to make her left turn.

Just as she was making her left turn, a car was trying to make it through against the red light. The driver ran right into her passenger side. She slammed on her brakes. Tibby could see Tammy's mouth form into a scream. He saw her freeze, but he had to go meet with Sara. He knew Sara needed him, not the next day, but right then. Tibby eased out of Sally B's car.

"Tibby," Sally B said before he closed the door all the way. He kneeled down so that Tammy wouldn't see him.

"I'll ring once, hang up, then ring again if it's late and you're home. If it's still early, I'll drive by and face the bar and I'll have my flashers on. Keep an eye on the front window tonight when you work. Have someone there to take over just in case."

"Okay," Tibby said.

Tibby closed her door and duck-walked to his car on the passenger side. He unlocked the door and crawled inside. He started it and slid over behind the wheel. He took a look at the minor accident Tammy was in.

"You'll have to handle it, baby, sorry," he said to himself as he drove backwards to escape the scene unseen.

CHAPTER THIRTY-SIX

SARA'S DRIVE TO THE rendezvous spot was only five minutes. Bishop McGin High School was on Slingerland Avenue, a short street.

Sara took a left onto Slingerland Avenue from Morton Avenue. She went this way because it was where the back side of the school was located. She drove one block onto a small street called Lane Avenue. Lane led to the back of the football field. Sara looked at each of the four modest houses that lined both sides of the sidewalk. She wasn't looking at the decor of these homes, she was checking to make sure no one was on the steps to see her driving up this block, which was a dead end street. After passing all the homes, she parked about thirty yards away from the homes at the back of the school. She sat in her car and waited. This area could not be seen from the end of the street.

A few minutes passed by, and still no Tibby. Sara looked at her car panel clock. It said 1:30, definitely time enough for Tibby to have been there. She needed to hurry and return home before Jim or the kids got back. She became impatient. She started up her car and was about to leave when Tibby pulled up behind her in his new blue Lincoln. Sara turned off her car and stepped out. Tibby did the same.

They approached each other like long lost friends. They embraced and kissed on the lips.

"Thanks for coming, Tibby. I'm sorry for getting you out, but I had to talk to you."

"What's wrong, Sara, you don't look good."

"Well, you know Tammy came to visit me."

"Yeah, you told me that. What did she want?"

"She wanted to know if Corey was your son."

"What did you tell her?"

Sara started to walk into the field, away from the cars.

"I told her the truth."

Tibby didn't expect this.

"Why? Why did you even let her in your house?"

"Never mind that, how'd she know to even come to my house?"

"Every time Jim comes to the bar, he questions me about it. I tried to keep it low key with Tammy, but after Jim kept coming there and bringing it up, I guess she got tired of the suspense and wanted to find out for herself. Then I finally told her that he was our son."

"But why?"

"Because that's what she wanted to hear, Sara."

"But that's a--"

"Well, I was angry. Jim had been starting trouble. Anyway, the child part was the truth."

"We both know who Corey's daddy is, Tibby."

"Yeah, too bad Jim doesn't."

This brought silence for a minute between them. Tibby walked over to Sara and put his arm around her. Sara had her head down and shoulders slouched.

"Do you ever think about our child we did have?"

Tibby took a few seconds to answer.

"Sometimes."

"You ever wonder if things had been better. . . ." she paused, "maybe it would have been you and me instead of me and Jim."

"We had a good time, Sara. But you know we wouldn't have lasted. I was too wild and you wanted to settle down. I just thought you were too young."

Tibby put his arm around Sara's waist and escorted her back to her car.

"Eh, that was a long time ago, Sara."

"Yeah, you're right. Ever wonder about it?"

"Sometimes."

Tibby abruptly changed the subject.

"But I think more about our last fling before you married Jim."

"Yeah, if it weren't for that fling. Oh well, can't go back and change time."

"Your wife is sweet, take care of her," Sara said.

Sara got into her car and started the engine. Tibby leaned into her driver's side window and gave her a kiss.

"Ya know, thinking back on it, I was too young to be thinking about a kid. You were fifteen and pregnant. I don't know what we were doin'," Tibby smiled.

"Being crazy," Sara said.

"Hey, by the way, did you ever tell Jim about that baby?"

"Are you crazy? He wouldn't have married me. I gotta go."

Sara drove off, leaving Tibby walking in the dust toward his car. Tibby smiled and got into his car, started it up and drove off.

CHAPTER THIRTY-SEVEN

UNCLE HENRY AND I were at Ravena Lake, where we always fished. We both had our lines in the water and sat next to each other.

"Uncle Henry, have you ever had anything bad happen to you as a kid?"

"Bad, like what?"

"Bad like, anything you thought was bad, but maybe somebody else didn't think was so bad?"

"Well, you're kinda not making sense, Corey. Just what do you mean?"

"I don't know, maybe someone did something to you that you didn't like, but they thought was funny."

"Sure, that happened a lot. But I don't think that's what you wanted to ask. Why, has something bad happened to you that you're not telling anyone?"

My fishing line jerked.

"Got one!" I shouted excitedly.

"Reel 'em in. Do it right or you're gonna lose him," Uncle Henry said, just as excited.

"How do you know it's a him? Maybe it's a her. Or maybe it's a him and a her. Maybe the fishes' parents had sex with a relative and caused a double sex baby to be born. Is that possible?"

I was fighting to reel the fish in. Uncle Henry was mystified by what I had just asked. "Boy, you say the damndest things sometimes.

C'mon, reel 'em in, be careful."

"Woooowe, look at that sucker!"

Uncle Henry had a big smile on his face, and was proud of my catch.

"Haven't you seen in those inquirer magazines where some guy was cross-breeding cats with kittens, and kittens' brothers and sisters breeding. The cats were coming out crazy and cockeyed."

Uncle Henry put his fishing pole down and helped me unhook the fish.

"Haven't you, Uncle Henry?"

"Here, take the hook out. Ya know, you been watching a little too much TV for me."

"I read about that in Time magazine, too."

I was about to tell Uncle Henry of my bizarre incident, but I had to be careful. I thought that the best way for me to tell Uncle Henry was to mention stories that I'd heard about on the news. That way, maybe he would have seen the same news story and would figure out that the same thing could have possibly happened to me. I couldn't tell him directly, because he could be the person who molested me, and I wasn't about to take that chance out here alone in the woods.

"Oh, so you do read?" Uncle Henry said, playfully.

"For real, Uncle Henry. Then there was this story about this hillbilly who had sex with his daughter and she got pregnant and the child was retarded, and about how he made the brother and sister have a child and it came out retarded. The boy said his dad always had sex with him. It said the boy was molested, sometimes three times a day. Then one day, the father killed the whole family, then he shot himself."

"Like I said, you dream up some real doozies."

I stopped with the fish, and my face grew more serious as I stood.

"These aren't stories, Uncle Henry, the father really was molesting his son."

Uncle Henry put the fish on the ground and looked up at me. He pulled me down and hugged me.

"I'm sorry, Corey. I believe you."

Uncle Henry playfully wrestled with me for a moment, then stopped.

"Now, let's catch some more of those fish so we can get them home to your mom in time for dinner tonight."

I thought to myself. I couldn't tell him that someone was molesting me.

We both rewormed our lines.

"Uncle Henry, you don't like Justin, do you?"

"Not particularly. Why?"

"Oh, nothing."

I thought for a minute.

"Well, what if you and I went into the attic to see what's behind that locked folding door. Maybe we can find out something."

"Nah. For what? He hasn't done anything wrong."

I went back to looking out at the lake, just like Uncle Henry. But my brain was cooking.

"Suppose we could find out something that would help you figure out what's wrong with your friend, Sally B. Remember, you said she never used the word 'great' with you before. The answer could be in that room."

This got Uncle Henry's adrenaline flowing, but he didn't want to let me know, so he kept his cool.

"Maybe so, but I doubt it."

But I was smarter than that. I knew I had touched a nerve when I mentioned Sally B's name. I remembered the way Uncle Henry looked in her eyes. I would do anything to help find the person who violated me, and Justin was another person to check out. At that moment I was sad because I couldn't even enjoy time with my uncle without thinking about my plight. I had to hurry to expose the sick bastard because I became more and more angry. I had to try to keep my cool.

"You and Sally B ever do it before, Uncle Henry?"

"None of your business."

"I know you care about her. I know if I cared about someone as pretty as Sally B and they looked sad, I'd want to know why."

Uncle Henry looked at me with a slight grin.

"Well, I would," I reiterated.

Uncle Henry's line jerked.

"Ooops, got one," Uncle Henry said as he carefully reeled in his catch.

Uncle Henry did care about Sally B, even though her lifestyle wasn't what he particularly cared for. She was about the only woman who made him laugh. And lately, she wasn't doing so.

I wondered if Uncle Henry would take heed to what I'd said and maybe check out Justin.

"So I take it you don't like this Justin guy?"

"It's not that I don't like him. It's just that well, he's been living up there for so long, but Mom and Dats never talked about him. I just think it's kinda strange. And why would they owe him a thousand dollars?"

"How'd you know about that?"

I realized I had said too much.

"I overheard Mom and Dats telling you."

"But you were downstairs when we were talking about that."

"I eavesdropped. You thought I was downstairs."

"Can you remember your Mom and Dats buying anything new lately?"

"No. Maybe they paid the school tuition with it."

"But the car, it's brand new. If they can afford that, why would they need to borrow?"

"I really don't think they borrowed money from him. There's something strange about him, that's for sure."

"And just because we talked about this doesn't mean you go up there snooping around."

I sighed.

"You understand me, Corey?"

"Yeah. Yeah."

"I don't want you getting in any trouble with this guy."

I frowned.

"We'll go up there together."

CHAPTER THIRTY-EIGHT

SARA PACED FROM THE BEDROOM to the kitchen and back again. She looked at the clock on the refrigerator. It read 2:38 p.m. Randy and Tony would be home shortly.

Sara's meeting with Tibby had raised thoughts about days with him and, as a result of their time together, the child they produced. She'd decided the best thing to do was to give up that child because her life would not be normal, and she wanted what was best for the child. Like all mothers who give up their children, at some time or another they wonder where their child is. All she knew was that the child was somewhere in New York, or at least she hoped.

Sara heard a key in the front door and went to greet her two sons. Randy opened the door, and Tony was directly behind him. Sara gave them a big hug, simultaneously. The boys returned the hug with a smile, but looked at each other knowing this wasn't the way she normally greeted them.

"Mom, what's wrong?" Randy asked.

"Oh, nothing. I just love both of you and I realized I hadn't told you in a while."

"You didn't work today, Mom?" Tony asked.

She entered the dining room behind the boys, with her hands on their shoulders.

"No, I stayed home. I'm trying to get this house straightened up a bit."

"Mom, where's Corey?" Tony asked.

"Your Uncle Henry took him fishing."

"He always gets to go fishing."

"No, he doesn't, he's just keeping himself occupied while his eye heals."

"But it's been almost a week. I never get to go out on a week night. Can I go over to Aunt Rebekah's tonight, Mom, please?" Tony asked.

Randy went into his room.

"Tony, it's a school night," she said.

"But Mom, she said we could come over any time we wanted," Tony reinforced.

Randy was in his room, looking through a basketball magazine.

"I suppose you want to go see your aunt too, huh, Randy?"

"Yeah, I'll go!" Randy answered, with divided attention.

"Tony, call her and ask if it's okay"

"Oh, it's okay, Mom. Can't we just walk over there?" Tony said.

"No, I said call, or stay here."

Sara looked in Randy's room.

"Bring your homework."

"Yes, Mom."

Tony was on the phone near the kitchen, dialing Aunt Rebekah's number.

"Hello, Aunt Rebekah, can we come over?"

The voice was soft but strong on the other end.

"Yes."

"Okay. We'll be right there. Bye," Tony said excitedly.

"Wait!" Sara yelled. "Let me speak to her."

Tony handed Sara the phone.

"Hi, Rebekah. Is it okay if they come over this evening?"

"Yes. I have fried chicken."

"If they come now, they're gonna bring their homework. I

might be going out shortly, so I'll drop them off. I'll blow the horn when I get there. Bye."

Sara hung up the phone and looked at her wristwatch. It was 3:00. She stood in thought, momentarily.

"Mom, what time can we go?" Tony asked.

"As soon as I get ready I'll drop you off."

Sara walked to Randy's bedroom doorway as Tony escorted her.

"You going with Tony, Randy?"

"I don't think so, Mom," Randy answered.

"She's having your favorite. Fried chicken."

Randy looked up from his basketball magazine at her.

"Fried chicken!" Sara said convincingly.

This brought a smile to Randy's face.

"I'm there."

Randy threw the magazine down and proceeded to take off his school uniform.

"I'll be glad when I get to high school. I won't have to wear this stupid blue tie," Randy said as he laid it neatly on his dresser.

"Go get changed, Tony," Sara said. "And bring your books. I'm gonna drop you off because I have a stop to make."

Aunt Rebekah Waters was actually a cousin of Mom's. My brothers and I referred to her as 'Aunt Rebekah'. She was in her late fifties. She was retired from secretarial work, due to a work-related accident that practically blinded her. She'd lived in the same house for thirty years, and had no intention of moving. She was known for her fried chicken meals. Mention that, and maybe the President would show up for dinner. But to me, Aunt Rebekah was no Uncle Henry. I didn't care for her. Especially her grouchy ways and occasional outbursts, which always seemed to be directed toward me, even when it was Tony's fault. Randy and Tony were Aunt Rebekah's favorites.

Aunt Rebekah never had any kids of her own. Sam, Aunt Rebekah's late husband, had been dead for three years. From what I can remember, he was a nice guy. Whenever I was around him, he made me laugh. It was probably Aunt Rebekah's bitching that drove him to the heart attack that killed him. Mom told us that it bothered him that Aunt Rebekah couldn't have kids. Aunt Rebekah used to tell me she was glad she never had a son like me. To this day, I believe she's gay. Yeah, that's right, gay. I think her husband knew it, but never talked about it. Once, a few years ago when Uncle Sam was out of town visiting his cousin, the three of us spent the night with Aunt Rebekah. It was very late at night. I could never sleep sound there because I was never totally comfortable. Randy and Tony were sound asleep in the extra bedroom, while I laid awake on the living room sofa. The living room was adjacent to Aunt Rebekah's bedroom. I heard the front door open and saw this large silhouette of a woman storm into Aunt Rebekah's bedroom. A fierce argument began. I could hear three voices. After about ten minutes, a smaller woman came out of Aunt Rebekah's bedroom in a hurry. She struggled with the door before she left. The only people left in Aunt Rebekah's room were the large woman and Aunt Rebekah. It got really quiet. I tiptoed to her door and peeked through the keyhole. I was right. The light was dim, but I could see the two of them kissing. I still couldn't see the other woman's face. I went back to the sofa. I tried to stay awake to get a look at her, but I dozed off. She must have left before I woke up. I do remember vaguely someone coming to the sofa that night and rubbing my back. Whoever it was had a rough hand.

"Okay, boys, are you ready?" Sara said as she made her way from the kitchen to Randy's room, where Randy and Tony were.

Randy and Tony were ready and armed with their school books. They followed Sara out of the kitchen back door. For Tony, it would be an evening of freedom. Aunt Rebekah iet Tony do whatever he wanted, even if it meant she would have some cleaning to do after he left.

Elm Street was a one-way street that spilled onto Grand Street. They stopped in front of number eighteen, a red, three story, brick house. Most of the houses on the block matched the plain style of Aunt Rebekah's on the quiet block.

Randy and Tony ran up the red wooden steps that led to the front door. Tony rang the doorbell repeatedly. Finally, Aunt Rebekah showed up at the door and opened it.

Sara blew the horn twice, waved goodbye to them and drove off.

For Sara that day Aunt Rebekah was a lifesaver. The stop she had to make she needed to make alone, and without anyone else's knowledge. She took a left onto Grand Street and stopped at the red light on Grand and Madison Avenue. The Avenue was actually the lower two blocks of Madison Avenue. On these two blocks were drug dealers, liquor stores, homeless people and prostitutes who occasionally came to pick up a trick.

Jim would come to the Avenue sometimes to hang out with old friends near the local bar called 'Dee's'. It was a hot spot most of the time, but it slowed down during the daytime hours.

Sara wasn't really worried about seeing Jim. As a matter of

fact, it would be sort of a relief if she saw him, then she would know where he was. She could always lie and say she'd been somewhere other than where she was really headed. After a minute at the stoplight at the foot of Madison Avenue, she turned onto South Pearl, headed north toward the business section of town. She glanced at her watch, which said 4:15, and knew she was losing time. She sped up, beating two lights before they turned red. She stopped at Pearl Street and Wilson Street.

She took a left and pulled into an open space. She took the space from an oncoming car, but apologized with a wave and a big smile.

Sara quickly parked and got out. She headed toward the Adoption Agency at 17 Wilson Street. She hustled through the double doors and began looking at the office listing on the wall directory. She couldn't find what she was looking for.

She went to the receptionist's desk that was toward the center of the hallway. The receptionist was a woman in her early fifties.

"Yes, may I help you?" the receptionist asked.

"I would like to find out who I need to speak to about finding my son." The receptionist pointed down the hall.

Sara walked down the hall and up the stairs to room 217. The lights were bright in the hallway of the second floor. There were a few people milling about, but most everyone was preparing for five-thirty to come so they could go home.

"Hello, I'm Sara Harris," she said to the secretary who opened the door.

"Yes, can I help you?"

"I gave my child up for adoption several years ago, and I wanted to find out where he is."

The secretary, Casey, was a jovial woman in her forties. Casey never wore makeup. To her, beauty came from within and worked its way out, and for anyone who didn't see it, they were the ones who lost out. She believed she could add another piece of quality clothing to her wardrobe instead of wasting money on makeup. Casey kept herself in good physical condition. Her cream colored, long sleeve silk blouse was kept buttoned at the collar. Her black, loose fitting skirt fell an inch below her knees. The click from the heel of her black, three-inch pumps was loud because she walked fast and heavy. She had a soft, rich voice.

"Feeling a little remorseful, huh?" she said as Sara followed her to an empty couch where she motioned for Sara to sit.

"How long has it been, honey?" Casey asked.

Sara didn't care for all of the questions initially but figured the lady was only being nosey because she didn't have anything else to talk about. After all what else went on in this office?

"About twenty-five years," Sara said.

"Wow, is this the first time you're checking?"

"Well, I started to after about seven years, but I never followed up."

"Yeah, you weren't too far off then. It's usually after about five or six years when the biological parents get itchy. Been havin' bad dreams about him? Oh, you did say it was a boy, right?"

"Yeah, he's twenty-five now. If he's still alive," Sara said.

"Mr. Linton is on the phone right now. As soon as he gets off, I'll tell him you're here."

"Oh, my name is Casey. And you're?"

"Sara Harris."

"Nice to meet you, Ms. Harris."

"That's Mrs. Harris," Sara said.

"Okay, *Mrs.* Harris. You can call me *Mrs.* Casey," Casey said, with huge laughter. Sara only etched a short smile, straining to join in on the humor.

Casey reached around her desk to shake Sara's hand, then sat back down after doing so. Casey began shuffling papers at her desk, then glanced at her watch. It said 4:30. Casey got up and knocked on Mr. Linton's door, then gently opened it.

"You have someone waiting," Casey whispered.

Mr. Linton motioned that he'd be right with her. Just as Casey closed the door, Mr. Linton was out of his seat and opening it back up. Casey sat in her chair and made introductions, with charisma.

"Mr. Linton, Mrs. Harris." Casey went back to her paper shuffling.

Mr. Linton's phone rang again.

"Excuse me," Mr. Linton said as he darted back into his office.

Casey purposely dropped papers on the floor near Sara, then went around her desk to pick them up.

"I know what you want, but you'll never get it out of him— plays strictly by the rules," Casey whispered.

Mr. Linton stood at the door of his office and called Sara.

"Mrs. Harris, you can come in now."

"Don't let that handsome charm fool you," Casey said, barely audible to Sara. Mr. Linton was an attractive man in his early thirties.

Mr. Linton had a big smile on his face as Sara entered his

office. She sat in the cushioned chair that faced his desk. She noticed a lone plaque on the wall that had his Masters degree from Columbia University. He closed the door behind her

Mr. Linton took his seat behind his desk. His attitude was of royalty. He believed he worked hard to get to this position, and he acted the part. He wore a dark green, wool suit with a flashy green tie. He always wore a white cotton long-sleeved shirt. His black leather belt matched his shiny black leather wingtip loafers. He pulled up his black nylon socks. He believed he had the best job in the world.

The office was plain looking and small, and the sunlight coming through the blinds brightened the room, but not enough to take away the dullness of the old steel green desk. After making sure his desk was in neat order, he spoke.

"Now, what can I do for you, Mrs. Harris?" Mr. Linton said, slow and deliberate.

"Well, a number of years ago I gave up my son for adoption and now I would like to contact him."

Mr. Linton stood, as always erect with his nose in the air, and began to pace about the room as if he were giving a speech that he had repeated many times before.

"Mrs. Harris, first, how long ago are we talking?"

"Twenty-five years, at least."

Mr. Linton paused in his pace, then started again. He admired himself while doing so. "That's a long time ago. Even if we do still have the records, which I'm quite sure we do somewhere around here, it's against the law to open sealed files leading to the whereabouts of adopted children."

"Isn't there any way for you to bypass the rules for special occasions?"

"The only occasions are for death and inheritance purposes. Official documents must be provided in both cases."

"And there's no other way?"

"I'm sorry, Mrs. Harris. I wish I could be more help to you," Mr. Linton said as he went to his office door and opened it for Sara.

Sara sadly rose from her seat and left the room. Casey shook her head. She too was sad at another failed attempt by a lost parent trying to locate her child.

"Casey, please come into my office."

Mr. Linton slammed the door and yelled at her.

"I have told you time and time again to screen these people. I do not have time to baby and pamper people who have 'sold' their children and now want them back."

The yelling faded as Sara walked further away from the door. She had nowhere else to turn, and realized she'd never find out where her son was. She resigned to the fact that she'd made a mistake in giving up her son, whose name she didn't even know. At least she still had her other three boys, even if she thought one was a little different. However, she was still hurt from the emptiness she felt for giving up her first child, and not knowing if he was dead or alive.

CHAPTER THIRTY-NINE

HENRY DROPPED COREY OFF at home with the bucket of fish they caught at Ravena Lake. No matter how hard he tried to forget Corey's words regarding Sally B, they rang loud and clear in his mind as he sat on a stool at Bruce Banes' restaurant. Banes and his wife, Ella, were hustling about as usual, getting to-go orders.

Henry had his hand on his chin in thought. Banes closed the cash register from a sale.

"Okay, thanks," Banes said to the departing customer. The customer waved goodbye as he walked out.

Banes went towards Henry and stared at him. Henry never even blinked.

"Wow, you are in a different time zone this evening," Banes said to him. Banes even whistled in front of him to snap him out of it.

"What? Oh, what is it?" Henry said.

"Banes, what do you know about that guy Justin who comes in here occasionally?"

"I know him. Him and Sally B sat in that corner booth for a few hours talking the last time I saw him."

"What booth?"

Banes nodded to the corner booth, farthest from the front door.

"You remember, you were sitting with Sally B first, then he came in."

"What kind of work does he do?"

"I don't ask and he don't tell. Why you ask?"

"Oh, just checking."

"Well, why are you checking? That girl in trouble or something? He comes in here, eats and leaves. The only words he says are what he wants to eat."

Banes leaned in close to whisper to Henry. Then he looked around, making sure his wife wasn't within earshot.

"From what I hear, he might be into some illegal stuff."

"Like what?" Henry asked, curiously.

"No idea. He's just too quiet for me.

"Is he always alone?"

"Mostly. Sometimes he'll come in with a stranger."

"Yeah?"

"Yeah, like one day he came in with this Asian girl."

"Who was she?"

"Never mentioned any names." Banes realized he was talking a little too much.

"Wonder if he has any relatives or anyone close to him here?"

"Told me he only had two real relatives up here."

"Yeah? Who?"

"Why you askin' so many questions about him?"

"Oh, come on, Banes you wanna know just as bad as I do."

"Look, I'm just fillin' in the blanks for you. I don't know much about him at all," Banes said with laughter.

"Oh, come on, Banes this is serious," Henry said, chuckling. "Tell me about the guy."

"All I know is what little he tells me and what I see. One day I see a kid, the next time I don't. What am I suppose to make something of it? No. You're making a big deal outta nothing. Now quit asking me so many questions about this guy. Go get laid or something."

They both chuckled.

Henry was persistent.

"What was he doing with an Asian, I wonder?"

"Ohhhh!" Banes said in a joking manner.

A female voice yelled out from the kitchen. "Banes, while you're standing there talking, people are waiting for orders."

Banes looked up at the line of five customers waiting for their orders that were piled on the kitchen window.

"Henry I gotta get these orders. Lemme talk to you later."

Banes put on his fun-loving smile and went back to his customers, who were patiently waiting.

"Hey, good things come to those who wait," Banes said to his first customer, with a smile.

"Yeah, and when we get home tonight, I'm gonna see how long you're gonna wait to get some," Ella said from the kitchen, drawing howls of laughter from the customers.

Henry chuckled and waved at Banes as he left the restaurant. "Let me get right back to you. I gotta make one call," Banes said as he went to the phone on the other end of the counter.

He picked up the receiver and dialed a number. It rang once

and a male voice answered. He got into a secretive stance before he spoke, turning his back to the customers.

"Friend of mine came in asking questions about you, Justin."

"Like what?"

"Just about how often you come here. Who's with you. Do you have family here. Stuff like that. But I didn't tell him anything."

"Who was it?"

"Henry You might know him. He's Jim's brother-in-law."

"That's all?"

"Well, there is something else."

"What's that?"

"We've been working together for a long time now, right?"

"Right, right."

"Don't you think it's about time for a raise? After all, I've put you with some very good people, politically."

"Banes, don't get greedy. You've done very well by me--"

"Yes, that's true, and you've benefitted a great deal because of my contacts—"

"And I've paid out great sums of money, Banes. Don't do this."

"I just can't remember the last raise you've given me. Cost of living goes up every day."

"Yes, the cost of living does go up, doesn't it."

"Now, I always keep my mouth shut, and I always will. But, it would make me happier knowing that as you got richer, you'd take care of the people who keep quiet for you. See what I'm saying?"

"Don't worry, I'll take care of you," Justin said as he hung up. Banes hung up with a smile, but unsure.

"Banes, what are you doin'? C'mon now, we got work to do. Who's so important on that phone?"

Support for Ella was heard from the customers seconding her pleas to get back to work. Banes hung up and smiled.

"Okay, here I come." He looked through the kitchen window and pointed to Ella.

"I love you, sweetie."

She frowned and banged on the tin counter of the kitchen window, signaling for him to get the orders out.

CHAPTER FORTY

I WAS IN THE KITCHEN with Mom. I stood in front of the stove, monitoring the fish that was frying in the fryer.

My thinking was that Mom really was pondering hard about something, but I'm not sure what. She was awful quiet.

"Mom, why are you so quiet?"

"Oh, nothing, just thinking."

"About what?"

"About your eye and letting you go back to school tomorrow."

"School, oh, Mom."

"Oh, Mom, what?"

"I just think I'm better than that school. I mean, I get A's without studying and I've already skipped the second grade."

"Well, we're working on getting you into a better school. But you better be thankful you're in that school. Do you realize how many people are waiting in line to get in Cathedral?"

"Maybe we can give somebody my spot and I'll teach."

Mom frowned, but then smiled.

"Just a joke, Mom."

"Awful cocky, aren't you?"

"No, just confident. That's what you taught me."

"Wish ya brothers would catch on."

"They're all right. They just do what they have to do. Randy, he studies, but none of us really likes school. You know how that is, we'd all rather be somewhere playing video games."

"I know you would."

Mom and I had grown silent for a moment as I turned the fish. She then dumped the fish into flour. I think she knew that I was going to ask her more questions; questions that she didn't want to answer. I stopped her from dumping more fish in the brown grocery-size paper bag with the flour.

"Mom, I need to re-season that."

Mom stopped in mid-stroke, took the fish she had in her hands and put it back on the kitchen sink with the other uncooked fish. Then she leaned on the kitchen sink, rather sadly.

I promptly mixed my oregano, garlic powder, salt, pepper, hot'n spicy seasoned salt, paprika and celery salt. I dumped a cup full of this in a small bowl and added a tad of Louisiana hot sauce. I mixed it, stirred it, then poured it in the flour bag.

"Now you can pour the fish in, Mom."

She poured the remaining five pieces of fish into the flour bag, closed the bag up and shook it several times.

I went back to the fish in the fryer. It was getting brown, so I turned it again.

"Mom, what's going on with the guy upstairs?"

Mom didn't stop cleaning the sink, but she slowed down a bit. She was wiping it with a sponge.

"What do you mean?"

"I mean, like what does he do? I hardly ever see him."

She turned and faced me, and leaned on the sink with both of her hands, tightly gripping it.

"Well, I really don't know much about him. He's in and out all the time."

She turned around and started back to cleaning the sink.

"Mom!"

She turned back toward me in a snap.

"He pays the rent and doesn't start any trouble and that's all that matters. Now leave it alone, Corey."

She was upset by my questioning. She grabbed the white dish-cloth from my hand and stormed into her bedroom.

I took the fish I had in the fryer and checked to see if it was done. I looked at it, used the long fork to take it out and laid it in the bowl that was lined with paper towels to soak up the vegetable oil. I gently laid the fork on the stove, took a quiet, deep breath and went to Mom's bedroom doorway. She slouched on the edge of the bed with her head hung down.

"Mom, are you all right?"

She didn't say a word. By looking at her posture, I knew she was feeling bad. She didn't need to answer. I slowly walked in and sat next to her.

"Mom, what is it? Tell me! I hate to see you like this."

A lone tear rolled down her face.

"It's that Justin, isn't it? I know it is, Mom."

I was angry and had to tell Mom what I'd seen.

"Mom, I saw him."

"What?"

"Justin carrying a black bag out from upstairs. I know it was that kid that I saw who was crying. I know it, Mom . . ."

Mom was shocked at what she was hearing. She turned to me, covered my mouth and put my head on her chest.

"Don't say anymore, Corey, please," she said in fear.

I tried to lift my head, but Mom had a tight grip.

"Don't, Corey, not another word. No, Corey, stay out of it. Just leave it alone. There's a lot going on that you don't understand."

I stood frustrated because she wouldn't tell me. Mom sat.

"Like what, Mom, what's so hard to understand? That you and Dats owe this man a thousand dollars?"

Mom jumped to her feet, towering over me, angry.

"Where did you hear that from, Uncle Henry?"

I just stared blankly for a minute, thinking carefully about my next words, because I didn't want to get Uncle Henry in trouble. That minute seemed like an eternity to Mom because she took both of her hands, grabbed me by my shoulders and started to shake me hard back and forth.

"Did you hear what I asked you, Corey, huh? How did you know that?"

"Mom... Mom... Mom. Okay, okay, stop!" I yelled. Mom stopped shaking me and stood there, waiting for an explanation.

"I listened at the door while you and Dats were talking to Uncle Henry."

"I'm sending you over to Aunt Rebekah's with Randy and Tony. All you want to do is sit around and listen to grown folks talk. I'm sick of it. Just like an old hag."

"Mom, please, I don't wanna go over there. I can never get any homework done over there."

"Homework! You haven't been in school for almost a week. And when's the last time you did some homework?"

"But I'm behind and I gotta catch up with the rest of the class," I said, trying to get her to have sympathy for me.

"Don't give me that pitiful look. It don't mean a hilla beans to me!"

Mom moved away from me, with a slight grin. Even though she was still a little upset, her grin was a sign that she wouldn't send me to the witch's house. Really though, Aunt Rebekah was an okay person to herself and Tony and Randy, I guess. But to me, she had this attitude. It was like she was out to get me. Everyone must have at least one aunt or uncle who just didn't seem to get along with them. Simple things, like when it came time to eat at her house, she would let Randy and Tony fix their own plate, but she always fixed my plate. I would try to trick her by moving my plate around, because she was practically blind. That really irritated her. Then she would monitor how much food I ate. She said she was just making sure I didn't waste any. But Randy and Tony threw piles of it away, then she would offer them more. Sometimes I felt like the cat that I cooked. I used to kick it around for no reason, just because it was there. Because of what had been going on, I knew how it felt. I hoped Aunt Rebekah didn't have thoughts of cutting me up and feeding me to the dogs.

Mom's tear had dried up by then.

"Mom, is everything gonna be okay?"

"Yes, Corey, we'll be just fine."

"I'm gonna get back to the fish, Mom. When's Dats coming back? I wanna be finished before he gets home."

Mom glanced at the clock inside the shelf of the bed head-board. It read 6:00. I knew Mom and Dats weren't going to be all right. I wasn't some kid she could just tell that and I'd go away and forget it. Nope, I decided to do something. Besides, I thought Justin might lead me to the answer of some of my own questions. I wondered if I should get Uncle Henry to help me or just go solo. With him, if we got caught by Justin, I wouldn't get hurt. Without him, what if he kidnapped me and killed me? I needed to think about it.

"Your father should be home soon, Corey."

Mom looked at the floor as if she were looking for Max, our missing cat.

"Corey, have you seen Max yet?"

"No, he's probably found another home."

I'm sick of this. I wish I could find another home. This one sucks. I hate it here. As soon as I find the idiot I'm looking for, I'm outta here. It stinks! My life is shit and I've got nobody to turn to.

CHAPTER FORTY-ONE

JIM HAD BEEN DRIVING for the better part of two hours on the New York State thruway. He'd gotten off at exit 17, into White Plains, New York.

He drove up the single lane road, headed toward the Brookbridge Nursing Home. He stopped at the security guard gate. The armed guard's quarters were made with solid stone. In front was a large window that circled around the entire octagon-shaped building. The guard could see from every angle, except the roof, with his naked eye. The surveillance camera allowed him to see his roof. These cameras were positioned throughout the surrounding ten-acre area. The eight foot high stone wall surrounded the entire area. It was hard to notice the walls around the place in the back because there was enough shrubbery to help decorate it.

The guard and the camera weren't used to keep people locked

in or monitored, but for security. This was part of what the high price tag that came with the place paid for.

"Yes, sir, can I help you, sir?" the young, husky, blue uniformed guard said enthusiastically, yet with a serious tone. He moved toward Jim's driver side, carrying a clipboard and ink pen.

"Yes, I'm here to see Mrs. Jackie Harris," Jim said, with a forced half smile.

The guard jotted down Jim's license plate, then gave him a blue parking pass. There was a different color pass for each day and all three shifts. There was a guard on duty twenty-four hours a day, seven days a week.

"Put this on your windshield and park in the lot to the right of the building, please, sir. Do you know where to go?"

"Yes, thanks," Jim said as he passed a road sign that read 'five miles per hour'. Jim adhered to the speed limit. He looked on both sides of the wide blacktop road. He always enjoyed looking at the beautifully manicured lawns that surrounded the mansion-size home. There were benches for lounging throughout the lawns, positioned under trees. There was an old couple sitting under a tree on a blanket watching as Jim drove by. That was what Jim wanted for his mother, and why he continued to deal with the likes of Justin. Jim had seen his mother in a less-equipped nursing home, and swore to her and himself that he would do better for her no matter what the cost, and he had paid dearly in his association with Justin Lord.

In the center, in front of the large building that housed about one hundred people, was a ten foot high marble water fountain with smaller spouts surrounding it. Water flowed from the top and from each marble spout.

Jim admired the master crafting it took to construct such a piece of artwork. The large mansion was an old Elizabethan house from the 1800's that was renovated and expanded upon. It came equipped with the latest in technology, from room-to-room speaker phones to automated carriage service, for those who found it difficult to get from one room to the next.

Jim parked his car in the lined space designated for visitors. On the opposite side of the building was assigned parking for the residents.

Jim had supplied his mother with the very best in nursing care. Her medical bills were all paid in advance for the year, which is why it was hard for him to use the money he made from Justin to get ahead. And there was a possibility that it would all come to an end. An end that was inevitable.

"Does she know you're coming?"

"No, I'm surprising her."

"Your name, sir?"

"Jim Harris. I'm her son."

"I'm gonna have to call her first."

"Sure."

The guard dialed the number 110 for her room. The phone rang twice.

"Hello, Mrs. Harris. You have a visitor. A Mr. Jim Harris," the guard said loudly. Not because Jackie couldn't hear that well, but because a lot of other residents couldn't hear well and so he made it a habit to speak loud and clear whenever he called or spoke to one of the elderly residents.

"Okay, thank you."

"I'm doing fine. How about you? Good. Yes, the family's okay, thanks. Right. I'll send him right in. Bye."

The guard hung the receiver up with a smile. Most of the elderly people were always eager to talk, since they never had regular visitors. The security guards knew this, and always tried to be cordial.

Jim casually got out of his car and walked around to the front of the building. He looked up at the sky. The sun was beginning to set. Shadows were cast everywhere against the trees and buildings, which made the place that much more enticing. As he opened the glass double door leading to the large hallway, he thought about how he wished he could live in such surroundings. A guard on a motor tram stopped in front of the building and watched Jim as he entered. All guests had to report to the reception area.

Jim approached the marble encasement where the armed guard sat behind a window. No one could get beyond this point unless the guard let them in.

"Hello, I'm here to see Jackie Harris!" Jim said through the opened window.

The older guard stayed seated in his swivel chair, only shifting his eyes up from the book he was reading to glance at Jim. The counter he sat in front of, surrounding the encasing, had control panels for every door that wasn't guarded. These doors could be automatically locked and unlocked from this panel. You could see every stairwell and every hallway that existed in the building. Even the janitor's quarters, indoor Olympic-size swimming pool, two indoor tennis courts, large exercise room, dining hall and the basement were monitored. This monitoring was all for the safety of the residents. The feel of the place was one of a year-round secured resort.

"Your mom loves to talk. She's a real nice lady."

"Thanks."

The guard pushed the button to the east end glass door that opened to the right of the guard's quarters. The guard waved and immediately put his head back down and began reading his book.

The mansion was separated into three floors. The first and second had a north, south, east and west end, with each having ten very comfortable six hundred square foot rooms. Each were fully equipped with a living room, dining room, bedroom and kitchen. The third floor consisted of twenty suites. These were twelve hundred square feet each. They were for anyone who could afford them.

The nursing home was full to capacity, and a three-page waiting list was kept. The wait usually wasn't that long for someone to move in because at least one elderly person died per month.

Jim slowly walked down the well-lit hallway. He admired paintings that partially lined the walls. There was an elderly couple riding in a two-seat, automated tram that resembled a golf cart. It ran no faster than five miles per hour, and didn't use much gas. It could take them anywhere on the ten acres. As the tram got further down the hall, all you could hear was the echo of Jim's shoes hitting against the marbled floor.

The light of dusk shone through the window at the end of the hall he was approaching. Each room was sequentially numbered. The right side of the hall had even numbers and the left side had odd numbered apartments. He got to apartment 110 and knocked on the door three times.

"Oh, come on in, who else would be coming in here, boy?"

Jim slowly walked in and looked around. The place was in immaculate condition. Jackie, Jim's mother, sat in her black leather reclining chair in the living room, watching television.

"Mama, you look great. Your face looks like you lost some weight." She waved her hand at Jim with an appreciative smile.

"Yeah, a pound or two."

"That's good, the more you lose the better to keep your blood pressure down." Jim looked at Jackie's navy blue and white polka dot rayon dress.

"That's the dress I bought you."

"Sure is. Got another for me?" she said with a smile.

"Stand up, let me look at you."

She stood up with Jim's help. Jim took two steps back, admiring her smaller body. He smiled, even though she was still overweight.

"Gimme a hug, Mama."

They embraced cheerfully.

"Now, can I sit down before I fall down?" Jackie asked with a smile.

"Sure, let me help you." Jim ushered her back in her favorite chain. She took a deep breath.

Jim looked at a new picture on the wall of Martin Luther King, Jr.

"Who gave you the picture, Mama?"

"Oh, a friend down the hall. He's trying to get me to take a tram ride with him, but I'm playing hard to get."

"That's why you're losing weight. You can't fool me." Jackie raised her eyebrows and smiled.

"Is he a nice guy?"

"He's okay. Oh, don't worry about that. Come over here and give me a hug," Jackie said with outstretched arms from her recliner.

He went and gave her a kiss on the cheek and a hug.

"You should have told me you were coming. I would have had the cook prepare something. Our night shift chef is coming on duty. I can still order something for you."

He walked around, checking to make sure everything that he'd been paying for was in order.

"No, that's all right, Mama. I'm not hungry"

He walked over to the terrace and stood by the dark green, steel, short railing. He was impressed by the greenery and the neatness, once again.

"Mama, you sure live good."

"That's what you want, right?"

"Yeah."

"It does beat that other place I was in by leaps and bounds."

Jackie turned up the volume on the television to hear Jeopardy's Alex Trebeck give an answer.

"The Greek town where the first Olympic competition was held." Then a bell was heard from one of the contestants. Then a click was heard as the screen went blank, because Jackie had turned the television off.

"Ah, who cares," Jackie said, then she put the remote on her lap.

"So, what'd you come all this way for without calling me?"

"How's the medication?"

"Poison, as usual."

"Everybody treating you okay?"

"Like a queen."

"Getting along fine with everyone?"

"Except for that guy down the hall who's trying to get my 'money pie'. There's this other gal down the hall there. She must be sixty or so, but she looks more like forty-five. She's hot on him like a six-shooter on openin' day of huntin' season. Says he don't want her though, because she don't have the personality like me," Jackie said with laughter. "Isn't that something? I still haven't lost my touch."

Jim smiled and sat on the new, navy blue velvet sofa. There was a knock on the door.

"It must be him now. He probably heard you walking down here. And talk about jealous. Might have to wind up giving him 'some'. I don't want the poor man to go crazy over me," Jackie laughed.

"Well, go open the door for me, son." Jim walked briskly to open the door.

To his amazement, there stood an elderly woman with light brown, Indian-like skin that glowed. Her body was very curvy for an older woman with bowed legs, and she wore a somewhat tight black short-sleeved dress that opened at the collar, where cleavage showed just a tad above where her wrinkles began. Jim was impressed.

"Oh, hi" Jim said. "You must be Molly. I hear you're the only one in this building who makes most men have a heart attack." Molly smiled.

"Well, come on in, Molly. This is my son, Jim. Jim meet Molly."

He extended his hand to shake with Molly. Her touch was not as soft and delicate as her looks would indicate. Jim looked at her hands, and was a bit shocked to see they were very wrinkled.

Jim ushered Molly into the living room. In Molly's left hand was a saucer, with aluminum foil covering it. Her youthful looks didn't resemble her slow, slurred speech.

"I just finished baking this chocolate cake, and I know you like chocolate," Molly said.

"See, son, I told you, she's gonna kill me yet. She knows I'm not supposed to eat sweets like this with my diabetes. She's just trying to get me outta the way for that man so he'll go after her."

Molly started to smile.

"But I'll take it anyway."

"It only has a little sugar!" Molly said. She put the cake on the kitchen counter. "Well, I'm gonna leave you to your son."

Molly turned to Jim and extended her hand to shake. He gladly complied.

"Nice to have met you, Jim," Molly said with a smile.

Molly left the room, and Jim couldn't help but notice her sway as she walked. She closed the door gently.

"Mama, how many face lifts has she had?" Jim asked in a low tone.

"Now, now, it's all her."

"She's beautiful," Jim said.

"Uh-huh, but did you see those hands? Rougher than the roughest spot on an alligator."

They both laughed hysterically. After they both stopped and settled back down, Jackie pressed Jim.

"So Jim, what is it?"

"What?"

"Now don't act dumb. I raised you better than that."

Jim leaned back on the sofa.

"Mama, I've got a problem."

"Um-hm."

"But I don't want to make my problem your problem."

"Yes, ya do or you wouldn't have come. Now speak up, boy."

"Mama, if you had to move from here, how would you feel?"

"I gotta go some time."

"No, I mean live somewhere a lot cheaper, maybe even moved in with us."

"No! I am not moving to Albany. I have more fun in my living room than I ever could in that whole city. No!"

"But it'd just be for a short while."

"Jim, what's wrong? You goin' broke or something?"

He sighed a deep breath.

"It's more complicated than that. The guy I'm working with may not be around much longer, and I might have to cut back on some things."

"Well, I'll move, but I won't move to Albany."

"But Mama, you'd be safer with me."

"Safer? And why don't you just get another job?"

"But I have a job already. I'm just making some extra money on the side, and this guy I'm working with might leave or . . . or even die."

Jackie looked at him with suspecting eyes.

"What kind of trouble are you in, Jimmy?"

She hadn't called him Jimmy in about twenty years, since the last time he got into trouble in Brooklyn.

"This guy isn't the most savory customer. He's got money,

and money buys power. Look at where you live."

"I'm lookin'. How could you get caught up with people like this anyway? I'll move as long as the kids are all right."

"The kids are fine. Except . . ."

"Except what?" snapped Jackie.

"Except, you see, it's Corey."

Jackie's heart rate began to accelerate as she eyeballed Jim.

"What about Corey?" she asked sternly, with a hint of fear. Sweat beads mounted up on her forehead in soldier formation.

"Sara and I believe his life is in danger."

Her breathing began to speed up noticeably. Jim took her hand.

"Calm down, Mama. We're keeping a close eye on him."

She grabbed hold of his hand firmly. She began to hyperventilate uncontrollably.

"Mama, Mama, you all right?" Jim said, standing.

Jackie pointed toward her room.

"Pills . . . dra . . . draw . . ."

Jim ran to her spacious bedroom in a panic.

"Where?" Jim shouted, opening dresser drawers, rambling through them, still not finding her heart pills.

"Where, Mama, where?" he shouted.

Then he rummaged through the medicine cabinet off the living room, above the sink that was outside the bathroom. Jim looked near her bed and saw a pill bottle on her night table. He ran to it, grabbed the bottle and raced back to her.

"Here they are, Mama."

He tore open the top, threw the cap down and dumped the pills in his hand. He took out two and forced them into her mouth. She was almost out of breath.

"Mama, swallow it, please!"

Jim put her head in his arms and leaned her head back.

"Swallow, Mama, hurry please swallow."

She took a big gasp of air and swallowed the two pills. Jim held her head in his arms as she slowly began to catch her breath.

"I'm sorry Mama," he said, rocking her.

Jim gently laid her head on the recliner. She was unconscious. He got up from the arm of the chair and went to the remote control. He pressed the emergency button and went back and sat on the arm of the chair, this time he rubbed her hand vigorously, trying to help her gain consciousness.

Every room was equipped with an emergency remote control button. If pressed, this button alerted the nurses' station at the end of the hall. Jackie's was at the opposite end. There were two certified nurses on each floor, twenty-four hours a day, seven days a week. A doctor was on call at all times, in case one was needed.

The nurse arrived and used her staff key to hurriedly open the door. She was in her mid-thirties and average looking. She wore a white uniform dress. Her name was Jessica. She immediately took over upon entering the spacious apartment. Jim felt responsible and helpless as he paced nervously about the room while Jessica waved smelling salts to Jackie. She remained unconscious.

"Is there anything I can do?" Jim asked.

"Did she have anything in her mouth?"

"Yes, I tried to give her her heart pills."

"Dial this number, 777-DOC-A."

"An eight hundred number?" said a dumbfounded Jim.

"Did I say eight hundred? Just dial it."

Jessica feverishly continued to wave the salt under Jackie's nose. She was beginning to regain consciousness, although her breathing was erratic.

In minutes, two male paramedics dressed in blue uniforms had arrived with a stretcher. One quickly opened his medicine bag.

"Heart?" the one paramedic asked.

"Yes," Jessica answered.

With that information, the other paramedic promptly set up an instrument that gave out heart readings.

The one paramedic put an oxygen mask on Jackie to help her breathe better.

Jim was still pacing as he glanced at his mother lying on the floor, helpless, but alive. He rushed into Jackie's neatly decorated bedroom. He sat on her bed and glanced at the clock. It was 7:30 p.m. He picked up the receiver of the phone and frantically dialed a number. The phone rang four times before someone answered.

"Sara, good, you're home. Where were you?"

"I was . . ."

"Look, never mind. I'm down here at Mama's. I think she just had a heart attack.

Mom was at the wall phone near the kitchen entryway with her pants unzipped. She held the phone between her cheek and shoulder as she held her blue jeans at the waist to hold them up. She was shocked at the news.

I walked in from the backyard. I looked at Mom's unbuttoned jeans. Mom saw this and began to button up while she continued.

"Is she gonna be all right?" Mom asked.

Dats was speaking so loud that Mom had to move the receiver a few inches from her ear.

I began to key in to Mom's conversation.

"What's wrong, Mom?" I asked curiously.

Mom mouthed that it was Dats on the phone. She waved me off with her free hand. But I could tell something was wrong.

"The paramedics are here now and they are probably gonna take her to the hospital. Oh, the doctor just arrived. Perfect timing, took him ten minutes, get what you pay for." Jim had rambled this last sentence. He was nervous.

"What did you say, honey?" Mom asked.

"Oh, nothing," Jim said.

"Is that Dats?" I asked.

Mom nodded yes. This was of grave interest to me, because if he was two hours away, that would give me time to get upstairs.

"Love you, bye," Mom said sadly.

That was the first time I heard Mom tell Dats she loved him in a long time. She just stood and leaned on the wall, in thought. She had a look of hurt in her eyes as they began to water up. Mom didn't see Grandma as much as Dats, but when she did they always had a good time. I ran up to her.

"Mom, what's wrong?"

She closed her eyes for a second, trying to catch the tear.

"It's your grandmother, she's had a heart attack."

I was sad. I hugged Mom around her waist, rested my head on her stomach and began to cry.

Grandma was my favorite. She always talked to me, and when I wasn't doing too well, I always called her. The summer that followed after I first got molested, I stayed with her from the time I got out of school until it was time to return for fall. But I could never tell her what happened. All I knew was that I was safe with her, and I learned a lot about people and survival that summer. She taught me how to cook, sew, and she let me do things, within reason, that Mom and Dats wouldn't. I got to do things like go to the store for her. It was only five doors down the street from her old apartment, but it seemed like a long way to me. She knew she was taking a chance in letting me do that at six years old, and she knew I might get in a fight or two, but that was her way of making a survivor out of me. But the two fights I got into that summer, I kicked the shit out of 'em. I never stayed another summer, for one reason or another, but I did visit her occasionally with Dats or Mom. We always had a good time, but nothing like that summer we spent together.

"Is she gonna be all right, Mom?" Mom and I walked, embraced, into the living room.

"I hope so, Corey. Your father said they were taking her to the hospital."

"Is Dats staying with her?"

"Yes," Mom answered, as my eyes lit up beneath my sorrow.

It was very quiet in our house while Mom and I hugged each other, hoping the best for Grandma. My eyes shifted towards upstairs because I could hear a sound, like a bag or something was being dragged across the floor. Mom had to be able to hear the dragging too, but probably ignored it, hoping that I would do the same.

As much as I wanted to help Grandma, I knew I really couldn't. Besides, I think if she knew what had been happening to me over the past five years, she would tell me to find the bastard and get rid of whoever it was. That's exactly what I'm going to do. After all if it wasn't for all my suffering, poor Max would still be here. I miss you, Max.

CHAPTER FORTY-TWO

THERE WAS SOMETHING being dragged upstairs in Justin's apartment, all right. It was Angie's dead body. Sally B dragged it in a large, black, plastic garment-type bag. She had grown weary from the day's events, and decided it would be best for her to conserve her energy for when she would have to quickly carry the bag down the stairs and to her car, without anyone seeing her, especially Corey.

Sally B was in the kitchen. She let go of the bag, stood up and bent backwards to flex her back, exhaling deeply while doing so. She sat at the kitchen table, then her eyes became fixed on the black bag. She was in a daze.

Justin yanked open his bedroom door, which jolted Sally B. He had a lit Kool cigarette dangling from his lips. He coughed a couple of times from the smoke. He stood and looked at the black bag near his bedroom door, then looked over at Sally B as he slouched. She was surprised to see him with a cigarette. He was never a regular smoker, only lighting one up when he was really nervous. This was the only sign that Justin exhibited indicating any emotional disturbances. Sally B was the only one who knew this. She knew things were making him uptight.

"What's wrong?" Justin asked.

"You tell me," she replied as she flicked her head up wearily, motioning with her finger like she was holding a cigarette.

Justin snatched the cigarette out of his mouth, stepped over the black bag, and walked by Sally B towards the kitchen back door.

"I got a call a little while ago from Banes. He told me Henry was asking questions about me."

There was silence for a moment. Justin put the cigarette back into his mouth and went to the stove near the refrigerator. He turned it on and proceeded to light his cigarette without looking. Sally B watched him, noticing it was already lit.

"It's already lit, Justin."

Justin's mind was elsewhere. He walked away from the stove and back to the kitchen door window, peering out. Sally B reached around from her kitchen table seat and turned it off.

"I do business with people all over the world, and the thought of them questioning me or my business could get them killed. Now I get some stupid port banana boat loader asking about me'n my business. And that's not even the worst of it," Justin said, pausing. "Banes threatened me."

"How? What did he say?"

"Implied that if I didn't give him a raise he would expose me."

"What!" Sally B said. She knew Banes had signed his death sentence.

"Said the cost of his living was going up and he needed more money."

"So what are you gonna do?"

"Pay 'em."

Sally B nodded, but she knew Justin wouldn't take being bullied.

"Take care of things. I gotta make a few calls," Justin said.

Justin walked toward the door to leave. He looked at the body, blew smoke, dropped the half-smoked cigarette and stomped it out. He pointed down at Angie's body.

"Look, take care of that. I'll be back later."

Justin turned the doorknob and opened it with a strong yank. He stuck his head back in the door, looked at Sally B and began to sing.

"Can ya handle it, wooo, but can you handle it . . ."

He slowly closed the door on his last words as Sally B shook her head, wondering when he would snap and all hell would break loose.

I'd heard footsteps from the basement as I sat in my eavesdropping chair. I turned off the room light and got up on my knees in the chair. Then I leaned over to the window, perched my elbows on the shelf area in front of the window to get comfortable and peeked out one of the blinds. I slowly opened one blind to a small crack. The front door slammed shut. I saw Justin's feet making their way to the middle walk area of the stairs. Then he paused, looked around and walked the remaining six wooden stairs to the ground. Although he had on hard black leather shoes, he made sure to walk lightly around the corner toward his car. Since I saw he was gone, I cracked the blind open a little further and bang!

"Having fun watching me?" Justin said as he knelt down to the basement window, startling me.

I let the blind go and fell back into the chair. He began to laugh loudly. The laughter became faint as he walked away. He had outsmarted me. I caught my breath and shot out the basement door, then ran up the stairs. I wanted to get a good look at the car he was driving. I got to the top of the stairs and didn't see Mom. I slowed my pace, then I was steadfast to the living room window. I ran to the window on the Myrtle Avenue side. He was stopped at the corner of Myrtle Avenue and Grand, letting a car pass by. Well, at least I thought he was gonna let him pass by. At the last minute, just missing impact, Justin accelerated as he made a right turn. The other driver of the car slammed on his brakes and waved his hand furiously toward Justin as he sped away. I swiftly moved to the Grand Street front window to see if Justin was turning up Park Avenue. He was.

"Asshole."

"What was that you said, young man?" Mom said, standing at the living room entrance. I was surprised and had to cover, but then I decided not to lie.

"I was calling that Justin guy an asshole for cutting that car off."

Mom's eyes got big, and she stroved toward me with her hand raised. I covered up. At the last second, she grabbed the string to the blinds and opened them to see where Justin was.

"You watch your mouth."

Then she turned toward me.

"Look, Corey, you stay away from that man. What he does is his business. He doesn't bother anyone."

She started back toward the kitchen.

"Yeah, except kids," I said under my breath.

I didn't realize it, but Mom had that mother hearing. She returned to the living room.

"What was that about kids?"

"I think he mistreats kids."

She was getting irritated. She pointed her index finger in my face.

"What you think and what you know are two different things. And until you know, keep your mouth shut. Understood?"

"Yes, Mom."

Mom left the living room. I plopped down into Dats' favorite chair and slouched, while reaching for the remote on the lamp table that separated his chair from the love seat. I laid my finger on the channel changer and the stations continued to shift from one to the next.

"Corey," Mom yelled from the kitchen.

I put the remote down and looked at her standing in the kitchen doorway.

"Yes?"

"You forgot to finish cleaning the kitchen. Wrap the fish in plastic and leave it out just in case your father decides to come home early in the morning. Oh, that reminds me, I need to call his job."

I reluctantly went to do my kitchen chores. My mind was on getting upstairs. My walk was defiant.

Mom picked up the phone and dialed Dats' work number.

"Hello, I'm calling for Jim Harris. May I speak to his supervisor? Well, any supervisor. Yes, Jim's mother has had a heart attack. He won't be in this evening."

I was at the kitchen sink with my hands in the sudsy water. I picked up a plate and washed it. Mom got off the phone.

"Okay, bye," she said, hanging up the phone.

"You goin' to see Grandma?"

"I don't know when, but soon. Maybe we'll all go if she survives. It's a good time to get away."

Mom walked back into her bedroom and closed the door behind her. I knew she wanted to get away from Albany to see Grandma, but also to avoid any contact with Justin. But if I'm not mistaken, he seemed like he'd know where to find us if we left. I looked up toward the ceiling, shook my head and said to myself, "tonight's the night."

I knew there were other kids being molested or even killed. If I could help stop one or two people responsible, then I would feel like I had done something to help, even if it cost me my life.

CHAPTER FORTY-THREE

IT WAS AFTER 9:00 and Justin was headed up Park Avenue. He stopped at the red light at Park and Delaware. There were two homeless men with grocery baskets from the Price Chopper on the corner, directly behind them. One of the panhandlers left his grocery cart and staggered to Justin's driver's side window.

"Gotta quarter, man?"

Justin rapidly waved the bad breath air coming from the panhandler. He dug in his pocket, pulled out a quarter and handed it to the man.

"That all ya got?"

Justin cut his eye and frowned, then made a swift right on red, leaving the man hanging. He made his drive north on Delaware Avenue a speedy one. He took a right, onto Arch Street going up a small hill onto what was known as Arbor Hill. Some parts of this area were very seedy, but mostly uptown was an okay area. Arbor Hill, like Bunker Hill, was where most of the fights took place. Justin drove past St. Joseph's school, which was then used as a boxing and recreation hall of sorts for the locals, or anyone who wanted to come in. It usually closed at seven or eight o'clock in the evening. Opposite St. Joseph's was a local basketball playground. The lights were still on and a couple of guys were playing two-on-two basketball. In a dark corner of the playground, two teens were huddled up, smoking pot. There was a card game going on with two men and a woman sitting on the small steel bleachers that were set on the boundaries of the basketball court. Music blared from a boom box being held by a teenager who stood at the gate entrance surrounding the court. A panhandler talked to himself and paced back and forth on the corner near the playground.

Justin drove to the fourth block of Swan Street and passed by an assortment of people, from pushers to hookers to crackheads to small-time pimps. They were lining both sides of the street and hovering around the most popular bar in Arbor Hill, Joe's Tavern. Justin slowed down as he approached the bar, then looked around. Almost at the end of the block, he pulled over and parked on the left side of the street in front of Banes' restaurant. Justin got out of his car, and as he entered the small restaurant, there were two men leaving.

"Yo, man, got dat dime," one of the patrons said, hoping for the right response. Justin could have walked to the side with him and bought a small hit of crack cocaine for ten dollars. He just looked the man's way and kept walking inside the restaurant.

Justin closed the door behind himself and discreetly made his way to the corner of the counter. He wanted to be out of earshot of Banes' wife, and away from the kitchen window where she could look and see him.

Banes finished up with a customer at the cash register. He smiled at the customer, then cut his eyes at Justin who scanned the menu, something he normally never did. There was another customer who was taking his order to go.

"I'll be right with you," Banes said to the customer.

Banes went down to the end of the counter where Justin sat. "Coffee?"

Justin's eyes gradually veered from the menu to Banes.

"We need to talk," Justin said softy, with a definite edge. This sent a chill through Banes' body.

"Okay, I'll be right with you."

"Your coffee's coming right up," Banes said a little louder.

Justin's eyes immediately went back toward the menu. Banes then went back to the other customer.

"Banes, c'mon, it's getting late," Ella said from the kitchen.

Banes looked at the clock above the front door. It read 9:40. They would close at 10:00.

"How many we got left out there, Honey?" Ella asked from the kitchen.

"Oh just a few," Banes said as he nervously glanced over at Justin.

Even Ella going over to Justin irritated him, but not as much as Banes.

He knew Justin thrived on secrecy, but Banes wasn't sure if he should pay more attention to Justin at certain times. This type of confusion would have surely gotten him killed if he wasn't careful. As far as Justin was concerned, the few dollars he made off of Banes from the prostitutes he sent to him were peanuts compared to what he was making in New York City. Justin was in deep thought, and Banes knew it. This made Banes nervous.

Justin was deciding whether Banes' legislative ties were strong enough to keep him working. You see, the Mayor was in complete control of the county legislature. Even though they used a voting system to decide issues, the Mayor got most of what he wanted enacted. He used some of the campaign donations that Justin bestowed upon him to fill the pockets of the necessary county legislators and other politicians.

Banes was an independent and he could swing to the Democratic or Republican side any time he wanted. He had the full support of Arbor Hill, and this was enough to keep him in office and kept a weekly check coming for the past two four-year terms. The check was only $250, but it was something.

To Justin, if Banes had ever decided to go over to the staunch Republican side, it would have been a blessing and he'd always have protection. The Democrats were easy because of the mayors they put into office. At least on the outside they were more understanding toward minorities. Whereas, for the Republicans, it was all about the dollar bill. Oh, the Democrats liked money too, but they used minorities to shield behind. The Republicans let you know they were about money right up front, and if you didn't have or potentially have it, you could join of course, but you'd be ignored until it was time to vote.

Justin always needed a front man. Banes was a good one and they both knew it. The question was, did Justin respect that enough to want to continue to work with him? Banes definitely wasn't making enough on his salary to afford a new Lincoln Continental every year. Nor was he making enough to afford the two bedroom house on an acre of land in Loudonville, New York. Banes needed Justin more than Justin needed him. The house was a ten to twenty minute drive, depending on where you're coming from in Albany. Loudonville was considered the upper crust section for people to live in. If you lived there, you had social status, not much compared to how Justin was living in New York, but status nonetheless.

You had to be a resident of Albany to be an Alderman and actually live in the ward, which is a small section of the county that each Alderman was responsible for. Banes covered this by listing the restaurant's address. On the second floor of the restaurant was an apartment that Banes and his wife used occasionally, but only to cover themselves because of Banes' political career.

Justin looked at Banes who stood at the cash register tending to a customer. Banes glanced his way and Justin, with a light nod of his head, motioned for Banes to come to him.

Banes finished with the customer and motioned with his index finger for the next customer in line to wait a minute. He feigned like he was going to check on the coffee pot that sat on the counter on a hot plate across from Justin. Banes turned the heat down low. He then turned toward Justin and leaned down to get a cup from the shelf on the rack stand behind the counter. It stood about three feet high and was full of clean glasses and coffee cups.

"Meet me at the Hudson," Justin said, barely audible.

Banes didn't even look Justin's way, but he heard what he said and knew what the next question was: Was he going to meet him? Justin got up and left the restaurant abruptly. Banes went back to one of the two final customers at the cash register.

Banes knew the time would be midnight, just like the prior two times they met there for Justin to pay him off.

Ella wasn't aware of Banes' affiliation with Justin because that's the way Justin wanted it. Banes didn't mind because he didn't want her involved. Ella didn't care to know where money came from, as long as the bills were paid. She figured the less she knew, the better.

Ella reasoned that if the First Lady of America and the Queen of England could live like royalty without lifting a finger all day, then she could at least enjoy some of the fruits of her labor with a home and car, plus have a little excess. After all, those people's forefathers got to be wealthy in the first place by slavery and stealing. Whether it be dirty or clean, it's still green.

Before Banes waited on his last customer, he smiled and asked her a question.

"Excuse me, would you mind waiting just a minute? I just want to lock my door."

"Sure," the attractive woman replied.

Ella looked out the kitchen window at the woman.

"And make sure you unlock it to let her leave, too," she said with a tad of jealousy.

Banes walked to the end of the counter, passing by the kitchen door that swung in and out. He checked out the front glass door, turning the plastic sign that hung from a small nail from 'open' to 'closed'. He pulled the white shade down covering the glass. Then he locked the door. He briskly made his way back to his female customer.

"Okay, you had the fried chicken dinner right?" Banes said to the woman.

"Yes," she said.

Banes turned slightly to his left toward the kitchen window, keeping one eye on the woman.

"Honey, how long before that chicken dinner is ready?"

"Now," Ella yelled while she put the flat brown grocery-sized bag on the kitchen window counter. Sweat dripped from her forehead and fatigue had set in, but she still managed a broad smile to the customer.

"Hi," the woman said.

Ella nodded and rapidly went back to work cleaning the small kitchen. Banes hit the five-ninety on the cash register and it rang as it opened. The woman handed him a ten dollar bill. Then he felt like he was moving in slow motion as he looked down and counted change for the ten dollar bill. His smile faded half-way as he thought about his rendezvous with Justin for midnight.

The woman cleared her throat, hoping Banes would take the hint. Then he snapped out of it and smiled bigger again.

"I'm sorry."

He gave the woman her change. She picked up her dinner, then her purse and slung the strap over her shoulder. She counted her change as she slowly walked to the door. Banes got to the door and unlocked it. He opened the door and the woman slowly walked out. Before he could close the door, the woman stuck her foot back in and said, "Oh, excuse me, you gave me too much change."

Banes opened the door wider, moving in the doorway

"Thank you, you are so kind. I musta been daydreaming back there."

In a blaze the woman, still carrying the brown bag on her forearm, pulled out a .38 caliber pistol with a silencer and pointed it right between Banes' eyes. His smile dropped like a ton of bricks, and the woman blasted him twice right between the eyes, killing him instantly.

The woman smiled, held on tightly to her package and put the gun in her purse, then casually walked down the street at a brisk pace.

CHAPTER FORTY-FOUR

I WAS IN THE LIVING ROOM sitting in Dats' chair.

Mom was sound asleep in her bed. She'd laid across it about a half hour ago and was still out. I wasn't about to go in there to wake her to tell her to get under the cover. I was up watching the Playboy Channel all to myself.

I heard the door open upstairs. I turned down the volume of the TV, using the remote.

I got up on my knees slowly, so as to not ruffle the torn plastic that covered the olive green velvet chair. Sweat rolled on my forehead as I leaned on the back part of the chair. The chair tilted back and I had to put my hands on the wood panel that surrounded the door to support myself so that the chair wouldn't bang into the door, which would have made noise while Sally B came down the stairs.

I knew she was the only one still up there because Justin had already left.

Her steps coming down the stairs were slow and heavy. Her breathing was louder and faster than normal. She was definitely carrying something that was heavy I heard the sound of thick plastic crumple a couple of times. I wanted to go out to the dining room door and see what she was carrying.

Sally B got to the bottom of the steps and paused for a moment to catch her breath. She was careful to breathe slowly and without a lot of noise.

Sally B wanted to lean the bag against the wall as she opened the door, but she thought it might make too much noise. She strained while maneuvering the bag on her right shoulder. She put her purse on the radiator and opened it to take her keys out. She thought she'd better take them out and have her trunk key ready to make a fast getaway.

I heard Mom getting up in the back. I calmly sat back down in the chair, faking like I was watching TV.

"Corey," she said, as she stood in the kitchen entryway, squenching her eyes.

Sally B became paranoid and sped out the front door and down the porch steps, using all her remaining strength to get to her car.

"Yes, Mom."

"What are you still doing up?"

"I dozed off for a minute."

"Well, doze off to bed."

"I was thinking maybe I would sleep up here." I said it nonchalantly, so as to not alarm Mom, and went to the front window and peeked out. I saw Sally B dump the black bag into the trunk of her car.

"Mom, can I sleep in Randy's room? They're not coming back tonight, are they?"

"Go ahead."

Aunt Rebekah had called earlier to say that Randy and Tony had fallen asleep and that she didn't want to wake them just to walk home and go back to bed.

This was good and not so good, because I didn't want that crying Tony to come while I went upstairs to check things out. But I needed Randy to help hoist me up to the ceiling door.

As I headed toward Randy's bedroom, Mom turned off the kitchen light and went back to bed.

I didn't bother taking off my clothes because in about twenty minutes I was going upstairs.

In my heart I felt it was Justin or someone upstairs that had something to do with what has been happening. I really don't want to let myself believe it was someone in my family raping me. I would stop at nothing to find out.

CHAPTER FORTY-FIVE

ELLA HAD FOUND BANES' body and all hell had broken loose. Police cars arrived and detectives were there taking fingerprints. The prints were almost unusable because there had been so many people in and out of the restaurant. Pictures were being taken.

The area where Banes' body had lain dead was already chalked and roped off. His corpse was on the way to the coroner's office.

A small crowd of locals had gathered around. They were trying to get a peek inside. The body was gone and Ella hunched in a corner booth and was consoled by Henry. Ella had called him after she found Banes' body.

Henry had his arm around Ella. She laid her head on his broad shoulder while she cried. As she cried, she tried to speak, uttering in an almost babbling tone.

"I can't--I can't understand why. He was liked by everybody."

Ella started to cry again, and then she sunk deeper into Henry's arms.

"Why would she do it?" Ella mumbled.

"What? Who?"

"Some Asian girl was the last one in here. I've never seen her before."

Henry shifted Ella up so that he could see her face.

"Was she Asian, Ella?"

"Yes."

Henry thought that Justin was involved because he remembered that Banes had told him jokingly that Justin was in there with an Asian.

Justin sat in his car parked in the parking lot, near where the jogging path ran along the Hudson. It was a secluded area at this time of night. At approximately 11:55, Justin walked to the boat loading area where the water current was rough.

Then another car pulled into the parking lot and turned off its lights as it headed straight for Justin, who stood at the edge.

The closer the car got to Justin, the faster it went.

Upon reaching Justin, the car stopped and the ignition was turned off. Justin never turned around to face the car as it pulled up behind him. The driver got out of the car and walked toward him, with caution. Only soft footsteps could be heard coming from a pair of sneakers rubbing on the concrete.

Justin was positioned on the end of the parking area where the grass was. It was almost ankle high.

"The job is complete," Sally B said as Justin turned toward her.

At the time Banes had made his paranoid call to Justin was when he'd decided to eliminate him. It was going to happen eventually, but not this soon.

"Two shots?" Justin asked, making sure his instructions were followed.

"Yes. Two in between the eyes."

"Is she in the car?"

"Yeah. She said you called her."

"Just bring her here."

Sally B went back to the car and motioned for Nicka to come out of the car. Sally B went to the trunk and opened it with her key.

"Help me with this, Nicka," Sally B said wearily.

Nicka went to the back of the trunk, reached in and grabbed an end of the bag while Sally B grabbed the other.

As they carried the bag towards the river, Sally B looked over her shoulder a couple of times, making sure they weren't seen.

Sally B and Nicka put the bag down. Sally B motioned for Nicka to follow her behind a small bush. They went behind the bush and emerged carrying a hundred pound brick. They carried it to the black bag and put it down. Obviously, Sally B could have carried the boulder herself, since she had put it there earlier that evening. Since Nicka was there, Sally B thought, why not work smarter instead of harder and have Nicka help her.

Sally B unzipped the black bag. She went to lift the brick, and Nicka helped her. They placed it on top of Angie's cold body, and Sally B zipped it back up. They picked the bag up again. This time the bag was a hundred pounds heavier. Justin watched as they swung the bag, throwing it into the rough river waters.

There was a small glimpse of satisfaction in Justin's eyes. The bag began to sink beneath the surface.

Justin sighed a slight air of relief. He then turned toward Nicka and looked in her eyes. He gently caressed her forehead with both hands. For a long moment, there was silence. Justin, at that moment, was flooded with compassion for Nicka.

He embraced her.

"Go back to New York," Justin whispered softly to Nicka. "You've done a good job for me, but I no longer need you. You know what to do."

Justin nodded as he looked blankly at Nicka. She slowly returned the nod, smiled and headed back to the car.

"Corey's next," Justin said.

Sally B went to the car. Justin turned back toward the river, looking at the hundred foot high bridge that connected Albany to Rennessler, New York. Rennessler was a small town that was considered a city, but with a more countrified vibe than Albany.

Sally B got in the car and drove off. She made her way out of the parking lot. Nicka sat in the front.

Justin was still looking at the center of the bridge, about a quarter of a mile from him.

The bridge was well lit. Justin stood there in thought, with his hand grasped behind his back. He saw Sally B's car pull to the center of the bridge and stop.

He watched both of them get out of the car. Sally B seemed to be talking to her casually as they walked along the edge of the bridge railing. Nicka stopped and looked down towards Justin and waved. At that instant, to Nicka's surprise, Sally B raised her up by her legs and pushed her over the bridge railing. She plunged to her death. If the impact didn't kill Nicka, she would surely drown. She couldn't swim. Justin knew that.

Justin had met Nicka a few years ago. She had gained his trust because she had done something for them in the past. Justin had called on Nicka to eliminate Banes because he knew she owed him a favor. He had called Nicka up from New York days before. He wanted her in town just in case he needed her. Banes was one of those reasons, as it turned out.

Sally B drove away, sadly. She thought another life had been taken for no real reason, except for what Justin wanted to justify. She felt disgusted in not having a choice but to do what Justin instructed her to do. When would it be her, she wondered. How long before Justin would begin killing everyone off.

CHAPTER FORTY-SIX

HENRY HAD LOCKED UP BANES' restaurant for Ella and driven her home. They were in the kitchen sitting and drinking coffee. They were in the Loudonville house in suburbia. It was very quiet. All you could hear were the crickets.

The kitchen was very modern and spacious. It had the neatness and cleanliness of a surgeon's lab.

Henry rubbed Ella's hand to comfort her as tears rolled down her chubby cheeks. Henry had persuaded the police to wait until tomorrow morning for her to come down to answer extensive questions.

"Ella, I know this is a hard time for you, but I need to ask some questions."

"No, not now, Henry, please."

He grasped her hand firmly, but with affection.

"Look, Ella, I don't know who or what got Banes killed, but I got a feeling the killing is not over."

She looked at him sadly, concerned and scared.

"What do you want to know?" she said softly, between tears.

"Did Banes ever mention the name Justin?"

Ella thought for a few seconds as she used her Kleenex to wipe her tears away.

"No, not that I can remember."

Henry sighed and thought for another question.

He put his elbows on the table and leaned his head into the palms of his hands, desperately thinking of another question.

"Was he doing anything out of the ordinary lately, like staying out late, spending a lot of money that you couldn't account for?"

Ella looked at Henry with knowing eyes.

"What, what is it?" she said as her voice cleared a bit.

"The car, how'd you guys buy it?"

"I really don't know. I never questioned him about the car or this house," Ella said while looking around, realizing whatever her one and only husband did to get these luxuries wasn't worth his life.

"Sunday's he would disappear all day and sometimes all night. I think it was just a cover. He'd tell me he was out hustling. Do you have an idea who's responsible?"

Henry got up from his seat. He was convinced in his gut that it was Justin, but he still wasn't absolutely sure.

"Ella, I gotta go, okay? I'll be back to you tomorrow."

He left in a hurry.

I had my hand on the knob of the dining room door that led to the hallway.

Mom had gone back to sleep, but she slept with one eye open sometimes, and then of course there was that 'mother hearing' that most all moms possessed.

It was pitch dark throughout the house, and quiet enough to hear a rat pissin' on cotton.

I was a little nervous about going upstairs that night, but I didn't think I would get another chance anytime soon. Sally B, carrying that last bag out, made me feel like I had to see what was going on up in that attic behind that door.

It probably would've been better if Uncle Henry were going up there with me, but there just wasn't time.

I slowly turned the knob. I knew that when the door opened it would squeak a little. That squeak might be just enough noise to wake Mom. What I had to do was lean down on the doorknob as I opened it. My weight muted the squeak.

I opened the door just enough to slide out. I tiptoed out in my white tube socks and pajamas. I had my pj's on just in case I had to rush and jump in bed.

As I made my way around to the upstairs steps, I noticed a purse on the radiator. I wondered whose it was. I knew it wasn't Mom's. Maybe it was Sally B's. She must have forgotten it when she was rushing out the door.

Nobody knew it, but earlier that day I'd stole Mom's key to Justin's door and had a copy made. I used some of my weekly allowance money. It only cost one dollar and twenty-nine cents. Somehow I'd get it back from Justin, since this was all his fault anyway. I quickly opened his door and went straight to the room off the living room, where the ceiling door to the attic was. I knew my way around his apartment pretty good by then. It was my third time up there, and I was hoping to get enough information to make it my last.

I pulled the step ladder over underneath the ceiling door and climbed the ladder. I had to stretch on my toes to reach the latch. I pushed open the door. It stayed erect once it opened, never touching the ceiling floor because it would have made too much noise if it fell open on the floor of the attic. I jumped up, grabbed the floor of the attic and hoisted myself up.

I smelled fresh Pine-Sol. Somebody had just cleaned up the floor. It was dark. I felt my way through the dusty furniture, working my way to the back.

I got to the back door, and it was locked.

"Dammit!"

I leaned my back against the wall and slid down to the floor.

"Damn!"

What was I going to do? I had to get in there. I wasn't giving up. I was becoming exhausted from living in constant danger, wondering when I would be attacked again.

It was scary, feeling alone and having no one to trust.

No matter what though, I had to keep pushing. I had to figure out a way to get in that room. I thought maybe some of my questions would be answered once I did.

CHAPTER FORTY-SEVEN

SALLY B HAD WATCHED NICKA plunge to her death. She knew that Justin would soon begin his reign of terror on the Harris family.

It was quiet in the car, and on the streets. The only noises that could be heard were the car engine running and the dirt on the bottom of her shoe, from the grass near the river rubbing on the brake.

As she stopped at the red light at the four corners, she sighed a long breath. She was calm, in spite of what she'd just experienced, because she was accustomed to the life, but she thought about how tired she was growing because of it. She also thought about how some day she wanted kids. Thoughts of how she would some day like to have a family crept in her mind. Even though she couldn't have kids of her own, she wanted to adopt and raise them as her own. She was making great money and socking it away for that day she'd hope to walk away from it all. She thought about the skills with which she had used to help build and organize Justin's multi-million dollar empire, and how she could use those very same skills to organize and help her own family and others in need, like charities and church organizations. But she knew that to walk away from her present lifestyle would be declaring war on Justin. This would be something she would have to contend with, because he was not going to let someone with the knowledge of the intricacies of his organization walk away into the sunset and live happily ever after. She thought one of them would have to go.

Still deep in thought, Sally B was not moving as the light changed to green. An irate driver, who was close behind on her bumper, blew his horn. She slowly looked over her shoulder at the driver behind her. He motioned his hand toward her to move it. She put on her left turn signal and made a left turn.

The impatient driver sped away. There was a twenty-four hour AM/PM gas station and mini grocery store on the corner near where Sally B had made her turn. She looked at her gas gauge and it read half full, but she thought she would get a snack anyway. She pulled directly in front of the entrance of the building. There were four gas tanks, two at each island. The building was small. Sally B looked behind her before she got out of the car, like she always did. Looking over her shoulder all the time was part of what came along with her lifestyle. She never knew when that one time would be when, in her haste, she would leave that one stone unturned, causing her to be caught by the law and jailed for life.

After making certain no one was following her, she casually leaned over and reached down to the front passenger side floor to get her purse. This was where she always kept it while driving, for no particular reason. It was just a habit. Not feeling it in the dark, she moved her hand around more swiftly, hoping it was in the corner of the floor. Still not feeling it, she sat up and turned the panel light, switching on the car's interior lights at the front panel and in the center of the ceiling. It wasn't there. She turned around and looked in the back seat and on the floor. It wasn't there either. Her heart rate began to accelerate, almost to the point where she could hear it beating. She then snatched the keys from the ignition and hastened out the door toward her trunk. After nervously finding the trunk key, she shoved it into the lock, turned and opened it, letting the door fly open.

Her worst nightmare had happened. She had lost her purse. Her heart pounded. She could hear it, and she felt her veins fill with anxiety.

She put one hand on the trunk door, leaning on it, trying to calm herself.

Her purse had everything in it; her driver's license, credit cards, and a small black book with notes of her daily events and thoughts. This black book alone would surely convict her because it was well-documented with all the crimes she had ever committed with Justin. Justin had no knowledge of this book, and if he got hold of it, he would surely kill her. It also had the keys to Justin's computer room, which held all the hard, cold facts of who he dealt with, when and where. It listed his vast savings accounts and how his money was hidden. If someone got to this information, they could put Justin away for good, not to mention her.

Sally B closed the hood of her trunk, trying to trace her thoughts back to where she'd been that day, starting with the bridge. Then she thought about the area where they dumped Angie's acid-ridden body. Prior to that, she left the house. Before that, she went to get the acid, and that was the last she remembered having her purse, then she went home. Once there, she cleaned up the dead body and dragged it to Justin's front door. Then Justin left. She brought her thoughts back to her leaving the house with Angie and remembered having to open the front door. She also remembered Sara calling Corey's name. Not wanting Sara or Corey to see her carrying the black plastic bag with Angie's body in it, she put her purse on top of the hallway radiator to get a better grip of the bag. In her mind she could see it, sitting right there on the radiator in the dark.

"Oh, my God," Sally B said, exasperated.

In my mind I envisioned Sally B's purse sitting on the hallway radiator. I wondered if the key to Justin's computer room just might be in it. Bouncing to my feet, I swiftly made my way to the attic entryway. I jumped down from the ceiling door and hung on, trying to swing my feet onto the ladder.

As fast and quietly as I could, I made my way through Justin's hallway to his front door. I went down the stairs making a few cracking sounds on some steps here and there, but not enough to wake Mom up. I grabbed the purse and sped back up the stairs in a flash.

As Sally B sped across the bridge from Rennessler, she decided to stop at Angie's dump site to make sure she didn't leave her purse there.

A couple of cars were on the other side of the bridge, heading toward Rennessler. Sally B would have to exit the bridge at the Pearl Street exit to get back to where she dumped Angie's remains. She drove fast, wanting to get this over with, because if her purse really was on the radiator, she needed to get it before anyone went snooping in it, including Justin.

She stopped at the green light at the exit. There was a homeless man standing in the middle of the street, blocking Sally B's way. He was singing his praise. Sally B frowned, but understood his plight. She forgot for a moment as she instinctively reached down for her purse, but it wasn't there.

Coins jingled against the ashtray compartment as she opened it. She took out the few coins that were left. She pushed the automatic window button and down it came. She stuck her arm out the window and jangled the change in her hand. The homeless man stopped singing upon hearing the familiar sound of the coins.

The man quickly made his way to her outstretched hand. She dropped the coins in his hands. The man gave a polite nod, smiled, allowed her to pass and then went back to the ramp exit and started singing.

Sally B normally didn't run red lights, but she was in a hurry, so two lights wouldn't matter. She kept a close eye on her rear-view mirror, making sure the police weren't behind her as she took a left turn from Pearl Street to Madison Avenue. The dumping site was only five minutes away. She glanced at her panel clock, which read 12:30. She hoped that Justin would still be down at the river when she arrived, using it as one of his deep thought locations, mulling over his next move.

* * * * * *

I was in the attic rambling through Sally B's purse. I took out her Gucci wallet, opened it and flipped through it. There were empty picture encasements, a few dollars, and a host of major credit cards.

I came to her license and read it softly.

"Sally B. Bellows, 4300 Park Avenue, New York."

I stopped and looked up from my floor seat toward the ceiling, in thought. I put the license back in the leather holder and rambled through her purse again. It wasn't that it was a big purse, but there were a lot of papers in it. I shook the bag to see if I could hear a key. Damn, it just hit me, I was messing up. What if there wasn't a key for the computer room door in there? Then I've run back up here for nothing. My pace quickened. I dug to the bottom of the purse and felt around for a key. Nothing. As I brought my hand along the side of the purse, I felt a zipper. I hurried to feel which direction to pull it. I pulled the zipper to the left, which opened a small pocket area on the side of the purse. I stuck my index and middle fingers in to see what I could come up with. There it was, the key. Or at least a key.

I promptly took it out between my two fingers. I put the purse on the floor and stood to see if this was my answer. It worked. I turned the lock and hesitated for a moment. Somehow, I knew bad things were going on up there before, but I wasn't one hundred percent sure. This time I would be, and the moment I opened the door and stepped in, I knew I'd stepped into a whole new world. This room would have all the answers.

The light from the computer glowed and enabled me to see throughout the small space.

I sensed that it was very clean and kept that way, unlike the room I'd just left. It was more like they were keeping everyone off balance by keeping the first room junky and dusty. This would usually keep the average person from wanting to take the time to make one step to get to what was behind the locked door. Climbing over all those chairs and dressers better have been worth it.

I didn't want to turn on any lights because they might be seen.

There was a laser printer next to the computer. The paper box beneath the printer was filled with used paper. The paper tracked from the box to the computer printer. Nothing was printing. I felt behind the switch and carefully hit the "on" button. I watched the screen come up. There was a swivel chair with arm rests. I noticed there was a miniature refrigerator to the right of the wooden computer table.

I gently rolled the computer chair up to the screen and took a seat. I'm sure there was a code to get in. I figured since Justin went to such lengths to keep this room a secret, it was hard to get into to see what the data was.

I'd fooled around with a computer at my friend's house, but most of what I knew about them was from taking a computer class at school, and the rest was pure luck.

I stared at the screen for a minute. To my surprise, a listing came up after I pressed the enter key.

1. NEW YORK
2. ITALY
3. THAILAND
4. JAPAN
5. CANADA

I didn't understand what this menu meant. I'd never seen anything like this. I was even surprised there wasn't a special pass to get into the menu.

I pressed the number one key. The screen showed:

I. NEW YORK CITY
   BOROUGHS:
A. MANHATTAN
B. BROOKLYN

I hit the letter 'A'. The screen showed:

MANHATTAN
1. PARK AVENUE
2. RITZ CARLTON

I hit the number one key again.

I went back to the beginning and viewed all these figures from all over the world. What did this mean? What was Justin buying? I looked at New York on the screen and Flatbush, remembering my summertime spent with Grandma in New York. I remembered Flatbush Avenue and the Fort Greene area. But there was nothing but drugs and prostitutes in this area. What did Justin want with drugs and prostitutes? Then I began hitting keys in different combinations. The screen showed a bunch of names:

NAME	AGE
1. NANCY MAY	13
2. SUZIE DAY	14
3. TAMMY TAY	16
4. BRENDA SAY	14
5. KIM WAY	15
6. ANGELA MAY	18
7. DORIS JAY	12
8. SONDRA FAY	16
9. KIM DAY	13
10. TONYA CAY	13

They were the 'A4' girls. All the last names were made up by Justin. But the names . . . that's it. I thought they were prostitutes. Justin was a pimp. He was selling women. And they were all kids. I understood why he looked at me the way he did, why I saw him carrying that kid from up here that night. That's why he got the kid out so fast. I had stumbled onto something, but he wasn't sure what might have leaked, so he cleaned up everything just in case. Well, I'd have to say he had good instincts because the police came to his house the next day. That's when all of this started. But where's all the money from his business going? I had found out. I was in the hot seat. With the kind of money Justin was making, he could buy information from anyone, like the police chief. Maybe he knew I made the call.

I hit the 'C3' key. On the screen rolled up:

PROTECTIVE SERVICES
1. POLICE
2. CITY OFFICIALS
3. OTHER

I hit key number one for police. The screen rolled to another page showing:

POLICE OFFICER

CAPTAN JOHN RAINES	50,000
CHIEF OF POLICE FRANK MALOY	100,000

These must have been payoffs. I knew Justin didn't care what their salaries were, so they must have been payoffs. My God, he practically owned not only people, but cities. This was valuable information. I realized that if they knew that I knew, all hell would break loose. I needed to get a copy of everything.

I needed to know more. Who else was on his payroll? I pressed key number 'C4'.

The screen rolled up and its title was: OTHER

OTHER
1. SALLY B
2. TIBBY
3. BANES
4. TOTTEN
5. MAYOR, NYC
6. RACINE
7. PONDIFF
8. LEE
9. JUDGE
10. HARRIS

As I looked at the last name, I glanced back up at the prior names. I was certain to find out more about each name. All I would have to do was hit the number indicated. The other names interested me, but the tenth name intrigued and scared me. I pressed buttons 'C3' and 'C10'. The screen rolled up and I was shocked.

JIM AND SARA HARRIS - COURIER
MARRIED: TWENTY YEARS
OCCUPATION: JIM, BUS MECHANIC AT CAPITOL DISTRICT
TRANSPORTATION LOCATED IN ALBANY, NY
COLLEGE: STATE
BORN: BROOKLYN
AGE: 40
AMT. TO DATE: $300,000
OCCUPATION: SARA, SECRETARY, URBAN AGENCY
DEVELOPMENT
COLLEGE: FORDHAM
BORN: ALBANY, NEW YORK
AGE: 40
AMT. TO DATE: SAME AS ABOVE
HISTORY: MET IN BROOKLYN. MOVED TO ALBANY.
MARRIED. HAS FOUR CHILDREN. THREE BOYS BY CUR
RENT HUSBAND. ONE CHILD BY EX-LOVER.
SPECIAL NOTE KEY: NUMBER NOT AVAILABLE

I was shocked. He knew everything about Mom and Dats. That meant he knew everything about me. I wondered what the special note key was. I scanned the board for the key. There was nothing that indicated what this key might be. I was angry at what was going on. I needed to know what was going on, especially about my Mom. I started to hit keys rapidly at random, using both hands. I'd been up in this room a little too long, as far as I was concerned. I could sense someone was on their way. I needed to hurry to get this printed.

I calmed myself and resigned to the fact that I wasn't going to get that special screen key. I started to look for the print button. I needed to hurry, it was getting close. I hoped I could get as much information as possible before getting caught.

Even if I did get caught it would be worth it as long as I got closer to the truth.

I left so dirty. I wished I was a snake so I could shed a layer of skin. It always felt like I had the filthy residue left on me from my abuser. Hot baths weren't helping anymore. I had to get the shit off me. The only way would be to get rid of my rapist.

CHAPTER FORTY-EIGHT

HENRY WAS FLYING DOWN the Arterial. The Arterial in Albany was just like any other modernly constructed highway or freeway of any other city. It got people from one place to the next faster than the city streets.

Through Albany, from the south end to Loudonville where Henry was coming from, it would have taken him thirty minutes. On the Arterial, it would take him about fifteen. He was nervous as he clutched the steering wheel with both hands. He leaned forward as he drove seventy miles per hour. He was anxious to get to Sara and Jim's. He was ten minutes away.

Sally B was just as anxious to get back to Justin's apartment. She had checked the area where she'd dumped Angie's body, and neither Justin nor her purse was there. She sped up Madison Avenue, thinking Justin might be in one of his hanging-out moods and come out to where there was some excitement. On the two blocks above Pearl Street headed to Sara and Jim's, there was plenty of that. From the bars, where music blared out in direct competition with a neighboring bar, to drugs, any kind you wanted was supplied by street hustlers roaming the street corners and standing outside the bar. And then of course there were the prostitutes lingering about, waiting for a cheap trick. Justin really wasn't interested in any of these women, but he always felt he could learn something to stay on top and keep his edge by occasionally hanging around them.

Just as she suspected, Justin was there sitting in his car. He was parked off of Madison Avenue. It was a side street called Ogden Place, where he was parked in a lot with other cars. He had managed to get in a spot where you could see who came in and out of Cutie's Place, the most popular bar on the street.

Sally B was initially relieved to have seen him, because she knew he didn't have her purse.

Justin and Sally B's eyes met as she cruised by the lot he was parked in. She would have to go back and talk to him. Unless planned otherwise, whenever she saw Justin by chance, it was a rule that she always made it back to talk to him. He felt secure in this because he would know, by talking to her face-to-face at that moment, if she was following him.

Sally B got to the corner of Myrtle Avenue and Grand Street and paused at the green light. She looked to her left, and wanted to go left to the house because she was only two minutes away. But she had to go back and talk to Justin, or he'd know that there was a problem. Not only that, he viewed it as disrespect for her not to return.

Sally B reluctantly turned right onto Grand Street. She went one block and it was a one way going in the opposite direction she needed to go. She stopped and contemplated going down the shortcut to where Justin was. If stopped by the police, she would be delayed. The police would occasionally park out of sight to catch people taking this shortcut down to Pearl Street. She decided against taking that right turn into the unknown. It was hard to see if the police were parked and waiting, because the street was narrow and only two short blocks. But the biggest problem was that on the southeast side of this street there was a fifteen-story nursing home, and opposite to that were the backyards of houses. At the corner was the hidden rear entrance to the parking lot where Justin was parked. This hidden rear entrance was where the police usually sat and waited for motorists to drive down the one-way street. They would catch them and the delay would be at least fifteen minutes. Sally B surely didn't want or need that problem.

She drove to the next corner and took a sharp right turn.

It was a small open area that the Arterial was connected to once you got to Pearl Street. There were no houses on either side of this street, just open area.

She took a left at the first intersection, and sure enough, two officers were sitting in the parking lot in a black and white. Justin sat and patiently watched and waited. Sally B drove parallel to the small lot. She stopped and pulled in an open space on the street. She got out and casually walked to Justin's car.

As she approached Justin's car, there were two guys walking by that said something to her.

"Hey, baby, what's ya name?" one of the men asked.

Sally B only looked and smiled as she approached Justin's driver's side. She thought about where she stood. Not wanting to look like some whore, which was what this area was known for, she walked to Justin's front passenger door and got in.

Justin liked Sally B's subtle awareness about small details like that. It was those qualifies about her that kept her around for so long. Despite what she was, in Justin's mind she was an astute, caring human being. The caring part was what Justin lacked in himself, and wanted so much to fill that missing piece in his heart. Sally B was the closest thing to him ever being there, and he hoped some day a fraction of it would rub off on him.

Justin stared at the people going in and out of Cutie's across the street while he spoke with Sally B.

"What's up?" Justin asked.

"I was headed back home," Sally B said with an almost nervous smile, looking at Justin.

"Home, where? You mean my house?"

"Yeah, yeah, back to your place."

"Is everything okay?" He twisted his body toward her. "I'm gonna miss Nicka," he said, his mind off in a distant place as he looked through Sally B.

"Yes, I am too," Sally B replied as her eyes became fixed on Cutie's. This got Justin's full attention.

"What do you mean, you will too?"

"I mean, she was a nice girl."

"Yeah, but she was my girl."

"I know, Justin. I was just saying she was nice."

"Oh, would you rather it'd been you who took a swim?" Justin asked as he turned to look at Sally B, who kept her eyes on Cutie's entrance.

"Look at me when I'm talking to you."

She cautiously turned toward him.

"That's better," he said, grinning.

"Are you just coming from Rennessler?"

"Yeah, I had to get gas," she said.

"Make sure you stay on full. We might have to move quickly."

Justin's eyes shifted down toward her hands, which laid on her lap. He then turned his attention back toward Cutie's entryway. Sally B followed suit.

"Look at them. Look at that. All day and all night. Eat, drink, and fuck. That's all that's on their minds," Justin said.

"Yep."

"Why don't you go and get some sleep," Justin said. With affection and a subtle sexual undertone, he softly rubbed Sally B on her thigh. She cut her eyes to his hand on her.

"Yeah, I think I will."

She opened the door half way.

"What do you think we should do with Corey? We know it was him who made the call to the police!" Justin said.

Sally B closed the door gently. She knew her answer needed to be the correct one. All Justin was doing was checking her loyalty.

"I think . . ."

"Think! Don't think, know!" Justin shot back.

"You make all the decisions, Justin. Whatever you want, I'll do," she said apologetically.

"If I wanted you to 'do' the family, would you?"

"Justin, you have a business to build. I think you're spending too much time on this whole Albany thing. It's small. You're too big for this place."

Sally B knew how to beat up on Justin mentally, then stroke his humongous ego. Justin was impressed and pleased by what she said, and by how she danced around his question.

"I am too big for this place, but that's what I like. I can be low key and fit in. But then again, maybe we should go out of the country for a while. Maybe Canada. We have business up there in Vancouver, right?"

Sally B nodded yes, a bit exasperated.

"Oh, but we couldn't leave here before we finished business."

"Justin, I've been with you for what. . . the better part of ten years, right? I've done a pretty good job with you, right?"

"Yeah."

"I think we should leave this smallness to Albany and get out. Things are getting too tense. You know you like things calm and relaxed."

"Yeah, but we need to clean up before we leave. That Corey might be on to something. He's a little too smart for me. It might be best . . ."

Sally B hung on and waited for Justin to complete his sentence, but he wouldn't.

"Okay. You can go get some rest now."

She opened her door and got out. She knew Justin would follow through with his plan. Before she closed the door, he spoke.

"Oh, Sally B."

She bent down and looked into the car before she closed the door.

"Yeah."

"Where's your purse? You never go anywhere without it."

She didn't know whether to lie or tell the truth. A million lies ran rampant through her mind. Justin was the type to check up on her right at that moment to see if she was lying. She knew that if she told him her purse was in her trunk, he might take her key and look for himself. But she thought it would be better to lie and take the chance. Then she thought, because he was relaxing and watching the Madison Avenue happenings, he wouldn't bother checking her story. If he did check and he caught her lying, he would go berserk.

"It's in the trunk," Sally B said.

"A lady should always carry her purse. Especially you, since you have all that information that's very private. We would hate to have you lose or misplace it and it get into the wrong hands, now would we?"

She began to perspire. She was surprised Justin knew about her black book. This meant that he had gone through her purse before. Time was running out. She knew she had to get to her purse as soon as possible.

"Okay, good night, Justin," she closed his door and started walking toward her car. She hoped like hell Justin wouldn't follow her and check the trunk. She trembled when she heard his car door open. This was it. She'd be caught in a lie and she would have to defend herself. Of course, he would try to kill her.

Justin started walking her way. Two men turned the corner and started walking towards Sally B's car.

Justin was moving in on her car. Then suddenly . . .

"Hey, is that you, Sally?"

Sally B looked behind her and saw Justin stop in his tracks as he was about ten feet away. She immediately acknowledged the two men who called her by walking towards them. She knew Justin would walk away, wanting to keep his identity a secret. She was saved. She sighed softly.

"Sally B, is that you?" the bigger man asked.

"Oh, hi, Bobby," Sally B replied, relieved that Bobby had saved her.

Bobby was an old friend of hers from New York. They exchanged pleasantries. Sally B looked back at Justin, who turned back toward his car.

"Is he bothering you?" Bobby asked, referring to Justin.

"No, no, just some guy," Sally B said, in a reassuring tone.

Justin got in his car and pulled off.

After a few words with her friend Bobby, Sally B got into her car and started home. She needed to beat Justin there, if he was headed that way.

CHAPTER FORTY-NINE

I HAD FOUND THE PRINT BUTTON on the computer. The printer had begun to print out information. Only two pages had printed.

Little did I know that at least two people, possibly three, were converging on the house.

Henry was stopped at the stoplight at the corner of Madison Avenue and Pearl Street, two minutes from the house. Sweat gathered on his forehead and under his armpits.

The light changed, and he passed by a prostitute who strolled up the street, trying to hitchhike. As Henry passed, he mumbled, "Aw, go home."

Then she flipped him the finger as he sped up toward Grand Street. He looked both ways, then turned left without waiting for the light to change to green.

Sally B parked on the Myrtle Avenue side of the house near Jim's driveway. She practically jumped out of the car. Her walk to the corner was steadfast. Just as she was about to walk toward the front stairs, Henry hung a right onto Myrtle Avenue. They made momentary eye contact, and Henry motioned for her to wait. She nodded, but wanted to go.

Henry promptly looked around on both sides of the street for a parking space. There weren't any. He paused in front of Jim's garage and sped into his driveway.

Henry hopped out of his car in a flash, slammed the door behind him and moved even faster toward Sally B. I heard the door slam. I stopped and looked around as I sat in Justin's chair. Then I jumped out of my seat, cautiously ran down the ceiling door and looked out the window. I saw Sally B on the corner and Uncle Henry walking toward her as I peered out of the Myrtle Avenue-side window.

"Oh, shit!"

I ran recklessly, but without destroying anything, back to the ceiling door. I climbed back up.

Sally B was prepared to be questioned.

"Sally B, I need to know what's going on with this guy Justin."

"Why? What's going on? Why are you asking, Henry?"

"Banes got shot a couple of hours ago. Right when he was closing."

"What! Banes? I mean, do they know who?"

"Well, Ella said some Asian girl was the last customer, and it happened right after that."

Sally B's heart raced, but she kept calm. She knew Justin would be rushing to get rid of everyone.

"Asian girl, huh?"

I tore off the computer paper that had already printed out. I hit the off button. The computer went blank. I hastily made my way down the ceiling door, closing the latch behind me.

The front door to the house opened. I stood and heard footsteps stop at the bottom of the stairs leading to Justin's.

I hurried to the front door, tiptoeing the whole way, and listened intently. Uncle Henry and Sally B were whispering, but it was loud.

"The police don't have any leads yet. They don't even know where the gun is or about the Asian girl."

"But I don't understand why you were asking me about Justin? How would he be connected?"

"I'm not saying he is for sure. It's just some things Banes said to me before that made me wonder, that's all. I thought I would ask you.

"And Banes told me that one day Justin came into his place with this Asian. I was wondering if there was any connection. He said he was joking, but I think he was covering for Justin." This was Sally B's chance to get out. She would tell the truth and be done with it.

"I don't know. He's never mentioned any Asian to me. And I've never seen one around."

Sally B took the first move up the step. Uncle Henry grabbed her arm, not letting her take the second step.

"Sally, what do you do for this guy?"

She looked at him blankly.

"Are you in some kind of trouble? If you know anything, you need to talk about it or you're gonna go down with him."

I was sweating heavily. How was I going to get out of this? I couldn't just walk out the front door. Hiding in the attic was out of the question, and I wasn't going to hide under a bed. Uncle Henry would surely check on me before he left the house. I had to get out, back downstairs, I thought.

Justin pulled up but couldn't find a parking place. He parked in front of the fire hydrant on the corner of Grand Street and Myrtle Avenue, opposite the house. This meant he wasn't staying long because he wouldn't want to get a ticket.

I heard a door slam outside. I ran to the bedroom door and looked out the window.

"Damn."

Justin was coming. I ran back to the door.

"Well, I'm gonna go in here and let Jim know about Banes," Henry said.

Sally B started up the stairs. Henry walked toward the dining room door. He looked up the stairwell toward her

"We need to talk tomorrow, Sally B, okay?"

She stopped and said, "Okay."

While stopped, the front door opened. Both Henry and Sally B turned and looked. Sally B knew who it was, but Henry had no idea. In walked Justin. Justin smiled.

"Ah huh, meeting of the minds, I see. Must be interesting, too, at this late hour," Justin joked.

Henry frowned.

"Friend of mine died tonight. We were just talking about it," Henry said.

"Dammit," I said as I gritted my teeth.

My thoughts ran wild.

Where was I gonna go? I looked toward Justin's kitchen back door I ran to it and carefully turned the knob.

Justin was loud as he talked and walked up the stairs past Sally B.

"Don't let me stop you. Go right ahead and talk," Justin said as he made it to the middle of the stairs.

Still in high gear, I quietly closed the kitchen back door as I made my way to the end of the back porch, furthest away from the Myrtle Avenue side. I knelt down in the corner. I had to pee real bad. I peeked over the railing into the neighbor's backyard. It was adjacent to our yard and separated by a wire fence. I thought about jumping, but I wasn't even that daring. No, I'd have to do something else.

Justin was in the kitchen. Sally B was close behind. That meant Uncle Henry was downstairs, about to talk to Mom.

"What the hell is going on, Sally B?" Justin vehemently asked. Sally B closed the door.

"What did he ask you?"

"If I knew about some Asian girl who was with you. That's it."

"Does he think it was me?"

"No, Nicka was the only connection he made."

Justin put his index finger to his lip, silencing Sally B. He looked over toward the kitchen back door. He motioned for her to continue talking as he quietly made his way toward the kitchen back door. Corey would surely be caught. Sally B kept talking.

"So we don't have anything to worry about . . ." her voice trailed off.

Justin yanked the door open.

Back downstairs in Jim's house, Henry had awakened Sara. They sat at the kitchen table.

"Do they have any idea who was responsible, Henry?" Sara asked.

"There was mention of an Asian girl. Ella mentioned to me that she was their last customer for the night. I'm not sure, but I think this guy Justin has something to do with it."

"What makes you say that?"

"Well, one day Banes was saying that Justin came in his place with an Asian girl, then he retracted it and said he was only kidding around. I think he was trying to cover."

"Well, Henry, I think you should let the police handle this. Don't get involved."

"C'mon, Banes was my friend. How could I not be involved. I'm sure the cops are gonna question me at some point."

"Where's Jim?"

"His mother had a heart attack."

"Heart attack?"

"Well, they aren't sure, but they rushed her to the hospital anyway. He stayed down there with her."

"Why didn't you go?"

"I didn't even know he was there. I got a call when she got ill. Maybe he had something on his mind and just decided to take a ride and wound up there."

Henry shrugged and sighed. "The boys asleep?"

"Tony and Randy are at Aunt Rebekah's. Corey is in Randy's room asleep."

After yanking the door open, Justin walked out onto the porch, and Corey was nowhere in sight. He walked to each end of the porch and looked. He looked at the side railing on the Myrtle Avenue side and didn't see anyone. He went back into the house.

"What was it?" Sally B asked.

"Nothing," Justin replied as he closed the door and locked it.

I hid on the side of the house. I was on the steel wall steps.

I looked down toward the ground a couple of times. Below me was our neighbor's backyard on the Grand Street side. The steel wall ladder that was cemented into the side of our house led directly to their yard. It must have been installed to be used as a fire escape for the second floor. I never even knew it was there until I found myself hanging from Justin's back porch.

Luckily the doberman and pit bull dogs that were owned by our neighbor were inside the house. The dogs knew me. I used to throw them bones every now and then. Hopefully, if the dogs got out any time soon, they'd remember those good ol' days and not try to bite me.

I was hasty about getting down the stairs. I thought about how I was going to get back into the house without Mom or Uncle Henry knowing I was ever gone.

I jumped to the ground from the last step. There were some old leaves on the ground, but mostly there was dirt. There were patches of grass here and there, and a picnic table nearby. My neighbor's sons had constructed a tree house that was in the top of the tree that branched into our yard. The tree was about three stories high. The tree house was roughly the second story, directly in view of Justin's back porch. I paused a second, making sure no one was awakened. From our kitchen window, there was a clear view if someone was walking in our neighbor's backyard, during the day, that is. But at night, it was a little difficult to see. I stood with my back almost melted into the side of the house, with both my arms extended and outstretched palms on the wall, feeling my way to the back edge of our house. I could hear the dogs barking next door. They usually barked if the wind blew on them the wrong way. Hopefully, nobody would pay much attention to them. I stopped for a minute and looked at the first floor window directly across from our house. I could see the Doberman's head in the window. He was looking and barking, but not viciously. Ten-year-old Billy and eleven-year-old Todd, my neighbors, were the ones responsible for the tree house. Their father owned the house. He had renovated it from a shell. Billy and Todd were always competing with their father, trying to out-build him. Because their dad was a construction worker, he taught them to build, hoping one day they would both own their own construction company.

Billy, half asleep, was trying to get the Doberman out of the window by putting his arm around the dog's neck. Billy spotted me and gave a half-hearted wave, not really caring what I was doing.

Then I was at the edge of our house. There was an open area of about twenty feet to our neighbor's backyard door. Beyond that door was my freedom. But if Mom or Uncle Henry decided to stand and look out the kitchen window, I would be spotted. My breathing accelerated.

Uncle Henry got up from his chair and looked out the kitchen window.

I dashed out. Unbeknownst to me, Uncle Henry had just turned back toward Mom, and I was in the clear.

I forged ahead and opened the backyard door as gently as possible, with extreme caution. The door opened into a small alleyway that led to other backyards leading up Myrtle Avenue. I ran down to the small driveway in back of the houses, toward Grand Street.

Henry and Sara were finishing up their coffee. Henry stood up and stretched.

"Well, I guess I'll let you get back to sleep."

He glimpsed at the wall phone near the kitchen entryway as he stood, stretching.

"I'm gonna call Jim."

"Henry, it's one in the morning. He's probably asleep or still at the hospital with his mother."

Henry sighed sarcastically, pinched his lips and picked up the receiver of the phone.

"Sara, since when does Jim care if I call him in the middle of the night?"

"Since his mom had a heart attack, that's when," she said adamantly.

"Aw, you don't know for sure. I'm calling anyway."

He dialed the number to Jim's mother's place. Jim sat in his mother's favorite chair, conked out with the lights and television on. He was fully dressed. The telephone rang loudly, alerting Jim as he jerked upright and snatched the receiver of the phone.

"Yeah, is she okay?" Jim asked, referring to his mother.

"Jim, buddy, it's me, Henry."

Henry talked very loud. Jim inched the phone away from his ear a bit.

"Oh, it's you. What's up? How'd you know I was here?"

"Who else, your wife told me. Is your mom gonna be all right?"

"I'm pretty sure, she didn't have a heart attack but they're keeping a watchful eye on her. Right now, she's fair," he said with an air of hope.

"Good. I just thought you might want to know that Banes got shot to death tonight."

"What?"

All sorts of thoughts were running through Jim's mind. The one thing that he hoped was that Justin wasn't connected.

"Do they know who did it?" Jim asked with great concern.

"No, but the last customer was some Asian girl. I had spoken to Banes a few days ago and he mentioned that Justin brought some Asian kid in there once before."

This was the last thing Jim wanted to hear. He squeezed his eyes shut and swallowed. He knew Justin had put out a hit on Banes. But why? Jim had no idea that Banes worked for Justin. He wondered who else was on the payroll. Then it hit him. He knew that Justin knew Corey made the 911 call.

"Henry, where are the boys?"

He sounded cool, but inside fear ran amuck.

"They're over at Aunt Rebekah's."

"Oh, okay."

"But Corey's here."

"Here, where?" Jim asked with concern.

"Here in Randy's room," Henry said, looking at Sara who nodded yes while she stirred the last of her coffee before drinking it.

"Henry, go see if he's asleep, now!"

"Why? What's wrong?" Henry asked, causing Sara's eyes to shift up from her coffee.

"Henry, just go and see, please!" Jim begged. He stood and paced around the recliner. He knew Corey was an adventurer.

As I ran from the alley up Grand Street toward our house, unbeknownst to me, Justin spotted me from his living room window. He smiled. I made my way to the basement door.

The basement door was located underneath the stairs that led to our front door. I stood on some paper that had blown in from the street. I stretched and got on my tiptoes to reach the top of the door to see if Mom had put an extra key there just in case she got locked out. Mom was good for hiding a key for emergency purposes. This was definitely one of those emergencies. There was no key.

Henry mumbled as he walked toward Randy's room. He was still on the phone, gesturing with his arms that checking for Corey in Randy's room was a waste of time. But anything to please Jim, because of his mom.

"Sara said he was asleep. She should know if her son is in his room asleep. Jeez, you're so paranoid."

Henry pushed open Randy's door as if this whole process of checking was a waste of time; the room was empty.

"My God, Sara, he's not in here."

Sara dropped her cup, breaking it on the table right before she was to take her last sip. She ran to the phone in hysterics and grabbed the receiver.

"Jim, he's gone. He's not in Randy's bed."

Henry was swift in getting to Sara. He tried to take the phone from her.

"Sara, let me talk to him."

Sara resisted more.

"No, no, Jim. What're we gonna do?" she shouted into the phone.

"Sara, check downstairs," Jim shouted as he too was beginning to panic.

She threw down the phone and charged for the basement door. Henry immediately picked up the receiver and talked.

"Jim, look, hold on, we're going to check downstairs."

Henry dropped the phone and rushed behind Sara, who was halfway down the stairs. Henry trucked down the thin hallway, with both of his hands palming the walls for support as he hurried. Sara opened the door to the bedroom. The covers were in a big ball on his bed. Sara went to Corey's bed and started pulling the covers off him and shaking him, crying.

"Corey, Corey, wake up," she said.

I acted like I'd been asleep for hours and pulled one of the covers back over me. I glanced at Uncle Henry who stood in between my door and the hallway. He looked at me like he knew I was up to something, then he looked at the dirty socks on my feet before I could get them back under the covers. He kept quiet. He then went to the phone near the window shelf, behind my eavesdropping chair. He picked up the receiver.

"Jim, he's down here. Everything's okay."

"Good."

"What were you so worried about anyway?"

"Never mind. I'm coming back as soon as I find out that Mama's okay."

"Okay. I'll see you when you get here."

Uncle Henry hung up the receiver. I had to stay on my back because I still had the computer paper stuck in the back of my pajama bottoms.

"Mom, what's going on?"

Mom was okay, and ready to pounce on me verbally.

"Why didn't you tell me you were coming back to your room?"

"You were asleep and I didn't want to wake you just for that."

My heart raced. I didn't know how much longer I could keep lying.

"Mom, can I go back to sleep? I'm pretty tired."

Uncle Henry calmly took Mom by her hand and ushered her away.

As Uncle Henry left my bedroom, he scanned the basement door from top to bottom, without making Mom aware of what he was doing, while she walked in front of him. He saw where I had moved a wash pail in front of the door to keep it shut because I didn't have time to lock it. He wore a slight grin as he headed back upstairs with Mom.

Mom had hid the extra key under the steps leading to the front door, under a brick in the corner. I had looked under the stairs and found it just in time.

As soon as I heard their footsteps upstairs, I sat up in my bed and sighed. I'd just made it. I pulled the printout from behind me and held it tightly in my hands, wondering what everything was all about.

My God, I was getting closer. Then, I thought, could Mom and Dats know that Justin had been molesting me? Maybe because they worked together and maybe I was part of the deal? What if all of them were in on it? Who could I trust? Who could I go to? Was Mom and Dats covering for Justin?

More than ever I realized I was alone in this. Why was I even born? It's so unfair.

CHAPTER FIFTY

JUSTIN TURNED ON THE LIGHT in the bedroom that led to the attic. Sally B was right behind him.

The light came on and Justin stopped in his tracks.

"I thought you cleaned up already, Sally B?"

"I did."

Justin stared at the step ladder that was not perfectly aligned in the corner where it was usually kept.

"Why is that step ladder out of place?"

"Looks okay to me," Sally B replied.

Justin angrily turned toward her, nose to nose.

"Look, I know when something is out of place!"

She was silent.

"Now, where's your key to the computer room?"

Sally B froze for an instant. With all the distractions, she'd completely forgotten about her purse. She had to think fast. If Justin found out, she'd be a dead woman. She sighed and headed for the kitchen, not knowing what she would do.

As she passed by the living room, out of the sight of Justin, she entered the hallway headed toward the kitchen. She reached down into her panties near her crotch area, pulled out a small PSP caliber gun that weighed 9 1/2 ounces and readied it to fire. If Justin was going to try to kill her, she thought, he'd better come to the showdown with the proper weapons. She was prepared to blast his ass.

She kept this gun with her at all times, except when she traveled through airports or other areas that had metal detectors.

She entered the kitchen with her thoughts heavy, causing her head to droop down. To her shock and surprise, she spotted her purse under the kitchen table. She glanced over her shoulder, then looked back to her purse and ran to it. But how did it get there, she thought.

Before Corey left, he had put the purse there with everything intact.

Sally B knew that one of the boys, probably Corey, had been in Justin's apartment. She knelt down and picked up the purse. She then put her gun back in her panties.

As she headed back to the front bedroom, she unzipped the inside pocket of the purse and took out her computer room key.

Justin stood on the mini step ladder waiting for her. He opened the latch and climbed up. He got in and reached back for Sally B's hand to help her up. After they were both in, Sally B handed Justin the key. He made his way through the dusty old furniture to the back door; it was unlocked.

Justin gradually turned to Sally B with a stoned look etched on his face. He was seething.

"Why, why was this left open?" he snapped.

Sally B wasn't sure who the last person up there was. But since she found her purse under the kitchen table and not on the radiator where she left it, she had a hint of who had been in the room. But she had to keep it a secret.

"Justin, you were the last one in here. You must have left in a hurry and forgot for the first time in your life."

Justin thought back carefully. He remembered he was in a hurry to Banes' and that maybe, just maybe, he was slipping and it was his fault.

He opened the sliding door, still in thought. He then went and turned on the light because it was dark. Then he realized something as he moved fast toward his computer.

"Hey, I'm always able to see when I walk into this room," Justin revealed.

"But how can you see in the dark?"

Justin switched on the computer, and the light from the screen illuminated enough to see a little.

"That's how," he said, pointing to the light from the computer screen.

"But that doesn't mean someone was up here. Maybe you forgot."

Justin was incensed. He pointed his finger in Sally B's face.

"Are you implying I'm irresponsible?"

"No, I'm just saying maybe you forgot in your haste," she said calmly.

Justin went to the computer and hit the enter key. The menu listing came up and he hit the special menu key. This special menu key showed:

PRINT STATUS
ACTIVE INACTIVE

The active light flashed on the computer screen. This was a special installment that Justin had implemented into the computer. It would indicate if printing had been done in the last 24 hours.

Justin pressed the enter key. The screen showed:

```
LAST PRINTS MADE AT 12:30 A.M.
WOULD YOU LIKE TO KNOW WHAT DATA WAS
PRINTED?
```

He hit the enter key, denoting yes. The screen came up and it showed:

```
ALL INFORMATION PRINTED REGARDING:
1. NEW YORK FILES
2. HARRIS FILES
3. WORLD NUMBERS
WOULD YOU LIKE THESE ITEMIZED?
```

Justin had an enraged look as his eyes went from the computer screen to being rooted on Sally B.

"I suppose I forgot I made a printout of my files, too, huh?"

He paced the room like a madman. He kicked and punched and grunted at nothing, a few times coming close to accidentally hitting Sally B.

Then abruptly he calmed himself, stood in the middle of the floor, and looked straight ahead at Sally B.

She didn't know what to do. She didn't know if this was the showdown or not. If it was, she knew Justin would kill instantly with one crushing blow, because she was too close to him to take out her gun. She froze, and waited. Justin sighed, walked to his computer and sat in his chair, in thought. Then he mumbled something to himself.

"It must have been Corey. Damn that kid!"

Sally B stood a few feet behind Justin with her gun in her hand, hanging by her side. She thought that this was the time for her to stop the madness. But she'd never shot anyone in cold blood. Could she find it in herself to murder Justin the killer, pimp and kidnapper, who vowed to never be taken alive? This was the question that ran rampant in her innermost thoughts. She raised the gun and pointed it at Justin's head.

CHAPTER FIFTY-ONE

JIM WAS WORRIED STIFF. He paced his mother's apartment like a lost gerbil. Who would be next? Who else worked for Justin? Does Justin own Albany? These questions clouded his mind. Would Justin come after his mother and then the rest of the family, or maybe he'd gotten to them already.

Jim stopped pacing near the phone, then grabbed the receiver. He frantically dialed home. The phone rang twice. Sara answered.

"Sara, is everything all right?" Jim asked.

"Yes, everything is fine."

"Look, I'm not waiting until the morning to come back. I'm headed over to the hospital to check on Mama, then I'm coming home."

"Good, I'll wait up."

"Is Henry still there?"

"Yes."

"Put him on."

Henry stood up from the kitchen table seat and took the phone from Sara.

"Yeah?"

"Henry, stay there tonight and keep an eye on things."

"Don't worry I'll be here. How long before you get here?"

"I'll be a couple of hours. I'm stopping by the hospital first."

"Okay. See you then."

"Bye," Jim said, then hung up.

"Sara, why don't you get some sleep. It's almost two in the morning. Are you going to work tomorrow?"

Henry went over to Sara and escorted her to her bedroom.

"No, I'm not working tomorrow. I took some time off."

Sara realized that she was in a semi-daze and snapped out of it. She lightly wrestled herself away from Henry's grasp.

"I can find my own way to the bed."

She sat on the bed and looked at herself in the mirror.

Henry went over to the locked clothing cabinet that was on the opposite side of the bed. He looked over at her and then knocked on the cabinet door.

"You guys make sure you keep this locked, don't you?"

She looked at him through the mirror. He smiled. She didn't want to respond.

She stood and headed out of the room.

"Please, Henry, not now."

She walked toward the living room and sat down in Jim's favorite chair. She sighed and slid down into a slouch, closed her eyes and began to doze off. Henry, always energetic, turned the corner from Sara's bedroom to the dining room entrance by storm, headed toward the living room.

"Hey . . ." his voice tapered off once he realized Sara was asleep in the chair.

He quietly went to the linen closet next to the bathroom.

Trying not to make a lot of noise, which is what the linen closet door made whenever it was opened, he surveyed the shelves and found a blanket on the top shelf. He grabbed it, partially closed the door and went to cover Sara. Then he went and cleaned up the broken cup that Sara had dropped on the kitchen table earlier.

After that, he headed downstairs to Corey's room.

"Hey, Uncle Henry," I said as he entered my room.

He sat on the edge of my bed.

"What are you doing sitting up so late?"

"After Mom came and woke me, it was hard to get back to sleep. What was wrong, why was she so upset?"

"Oh, she's just worried at the usual adult stuff, you know."

"C'mon, Uncle Henry, what is this adult stuff? You know we tell each other stuff."

"Okay, you can start by telling me about that basement door being kept shut with that pail. Now all of a sudden it's locked."

"Yeah, okay, I went and locked it after you and Mom went back upstairs."

"But what was it doing open in the first place?"

There was a brief pause as we peered into each other's eyes. I wanted to tell all, but I still wasn't sure about him. He knew I had some valuable information, and he didn't want to push me too much and scare me away. I broke the silence.

"So when's Dats coming back?"

Uncle Henry checked his watch.

"Maybe in an hour and a half. Why?"

"I just wanted to know how Grandma was doing. Thinking about her kept me awake, too." Because I had been molested kept me awake too, but I could not tell Uncle Henry, not yet anyway.

"At last count she didn't have a heart attack, but she's not in the clear yet."

Uncle Henry moved closer to me.

"You know, Corey, she doesn't have much longer. She's sick, and she's not getting better."

"I miss not being there with her; I hope I get to see her before she dies."

We both went to embrace each other, and I began to drown my sorrows on his shoulder.

"She lived a good life, Corey."

"It's not just that," I said, sighing.

"Well, what else?"

"Mom and Dats and. . .and that Justin."

Uncle Henry leaned me back and looked at me.

"Whaddya know about Justin?"

"I know Mom and Dats owe him a thousand dollars."

"Yeah, but you already knew that."

"And and . . ."

"And what, Corey?"

"I know he's doing something to kids."

"I know something isn't right either. Your father is rushing home because he thought something was wrong with you."

"I gotta tell you something, but you gotta swear you won't tell anyone else."

"Okay. What, Corey? What is it?"

Mom yelled down from the top of the basement stairs.

"Henry, is everything okay?"

Uncle Henry turned his head toward our bedroom door to answer Mom.

"Yes," he said, raising his voice.

"Can you come here, I need to talk to you."

"What's it about, Sara? Can it wait a few minutes?"

"No, it can't wait, it's very important."

Uncle Henry looked me in my eyes.

"Corey, we'll continue this after I'm done talking to your mother. Don't worry, everything is gonna be all right."

"Okay." I forced a smile.

Uncle Henry affectionately rubbed my head, then went upstairs.

I just wanted it to end. I couldn't take much more. I tried to remain strong but it was difficult. I had to hurry and expose the molester. I felt drained.

I didn't understand why anyone would want to take advantage of kids. Whoever the criminal was was very confused and needed to be put out of their misery.

CHAPTER FIFTY-TWO

BEFORE JUSTIN TURNED AROUND, Sally B had inconspicuously put her gun back into her underwear. She sat at the kitchen table with her face resting in the palm of her hand with her elbow on the table, contemplating her next move. She realized just how much control Justin had over her.

She thought about running. She had a little nest egg of money hidden away; money that not even Justin knew about. She never stole from him. Always believing that Justin and this lifestyle would eventually come to an end made her wise enough to invest in stocks, bonds and annuities. Some of her choices in the area of stocks had turned into a cash cow for a while. She even used an alias, because she knew Justin was keeping close tabs on her money. He always paid her well to make sure he kept her in a high lifestyle. He'd gotten her used to living this way. That way, he believed it would be hard for her to walk away to a life of nothing. Sally B realized this a long time ago, and she acted on it. With the stocks and bonds she would at least live comfortably the rest of her life, not having to ever work again.

She wanted to go somewhere far away, get married, and have some kids. Her time was getting short, she needed to make a decision. Planning was the important thing. Because everything that Justin owned or had was in her name, she needed to dump it or sell it. If she didn't do it right, the police would be after her.

Sally B looked at Justin. He seemed to be in another world. She called his name, but he didn't respond. It was like he wasn't even in the room.

The room was of medium size and dimly lit. It was very late at night and not a sound could be heard over the loud music that blared out from the boom box.

There was a full-size bed in the center of the room. Everything was very clean and neatly placed. There was a dresser with chains on top of it. A chair was in the corner, in it sat a woman dressed in a garter belt and holding a whip. She was looking directly at the boy who laid belly down on the bed. There was a man behind him.

"So, how do you like us now?" the woman asked. "Lucky we adopted you when we did," she said, smiling.

"Yeah, ya mamma didn't want you, whoever the bitch is," the man said.

"She could never put you in the school we've sent you to,"

the woman said.

The man behind the boy was naked, along with the boy.

"Boy, didn't I tell you to move to the center and bend? Now do it!"

The boy moved further to the center of the bed. The man penetrated him and the woman watched.

"You were supposed to bring us a friend!" the woman shouted as she snapped a whip towards the boy.

"But I don't want to get in any trouble. You could get in trouble too if I do that. Maybe if I brought somebody they would go and tell somebody and would try to come put you in jail. I don't want you to go to jail."

The boy was at the mercy of this man and woman, and had been for many years.

"Trouble, nobody's gonna get in any trouble," the woman shouted, darting up from her chair and getting in the boy's face. "Doesn't this feel good?"

"Yes," the boy said.

"Well, why would anyone get in trouble? Have you been talking to anyone about us?"

"No," the boy said fearfully.

"Well, I'm gonna give you something to remember to make sure you don't," the woman said.

The man moved away from the boy. The woman snapped the whip high and wide. The boy had a clear view of the whip and was terrified. He yelled out as she began to beat him.

"No, no, no, no, no . . ."

The boy's voice faded.

"Justin, Justin, are you all right?" Sally B asked as she patted him on his shoulder.

Justin sat in front of the computer screen, now sweating profusely, still stuck dreaming of his horrible past. Sally B kept patting him on his shoulder.

"No, no," Justin said.

He looked up at Sally B and wiped his brow with the palm of his hand. She was surprised to see him looking like this. It was a first.

Justin's thoughts ran wild. He was punished as a child when he didn't make things perfect. As an adult, things weren't perfect again. In his thoughts, Justin was being punished again by Corey with all the confusion he was causing. He had to make it right again. He stood and tucked his black shirt in his black trousers. Then he spoke.

"Just had a bad dream, that's all."

"But you weren't even asleep. You were just staring at the computer screen," Sally B replied in a concerned tone.

"Whoever said you had to be asleep to have a dream? Corey's got some information that belongs to us. We need to get it back."

"Justin, we can't just go barging in there. Henry's there and there's too much confusion. We should wait and plan it out like you always like to."

Sally B was stalling. She knew Justin was ready to commit murder. Henry couldn't really stop him either, but just her mentioning his name to Justin made him think twice. Not because he couldn't handle Henry, but because he always took Sally B's advice, the few times she offered it. Justin thought her advice was always correct, and never given too much, so why should he change? If he didn't listen to her, something could go wrong, especially since he was hesitating. During his rampages, he never had second thoughts. They were always done right at the moment he decided to do it, and all were successful.

He was faltering.

"You're right. We'll wait."

Sally B sighed to herself. Justin sat back in his computer chair.

"Tomorrow we will make our move, after I take care of a few things," Justin said.

"What things?"

"Just some personal business."

Justin began to key in on his computer. The telephone rang. Sally B and Justin both looked at each other. They thought it was strange for his private line to be ringing at that time of night. But it wasn't totally out of the question, because Justin did do business in other parts of the world. He hoped that it would be Stanley calling from Bangkok. The design that grew on his face spelled otherwise-- trouble. Only seven people in the world had his private number.

"Hello," Justin said.

"Hey Justin, this is your friend Captain Lee at Division II."

Justin covered the receiver end of the phone and mouthed to Sally B that Captain Lee was on the phone. Sally B nodded.

Division II was around the corner on Warren Street, and only a five-minute walk from Justin's apartment.

Captain Lee sat in his swivel chair at his desk looking at a faxed photo that resembled Justin. His desk was cluttered with papers. The rest of his office matched his desk. The desk light was low.

The place was relatively quiet at this hour.

Captain Lee held the fax up in front of him, with the phone clutched between his shoulder and ear as he spoke.

"Hey, Mutt and Jeff, two of my colleagues from New York, faxed me a photo, and I'd swear it looks just like you. But the name is different. Al Totten."

Justin was alarmed, but didn't let Captain Lee or Sally B notice.

"Well, you know what they say, somewhere in the world everybody has a look-alike."

"Yeah, I guess you're right. But anyway, this picture was taken after a woman housekeeper was found dead a few days ago."

"Yeah, really?"

"Really. I guess the video camera captured the photo of him going into the garage right after the murder."

Justin didn't want to sound too concerned, so he joked instead.

"You know how you guys think, all criminals look alike."

Captain Lee chuckled, but felt something eerie behind this.

"Yeah, you're right. So when are we gonna get together? It's been years. We always talk about it, but never do it."

"Lee, as busy as you stay, we'll do it one of these days. That is, if I don't get picked up for mistaken identity."

They both laughed.

"Oh, by the way, Lee, who's Mutt and Jeff? Sounds like two cartoon characters," Justin said laughing, but was every bit serious.

"I know it. They got their nicknames from around the station in New York. They are two older guys on their way to retirement. They're not a perfect match, but they work well together. Well, that is until they were working on a recent surveillance assignment. They were trailing a woman who's suspected of running the largest prostitution ring in the state. They lost the woman at the Park Plaza, where the murder took place. She was the first suspect that got away in five years."

Captain Lee's other phone button lit up.

"Hey I got another call. I gotta go. Gimme a call when you're free. It'll be like old times in New York."

"Yep."

Captain Lee hung up. He took a closer look at the paper picture and shook his head. Then he tossed the photo in a pile of other fax photos and answered the blinking phone line.

Justin slowly hung the phone up, and was deep in thought as

he peered at Sally B.

"Well, what is it?" she asked.

"Camera got a picture of me leaving the elevator on my way to the garage the day that housekeeper died."

"Well, did he think it was you?"

"No, but if it weren't for my sunglasses and hat, he would have known it was me. Now we've gotta move on Corey tomorrow. If I know Captain Lee, he just might start asking questions. He always wants to know what I do for a living anyway. He can be nosey."

"Seems like he would've come after you since the picture had your name on it."

"It didn't."

"Well, who's name was on it?"

"Al Totten."

"Al Totten, who's that?"

"We've got work to do."

Justin moved back in the computer seat, ignoring her question.

"I'm clearing the files," he said.

Sally B headed toward the attic exit.

"Damn kid," Justin mumbled.

As Sally B climbed down the attic ladder, she heard Justin shout.

"Nobody steals from me!"

By his yelling, Sally B knew the pressure was mounting on Justin. The stealing of his files was to Justin like a personal declaration of war. Nobody would be safe as long as his business information was in someone else's hands, and a picture of him in the hands of his boyhood friend, Captain Lee, just five minutes away this was too close for Justin. Too many holes.

CHAPTER FIFTY-THREE

JIM SAT AT THE BEDSIDE of his mother, whose time on earth could expire shortly.

Jackie opened her eyes and smiled at him.

"Hi, son," she said in a strained voice. He kissed her forehead.

"You feeling better, Mama?"

"Some. I guess I'm just old and tired. But I'm still here."

"The doctor said you're gonna pull through. But they want to watch you for a couple of days."

"Whatever they wanna do, I got time," she replied, with a painful smile. "I still hate this place. Seems like every two or three months I'm here."

Jim moved closer on the bed toward her.

"Mama, was there ever a time that maybe Daddy wasn't sure about things?"

"Things like what? C'mon, spit it out," she said lovingly, but impatiently.

Jim was trying hard not to insult his dying mother. He took her hand.

"Wasn't sure about kids or anything that was his?"

Jackie looked at him, knowing full well what he was referring to.

She sighed a bit, then answered.

"What your father owned, he took care of, and the kids under his roof he took care of, and loved dearly, no matter what. You've been doubting Corey since the day he was born. A child is a child and they're very precious, and all of them need somebody to watch over them, no matter how grown they act."

She coughed a few times and became stern as she pointed her finger toward the door. Jim moved closer to her.

"Now, you let me rest and get the hell outta here and go watch over your family."

She closed her eyes and drifted off to sleep.

Jim kissed her cheek.

"Yes, Mama," he said softly.

He pulled the blanket up to her shoulders and hurried out, checking his watch. It was getting late.

CHAPTER FIFTY-FOUR

I WOKE UP and found Uncle Henry asleep in Tony's bed. I must have fallen asleep while he and Mom were talking.

Uncle Henry snored louder whenever he laid flat on his back. I looked at him from head to toe. He was a very big man. He and Mom were definitely brother and sister. I looked at his large, thick hands. Both he and Mom had a little mole not quite in the center of their right palm. I looked closer at Uncle Henry's. His protruded out a little more than Mom's. I leaned over onto him to touch it.

He woke up, still half asleep.

"What, what? What is it?"

I leaned back and sat up in my bed. I was scared again and didn't want to tell him what was really bothering me.

"What was that you wanted to talk about earlier, Corey?"

"Nothing, never mind. Uncle Henry, why is your hand like that?"

He looked at his hand, first his palm, then the back.

"What's wrong with it?"

"It's so big."

"Same size it's always been. Get some rest, Corey. Don't forget you're going back to school tomorrow. How's the eye anyway?" Uncle Henry asked with closed eyes. I'd forgotten all about my eye since the pain went away I touched around my eyelid.

"It's fine, I guess."

"Good," Uncle Henry said, grasping his hand across his flat stomach and going back to sleep.

"Uncle Henry, when did Dats say he'd be back?"

Uncle Henry was getting a little annoyed. He sat up and made an announcement, sarcastically.

"Your *Dats* will be back in about an hour or so. Now, I'm going upstairs and use the bathroom. Then I'm gonna sleep in Randy's bed. You stay put, okay?"

I knew he was going upstairs to sleep in peace. In a way, I was kind of glad because I wanted to look at the computer printout I stole from Justin's. His last statement was more of a playful directive. I really didn't understand why. At least I knew he was up there with Mom, so I wasn't so scared. The thought of Justin possibly knowing that someone was tampering with his computer didn't sit too well with him. I knew he would think it was me. If he had files on Mom and Dats, then he knew I liked computers. Justin's silent spirit struck me more like it was an act, that he knew everything going on around him, even though he acted like he didn't.

It didn't matter to me what Uncle Henry or anyone else thought. I only cared about stopping a mad person. Hopefully the police would discover this, this crazy, sick person before I did. They would carry out the more civil punishment for their crimes against me and who knows how many other poor kids they destroyed. Me, I would surely punish them for an eternity once exposed.

CHAPTER FIFTY-FIVE

TAMMY AND TIBBY were fast asleep in their king-sized bed.

The comforter was half-way on Tibby, while Tammy was balled into a knot with a blanket over her head. There was a shred of light shining through the window facing them, illuminating from the moon's glow.

Their sixteen-month-old son was in the baby room, adjacent to theirs.

The telephone on the night stand near Tibby's side of the bed rang loud. Tibby slowly turned from his back onto his side toward the phone. By the second ring he blindly reached for the receiver, and in the process, knocked an empty water glass to the floor. It didn't break on the thick, wall-to-wall, dark golden carpet. Still half asleep, he put the phone to his ear and spoke.

"Yeah?"

"It's me," Sally B said.

Tibby recognized her voice. He nervously sat up with his back parallel to the black headboard. He turned his head slightly toward Tammy to look and make certain she wasn't awake.

"Go ahead," he said.

"Look, things might get crazy tonight with Justin. Be ready today. Stay at the bar."

Tammy turned over toward Tibby.

"Sorry, you got the wrong number," Tibby said.

Sally B had already hung up, then Tibby followed suit.

"Who was that?" Tammy asked mumbling, half asleep.

"Wrong number," Tibby said, sighing loudly.

Fear had caused Tibby to become wide awake.

He stayed sitting up in bed as Tammy rolled over to him. He was in thought. Tibby loved his wife and son, and didn't want to risk anything happening to them. He could ignore Sally B and risk keeping his family safe, or help her like he was paid to do.

Sally B still had her hand on the receiver of the phone. Justin came up the ceiling door. She subtly took her hand off the receiver. As he entered the computer room, she acted as if she were simply reviewing the printouts.

"Get me Stanley on the line, then Anthony in Italy, and Yurvoc in Russia."

On Anthony, Sally B looked up. She knew this meant Justin was about to make a major move.

Just as Sally B put her hand on the telephone receiver, it rang. She looked at Justin. She always looked for his approval to answer his phone when he was present. He nodded. She answered it.

"Yes?"

"Sally B, it's me, Jim."

"I know it's you. What's up?"

"Where's Justin?"

"Here."

She handed the phone to Justin.

Justin mouthed, "Who is it?"

"Jim."

A smile swept across Justin's face while he took the phone.

"Jim, where are you?"

"I'm on the 'Thruway'." It was a toll highway that anyone could use to get almost anywhere in New York state.

"I know it was Corey who made the 911 call, Jim."

"How do you know?"

"I have my sources. Not only that, he's stolen some valuable information from me that could put me away for a very long time. I want it back!"

Jim stood at a rest area, just off the Thruway.

"Look, how do you know Corey has it?"

"Corey is the only one curious enough to find his way up here, break in and steal from my computer."

Jim was exasperated and defenseless at that moment. He banged his hand on the phone shelf.

"How far away are you, Jim?"

Jim looked back at the highway. Cars rushed by.

"At least another hour."

He lied. He was only a half hour away but he wanted to get there before Justin would make any moves.

"I'll see you when you arrive."

Jim was about to hang up.

"So Jim, by the way, where are you coming from?"

"Seeing my mother, she's sick."

"Poor mama, send my condolences."

"I said she's sick, not dead," Jim shot back.

"Like I said, send her my condolences," Justin said, followed by a sinister little laugh as he hung up.

Jim slammed the phone down, raced to his car and pulled away fast, headed north toward Albany. He knew Justin could and would kill his entire family if he wasn't careful.

Justin was still smiling as Sally B dialed a number. She handed him the phone. Sally B would never talk to an overseas contact unless Justin gave her the phone after he had already spoken. This was to ensure his partners that no one else knew their phone numbers. They valued their privacy and they didn't want people to track them.

Justin was sure they were doing the same thing to him. The only difference was these were family men he was dealing with, so their private lines usually stayed the same for at least a couple of years. For Justin, it was different. He was single with no children. This allowed him to move around at a moment's notice. His private line number would change too. It was harder for his associates to track him down. It wasn't totally fail proof, but it was Justin's system, and it worked for him.

Forty minutes had gone by, and everyone was asleep. It was almost 4:00 a.m. Jim came in through the front door because he didn't want to wake the entire house. But mostly he didn't want to alarm Justin.

He peeked in Randy's room and saw Uncle Henry stretched out on the bed, asleep and snoring, as usual.

After Jim closed the door, Henry raised his head up and looked toward the door. He was fully aware that Jim looked in.

Jim eased toward his bedroom door, opened it and smiled, while Sara laid sound asleep.

He really wanted to wake everyone and get out. But he'd wait, not wanting to alarm his family. He'd decided not to run away, especially since he could easily be found by Justin.

The floor crackled a little with Jim's every footstep in route to the living room. He decided he was going to stand guard the remainder of the night.

He took his navy blue zippered windbreaker jacket off and laid it on the couch. He plopped down in his favorite chair and picked up the remote from the lamp table that was to his right. He began flipping the channels, then slouched down in the chair. After about ten minutes of fighting sleep, fatigue took over. He was out like a light.

The time was about 5:00 a.m. It was still dark throughout the house. The sun's rays would be shining through the cracks in the blinds of the front windows soon.

Although everyone was asleep and all was quiet throughout the house, there was an eeriness about the serenity.

Two people were awake: the molester and me.

In the basement, I had been bound, gagged and blindfolded by my attacker. All I felt throughout this horrible ordeal was the pain of being molested at gun point, again.

I tried to wrestle away, but I was overpowered. I laid there and took it. The pain was excruciating. Tears soaked my blindfold as every minute ticked by. Although it lasted only a few minutes, it seemed like an eternity.

My assailant climbed off of me and got dressed. I was too distraught to even kick. I stayed on my stomach. I felt the ropes being taken off. The barrel of the gun was pressed hard against the back of my head as the blindfold was taken off. I knew this meant if I moved or made a sound I would die. I thought about yelling when the gag came out of my mouth, but I would surely be killed. I knew my attacker wouldn't be stupid enough to shoot me, because that would surely put them in jail. No, they would suffocate me with my pillow, and the news would say that I died in my sleep. It would be better for me to be patient. One day the bastard would slip, and then it would be my day.

My covers were thrown over my head, and the molester ran out of the room and up the stairs. I heard the dining room door that led to the hallway open. It was gently closed. Then all was quiet.

All I could do was cry.

CHAPTER FIFTY-SIX

IT WAS 6:30 IN THE MORNING. The water in the tub was hot. I had been soaking in it for the past half hour. My eyes were closed and my head rested on the tub wall. I tried desperately to put my mind elsewhere and forget my physical and emotional pain. Soaking would help ease my physical pain. Hopefully time would heal my emotional wounds.

Another thirty minutes passed by and I decided to get out of the tub. I looked in the mirror, not really seeing my reflection, but rather trying to find my soul, which had been taken away from me again. It was as if I couldn't see myself, like being caught in a dark hole and searching for my way out. I looked in the mirror above the sink and saw fear and sadness. My whole world had been rocked and I couldn't do a thing about it, not yet anyway. I had to get myself together and at least appear strong. I didn't want to appear like anything was wrong. Helping Mom would be a good way to hide my pain, even though it would be very difficult. As I headed toward the kitchen, my feet felt like a ton of bricks.

I didn't want to move. My mind was gone. I was in a daze. No way would I, or could I let my family see anything externally. My heart cried over and over. I wanted to just stop and shout. I was slipping. How could this have happened to me again? My silent torment was undetectable, and it was imperative that I kept it that way. I looked at everyone with only short glances and an occasional small grin. To my family, my actions were normal. Whenever I cooked, I more than not went into my own little world. But that day I hurt, I hurt bad, and wasn't able to do one thing about it. From that day forward, I knew that I would never be able to sleep comfortably again. Really, this would be good, because maybe I'd have a better chance of defending myself, should the molester show up again. We were making my favorite: turkey sausages, scrambled cheese eggs, oatmeal and toast. Only Dats and Uncle Henry liked grits as much as I did. Randy and Tony preferred oatmeal to eggs. Mom would be happy just drinking her cup of light coffee and nibbling the eggs.

Dats and Uncle Henry were in the living room watching television. Dats had called work earlier and taken the day off. I didn't know why Uncle Henry was still there.

Mom stood near the kitchen sink with one hand on her hip and the other slowly tipping her coffee cup to her perfectly-shaped lips.

I poured the scrambled eggs into a large bowl on the table.

"Breakfast," Mom yelled.

She glanced at the clock atop the refrigerator. It was 7:20 a.m.

"Where's Randy and Tony? They know I told them to be here for breakfast," Mom said, bothered by their tardiness.

"Maybe they overslept, Mom."

The doorbell rang.

"There they are, Mom."

"It better be," she said as she walked out of the kitchen toward the front door "They always forget their keys."

Dats had already beat her to it. He glanced at the overcast sky. It was Randy and Tony. Mom made an about-face back into the kitchen and leaned on the sink, sipping her coffee again.

Randy and Tony came to the kitchen doorway.

Like always, Tony charged to Mom like an uncorked ballistic missile and gave her a big hug.

"Hi, Mom," Tony said, burying his head into Mom's abdomen area. Mom matched his embrace after she placed her coffee cup on the sink. She lovingly kissed him on the top of his head.

Randy looked at what was for breakfast and smiled as he spoke to Mom.

"Hi, Mom."

Mom, with a sympathetic smile, motioned for Randy to come and give her a hug. Randy did. She cuddled them. After a minute she released them.

"Wash up and come eat," she said. Tony went to the bathroom. Randy headed toward his bedroom, looking at me as he walked. He caught me staring 'out'. He knew something was up. "Corey, c'mere. I wanna tell you what Julie told me," Randy said.

I knew what he was saying was only a cover, because neither one of us knew a Julie. He just didn't want anyone to know we were going into his room to talk.

I left the kitchen and ran into his room. He closed the door behind me. I was sad, hurt and dehumanized. I was still hesitant, but right then I needed to talk to someone.

"What's wrong, Corey?" he asked as he began to change his clothes. He'd never wear the same school clothes two days in a row-- bad for his image. He reached into his closet and took out one of three clean school uniform sets. Mom and Dats had bought him one set, and he hustled newspapers in the mornings during the past summer to buy the extra sets. I sat down on the bed. I really wanted to tell him what had happened.

Tears rolled down my cheeks. Randy finished putting on his pants and looked at my teared face.

He sat on the bed next to me and put his arm around me.

"What's wrong?"

I began to sob more. It was the first time Randy had ever seen me cry like this.

He shook me affectionately a couple of times. I wanted to tell him what happened, but he would say something to Mom and Dats immediately. This would blow my strategy to catch my abuser. I had to lie. Well, it really wasn't a lie, but it really wasn't what I was crying about at that moment.

"Grandma, she's gonna die."

"Die?"

"Yeah, she's sick. Dats was there with her last night and she's not doing well."

He embraced me tighter.

"She'll be all right. Grandma's been sick for a long time. She'll survive."

He used the palm of his hand to wipe my tears away. "Look, Grandma is a survivor. She wouldn't want you to be like this. Be strong. No matter what, think about everything she's taught you. If she does die, she would want you to do the things she showed you." He was saying some nice things, but I still hurt badly, both mentally and physically.

"C'mon, let's go eat some of your good cookin'."

Randy led me back into the kitchen. My eyes were a little red. Mom spotted this immediately.

"Is your eye bothering you, Corey?" Mom asked.

"No, I was just rubbing them."

She began to fix our plates. We were all seated at the table. The clock radio on top of the refrigerator was turned up by Mom.

"Shhh!" she said.

Everyone froze in their seats. The radio announcer gave the news.

"Fifty-year-old Bruce Banes was shot and killed late last night at his Arbor Hill diner. A full police investigation is underway. Police say a woman spotted the body of an Asian woman floating near the Hudson River shore just moments ago. Police are investigating possible leads into her death."

Mom turned the radio volume lower and went back to fixing our plates.

This news got Uncle Henry's thinking cap going.

He wondered if she was the same Asian girl Banes served before he died.

"Banes died?" I asked, surprised.

Uncle Henry looked quickly at Mom and Dats before he would answer, looking for their approval to continue. They gave him a questionable look.

He continued to wolf down his eggs and talk.

"Banes shouldn'tve died last night. He was a good guy."

"How do you know he was a good guy, Uncle Henry?" I asked defiantly.

"Corey, that's mighty bold of you," Uncle Henry said sarcastically.

I'd had enough of 'building up' people, especially since someone either at this table or upstairs was taking advantage of me.

"But it's like you never know what people are really into."

I was gonna lower the bomb and tell them while they continued to eat.

"Take me, for instance."

Everyone looked at each other, then kept eating, but listened intently. I guess they thought I was losing it.

"The cat. Yeah, Max, that's who I'm talkin' about. Does anyone know what really happened to him?!"

"He ran away, Corey," Mom replied.

"No, you all ate him." Everyone looked at me in mid-bite, stunned. "That's right, for dinner. Why? Why did I tell you all? Because nobody is without some kind of shame or wrong."

I was getting to the point of telling everything that happened. I stood from the table. I paced in one place, fuming.

"And you know what, that's not all."

They were waiting impatiently as I contemplated my next revelation. Everyone slowly lowered their forks from their mouths.

"Know why I did it? Because I just did it. That's all. Because I was mad. Nobody knows what anyone's capable of when they're mad or crazy or happy or sad. So, Uncle Henry, nobody but Banes knows what he did secretly. Maybe he did something to that Asian girl, like molested her or maybe he was having sex with her. I don't know, nobody really knows. But maybe some day we'll find out. And if she was connected to Banes' death, we'll never know because now she's dead, too."

All was quiet. Tears rolled down my face. Nobody but my molester knew the real reason why.

I stood there crying. Mom came and held me tightly, close to her midsection.

"It's . . ." Mom couldn't finish because she just couldn't. She had an idea what was bothering me; she thought maybe it was Grandma. But ultimately she knew that I was right in what I was saying. Dats and Uncle Henry knew I was right, too. They couldn't even finish eating. Tony sadly looked over at the late Max's cat dish.

There was no more talk, just thought. Mom led me into the living room and held my head close to her bosom.

This was one breakfast no one could ever forget.

* * * * * *

"I think it's time we paid our landlords a little visit, and I don't mean casual either," Justin said.

He had his hand on his apartment doorknob, with Sally B nearby.

He opened the door and started out. He turned to Sally B. "You wait here."

Then he closed the door on her. He took out his gun and checked to make sure it was loaded. Then he tucked it in the back of his pants under his shirt. He confidently made his way down the stairs. Sally B became nervous.

Mom and I were still in the living room. Randy and Tony were in their bedrooms, stalling about getting ready for school.

Then the dining room door flew open and Justin casually walked in like we were his tenants. As he made his way toward the kitchen, he looked back into the living room with a smile. I frowned at him. Mom was scared.

"Jim, I need to speak with you."

"Oh, Justin, nice to see you. I didn't hear you knock," Dats said.

"I didn't knock, Jimmy!" Justin said. He knew Dats didn't like to be called that. Dats had an irritated look.

I stormed into the kitchen. Justin stood in the doorway.

"Who do you think you are, barging in our house!" I yelled.

Randy came and stood in his doorway. Tony stopped at the top of the basement entrance and watched.

Mom ran toward me and put her arms around my shoulders from behind.

"Well, well. We're all together now," Justin looked at me with his stupid grin, then turned back to Dats.

"Didn't you hear me? This is not your house," I said as Mom pulled me back toward the basement door

"Corey, come on now, let's go downstairs," Mom said.

I tried to resist, but Mom was too strong for me.

Uncle Henry stood up.

"What's going on, Jim, is there a problem?" Uncle Henry asked.

Justin cut his eyes at Uncle Henry, showcasing a detesting glaze.

"I think you should learn to knock," Uncle Henry said, raising his eyebrows.

"Nobody pays you to think," Justin retaliated.

Uncle Henry moved closer to Justin.

Then Dats stepped in.

"Let me handle this," Dats said, escorting Justin to the living room.

Uncle Henry just looked from the kitchen into the living room.

Dats closed the glass door as he went into the living room. Uncle Henry tried to look through the glass door, but there were white curtains hanging on it.

Mom had told me to stay in the basement until Justin left. She ran up the stairs. I angrily grabbed my eavesdropping pipe from behind the radiator, sat in my chair and listened.

Mom was just entering the living room with Dats and Justin.

I could faintly hear the door close as Justin began to talk.

"I know it was Corey who made the 911 call. He also broke into my computer room and stole some documents."

They looked at each other. "You both know that I can't leave any stones unturned. Now, I need that printout back."

"How do you know Corey has it?" Mom asked.

"Who else would pull something like this? You know I have very incriminating evidence against both of you locked away in a safe place, so it'd be stupid of either one of you to have done this. And I know he was the only one home while I was out. Now, I don't care what you do to get my printout back, but get it! And if you can't, I'll do it myself. I pay both of you very well to keep your boys in that school. And Jim, your mother has been very well taken care of because of my generosity"

"We've always earned whatever money we accepted from you. You wanted protection, we got that, girls, everything you asked for, we got it," Dats said.

Justin went to the living room door.

He thought for a few seconds. He could have killed all of us right then, but he had his reasons for letting us live.

I heard him making his exit as I continued to listen. I knew

Mom and Dats would come down here asking me for the printout. I put my eavesdropping pipe back behind the radiator.

I went over to my bed, lifted my mattress and grabbed the printout. I stuck it down the back of my pants. I heard the dining room door close and footsteps going back up to Justin's place. Then I heard several footsteps coming down the basement stairs to my bedroom. I quickly fixed the covers on my bed and went and sat back in my eavesdropping chair. Then my bedroom door opened. Mom entered, followed by Dats and Uncle Henry.

"Corey, did you go upstairs and take anything from Justin's computer room?" Mom asked in a frenzy.

"Corey, this is not some game we're playing," Dats reiterated.

Uncle Henry calmly sat on the sturdy wooden arm of the chair.

"Corey, this guy swears you got up into his place and just did whatever you wanted. I said to myself, how does a ten year old know where to look for a computer in a house he's only been in once?"

"What's the big deal about this guy, Mom?"

"Corey, that's not the issue here. If you have a computer printout, then you need to hand it over before you get us all in trouble," Dats said desperately.

"I don't have it."

They all looked at each other. Mom threw up her hands in frustration and left in a huff. Dats followed her.

"Get ready for school, Corey," Mom said as she walked out.

"Maybe we shouldn't send him to school today," Dats said.

"Today, tomorrow, the next day, what difference does it make?" Mom whispered angrily as she made it to the dining room.

"He's better off there. There are too many people around there for Justin to try anything. He wouldn't risk it!" Mom said.

"Boys, let's go get ready for school," she yelled to Randy and Tony, stood at the top of the basement stairs.

Uncle Henry had me cornered in the basement. He wouldn't leave the arm of the chair.

"Corey, I don't know what that little outburst you had in the kitchen was all about, but whatever's bothering you, you can't take it out on the guy upstairs. If you have something of his, you need to return it."

There was silence as Uncle Henry peered down at me.

"And I'll tell you something else, Corey, I don't think it was a coincidence they found that Asian girl's body in the Hudson this morning. My gut feeling is, she had something to do with Banes' death."

"But how do you know . . ."

Uncle Henry raised his hand to silence me.

"Let's just say I know something. I know that basement door didn't just get open by itself and a pail moved in front of it to keep it closed."

Uncle Henry put his hand down and knelt in front of me.

"I'll make a deal with you, you share your secret and I'll share mine," Uncle Henry proposed. A million thoughts ran through my head. I really wanted to trust an adult. But I couldn't. I remembered meeting this con the summer I stayed in Brooklyn with Grandma. I would see him on the corner watching houses when I would go to the store for Grandma. One day I asked him why he was watching the houses. He then asked me how did I know he was watching houses, and I told him he was always on a different side of the street whenever I came to the store. He talked to me and we became friends.

After a while he told me that he had blown his con because I had seen him too often at too many different times, and that secrecy was the only thing that worked. Anybody could plan a con, but could they pull it off without a hitch. He told me that's why he always worked alone. That way, he knew nobody else would talk.

"I don't have nothing, Uncle Henry. I opened the door and got scared and ran back in bed because I thought I would get in trouble for being up. Mom and Dats doesn't want us out without them knowing, especially early morning."

Uncle Henry knew I was lying, but he went along with it for then. He smiled.

"Okay, buddy."

"Corey," Mom yelled from the top of the stairs.

"Let's go. Walk to school with your brothers," she said.

"Okay, Mom," I yelled back to her.

Uncle Henry stood and followed me up the stairs.

"You be careful with that eye at school today. No roughhouse playing," Uncle Henry warned.

"Yes, Uncle Henry."

Randy and Tony were waiting for me in the hallway leading to the front door. I trotted out the door behind Randy. Mom and Uncle Henry watched us leave from the dining room door.

Randy and Tony headed up Myrtle Avenue toward school.

"Let's go up the alley!" I demanded, whispering.

Randy and Tony stood on the corner and looked at me for a minute.

I motioned for them to follow me. They reluctantly followed

me because when we first moved on Grand Street there was this bully who lived on Myrtle Avenue, about half-way up the block.

He once warned me and Randy never to walk up his street again. That very next day we did, and the bully tried to take on all of us. Keep in mind that five years ago the bully was bigger than all of us. But even back then, Randy was stronger than the average eight year old. I wasn't much help at five years old, but Randy even at eight didn't need me. I helped anyway, and we kicked the shit out of him. He never bothered us again. We told Tony about it when he got older, because he was only two at the time. Even so, Tony felt like it was a direct threat to him and he felt he had to go up that hill. He threatened us, saying that he was going to get his gang on us if we came up the hill again. Even if we sometimes have to walk out of our way, we go up Myrtle Avenue hill. We may have done some silly things, but we weren't punks. To go the alley way, to Randy and Tony this was an act of cowardice. Once I explained to them the reason why we needed to walk up the alleyway to school, they were game.

"I want to show you guys something. And I don't want the whole neighborhood watching us."

We turned the corner from Grand Street up the alleyway. The width of the alleyway was large enough for one car to fit. Mostly only the people coming and going to their homes on either Myrtle Avenue or Park Avenue used the alleyway to pull in and out of their garages or driveways. I took out the computer printout from the back of my pants.

I kept looking behind me to see if anyone was following us. I opened the printout.

"Look at this, it has Mom and Dats in it. I took it from Justin's computer."

"How'd you do that?" Tony asked. He was impressed.

"Never mind that, what does it say?" Randy said.

Tony and Randy were jockeying for room to get a good look at the entire printout.

"That Justin is into some crooked stuff. This printout gives names, dates, money amounts, everything. It's only a couple of pages, but they must be important because he wants them back bad. I overheard him threaten Mom and Dats if he didn't get 'em back." I heard a car engine start up and I looked up the alleyway hill. There was a car pulling from the Tunney's backyard. It was Mrs. Tunney. I snatched the printout and refolded it back up because this was the nosiest old lady I'd ever met. If we smiled at her, she'd ask what we were doing.

We moved to the side to let her drive by. She nearly ran into the light pole on the left side of the street because she was breaking her neck to see what we were doing as she coasted down the alleyway.

We laughed at Mrs. Tunney's driving, then started back up the alleyway.

Two dogs started barking, one in Mrs. Tunney's backyard and the other one in a backyard almost at the end of the block. Mrs. Tunney's dog was a little mutt on a chain. It was really useless to anyone who owned it. After Mrs. Tunney turned onto Grand Street, we teased the dog a little, then kept going. The dog at the corner of Phillip Street and the alleyway was a big grey Husky. It was on the first back porch of the corner house, standing erect as he barked. The owner, a big white woman, walked onto the back porch and looked at us smiling, then she yelled at us.

"Betcha won't tease this one."

We smiled again and kept on across Phillip Street through the alleyway of the next block of Myrtle Avenue, which was the flat part.

"So, what're you gonna do with the printout?" Randy asked.

Tony adjusted his backpack on his shoulder with wide eyes, ran in front of me and continued through the alley walking backwards, sucking up my every word.

"That's where I need you guys to help me."

Tony tripped on a rock, but he didn't fall.

"What?" Randy asked.

"Nobody else can know that I have this printout, but I need to get a copy of it."

"But there's always somebody in the principal's office. The copy machine is outside her office, and Mrs. Hillzinger never leaves the office counter."

"Yeah, how you gonna do that, Corey?" Tony asked.

"We gotta create some kind of diversion," I said.

"Why don't you go to the copy center downtown?" Tony suggested.

"Good idea, Tony, but what are we gonna do, skip school to go down there? Plus, we can't take the chance of somebody else seeing what's in the printout. It wouldn't be good for them. We can't leave a trail. Justin would find out and it could hurt them."

"We could go to the library, Corey," Randy suggested.

I pondered my thoughts for a few seconds, while looking into Randy's eyes.

"Nah, we need to do this now, today, in school. Like right away. To have to go all the way to the library is too much time after school. Justin could be waiting with Mom and Dats to come get the printout after school. Who knows, they could be on their way to school right now to get it. Nope, I think the principal's office is our best bet."

"So what if they come while we're in class and we haven't got a copy made yet?" Tony asked.

"Let's hope they don't," I said.

"I think we're making too big a deal of this whole thing. Just give me the printout.. I'll get it done," Randy said, with a tad of machoism.

"Randy, this isn't the time to poke ya chest out. People could get hurt," I said.

"Yeah, Randy, put ya chest back in ya chest," Tony said, as he tried to make a joke.

Randy and I shot Tony a look.

"Shut up. That was corny, Tony," Randy said.

I rolled my eyes.

"So what's the plan, Corey?" Randy asked.

"Maybe you guys can start fighting or something, and then everybody'll come to break it up. But you gotta do it right in front of the office," Tony suggested.

"Strike two, Tony. I don't wanna beat up Corey, and anyway somebody will break it up, and who's gonna make the copies? We can't bring anybody else in on this," Randy said.

"Yeah, we gotta think of something. It won't be hard!" I said.

We were at the end of the alleyway, standing at the corner that was across the street from the school. The street we had to cross to get to school was Eagle Street, which ran north and south. We stood on the corner and watched the other kids play. There we were, trying to figure out a way to make copies to save our mother and father, and probably me too. All the other kids were playing, like they didn't have a worry in the world, which is what we should have been doing. We didn't have a clue, but I knew we needed to make copies that day. I just had a feeling that a lot might happen and I needed to get a copy of the printout, but it looked gloomy, and so did we. A fire truck roared by us as we dejectedly crossed the street.

Randy and Tony went to the playground area of the school as I sat on the school rail, watching the fire truck speed away with its sirens blasting. The school bell sounded. Everyone scattered, bumping into each other, laughing and talking as they hurried for their designated door. I wished I could be so happy. I knew I would have some leverage to get Mom and Dats out of this, if I could just get a copy. And I would. I jumped off the railing and headed into school.

CHAPTER FIFTY-SEVEN

SARA HAD GONE TO the adoption agency she visited before, at the request of Casey, the secretary. It was only about 8:30, but Casey needed to see Sara before work because she couldn't do what she was going to do during work hours or she would lose her job.

Sara waited at the far end of the parking lot in her car, as Casey had instructed..

She noticed a car pull beside her driver's door. It was Casey. Casey got out of her car and quickly got in Sara's front passenger side.

"Hi," Casey said with a small smile, trying to hide her nervousness.

"Hi," Sara said.

"I know you have no idea why I'm doing this, and neither do I really. I will say that my boss is an ass and I don't really like him, but really he's just a puppy. Anyway, enough of that. After you left that day, Mr. Linton called me into his office and belittled me, and then asked me out. How dare he! So I got mad and remembered you were so insulted by him, and I decided to take matters into my own hands."

"But why me?" Sara asked.

"You just happened to be the last person in that day and I like your quiet spirit."

"Quiet spirit?" Sara asked.

"Yeah. See, I study astrology and . . ."

Sara gave Casey a strange look that cut her off.

". . . Never mind." Casey said, knowing Sara didn't want to hear it.

"Anyway, your son is still in New York City somewhere."

It was getting close to 9:00. Casey saw her boss pull into the parking lot. She slid down in the front seat.

"There's my boss. I gotta beat him upstairs."

Sara looked around.

"Don't look back. Here, I made a copy of your file." Casey handed Sara the large folder.

"You're gonna have to read it," Casey sighed. "Try not to call the office, but in case you have to, use a password." Casey thought for a few seconds. "Ah . . . red, say red, and I'll know it's you. If I don't respond, hang up and call back. That's only if you need my help, which you shouldn't." Casey put large, dark sunglasses on.

She crept out the door.

Sara watched her go into another door of the building.

Sara started her car and pulled out. She drove by Mr. Linton, blew her horn and motioned seductively for the boss to come to her car.

He looked around, checking to make sure no one was watching, because he was a married man. He smiled as he went closer.

Just as he was about to lean on the passenger car door, Sara sped off, leaving him hanging. She only did it to give Casey time to get up to the office before he did.

Mr. Linton was embarrassed as he meekly looked around, then tucked his tail and walked toward the building.

Sara needed to find somewhere quiet so that she could go through the large file.

Back home, Henry and Jim were at each other.

"Look, Jim, how can you let this guy come into your home and boss you around? What else is there to this guy that you aren't telling me? It's gotta be more than that grand you owe him."

Jim walked away from Henry and stared blankly out of the living room window.

Henry walked up behind Jim.

"What? Did he catch you with Sally B or something?"

Jim slightly turned his head toward Henry, rolled his eyes in the process, then looked out of the window. Henry was put off by Jim's nonchalance.

Henry took Jim by his arm and attempted to get his attention. Jim abruptly turned toward him and grabbed him by his collar.

"Now, you look, Henry just leave well enough alone, dammit! I can handle this."

Henry easily overpowered Jim and calmly took his hands from his blue flannel shirt collar.

"Okay, okay, Jim, calm down. That's what you should've done to Justin, not me. I'm your friend."

Jim backed off and sat in the loveseat near the same window he was staring out of.

"Look, I'm sorry. A lot's happening right now."

"Don't worry about it. I know where you're at."

"Banes got shot, Mama's sick, now this guy's accusing my son of being a thief!"

"Well, at least you're finally clear on that."

Jim cut his eyes at Henry.

"Well, you were questioning whose son he is."

"Do you think this guy will try to hurt Corey?" Henry continued.

"No telling what he'll do, Henry. He's a dangerous man."

"What do you mean 'dangerous'?"

"Let's just say he's not the putz you think he is. It's all a show."

"I kinda figured that. But what is it that makes him so special?"

"What else? Money!"

"Money?"

"And he's got plenty of it."

"But that doesn't make him special, Jim."

"I'm willing to bet you Banes was on his payroll. He must have stumbled onto something, or started talking too much. You know how Banes could get at times. Then Justin just got cold feet and decided to get rid of him."

"Well, you know what's strange about that is this Asian girl? Why would she want to kill Banes?"

"I don't know."

"Well, let's go to the police, Jim," Henry said, standing up.

"No, we can't. We don't really have anything on the guy."

"But you really do have something on him, Jim."

"No, we don't have nothing that can be proven."

"Are you on his payroll, Jim?"

"What makes you ask that?"

"You're just letting this play along too easy. Why did the police go up to his apartment the other day?"

"Because Corey was playing a prank."

Jim was lying.

"No, I mean, why would Corey play a prank like that? I mean, the kid likes excitement, but to call the police, that's a bit much, don't you think?"

Jim stared blankly at Henry.

"C'mon, Jim, in order for Corey to call the police he must have seen something that he didn't think was right. And he must have seen something more than once."

Jim stormed to his feet and walked to the window on the Myrtle Avenue side of the house.

"All right, all right. The day we took Corey home from the hospital, he told us he saw Justin bring a bag from upstairs and that he was carrying it like it had a body in it."

"But what would make him think that it had a body in it?"

"Because he snuck upstairs and heard a child's voice. But he didn't have a chance to see who it was because he heard footsteps coming and ran out of the apartment."

"So why didn't you ask Justin about it?"

"I did ask him," Jim shot back.

"So report it to the police."

"It's been reported, Henry! Look, if there isn't proof, then nothing's going to happen, and as long as that man is out there running loose, I'm not going to antagonize him and have him touch my family. Got it!"

"Enough said, Jim."

Henry rubbed his chin in thought. He was only backing off temporarily.

CHAPTER FIFTY-EIGHT

SARA SAT IN A BOOTH in the rear of the Central Avenue Gateway Diner. Central Avenue ran from downtown Albany right straight through the town of Colonie to the neighboring city of Schenetady. It was Albany's main drag. Most people used Central to go from one mall to the next.

The diner was where a lot of people went mostly for breakfast or late night snacks. There was a waiting area as you entered through the front door, before you got to the inside of the diner. To the left of the front door was the cashier's booth. They made sure that everyone paid so they couldn't run out on the bill.

Party people who came in late at night from local dance clubs would be the ones who tried to run out on their bill. These party people, mostly teenagers and college types, would sit at the five booths that were near the cashier's booth. These booths were adjacent to windows that lined the restaurant from the front door to the rear of the restaurant. There were other two-seater booths that ran down the center of the restaurant. Usually young and old lovers would sit there. Occasionally early mornings and late night panhandlers would stroll in. They would ask for money, or take a seat where food was left over and eat. Sometimes they'd sit at the ten-stool counter that was opposite the booths. Truckers would come in early mornings and sit at the counter for breakfast before they got back on the highway.

Mostly during the week, in the middle of the day, the place was quiet. The elderly frequented the restaurant, and usually sat at the center booths because the sunlight from the windows near the wall booths was too bright for them.

In the very back at the last corner booth, Sara had papers scattered about her table as she sat facing the entrance. She occasionally glanced up toward the front door to see who was coming and going. Not that it mattered, but she wanted to make sure no one came in that she knew. But if that did happen, which was highly unlikely, she wanted to put away her papers and be pleasant toward them. She hoped most people would go to the side where the sun shined in the windows and leave the back to her

She intermittently sipped her black coffee while she scoured the papers that Casey gave her from the adoption agency. Most of the forms were from years ago that she had to sign when she gave up her child for adoption.

Frustration began to set in because she wasn't finding any information that told her where her child was, twenty-five years later.

Sara took her last sip of coffee and motioned for the waitress to come.

The thin, pretty woman hurried over to her.

"Yes?" the waitress said.

Sara put her arms on the table covering the papers, smiling at the waitress as she spoke.

"May I have more coffee, please?"

"Yes, right away!" the waitress replied.

Sara went back to reading the forms. What she was looking for was something that gave her a hint as to where her child was located. She wanted to know so that she could inform his adoptive parents that she might be leaving Albany, not that the adoptive parents knew Sara was in Albany or if she was even alive. But for Sara just to know and maybe meet with her full-grown child would be satisfying for her.

The waitress returned with the coffee and poured Sara a full cup.

Sara nodded, smiled at the waitress and went back to her work. The waitress went back to serving her customers.

Sara finally came across one of the papers that gave her a clue as to where her search might begin.

"Summers," she said to herself. But the form only listed the names of the adopting couple as Jonathan and Emily Summers.

Sara jerked her head up from her papers and scanned the room. She hadn't spotted what she was looking for. Then she got up from her seat and went to her waitress, who stood behind the counter preparing coffee with her back to Sara.

"Excuse me," she said.

The waitress quickly turned toward Sara with a big smile. "Yes?"

"Do you have a phone here?" she asked anxiously.

The waitress pointed toward the rear area of the restaurant. "Yes, in the ladies' room."

Sara looked in the direction and headed there. "Thanks."

She walked briskly toward the ladies' room and pushed open the door, almost hitting a woman who was leaving.

"Excuse me," Sara said apologetically.

Sara pushed open the heavy wooden door. She looked around and spotted the phone, opposite two sinks. She went to the sink and washed her face with cold water. She wiped her hands, using brown paper towels from the towel box hanging on the wall between the two mirrors above the sinks. She looked at her face momentarily. Water dripped down her cheeks. She sighed, then dried her face. She took a longer look at her tired eyes. She fingered through her black hair, trying to fix it. It was still better looking than most women. Even though she didn't know it, she still looked good. She tucked her white cotton blouse into her blue jeans. She snapped out of it, then hastened to the phone.

She dug into her pocket for a quarter.

Quickly finding one, she inserted it into the phone.

She dialed a number. She waited impatiently as the phone rang three times.

Before the person could say hello, Sara blurted out "Carpet Red."

There was a short pause on the phone coming from the other end. Then Sara jumped back in again.

"I mean 'Red Carpet'." She paused.

"Code Red," Sara said again.

Casey, on the other end of the phone, sighed and whispered.

"Red, just red, Honey. It's me. What can I do for you?"

"I need to find out where the Summers live, or a phone number and whatever else you can tell me. These papers don't give me information."

Casey sat at her desk, whispering.

She had the phone between her shoulder and ear as her eyes scanned the room, making sure her boss was nowhere in sight.

"Listen, what I'll do is check the computer, but it might take some time. Did you check directory assistance?"

"Yes. Nothing."

"Figures."

"I don't have a lot of time, I may have to leave in a moment's notice."

"Leave where?"

"The country" Sara said. She only said this hoping it would help her get the adoption records.

"Why?"

"Never mind why. Just help me, please."

"Sure, okay."

"I'll call you back in five minutes."

"Five minutes?"

"That's all I've got!"

"Well, Honey, hold on just a minute. Who's helping who here?"

"I'm sorry, ten minutes?" Sara said.

Casey held the receiver away from her ear, flabbergasted. She stared at the device incredulously. Then she put the receiver back to her ear.

"Call back in a half hour and I'll have concrete information. Call back in ten minutes and I'll have mush."

Sara sighed. "Okay, you win."

"Bye," Casey said, like she had won the war of words.

Sara readied herself for a wait as she hung up the receiver.

She came back to the booth with her shoulders slouched. She plopped down into her seat and waited.

The remorse she felt for giving away her very first born could only be eased by finding him. It had been years since she saw him. But at the time she made her decision, she believed that it was best for the child. With the possibility of her family having to move away forever, she wanted to say good-bye for good, that is if he was still alive.

CHAPTER FIFTY-NINE

INSIDE THE SCHOOL'S first floor there was chaos.

Kindergartners through fourth grade students milled about talking and playing, while others ran to their classrooms.

Randy, Tony and I stood there in front of it all. We watched through a large two inch thick window. It was the school office window.

In the waiting area, three chairs with their backs beneath the window pane lined the wall. In front was the counter. Behind the counter was old Mrs. Hillzinger, the office supervisor. Mrs. Hillzinger was known for enforcing school rules and regulations. If someone needed to be paddled, it was done with a wooden, two foot long, three inch board, and she carried it out with pleasure. Mrs. Hillzinger was the only lay person in the school. The remainder were nuns and priests.

The school secretary was in charge of making sure all the administrative paperwork was in order. Her assistant did most of the work, though. They were both nuns. Mrs. Hillzinger was known for her organizational skills and stern disposition. She was a member of the church parish and worked with the priests, and came highly recommended.

Her face was thick and full of wrinkles. For some reason, she felt her thick black mustache made her look more youthful. That's why she never shaved it off.

She only stood five feet four, but weighted about one hundred and fifty pounds, and it was all muscle. Around her midsection was a little flab, but that was to be expected at fifty, as far as Mrs. Hillzinger was concerned. Otherwise, she was a thick woman with big bones. She would be our biggest obstacle because she guarded that office like it was Fort Knox.

We were watching as Mrs. Hillzinger moved gracefully about the office in a hurry. She stood behind the counter that went from one end of the office to the other, barking out instructions to the secretary.

Behind the counter were two desks; one for Mrs. Hillzinger and one for the secretary. The assistant had a smaller desk in the corner of the office.

Mrs. Hillzinger's desk was near the one and only copy machine in the school.

"God, how are we gonna get to it, Corey? That Mrs. Hillzinger guards it like she owns it," Tony said.

"Yeah, I know. We'll figure out something," I said.

"Well, we'd better figure it out fast 'cause you can't carry that printout around forever." Randy said.

The halls were emptied out finally. The first bell rang. It was time for all students to be in their second class.

Mrs. Hillzinger scurried like a penguin to the two windows near the secretary's desk and opened the blinds. Then she looked at the clock above the window pane where we stood. It was 9:30 a.m. She looked toward the principal's office.

She looked at us and pointed her finger, shaking it.

She frowned, fixed her bifocals, rubbed her thin black mustache with her thumb and index finger and made her way from behind the steel made counter toward the front door. We scattered.

"I'm outta here," Randy said.

"Come back at eleven," I said.

"Okay" Tony said, taking off down the hall opposite Randy and me.

Mrs. Hillzinger opened the door and watched us run away.

"Walk!" she yelled with resounding authority.

* * * * * *

Justin and Sally B rested in his car. They were parked on Morton Avenue, opposite Cathedral Academy, on the other side of Lincoln Park. They weren't even a quarter mile away.

Justin had his high-powered binoculars pressing against the passenger window of the car. He could see Mrs. Hillzinger through her window.

"I guess school has started," Justin said. He glanced at his wristwatch.

"Nine-thirty. We'll wait." He laid his binoculars on his lap and looked out the front windshield.

"Is everything ready, Sally B?" He turned toward her.

"Yes."

"What about New York? Are we closed up?"

"No. I thought you wanted me to keep them open."

Sally B remembered that Justin did say to close the two suites, but she was saving her own neck and keeping them open.

If anything went down against her, Sally B's old friend, Christina, was instructed to blow the lid and to plant drink glasses with Justin's fingerprints and other articles to set him up to be caught.

The knife that he used to slit Angie's throat would also be left for the police. Christina was told by Sally B to place the knife in the New York suite with a note detailing where the body was dumped by Justin, not Sally B. Of course it was a lie about who dumped the body, but if Justin was successful in killing her, Sally B wanted to make sure that Justin spent his remaining days on earth in prison.

"Are we gonna do it today or not, Justin?"

"We'll wait and see."

Justin cut his eyes at her running them from her head to her toes.

"It's been a while, hasn't it?"

She looked at him, knowing what he meant, but playing dumb.

"What's been a while?"

He stroked her thigh as if she were his possession.

"You know, me and you."

"I guess you could say that. But now isn't the time."

He slid over closer to her and put his arm around her.

"Who said so?" he asked.

Sally B leaned away.

"Justin, we need to be precise."

Justin moved away.

"Yeah. We'll have plenty of time for that."

Justin picked his binoculars up from his lap and looked toward the school.

"In time we'll get what I want and we'll be done here," he said.

Sally B stared straight ahead, looked up Morton Avenue and wondered where the end of the day would bring her.

CHAPTER SIXTY

CAPTAIN LEE STARED at the photo that had the name of Al Totten on it. He took the picture out of his "in" basket and studied it while leaning back in his chair in his police station office. He went to his personal computer and keyed in 013-28-7222, which was the social security number at the bottom of the picture.

Captain Lee was happy being captain, and whenever something came across his fax or desk that involved nabbing a criminal, he exhausted all his avenues before he discarded it.

Justin knew this character trait about Captain Lee. For Lee all police were brothers, and he felt if he could help a fellow officer, then his day was complete.

Captain Lee was already into overtime.

He hit the enter key on the computer keyboard.

The computer screen showed a number of criminal activities from Al Totten's early childhood.

The computer screen read:

1. Alan Totten
2. Age: 25
3. Place of Birth: Troy, New York
4. Parents:

This light blinked, which was strange.

5. Number of Juvenile Convictions: 3
   a) Time Served: 1 year
6. Other Convictions: 0
7. Current Address: Unknown
8. Next of Kin: Unknown

To Captain Lee, it wasn't so strange not to know next of kin because a lot of times when people are locked up they don't reveal relatives unless it's absolutely necessary. But for a juvenile to not list his parents was unusual, since police had to be able to call them in case of an emergency.

Apparently Al Totten didn't care for his parents, or didn't know if they were alive or dead, and didn't care to know. Since Totten was born in Troy and Captain Lee was working in the Division II Precinct in Albany, he wanted to know more about this potential killer.

He turned from the computer and rolled his swivel chair back to his desk. He checked his pad for the phone number listed on it. He picked up the receiver of the telephone and then dialed the number.

The phone rang one time and someone picked it up. Captain Lee heard a noise in the background as the person spoke.

"Jefferies," he said in the laid-back voice amid the turmoil that surrounded him at New York City's 3rd Precinct, on the upper west side of Manhattan.

It was Jeff, of the station dubbed Mutt and Jeff detective team.

Jeff frowned at the noise around him as he strained to hear Captain Lee speak.

"I'm sorry, you're gonna have to speak up. I got all these jerks running around my desk making noise. Wait, let me close my door."

Jeff laid the receiver on his desk and went to close his door. But before doing so he yelled out to anyone and everyone.

"Shutup!!"

This didn't draw any reaction from his busy coworkers. Obviously, they're used to such outbursts by Jeff. He shrugged, smiled, and closed his door behind him while he made his way back to his desk recliner.

"Yeah, Detective Jefferies speaking. What can I do for you?"

"Hello, this is Captain Lee up at Division II in Albany. You faxed me a photo of Al Totten the other night . . ."

"Yeah, you and about forty-nine other states," Jeff mumbled, interrupting.

"Excuse me?" Captain Lee said.

"Oh, nothing, just talking. Nothing," Jeff said impatiently.

"Anyway, what's going on with this guy Totten?"

Jeff paused for a moment, and frowned at the thought.

"What Totten?"

"The fax you sent me about the maid that was killed at Park Plaza and the girl you said you were trailing but lost her."

Jeff was reluctantly digging through a stack of papers that were sloppily thrown on his desk. He found Totten's picture.

"Oh, okay, this guy. We're still looking. We don't have too many leads. We're still trying to locate this woman, the woman we were trailing."

"Is she a suspect in the killing, too?"

"I don't . . ." He paused and thought for a second. "Ya know, I never thought about that. I'm gonna check into it."

Captain Lee had struck a nerve, and he was proud.

"Well, I'm glad I could be of help to you. Now go get those animals," Captain Lee said in a gung-ho tone.

Jeff moved the phone away from his ear and frowned, then shook his head at Captain Lee's last remark.

"Small town cowboy," Jeff mumbled.

He hung up the phone and pinned the picture on the wall to his left. He backed away from the picture and stared at it. He rubbed his chin, contemplating his next move.

CHAPTER SIXTY-ONE

IT WAS 11:00 A.M. Sara sat at the Gateway Diner on Central Avenue. She looked through the papers from the adoption agency, not because they had valuable information, but because she was nervous. Sara's nerves were almost shot because she was still giving Casey time at the adoption agency to look up more goods about the whereabouts of the unknown child.

She picked her head up from the table and looked around. She saw people, but she wasn't paying any attention to them. She began tapping her fingers on the table in a rhythmic fashion. After a few minutes of this, she began to stare at the areas leading to the bathroom where the telephone was.

She glanced at the clock on the wall behind the counter. It read 11:15. The minutes seemed like hours for Sara. Finally she got tired of waiting and bolted from her booth seat to the women's bathroom, where the telephone awaited her.

She dialed the seven digits to the adoption agency. She waited patiently as her partner, Casey, answered.

"Red."

"Ya got it this time," Casey said, somewhat surprised.

"Yeah, yeah," Sara said hastily.

"Slow down, haste makes waste," Casey said with a smile.

Sara could tell Casey was smiling over the phone. She cringed a bit and took a deep breath, knowing that Casey was right.

"Okay, what have you got?" Sara asked with a forced hint of calmness.

"Well, I was able to come up with the family who adopted your child. But the problem is that their number comes up unlisted."

With that information, Sara looked in the mirror. She leaned against the wall and propped her left foot against it, supporting her weight on her right foot. She stared at the mirror, wondering what to do next. She sighed, and was almost ready to throw in the towel.

"Well, I guess that's it then," Sara said in defeat.

"Hold on now, that's not all."

"Yeah," Sara said, almost excited.

"It seems that there were more records and I went through hell to get them."

Casey wanted some praise for efforts before she would give up any more information, and Sara sensed this.

"I know, you've done a fine job. Now, what is it?" Sara said wearily.

"Here's the number," Casey said.

"What?" Mom exclaimed as she bounced off the wall.

"You mean you have a phone number where my son might be?" Sara said incredulously.

"No." Casey dragged this out, and she felt justified in being dramatic with this information because she was never given a pat on her back by her boss for doing great job. She felt this was her moment of glory. "Casey, you're doing a great job helping me out like this. I know your job is on the line the more you help me. I really, really appreciate what you're doing. Now, can I please have that phone number?"

"Thank you, Sara, I really appreciate that. Got a pen?"

"No, give it to me. I'll remember"

"Area code 718-626-2688. Got it?"

"Yeah, thanks. Goodbye," Sara said, slamming the receiver

back on the phone.

She dug into her pocket for a quarter. Then she realized it was a long distance call. She went out to the restaurant counter in a hurry.

"I need change for five dollars," Sara impatiently said to the waitress behind the counter.

The waitress looked into Sara's darkened eyes. She knew Sara was desperate. The waitress patted her money apron, feeling for coins.

"I'm sorry, I don't have that much."

"Does anyone?" Sara asked.

"I'll check," the waitress said.

"No, see, I need the change, it's a matter of life and death. This is a restaurant. You have to have change."

"Can't you make a collect call?" the waitress asked.

"You don't understand, they don't know who I am .."

The waitress had a dumbfounded look.

"Look, it's too complicated. Just give me some change, please!" Sara begged.

The waitress took Sara's five dollars and went to the cash register near the front door. The restaurant manager was behind the register counting receipts. Even in his black tie, white shirt and dress slacks, all of which were tight on his flabby body, he looked sloppy.

"Sam, she needs change for a five in silver for the phone," the waitress said. Sam pushed back his oily black bangs from his forehead and adjusted his crooked, thick, black-framed glasses.

Sam didn't have the decency to lift his head up from his count to answer.

"Can't do it, I need change for the rest of the day," he said.

Sara banged her hand down hard on his stack of receipts.

"I'm up here!" Sara said authoritatively. Sam stopped counting to look at her.

"Look, I'm a paying customer and I need to make a long distance emergency phone call. I have to! After you give me change, I'll go out and bring more back when I'm finished making my call. I need the change, please."

Sam looked into Sara's desperate eyes. He sighed, opened the cash register and took out five dollars worth of quarters. Sara smiled as the manager took the five dollar bill from the waitress and gave her the quarters.

Sara headed toward the ladies' room and had to get in a jab, but to herself.

"Asshole!"

She dashed into the ladies' room and put in a quarter, then

dialed the number from memory. Her heart pounded as she waited
for an answer. An automated voice told her to add more money. She
inserted three dollars worth of quarters. After three rings, someone
answered. It was a raspy female voice.

"Yes?"

"Is this the Summers residence?" Sara asked.

There was a brief pause as the woman in her sixties contemplated.

"Hello?" Sara said.

"Yes, this is," the raspy voiced woman replied.

"I'm Sara Harris. You don't really know me. I'm calling about
your son."

"What about my son? Is there something wrong at school? We
sent him to school . . ."

"I guess I have the wrong number. I'm sorry." Sara was about
to hang up when someone snatched the phone from Mrs. Summers.

"Who is this?" Mr. Summers asked in a dictating tone. He
was in his mid sixties.·

Sara pressed the receiver back to her ear.

"Yes, oh, this is Sara Harris."

"What do you want?" Mr. Summers barked impatiently.

"Your son, where is he? Is he really at school?" Sara asked.

"You have to excuse my wife. Ever since our son left, she
hasn't been the same. She almost lost her mind. She blames herself
for him running off."

"Have you heard from him?"

"Wait. Who are you anyway?"

"Sara Har . . ."

"I know that. But who or what are you asking these questions
for?"

Sara didn't want to tell because she knew she would probably
get hung up on. But she figured she had nothing to lose and that she
had gotten this far. She took a deep breath.

"I gave my child up for adoption years ago . . . now I'm trying to locate him before I leave the country"

"Well, why?"

"Just to tell him I love him and that I was sorry for giving up
on him the way that I did."

Mr. Summers sighed and paused a few seconds before he spoke
again.

"How do we come into play with all of this?" Mr. Summers
asked.

"Well, this is how far I got with the agency . . . and I know that this information is confidential, so don't blame the agency I pushed."

"We don't know where he is," Mr. Summers said.

"Thanks," Sara said.

Just as Sara was about to hang up, Mr. Summers looked over at his wife rocking herself in the stationary chair while staring at him. She'd hoped that he would give Sara all the information. Mrs. Summers really wanted to know for herself, even in her lopsided state of mind, where her only son was.

"Hey!" Mr. Summers yelled into the phone so that Sara could hear him before she hung up. She put the phone back to her ear.

"You might try some lady's house on Elk Street in Albany. He was fond of her. That was the last number he left with us, then he disappeared again. We haven't heard from him in ten years," Mr. Summers said.

"Okay thank you, Mr Summers. Oh, by the way, what's his name now?" Sara asked.

"Alvin Summers. Goodbye."

"But what address number?"

"Sixteen," Mr. Summers said.

"Thanks. I wish the best for you and your wife," Sara said, then hung up the receiver.

Sara rushed out the door and back to her booth. She gathered her papers and put a five on top of the check that was for two dollars and seventy-eight cents. She packed her papers across her chest and put both arms over them, then ran out of the diner.

Sara was equally as worried about Corey, Randy and Tony, but for the moment her next stop would be 16 Elk Street, no doubt.

Mom sped east down Central, headed toward Downtown Albany. A motorcycle policeman pulled up beside her, and she got the hint to slow down, even though she was only five miles per hour over the limit of thirty-five.

"Go arrest somebody," Sara said under her breath as the police sped away. At Central Avenue and North Allen Street, Sara stopped at a phone booth on the corner near a flower store called Central Avenue florist. She quickly got out of her car and reached into her pocket for a quarter. She inserted the quarter and dialed a number. The phone range once and a loud voice answered.

"Tibby speaking."

"It's me, Sara."

Tibby stood at his bar near the cash register. Tammy, his wife, was in the bar office. Tibby looked around to make sure Tammy wasn't in earshot. He lowered his voice as he spoke.

"Sara, what's up?" Tibby asked, to try to appear calm.

"Tibby, I know where he is."

"Sara, who?"

"Our son.

"How do you know?"

"I called the people who adopted him."

"Yeah."

"Yeah, I need you to meet me at 16 Elk Street."

"Sara, do you think these people are really gonna tell you where he is? It's a wild goose chase."

"I believe him, Tibby, and I want you to meet me there in the next twenty minutes."

"But Sara, Tammy is here and she's gonna want to know where I'm going."

Tibby really was just using Tammy as an excuse.

"Tibby don't make me come there and get you myself. If you can't take care of it with Tammy the same way you do when you need to go out and see one of your whores, then I'll come and get you. We'll see how Tammy likes that. And I'll do it, too. Quick, what's it gonna be?"

Tibby was cornered, but he knew that between Tammy and Sara, Sara would deliver the hardest bite.

"All right!" Tibby said, whispering loud and tersely into the receiver.

Sara hung up without saying goodbye. Tammy walked out from the rear office.

"Who was that, Honey?"

"Oh, that was the Johnnie Walker distributor. They need to have a pow-wow about the late payment."

Tibby was a fast thinker. He moved toward Tammy from behind the bar.

"I need to go see him pronto. I'll only be about an hour. You wanna wait here or come with me?"

Tibby felt he had to invite her like he always did, and just hope she would continue to say no like she always did.

Her long pause caused Tibby's heart to pound. He thought, come on, woman, make a damn decision.

"Nah, too boring for me."

"Okay."

Tibby swiftly headed for the door while Tammy's eyes followed him.

"I'll see you when you get back," Tammy said.

Tibby hadn't said bye to Tammy like he normally did. Then he stuck his head back in the front door.

"Bye, Honey,"

Tammy smiled.

"Want me to bring you something back?" Tibby asked. "No, just you," Tammy said. Tibby forced a smile, matching Tammy's, and left.

CHAPTER SIXTY-TWO

ALL HELL BROKE LOOSE at Cathedral Academy. The school fire alarm rang, piercing the ears of all the scrambling students who were in crooked lines moving hectically toward the nearest exits. Some students were running through the first floor hallway, panicking.

Mrs. Hillzinger was still in the school office, looking out of the window blinds as the students scurried into their designated lines.

Mrs. Hillzinger came into the hallway and put her hands on her hips, barking out orders to the teachers and students, trying to be the voice of intelligence and authority.

"Move quickly and quietly to the exits, children. Come on, hurry!"

She wouldn't move from in front of the school office until the very last minute.

Randy, Tony and I waited in the gym. It was a short walk from the school office.

Randy peeked through the crack that separated the two doors, then came back and sat in the chair along the side of the basketball court. We were the only ones in the gym. A few more people, and the school would be empty.

"She's still there," Randy said.

"I think we should think of another way to make a copy," Tony said meekly.

"It's either now or never, Tony" I said with authority.

"But we could sneak down to the copy store tonight," Tony attacked.

"Do you have money for that, Tony?" I said in retaliation. "Plus there's no time for that."

"No, but we could get burned up in here."

"Stupid, who do you think pulled the fire alarm switch?" I said.

Tony shrugged his shoulders. I sighed, and glanced at Randy "I did, dummy. There's no fire."

"Oh," Tony said, more secure.

"Oh, he says. Listen, as soon as Hillzinger leaves I'm gonna make the copies. We got time to make two copies, tops . . ."

I stopped to listen to the sirens as the fire trucks got closer. I could hear them from a distance.

"I'll be right back," I said.

I ran and peeked through the double wooden door crack. Mrs. Hillzinger looked at both ends of the empty hall and left the building through the front door.

I scampered back to the place in the gym where Randy and Tony waited. My breathing was hard and I was scared. Not so much scared at being caught, but more at not getting the copies to protect Mom and Dats. I even thought that I could be protecting someone who was molesting me. No matter, I still had to protect my family.

"Look, the fire trucks are almost here. I'm guessing, but I think we've got about two minutes to get in that office, make the copies and sneak outside before the firemen get in here and see us. Tony you watch the front door. If anyone sees you, just start walking out the front door and just say you were scared and didn't know what to do. Got it?"

Tony nodded. "Corey, why do you need the copies anyway?"

"Trust me, I just need them."

"Randy, I need you to stay with me. That way if we're caught you can say you wanted to make sure your brothers were all right and you came back in school to find me and Tony when you didn't see us outside with everyone else. Okay?"

"That's what I would've said."

Randy's ego was working a little here.

"Let's go. If we don't get caught we'll just split up like nothing happened. And I'll see you at home after school." I was the first to leave the gym. The double wooden doors squeaked a bit.

All that could be heard was the school fire alarm running constantly. We ran from the gym. Tony stopped at the hallway that faced the front door. He peeked around the corner, and no one was there. He waved us by. We ran across the open area to the school office. I sped into the office, hopped up on the office counter, and jumped over to the other side near the copier. It was humming loud and clear, ready to go. I looked back at Randy who watched from the hallway through the office hallway window. I ran to the window and peeked out. The fire trucks had arrived. I raced back to the copier and pulled the printout from my back pocket. I laid the printout on the copier and pressed the print button. A green light flashed. It needed more paper.

"Shit!"

I looked at Randy who mouthed, "What's wrong?"

"Paper," I said.

I ran to peek out of the blinds again. The firemen were on the school grounds, about thirty yards from the front door. I ran back to the copier and looked under the machine in the cabinet area, trying to find paper. There wasn't any I ran back to the window and peeked out. The fireman was on his way, about twenty yards from the front door. I would surely be caught.

I waved at Randy to go. He stuck his head in the office door

"What?" Randy asked.

"Go," I said.

"No, I'm staying," Randy said, wanting to help me.

"Go, Randy."

"No, we're gonna be caught. I can't find the paper."

"No, I'm staying." Randy said.

"Okay. We gotta stall 'em. Send Tony out and tell him to say what we said."

Randy ran out of the office and into the hallway to Tony.

"Tony, go out the front door; tell 'em what we told you, and nothing more," Randy yelled.

Randy ran back into the office, hopped over the counter and we both looked for paper.

I stopped to think for a second and realized it could only be in one place--Mrs. Hillzinger's desk drawer.

I went to her desk, and there it was. I grabbed a handful of paper and put it in the copier.

"Is Tony with the fireman, Randy?"

Randy looked out the window to see.

"I guess."

"Are they buying the story?" I asked.

"Yeah. Hillzinger's got her arm over Tony's shoulder. The fireman is almost at the door."

"Okay. One more copy and we're out. Go, Randy, I'll see you at home after school."

Randy looked at me. I knew, out of all the misunderstandings and bitter fights we'd had, that we loved each other and that he could have easily left me there, but he didn't. Like him, if we were going to go down, it would be together.

"Got two copies, we're outta here," I said.

I peeked out and I could hear the heavy voice of the fireman in the front entryway. Randy ran to the opposite end of the hallway. With his great speed, he was already waiting for me at the end of the hall. I wasn't nearly as fast as Randy, but I made the hallway corner just as the fireman turned the corner from the front entryway to the school office.

"Here, Randy, take these two and hide them in our hiding place," I said as I gave him the two copies of the printout. I kept the original.

"I'll see you at home after school," Randy said, smiling.

"You go that way and I'm going out this way." I said.

"But I thought we were gonna go out together?" Randy asked, not wanting to part.

"It's better this way. If I get caught, they'll have more sympathy for me because of my eye. They'll figure there's no excuse for you because you're in the eight grade. Now go!" I yelled.

Randy nodded and obeyed, not because he wanted to, but because he knew that I was right. He ran out the back door to the schoolyard, and I ran out the school door at the front end on the east side of the school closest to Park Avenue.

Sitting there in his car in the driver's seat was Justin. Across from him in the passenger seat was Sally B. They had watched the entire false fire alarm. They waited. Justin watched Corey leave the school grounds.

I crossed Eagle Street and began walking down Park Avenue, headed toward the store. I thought this was the perfect time to skip school for a minute and run down to the beverage store around the corner on Warren Street. It was a five-minute walk, and I figured I could be back in time.

Justin watched Corey quick-walk his way down Park Avenue. He got out of his car and followed him on the opposite side of the street.

Sally B turned the car around and slowly followed behind Justin.

I looked back a couple of times, but I was looking for someone from the school, like Mrs. Hillzinger, to be following me. As far as I was concerned, the coast was clear.

Sally B got nervous from Corey looking back, thinking that he spotted her. She sped up and drove past Corey. She had stopped at the stop sign.

I crossed the street. Before I could do anything, Justin grabbed me. Sally B pulled up. Justin snatched open the rear door and threw me head first on the seat. He jumped in right behind me. As Sally B drove off, he blindfolded me. Before I knew it, I was gagged, hogtied and on the floor of the car. Justin propped his feet up on me, then leaned forward on the back of the front seat.

I was certain I would die. I thought first he'd rape me then kill me. I always figured it was Justin.

After all my big talk, I was helpless. I was really scared and didn't want to die.

CHAPTER SIXTY-THREE

ELK STREET WAS AT the border of midtown and uptown Albany. This small one-way street ran behind Washington Avenue and the Albany Public Library. One block of the street was taken up by the rear parking lot of the library. The other block had two-story homes on it. All this was across from about three acres of grass and weeds. Sara waited in her car, impatiently for Tibby to arrive. Tibby's bar was not more than a ten-minute car drive away. Sara couldn't conceive what was taking him more than fifteen minutes to get there. Then she thought because she told Tibby twenty minutes, he would use the entire time to get to her.

Tibby did it this way because he didn't want to let Sara think she was controlling him, even though she really was. The fact that he jumped when she said so was the proof of who was in control.

Sara gnawed at her index fingernail. There wasn't much left to it at that point, but here was always flesh to nibble.

She sat behind the steering wheel, watching intently in her rear-view mirror. She checked her watch, then turned to look behind her and saw Tibby in his car.

Tibby drove only about ten miles per hour. Two cars passed by him doing about thirty up the one-way street.

Sara got out of her car and waved Tibby down from the sidewalk. She pointed to an empty space in front of her car. Upon passing Sara's car, Tibby gave her a short roll of his eyes, just to let her know he was put off by all of this. But he parked his car in front of Sara's anyway, and would follow her lead.

Tibby emerged from his car. Sara stood directly in front of him.

"Okay, Sara, you got me here. Where do we go?"

She turned her head toward the house directly behind her.

There was an old, worn, red wooden staircase of about ten steps leading up to the two-story red brick house.

"Up there," Sara said as she motioned with a nod.

"Let's get this over with," Tibby said sharply.

Tibby left Sara standing there as he grabbed the wooden stair railing and headed up the steps. Sara followed, and looked down toward the basement steps at the ground level apartment where old trash and newspaper was strewn about. Nobody lived in the basement. Sara looked at the basement apartment blinds and they were dirty and rusty. Then Sara looked at the open field across from the house as she turned and walked up the stairs backwards, while holding on to the rail. There was nothing but an empty field across the street, with a steel fence from one end of the block to the other. She walked up the stairs, wondering if anyone was watching from the other homes.

Tibby looked at the first and second floor doorbells. No names were listed. Then he looked up and checked the mailboxes above the doorbells. One box had a dirty white name tag of Willoughby on it, and the other box had nothing. Sara joined Tibby in trying to determine which bell to ring.

"Which one, Sara?"

"I don't know."

Sara pressed both bells.

"There!" she said.

Tibby cut his eyes at her.

"What I want to know is why all of a sudden you're obsessed with this shit anyway?"

"Because I am. You'd never understand because you could never be a mother. You carried the sperm. I carried the child for nine months."

Sara turned toward the wooden double doors. Both of the doors had a window. Tibby shook his head in disbelief that he had joined the fiasco.

Sara pressed the doorbells again and again, hoping someone would come to the door. It was dark in the hallway and hard to see anyone until they were right in front of the door. Tibby and Sara heard a police siren headed up Elk Street. They both turned their heads to look at the speeding police car. Then they simultaneously turned their heads back toward the double door window. Both were startled when they saw and old white, wrinkled, scary face of a man with big green eyes pressed against the window. Steam began to build on the glass as he pressed harder.

"Oh. Excuse me, we're looking for Alvin Summers. Do you know if he's home?" Sara asked.

The old man opened his door with a slight grin. He had no teeth. Sara shot a look to Tibby, not understanding why the old man was grinning.

"Maybe he's happy to see another human being, or maybe he's just crazy," Tibby mumbled.

"Hey I heard that shit!" the old man snapped with a grin.

The old man was frail, and wearing only his pee-stained white boxers with red polka dots. His head was clean shaven and he had a scruffy beard, but wore a top of the line Rolex watch on his left wrist.

The old man continued to grin as he turned his back on Sara and Tibby, then motioned for them to follow him. They paused, looked at each other incredulously, then reluctantly followed.

CHAPTER SIXTY-FOUR

ALL THE STUDENTS were back in school. Corey's homeroom teacher took attendance, like she always did after a fire alarm; false or real.

The alarm was discarded by the fireman as a foul-up in the system. One of the students in Sister Raye's class was curious as to what had happened. Sister Raye was pale with rosy cheeks, and she wore a navy blue habit over her short, thin body. She wore it well.

"Sister Raye, why did the alarm go off?" the little girl asked.

"It was probably a foul-up in the system."

"Usually we know when we're gonna have a fire alarm. Why didn't we this time?" the little girl asked.

Sister Raye's attention was divided as she continued to count the students against her homeroom class list.

All students had to report back to their homerooms whenever there was a fire alarm. Classes resumed where they left off, once everyone was accounted for.

"Where's Corey?" Sister Raye asked.

All of the fifth graders looked around to the right corner of the room where Corey's desk was. Sister Raye headed for the door. Everyone began their own chatter in the class.

"Okay, class, I'm going to the office. You need to open your books to where you left off before the fire alarm."

The class wasn't paying any attention to Sister Raye as she left the room. Sister Raye knew her students heard her, but it was a test by them to ignore her, and she knew it. She would not allow her students to take advantage of her just because she was younger and more inexperienced than her co-workers. She stuck her head back in her classroom.

"I said now!" Sister Raye demanded.

In unison, the class stopped their chatter and heeded to Sister Raye's order. Sister Raye left with a smile and headed for the school office. She wiped her hands together, congratulating herself on a job well done.

Once in the school's office, Sister Raye stood at the counter talking with Mrs. Hillzinger.

"Hi, Sister Raye, what can I do for you?"

Sister Raye, being somewhat new, naturally figured she'd ask for the principal.

"I need to speak to Father Donnelly."

But according to Mrs. Hillzinger, she was in charge, and if anyone had to speak to the principal, you really needed to speak to her first. Most everyone carried on with Mrs. Hillzinger because she was good at what she did. But sooner or later they talked to the principal, if necessary, all on their own.

"Maybe I can help you?"

"But I really need to discuss this with Father Donnelly."

Mrs. Hillzinger sighed hard.

"Is there a problem with you discussing this with me, Sister Raye?"

"No, but . . ."

"No buts, what is it?"

"Well, one of my students is missing."

"Who?"

"Corey Harris."

Father Donnelly came from inside his office into the outer area after overhearing.

"Has anyone checked the gym or other classrooms?" Father Donnelly asked.

"No, we're going to look into that now, Father Donnelly!" Mrs. Hillzinger said matter-of-factly.

Father Donnelly pushed his black rimmed glasses up on his nose and headed back into his office. He wore his short sleeve black habit collar and matching black trousers with dignity.

"Let me know if he's not found," Father Donnelly said with a confident air that Corey was somewhere in the building.

Mrs. Hillzinger lifted the divider, came from behind the counter and took a left, heading straight for the school gym. She had a full head of steam. She was pissed, not only that a student was missing, but because Father Donnelly was involved already. Sister Raye sheepishly followed behind Mrs. Hillzinger.

Mrs. Hillzinger yanked open the gym door. It banged against the wall as she walked through.

"Corey?" Mrs. Hillzinger yelled.

Mrs. Hillzinger walked to the end of the gym, through the kitchen door and scanned it, only to find it empty. Sister Raye went to the opposite end of the gym where a theater stage was located, directly behind the old half-moon shaped basketball hoop.

"Corey?" Sister Raye said softly.

Then Mrs. Hillzinger came to the stage. She climbed up on the five foot stage and stomped from one end to the other, searching behind the stage curtain. She began to pull vigorously with her index finger and thumb on her dark, thin mustache. Coming from Mrs. Hillzinger, this was a sign of frustration.

Not finding Corey, Mrs. Hillzinger jumped down from the stage, sweating. She marched fast to the gym door leading to the school backyard. She kicked the waist high lever to open the door and looked out.

"He's gone. I'll call his parents," Mrs. Hillzinger said, storming off.

"Maybe he's in another classroom," Sister Raye said.

"Unlikely," Mrs. Hillzinger said adamantly. She headed for her office, very upset.

Mrs. Hillzinger knew there was trouble, because most of the time missing students could be found in the gym shooting baskets or just hanging out in the school backyard. If so, a paddling was in order.

Not finding Corey made Mrs. Hillzinger even more agitated. Sister Raye followed Mrs. Hillzinger to the school office. Heads would roll if Corey wasn't found.

CHAPTER SIXTY-FIVE

SALLY B CALMLY DROVE NORTH on Central Avenue. Justin sat in the back seat, leaning toward the front with his feet resting on me. He ripped the duct tape from my mouth. The computer printout that I had in the back of my pants was on the back seat.

"Corey, you'll never steal again in your life after I finish with you."

I was glad the tape was off of my mouth, even though it hurt when he took it off. I gasped for more air.

"You realize that back in ancient times, you lost a hand for stealing," Justin said while beginning to sing. "A hand, a hand, a hand," then he stopped abruptly.

I remained quiet.

"Not so talkative now, are you?" Justin said.

He pressed on my stomach hard with his feet.

"You're the thief!" I shouted, coughing.

"So you can talk," Justin said.

He eased up his feet off of my stomach.

"Why do you have my Mom and Dats in your printout?"

"They owe me."

"Where are you taking me?"

"Somewhere nobody will ever find you."

"Okay, so why can't you untie me? You scared of me?"

A slight grin covered Justin's face. I couldn't keep my mouth shut.

"And these are modern times. So if you don't know, you better ask somebody," I said sarcastically.

I knew I was starting to irk Justin even more than I already had in the past few days.

"Modern times, you say?" Justin said.

He reached into the left inside pocket of his black leather jacket and took out a straight razor. He flicked it open. I couldn't believe he was going to cut me loose, I thought.

"I'll untie you, but you'll pay," Justin said with a smirk.

"Yeah, right. The same way you make my Mom and Dats pay?"

Justin began to cut me loose.

"No, the way they had to pay in the old days. The old school way. But I'll make it `light' on you."

I flipped him the finger. Then in a flash, my middle finger fell to the floor of the car. I yelled in pain as I felt for my finger. I picked it up. Then I grabbed my left hand in great pain. Blood poured out of my new nub. I had underestimated Justin. Then I knew he was going to kill me.

Sally B wasn't shocked, only a little ruffled. She handed me her jacket that was on the front seat.

"The next time it'll be your hand," Justin said calmly.

He wiped the razor on Sally B's jacket. After thoroughly inspecting the razor, he closed it up and put it back in his jacket pocket.

Justin began to frown. Sally B looked at him through her rearview mirror. She knew as long as Justin was aware that there were other copies lurking around, Corey would live longer. Jail was not in Justin's plans--ever. But to be at the thumb of a ten-year-old wasn't either. I knew I was in control, and so did Sally B.

I really wasn't ready to die, but since I sensed that I had Justin by the balls, why not talk shit. He'd do the same to me. He was really no different from me. He'd just been through more because he was older. He probably killed a few people in his day. But I had killed a cat and had the disposition to kill a human being, the one who was sexually abusing me. And I knew if given the chance and pushed to the edge, I could kill my abuser. So we were the same. He knew, I knew, and Sally B knew.

I was really bluffing Justin, but he didn't know it. I had twenty-four hours to live. I knew he had the means to keep me as long as possible, but I had to make him think I had planned for something like this to happen. My only concern was that if Justin called my bluff, would Randy expose the printout or not? All I told Randy was to meet me at home after school. I knew he would probably not show the printout to anyone, because maybe he thought it would get me in hot water.

If this had been a week or two ago, Randy would have fed me to the rats, but since we made our peace, I knew he wouldn't turn on me—just a brother's love. Hopefully if twenty-four hours did go by, he'd know I was in some kind of danger.

"Are there are other copies?" Justin asked with disdain.

"You think I'm stupid enough to only have one."

"I could easily start eliminating your family until I get my printouts."

"But you won't, will you?"

"You're worse than the bastard you really are," Justin said as he grinned.

"I'm not a bastard. I know my daddy. All you are is a criminal."

"I supply services for people like your Uncle Henry and your 'Dats', too, for that matter. It just so happens your good ol' Dats wanted a piece of the pie. Henry is a disgusting old man, Corey. Get your faith off of him and into me so your life can be spared."

"What are you talking about? Uncle Henry's good to everyone."

"He's useless. End of discussion."

Justin put the duct tape back on my mouth.

"Okay, Sally B."

Justin pointed to the highway. Sally B nodded.

Sally B had gotten to the intersection of Central Avenue and Wolf Road. This was a fairly busy intersection. It was near Colonie Center Mall in the city of Colonie. She made the red light and got on the highway headed south on Interstate 87. Coming out this far was only a diversion. Justin didn't want Corey to have any idea where they were going.

CHAPTER SIXTY-SIX

A DIM LIGHT BULB hung from the ceiling of the kitchen, above a new round wooden table where Tibby, Sara and the old man sat. His name was James G. Crinkins. He called himself Crinkins. Sara was impressed with the art deco decor of the large kitchen. Tibby was just as impressed.

Crinkins banged his hand on the table. With the remote control near his hand, he pressed a button and locked the door to his apartment.

"Yeah, I fought in World War II. Killed enough people to demand respect. I was the best fighter the army ever saw. And I'm living damn good, too. I'm taking the government for everything they owe me. I'll be damned if I let them do me the way they treat those Vietnam vets."

"Look," Crinkins pointed to the plaque he received for a Purple Heart that hung on the wall behind the chair he sat in.

"I didn't get that for running scared. The government knows that, too. Ya see that over there?"

He pointed to his Army uniform hanging on the wall near the bathroom door.

"Look at those stars on my shoulders."

Sara and Tibby hesitantly looked, wondering if they had stepped into a lunatic's nest.

"That's right, five stars for General. I earned every one 'em. Twenty years in the service. Went in when I was eighteen, got out when I was thirty-eight. Youngest decorated General ever. And I'm getting paid for every bullet I took or ducked. I'm no stiff. Now, what the hell do you want? Coming in here disrupting my peace."

Sara noticed all the old and new Army paraphernalia that was laid neatly about the kitchen. There were rifles, handguns, grenades, knives, gold medals and flags on tables at each room entrance. There was a large world map on the wall behind Tibby's chair.

"Goddamned movies on the war, never was right."

Crinkins slammed his palms on the top of the table. He leaned in Sara's face with a menacing glare.

"Now, what the hell do you want with me, Private?"

He took what looked like a small version of a machine gun from a holster underneath the table and slammed it on top of the table. It was a Hammerli Model 280 that he had imported for fifteen hundred dollars.

Then Sara really didn't know how to react to this treatment, but she knew that she was tired of being dictated to. But with the gun in the hands of a shaky old man, she figured the odds were against her.

"What's the matter, Private, cat gotcha tongue?"

Sara's eyes shifted about the room to the table where the guns were.

"Think you can outdraw me, Private? Go ahead, try me."

He put his gun at the edge of the table near him.

"Go ahead."

Sara looked at Tibby who shook his head 'no'.

Sara mustered up all her strength and courage as she snapped her head back to Crinkins' eyes. She leaned toward him, and they were almost nose to nose.

"Look, I came here to look for my son, not trouble. If you want war, go to the Middle East, they'll oblige you, Mister!"

Crinkin's eyes shifted slowly toward Tibby, then as they made their way back to Sara a slow smile came across his face. Crinkins put his hand on the trigger of his gun and pointed it in Sara's face.

"You've got ten seconds to talk and get the hell out of my house or you and ya boyfriend here are gonna find yourselves buried in the backyard with the rest of the intruders."

Crinkins looked at his wristwatch. Sara and Tibby stood up and swiftly made their way to the door. As Crinkins stood, he used the remote to unlock the front door. He pointed the gun at them.

"On your mark, get set, go!" Crinkins said, laughing.

"Has Alvin Summers lived here before?" Mom asked, rushing.

She stumbled, making her way to the front door with Tibby leading the way.

"Hell no. And he better not ever show his face," Crinkins said.

He shot twice in the ceiling of the house as his watch came to ten seconds. He started to laugh hysterically.

Tibby and Sara scrambled for their cars, and burnt rubber getting out of there.

Sara followed Tibby as he took a right turn, headed toward uptown.

Tibby approached the corner of Lark Street and Clinton Avenue. Clinton Avenue was the main drag in the uptown section of Albany.

Tibby slammed on his brakes and rushed out of his car. He ran toward Sara who sat in her car parked behind him. Tibby was irate. He paced in a small circle near Sara's driver's side door while he spoke.

"I told you we were going on a wild goose chase!"

Sara looked at Tibby with sad eyes.

"How was I supposed to know?" she shot back.

She knew Tibby was right. Tibby put his hands on her door and leaned toward her as he spoke. He breathed hard and fast.

"Do you realize you almost got us killed over nothing? I can't believe I even went there with you in the first place"

"It wasn't for nothing."

"Well, what was it for then?"

"We found out that our son doesn't live there."

"You can bet wherever he lives I don't care or want to know. As far as I'm concerned, the day we gave him up was the day he no longer existed. And I'm keeping it that way"

"If it wasn't for your selfishness, I would still have my son. I shouldn't have listened to you. You made me do it," Sara said.

"Don't give me that. You wanted to give him up just as much as I did, or else you would've kept him . . . Good-bye, Sara,"

Tibby angrily went to his car, got in and sped off. He headed toward his bar. Sara was left sitting there. A tear rolled down her cheek.

Henry and Jim were watching Music Television at Henry's request, in Jim's living room.

There was an erotic video playing. Henry watched intently while Jim's mind wandered, even though his stare was on the tube.

"Look at that. They got everything on TV nowadays," Henry said.

"Yeah, you're right, Henry," Jim said, not really paying attention.

The phone rang. Jim relaxed in his favorite chair He hesitated as it rang two more times.

Henry sat on the sofa, leaning forward with his eyes glued to the tube. He became annoyed by the phone ringing.

"Aren't you gonna answer it, Jim?"

Jim looked at Henry, who still watched at the music video. Jim reached for the phone.

"Hello?" Jim said.

"This is Father Donnelly at Cathedral Academy."

"Yes, I know who you are. I'm Jim Harris. What is it?"

Jim leaned forward in his chair.

"Is Corey at home with you?"

Jim was silent. He moved the phone away from his ear as Father Donnelly was telling him what had happened.

"We had a fire drill and . . ."

Father Donnelly's voice became faint as Jim slowly hung the phone up while his eyes were fixed on Henry. Jim knew it was Justin.

"He took him."

Henry was oblivious to what Jim was saying.

The music video went off. Then Henry turned his head toward Jim.

"What's that, Jim?'

"He got Corey."

Henry rose quickly to his feet.

"Who?"

"Justin Lord," Jim replied.

"How do you know?"

"He warned me."

Henry reached for the phone.

"Let's call the police."

Jim put his hand on top of Henry, stopping him. Jim sighed and his shoulders slouched. "No. That's not the way."

"What are you talking about? Your son has been kidnapped and you don't want the police?"

Jim shook his head no. Henry was baffled.

"Sit down, Henry I need to tell you something."

Henry gradually removed his hand from the phone and took a seat.

"Talk," Henry said.

"There's a lot you don't know about, and that's on purpose."

Jim's words were beginning to crack and water welled up in his eyes. "Sara and I are in very deep . . . with . . . with," he sighed again, holding back tears. "With Justin." Jim hung his head and plopped down in a chair near Henry. "We just got in over our heads. "After I saw my mother in that filthy nursing home room I had to get her in a better place. And the kids schooling got more expensive. I worked overtime and that still wasn't enough. I had to go to Justin. He was just there. We did it all for our family."

Jim put his head on the table and covered his head with his arms. Henry could hear sniffles from Jim. "We're in too deep, Henry. If we call the cops, we all could die, or be put away." Jim closed his eyes as Henry consoled him by lightly rubbing his back. Jim knew that lives were at stake.

CHAPTER SIXTY-SEVEN

SARA WAS HEARTBROKEN. Her drive down Clinton Avenue was deliberate and thoughtful. She thought she would never again see her first-born. Trying to track him down and being unsuccessful made her remorse even heavier.

She stopped at a red light on Clinton Avenue and Swan Street. There was a phone booth on the corner. She glanced at it. She thought about calling Mr. Summers back and giving him a good cursing out for giving her bogus information. The red light changed to green and she drove on.

Sara looked around at the people walking up and down Clinton Avenue, thinking that any one of these nondescript people could be her son. She came to the corner of Clinton and North Pearl Street, and could have made a right on red, but decided against it. Instead she thought about the phone booth she'd just passed. Once again she thought about calling Mr. Summers to get some anger off of her chest. But the light changed to green and she drove south on Pearl Street.

Sara knew that if she was going to do something, it would have to be before she got home. Cars passed her by on Pearl Street, even though there was only one lane. That's how slow she drove. A couple of drivers blew their horns at her. She paid them all little to no attention. She passed by several stores from card shops to restaurants to drug stores to retail clothing shops to small and large grocery stores that lined both sides of the main Downtown Albany strip. There was a phone booth that she spotted on the corner of Pearl Street and Stuben Place. The phone was adjacent to the Steuben Athletic Club. This was a popular club for most of the white collar employees in the downtown area and Omni Hotel guests.

Sara held up traffic while she debated on whether to get out and make her call to Mr. Summers. She tossed and turned in her seat a few times, waving the other drivers on. She double-parked and looked at the phone, then at her car panel clock. It read 1:30. A car was speeding, heading toward her. She opened her door without looking first. The car veered off into the opposite lane at the last second, just missing Sara. She saw this, but ran to the phone. She felt her pockets for more change. She put in a quarter and dialed the Brooklyn number. The operator recording asked for two dollars and seventy-five cents more. Sara only had one dollar and seventy-five cents in quarters left. She hung the receiver up. She then immediately redialed Mr. Summers collect. She hoped Mr. Summers would answer because she didn't think Mrs. Summers would remember her, since she was suffering from a mental breakdown about her missing son.

"Operator, may I help you?"

"Yes, collect from Sara Harris."

The operator switched over to the Summers' line. The wait seemed like forever to Sara as she watched several people walk by her.

"Okay, go ahead," the operator said.

"Hello, Mr. Summers. Do you remember me?"

"Yes. We spoke a short while ago. What is it now?"

"Look, I know you went out of your way to help me and I'm sorry to keep bothering you, but that 16 Elk Street came up empty. There was some lunatic . . ."

"What street was that?" Mr. Summers said, cutting her off.

"Elk, 16 Elk, like you told me."

"No, you must have heard me wrong. I said Elm Street."

Sara dropped the phone and ran to her car without saying another word. She thought to herself that Summers didn't say Elm.

She sped down Pearl Street, headed toward Elm. She knew it could be another wild goose chase, but it was worth the try. She stopped at the red light in front of the Omni Hotel on the corner of Pearl and State Streets, then it dawned on her that this house number was familiar to her. The light changed to green and she forged ahead.

CHAPTER SIXTY-EIGHT

SALLY B DROVE TOWARD her turn-off from Pearl Street to Port Road. She stopped at the flashing red light at Port Road, and after a few seconds she took a left turn. Port Road was full of dirt and rocks. On both sides of the road was about two acres of open fields of undeveloped land. It was still daytime, and cloudy. There were Albany Asphalt Company trucks, cement trucks and tractors using this road to enter and exit the Port area. The Port area was a stretch of about two miles along the Hudson River. Other businesses were housed at the Port because it was cheap to rent. Dust flew everywhere. Most of the drivers paid no attention to anyone coming in or out of Port Road because there were so many businesses in the area. In this case, Sally B, Justin and Corey were going to Justin's storage warehouse.

Sally B came to a fork in the dirt road. A noisy tractor trailer coming in the opposite direction passed by Sally B took a left turn down the fork. The road had no name. Everyone referred to this particular road as 'storage' because of all the storage rooms that lined both sides of the road.

Sally B took a right into the third building driveway. She drove past the first building to the building in the back. She leaned over, opened the glove compartment and took out the remote control. Justin had a slight grin on his face. Sally B pressed the open button and the twenty foot high, thirty foot wide steel door slid open to the fight. Corey was still under Justin's feet. Because he was screaming from the pain of his finger he could hardly hear the noises from the area. Sally B demanded that Justin tie her jacket sleeve around my wrist to slow the bleeding. Justin was very hesitant but knew that if I lost too much blood I'd pass out or go into shock. He wanted to make sure I was conscious throughout the cruel torture that lie ahead for me. Sally B drove into the large, airplane hangar-like building. The sunlight shined in the doorway as it opened, lending some light for Sally B to see. Once inside, she hit the 'close' button on the remote control. The door began to close, and the room became dark as the door cut off the only light source. She hit a light switch on the remote. A small, dim light came on above a set of freshly painted wooden stairs that led to a second floor area. Sally B got out of the car. Justin untied my feet. He got out on the passenger side. Sally B opened the rear door on the driver's side and helped me gather myself as much as he could.

I sat on the seat momentarily to catch my breath after being stomped on by Justin the entire ride. He hurt me, but I'd never let him know how much.

"C'mon, Corey, time to see your new home," Justin said sarcastically.

Sally B helped me out of the car. I could hear what I thought were Justin's footsteps on the stairs as he ascended. Sally B held my arm and escorted me. We came to the foot of the stairs.

"You've got steps, Corey," she said.

I was still gagged and blindfolded. I nodded, and she led me up the stairs. I heard a loud bang and it caused me to hesitate.

"It's all right, Corey, it's only a door."

On the second floor, Justin opened another door. It was to his office.

Sally B ushered me through the steel door that I heard slam earlier, and then through a second door to the office. She sat me down on the couch. Justin snatched the duct tape off of my mouth. This was the second time. I was not quite numb from the pain. "You think you could take the blindfold off now?" I asked, pathetically.

I figured that at that moment Justin had the leverage, so I wasn't afraid to kiss his ass a little to get my way.

I sensed that Sally B looked to Justin for an answer.

Next I felt Sally B's hands behind my head untying the blindfold.

I blinked several times as my eyes adjusted to the dim light. Some blood came from where my stitches were. Sally B looked at my eye sympathetically.

Justin went and sat behind a wooden desk. The only thing on the desk was a portable cellular phone. Justin knew better than to have a phone line linked to the phone company. That was an easy way to find out who occupied a place. I looked around the room. It had only the desk, a couch I sat on, a love chair and a very 'cold' feeling. The dim light didn't help the bareness either. There was a small attempt to make it more comfortable with new, grey wall-to-wall carpeting, but it really didn't help.

I saw a small, portable refrigerator in the corner, near where Sally B stood.

"I'm thirsty," I said.

Sally B looked at Justin for an answer. He nodded. She went to the refrigerator. I leaned forward on the sofa, and looked when she opened the door. It was full of fruit juices. She grabbed one and opened the twist-off top, then walked toward me. Justin had retied me.

"If you untie me I can hold it myself."

"No! Pour it down his mouth," Justin yelled between his smile.

I opened my mouth and tilted my head back.

Sally B poured some juice down my throat. I swallowed hard. She sat on the couch near me and waited.

"So this is where you hide out when you're on the run."

"Watch your tongue or you'll be gagged again, boy," Justin said.

"Yeah, sure."

"Gag him, Sally B, now!"

Sally B put the bottle of juice on the floor. She went to get her purse from on the floor near the door. She took the duct tape from her purse and tore off a large piece. She came to me and put it over my mouth. I had been silenced again.

Sally B returned to the couch, next to me. She wrapped her jacket tighter around my bloody hand. I still had my finger in my hand. Blood came out steadily. I sensed that she felt for me and what I was going through, and what might happen.

I heard a beeping sound as Justin dialed a number on his cellular phone.

"Hello, Jim. You ready to play hide and go seek?"

"What is it you want, Justin? I'm busy." Jim was bluffing.

"Busy doing what?"

"That's none of your business."

"You wouldn't happen to be looking for Corey, would you?"

"Corey? Who said anything about him?"

"Oh, come on, Jim, let's stop playing this cat and mouse game. You know I have Corey and I know you would love to have him back, wouldn't you?"

"I don't believe you."

"Well, you'll have to."

Jim pulled the phone into the kitchen, and paced. Henry stood next to Jim, trying to listen in. Jim covered the receiver of the phone with his left hand and whispered.

"He's got Corey."

Henry had a surprised look. Jim heard a click. Justin had hung up on him. Jim gradually hung up the receiver and stared at Henry, but his mind was really on how to get him back.

"So what now, Jim?" Henry asked.

"We'll wait."

"Wait! Corey could get killed while we wait," Uncle Henry said in a panic.

"No! Justin wants something. He'll call back. Until then, we just sit tight."

"Why not have the police handle it? They're pros at this!"

"So is Justin."

I wondered when Justin would take me in some back room and have his way with me. At least I would die knowing my rapist. I didn't know how I was going to fight his crazy ass off of me but I would certainly try.

CHAPTER SIXTY-NINE

SARA ARRIVED ON ELM STREET two blocks from her house. She parked in an open space on the right side, just up from number 16 Elm. She backed into the car parked behind her, shaking it a little, but not doing any damage.

Sara straightened her car parallel to the curb and jammed on her foot pedal emergency brake. She rushed to open her door, and then slowed her pace.

Her eyes scaled 16 Elm Street from the basement apartment to the third floor window. Then she looked up and down the block. She was intrigued that her son was this close to her own house and she never knew it. She lightly grabbed the railing with her right hand and slid it up as she walked slowly up the stairs. She knew that Aunt Rebekah had owned the house for twenty years. Aunt Rebekah and her late husband bought the house cheap in an auction.

Sara made it to the top step of the red brick house and rang the doorbell. She turned around, put her back to the door, and watched a car drive down the street, bewildered.

Aunt Rebekah was in her sixties, and she looked it. She came to the double wooden door. She wore an oversized brown dress with a brown and white apron. More wrinkles formed on Aunt Rebekah's face as she strained to look through her door window white curtain to see Sara. She strained to see because she was practically blind. She adjusted her thick glasses up on her nose. They were silver framed, and always slid down her nose.

Most of the houses that lined both sides of this narrow street were similar to Aunt Rebekah's, except some were two-story homes and were painted different colors. Mostly the street was a quiet one. There was a racial mix of people living on this block. But there were mostly older Italians.

There was no one walking the block right then, but soon school children would make their way from Cathedral Academy toward Grand Street.

Aunt Rebekah opened the door.

"Hi, Sara. What's brought you here today?"

"Rebekah, I need to talk with you. It's important."

Aunt Rebekah stepped to the side, motioning Sara in with a warm smile.

"Come on in."

Adjacent to and a few feet from Aunt Rebekah's four steps to her door was a long dark staircase that led to the second floor. Sara stared to the top of the stairway as she made her way to Aunt Rebekah's four steps.

Aunt Rebekah closed the front door gently and put the double bolt lock on.

She wiped her hands on her brown apron that she wore almost all the time, along with her other clothes. She slowly walked the four steps to her place, and held on to the wall for support.

Aunt Rebekah's place was very cluttered. Her shaggy, wall-to-wall red carpet was kept clean. Her white poodle, Hap, went to Sara, looked at her, wagged his tail and walked back to his corner and sat. Sara sat at the dining room table. The table was neat. Around it were several hat boxes and a china cabinet full of expensive china. Near the cabinet was a large mirror. It was spotless.

"Rebekah, how are you?"

"Fine. Can I get you some coffee or something?"

"No, thanks."

Aunt Rebekah glanced at her wristwatch.

"Boys should be getting out of school soon."

"What time is it?" Sara asked.

"Two ten."

"Wow. The day's almost gone," Sara said, sighing.

"Sara, is everything all right? You seem a little nervous."

Sara's eyes slowly scanned the ceiling as she contemplated her next word. Then she propped her elbow on the table and rested her chin in the palm of her hand. She was nervous. Her eyes stared into Aunt Rebekah's eyes. She took her elbow down and grasped her hands together.

"Well, a few years ago, I had. . .I mean, I gave up a child for adoption."

"What?"

An enraged look swamped Aunt Rebekah's face.

"Rebekah, it was before I was married. I was a kid and didn't know what I was doing. Please . . ."

"Does Jim know about this?" Aunt Rebekah snapped.

"Well, no, not exactly . . ."

"Well?" Aunt Rebekah said.

At this point Aunt Rebekah felt Sara was capable of doing anything. To her, anyone who gave up their child had no conscience and would sell their soul at anyone's expense.

"I know what you're thinking. But I'm not cold-hearted, and I do love my children. It was a confusing time for me. I was so young."

"But that was a child you carried for nine months. How could you just give away your flesh and blood like that?"

Aunt Rebekah had a frown on her face. It would be an uphill battle for Sara to get Aunt Rebekah to side with her.

"I realize now I was wrong. That's why I'm looking for him."

"What do you mean?"

"I've been doing some research, and the last place he was officially documented at was here."

Aunt Rebekah had a curious look. Her forehead wrinkled.

"Here?" Aunt Rebekah asked.

"Yes. I called New York. His adoptive parents are the Summers. I spoke to Mr. Summers, and this is where he said was the last address on him. Wait,. I'll show you the papers."

Sara put her large black purse on the dining room table and began searching through it, then the phone rang. With Aunt Rebekah being almost fifty pounds overweight at five foot seven inches tall, this was a chore. The phone rang two more times before Aunt Rebekah got to it.

"Hello?" Aunt Rebekah said.

She leaned against the china cabinet.

"Aunt Rebekah, you haven't seen Sara, have you? There's an emergency."

"What kind of emergency, Jim?"

Sara's eyes shifted up from shuffling through the adoption papers.

"What is it, Aunt Rebekah?" Sara asked.

Sara dropped the papers on the table and went quickly to where Aunt Rebekah stood.

"It's Corey, he's sick," Rebekah said.

"Aunt Rebekah, let me talk."

Aunt Rebekah gave Sara the phone.

"Jim, it's me. What is it?"

"Can Rebekah hear you?"

Sara blinked, then glanced at Aunt Rebekah.

"No, it's okay," Sara answered.

Sara had gotten the hint that something terrible was wrong.

"Sara, you can't show any emotion toward Aunt Rebekah. It's best that as few people know about this as possible."

"Yes, okay," Sara said.

"Justin took Corey," Jim said.

There was a brief silence.

Sara could only cringe a little, but she wanted to cry badly. She glanced longer at Aunt Rebekah, then hung up.

Sara forced a smile and slowly went back to her seat. She knew she had to finish her conversation with Aunt Rebekah or she would suspect something.

Sara calmly sat in her seat, and Aunt Rebekah sat back in hers.

Sara picked up the adoption papers.

"You okay, Sara?"

"Yes. I was just thinking about Corey."

"He's gonna be all right, isn't he?"

"Oh, yeah. Probably just the flu. Jim can handle it."

"Can I get you something?"

"No . . . You were saying that nobody has lived upstairs?"

"Well, actually there . . ." Sara's attention was divided.

"I'm sorry, Rebekah, I've gotta get home."

Sara gathered her things and dashed out the door, leaving Aunt Rebekah behind, in thought.

"I'll call you and we'll finish later."

"But there was Al . . ." Aunt Rebekah yelled.

Sara heard Aunt Rebekah's last words, but she couldn't concentrate and rushed getting into her car. She flew down the street, screeching her wheels as she made a right onto Grand Street.

She burned rubber all the way down the two blocks headed home. At Myrtle Avenue, she turned right and parked a few feet from the corner fire hydrant.

Sara ran up the front steps, and Jim was there to open the door Henry stood behind him with an anxious look. Tears welled up in Sara's eyes. Sara and Jim embraced for a long moment. They held each other as they walked back into the kitchen. Henry pulled two chairs out for them.

"Sit. Both of you," Henry said.

Henry stood between both of them. He put a hand on each of their shoulders, forcing them to sit.

"Henry, this is no game," Sara said.

"I know, Sara. But we need a plan."

"The plan is simple. We wait," Jim said.

Sara looked at the clock on top of the refrigerator. It read 2:45 p.m.

"Randy and Tony will be home soon," Sara said.

"What're you gonna tell them?" Henry asked.

"No, it's what they're gonna tell me," Sara said.

"Whaddya mean?" Henry asked.

"I mean, they're brothers, maybe they know something that can help us."

"Yeah, I guess. I didn't think about that. You're sure you don't want to call the police?" Henry pushed.

"No! Don't! This man knows people we think he doesn't. Especially with Banes' death. I know Justin had something to do with it," Sara said. She was guessing.

They could hear footsteps on the front steps. Then they could hear a key turning in the front door. Sara stood up.

"Now let me handle this. I don't want to scare them off. I know they'll try to protect Corey and not tell us anything."

The phone rang. Sara ran to the wall phone near the kitchen entrance.

"Hello?" Sara said. She breathed hard.

"Sara, you sound out of breath," Justin said sarcastically.

"Don't worry about that. Where's Corey?"

"Corey's fine."

"I want him back now!"

"I think you've got something I want, too."

"You'll get your money."

A smile slowly spread across Justin's face. "Sara, do you think I would have taken your son just because you owe me some 'pennies'. Ohhhh, shame on you. Shame on you." Justin's face turned stone cold. "All I want is the printout and all copies Corey stole from my computer room."

Jim had run from the front door to the telephone in his bedroom, and listened intently.

"Justin, we just want Corey back," Jim said.

"Even swap," Justin said.

"You'll get your printout."

Justin hung up. Sara and Jim followed suit.

Randy and Tony came into the kitchen where everyone stood.

Sara knelt down in front of Randy. Randy loomed large over her.

"Randy, we need your help, Honey," Sara said.

"Where's Corey?" Randy asked.

"That's what we need to talk to you about, Randy," Sara said.

"What?" Randy asked.

"Randy, remember the man from upstairs?" Sara asked.

"Yeah."

"Well, he's taken Corey," Sara said.

Randy's eyes began to water, because he was scared.

Sara rubbed Randy's hand.

"Honey, I know it hurts. But maybe you can help."

"How?"

"Well, there is a missing printout that we want to get back to Justin. Justin said Corey took it from his computer room."

Randy wiped his teary eyes.

"Do you know where it is, Randy?" Jim asked.

Randy's eyes scanned everyone present. He remembered that Corey told him to keep it and not show anyone. But it was his call, and he needed to make the right decision.

Randy reached in the back of his pants and pulled out the printout. He slowly handed it to Sara.

"This is it, Mom."

Sara stood up, and Randy laid his head on her chest. He began to weep.

Sara looked at Tony. As his eyes were beginning to water, she pulled him toward her and the three of them embraced. Henry sighed.

"Now we wait," Henry said.

The telephone rang. Jim snatched the receiver.

"Hello," Jim said loudly.

"Why are you yelling?"

"Oh, sorry, Aunt Rebekah, I thought you were somebody else."

"Let me speak to Sara."

"Sara, it's for you."

Sara let go of Randy and Tony. They both sat at the kitchen table.

"Yes," Sara said.

"Sara, is everything okay? You left in a big hurry. Is Corey okay?"

There was a brief silence. Sara glanced at everyone before she would answer.

"Yes, Corey's going to be all right."

"Okay. If you need anything, let me know."

"I'll call you later, Aunt Rebekah."

Just before Sara was about to hang up, she remembered Aunt Rebekah's last statement before she left her house.

"Rebekah," Sara yelled.

"Yes."

Sara moved into the bathroom with the phone. She closed the door behind her and lowered her voice.

"You said someone lived with you by the name of Al."

"Yes, he was one of my great nephews. He never stayed long. He was mostly in and out. Then he just disappeared, left after we argued. He was grown, so I let him go."

"You said he was your great nephew. But why didn't I know about him?"

"He's Sam's great nephew."

Sam was Aunt Rebekah's late husband.

"Well, where is he now?"

"I don't know, Sara. He never calls."

"Where did he come from?"

"New York."

Sara sighed.

"Rebekah, what part of New York."

"Brooklyn."

"What's his name?"

The phone clicked. There was someone else trying to call.

"Aunt Rebekah, I have to get this other line. I'll call you later."

"Okay, bye. Call if you need anything."

"Bye."

Sara clicked over to the other phone line.

"Hello?" Sara said.

"Mom, don't give it to him. I'll be all right." I said hurriedly.

Sara ran from the bathroom and motioned for Jim to get on the phone in the bedroom.

"That's right, Sara, make sure Jim picks up the phone in the bedroom," Justin said. "Do you have my printout?"

"Yes, Justin. What next?" Sara said.

"Oh, you won't have to travel far."

The doorbell rang.

Henry trotted to the front to answer the door.

Captain Lee stood at the front door looking fit in his grey suit. He was accompanied by another officer in a navy blue police uniform.

Henry opened the door. He was surprised to see the police.

"Hello, I'm Captain Lee and this is Officer Weston. We were looking for the tenant who lives upstairs."

Henry wanted to tell them what was happening, but didn't.

"Well . . . I . . ."

Sara and Jim walked up behind Henry and propped the door open.

"Excuse me, Officer, what's going on?" Sara asked demandingly.

"Do you own this house?" Captain Lee asked.

"Yes, I'm Sara Harris and this is my husband, Jim."

Captain Lee reached toward Officer Weston for him to hand over the sketch of the man they were looking for. He showed Sara and Jim the 8x10 black and white sketch. It was the same picture that was faxed to Captain Lee by Mutt and Jeff from New York. The picture wasn't a good one, but Jim and Sara knew who it resembled, but something looked different.

"Have you seen this man before?" Captain Lee asked.

Sara and Jim studied the sketch. They had seen a resemblance to Justin.

"Nope," Jim said.

Jim handed the sketch back to Captain Lee.

"Officer, what made you come here?" Jim asked.

"After I did some digging, our computer gave this address from taxes you paid and you had your tenant's social security number listed. It matched ours. You know, your write-off?"

"Oh. Nobody by that name," Sara said.

"Okay, sorry to bother you. Thanks for your time."

The officers started down the steps. Captain Lee stopped and turned back toward Sara.

"If you see anyone who matches the sketch, please call me."

As Captain Lee walked away, Henry couldn't help but laugh at his pigeon-toed walk.

Captain Lee reached in his chest pocket, pulled out a business card, then ran back up the steps and handed it to Sara.

"Get the sketch, Sara," Henry whispered.

Captain Lee had started back down the steps.

"Captain, can I keep the sketch?" Sara asked.

Captain Lee ran back up the steps and handed Sara the sketch.

He returned to the squad car. He got in the passenger side, and Officer Weston drove off.

Everyone walked back into the kitchen.

"It's him, isn't it, Sara?" Henry asked.

"Of course it is. But if he finds out the police are looking for him, he'll think we sent them. This name, Totten?"

Sara knew she'd heard the name before, but she wasn't sure where.

"Jim, have you ever heard of this name before?" Sara asked.

Sara handed Jim the sketch, and he studied it for a few seconds.

"No, not that I know of," Jim answered.

Randy and Tony came into the kitchen.

"Mom, is there anything we can do to help?" Randy asked.

"No. You have helped already. Thanks. Why don't you guys go and watch television," Sara suggested.

"Okay, Mom," Randy replied.

Randy and Tony exited the kitchen. The telephone rang. Sara got up quickly from her seat and snatched the receiver from the kitchen entryway wall phone. Everyone else remained quiet. Tony and Randy stopped in their tracks.

"Hello?" Sara said. "Oh, hi, Father Donnelly. Corey came home a short while ago. He decided he was going to take the rest of the day off from school."

"Is he all right?" Father Donnelly asked.

"Yes, other than the punishment he's going to get for skipping school," Sara said.

"Okay, goodbye," Father Donnelly said.

"Bye," Sara said.

Sara slowly hung the receiver up. She had lied to Father Donnelly. Sadness blanketed her face.

"You think the boys might have more to help us with?" Henry asked.

Henry really didn't believe the boys could help more. He was only trying to give hope to Sara. Sara watched the boys walk toward the living room.

"No. I think they gave us all they had."

"So now we just wait, I guess!" Henry said.

"We don't have a choice," Jim offered.

Sara took a seat at the kitchen table. She turned to look at the boys watching television in the living room. Then she looked in her room, then at Jim.

"Jim, some changes are gonna be made. We can't keep living the way we have."

"I know," Jim said.

"I'm talking about everything, Jim!" Sara said.

Then Sara's eyes met Henry's.

Both Jim and Henry knew what she was talking about. Those wild sexual encounters would be a thing of the past.

"We might have to move after all of this, too. If Justin doesn't go to jail, we'll never be safe."

"I've thought about that too," Jim said.

Sara sat erect in her seat and looked at Jim and Henry while pondering her thoughts.

"And I don't think I'm ready to spend the rest of my life running from Justin Lord." She paused. "No, it's either him or us!"

CHAPTER SEVENTY

CAPTAIN LEE AND OFFICER WESTON were parked in front of the Division II Police Station. Weston took the key from the ignition.

"Do you think this guy is here?" Weston asked.

"If he is, I'll find him. If he's in my city, I'll find him."

"But the Harris family was our only lead, Cap."

Captain Lee got out of the car. Weston followed.

"I'm gonna make a few calls and if Totten is here, one of these guys will know."

They walked up the steps to the Division II precinct dark green wooden door.

They entered the police station. Weston went to the station desk to check for his messages, and Captain Lee hurried to his office.

He promptly went to his phone. He opened the top right-side drawer of his desk and took out his multi-colored phone book.

He flipped to the J's. He used his right index finger to move down the page, stopping at the name Justin.

Captain Lee dialed one of the two phone numbers he had on Justin. The phone rang five times, and he hung up. He looked in his phone book at the second number he had on Justin. He dialed it. The phone rang twice, and there was an answer.

"Yes, who's calling?" the female voice asked. This was one of the few times Justin allowed Sally B to answer his private line.

"This is Captain Lee calling for Justin."

Sally B, Justin and I were still in the upstairs room at his warehouse. Sally B covered the audible end of the phone with her hand and went to whisper in Justin's ear. He was leaning back comfortably in his wooden chair.

After telling Justin who it was on his cellular phone, Justin's eyes opened wide. Two thoughts ran through his head: one, maybe Lee was on to him, and two, maybe Corey's family had instructed Lee to call. But then the more reasonable thought dominated. He still had Corey, and his family wouldn't chance his life by telling the police.

Justin motioned for Sally B to take me out of the room. Then he motioned for her not to. She sat next to me.

"Hey, Captain Lee, it's me, Justin. What can I do for you?"

When I heard Captain, my eyes lit up.

"Wish I could afford my own personal secretary," Captain Lee said. Justin chuckled.

"It seems as though I have a small situation, and I was wondering if you could help me," Captain Lee asked.

"Go ahead."

"I'm trying to find a guy named Totten."

Justin sat up in his chair and leaned forward.

"What's he done?"

Justin knew the answer to that question.

"He may be linked to the murder of a hotel maid in New York City."

"I've never heard of this guy."

"Well, thanks anyway. We're getting close. I already made one stop from a lead."

"That's good. I'll keep my eyes and ears open for you," Justin said, brandishing a huge smile.

"Thanks."

They were about to hang up. Then Justin had another question.

"Oh, Lee, where was that stop you made? Maybe I can go there and find out a little more, seeing that I'm not the heat."

Justin just wanted to know for his own benefit.

"It was at the Harris' house on Grand Street. Ever heard of them?" Justin's smile fell off of his face and he swallowed hard. He gave me a long, hard, cold stare. Justin's mind became chaotic. He tried hard not to show it. He thought maybe Captain Lee's call was a trap and that the whole conversation was being recorded to find his whereabouts. He wasn't sure. He stood and paced for a few second in small circles.

"Hello?" Captain Lee yelled.

"Oh, sorry, Lee, there was some static on my end."

He was right, his mind was experiencing some static with Captain Lee's new revelation.

"Do you know where that is?" Captain Lee asked.

Without thinking, Justin answered immediately.

"Yeah, I'll check it out for you, Lee."

"Okay, let me know."

Captain Lee hung up the phone. Sally B watched Justin become nervous. To an extent, Sally B was glad because she sensed vulnerability. She thought maybe she could use whatever news Justin just received from Lee. She would choose her words carefully in finding out.

"So what does Lee want?" Sally B asked, carefully.

Justin's pacing slowed a bit.

"I don't know, but we can handle it."

Sally B stood. She knew something was wrong.

"Justin, let's take care of this business and leave."

Justin stopped pacing. He came to me, kneeled in front of me and violently ripped the tape from my mouth. I didn't wince from the pain.

"You'd better hope the police aren't on to us!"

I smiled in pain from the tape. Justin smiled back. We were both scared, but dared not let the other one see it. Justin stood and looked at Sally B. Then he used his foot to press on my severed finger. I yelled in pain. Justin laughed.

"Is everything set for us when we finish here, Sally B?"

"Yes. Whenever you're ready. We'll be outta here in no time."

Sally B knew something was bothering Justin. She knew she had to find out, because she didn't want anything to disrupt her secondary plans in case things went haywire.

"We may have to get outta here sooner than I really want to," Justin suggested.

"What's wrong?"

"Our Captain Lee stopped by the Harris' looking for Totten. They're linking him to the maid in New York."

Justin was speaking in code so that I wouldn't be able to figure out what was happening. The only thing I didn't know was whether Captain Lee was on the take to Justin or setting a trap for him. I knew the police were getting close to something, but I wasn't sure what. I knew if they were on to Justin they had a conversation long enough to trace the call and find us. I figured maybe ten minutes had passed by. I didn't know where we were. It was hard for me to tell if the police were on their way or not. For some strange reason, I knew every-thing would work out. At the same time, I was hoping that I would survive this because I needed to find out who was responsible for molesting me.

"Sally B, we're getting out," Justin said.

"Okay, I'll push everything up. How much sooner?"

"Now. Call Sara. We need to set the meeting. First call and confirm all of our arrangements."

"I did already."

"Don't argue with me, Sally B. Just do it!"

Sally B knew Justin meant business, and she had to act fast. Not only for Justin, but also because her own life was at stake, and she had to make sure that if she was killed by Justin, that her secondary plans were carried out by her long-time friend, Christina. She really needed an outside phone to call Christina. Or she could make her calls out of the room. But she knew if she went outside the room Justin might suspect something and kill her on the spot.

"I think it'd be better if I called Sara in private. That way Corey won't know what's going on."

I looked at Sally B. She was either smart or up to something, I thought. She gave me a look that I wasn't too sure about. Maybe she would kill me and Justin, and then get out.

"Yeah, do it. I'll keep an eye on him," Justin said.

Sally B hustled to get outside of the office. The door slammed behind her. She dialed a number. The phone rang once and it was quickly answered.

"Christina?" Sally B whispered.

"Who's this?" the female voice asked.

"Who's this?" Sally B asked.

Who's this, who's this, was Sally B and Christina's code for identifying themselves. Time wasn't on their side. Christina and Sally B had always kept in contact. They were last together when they en-tertained Dats and Uncle Henry.

"Christina, plans have changed. Do you still have the docu-ments?"

"Yes."

"Okay Look, I'm not sure when exactly I'm going to meet you, or if I will at all. But if I don't meet with you and I'm all right, I'll call you in sixty minutes at home."

"But I need to know what time you're supposed to meet with me, Sally B."

"But that's what I'm not sure about, because I'm not sure what time I'm supposed to be leaving with Justin. I gotta get off this phone, too."

"What phone are you on?"

Sally B looked at Justin's cellular. She knew she'd just made a mistake. When Justin gets the bill, if she was still alive, how would she explain this call at this particular time? Justin doesn't forget anything. He'd think something was wrong. Unbeknownst to Sally B, Justin always used an electronic chip in his cellular phone. This illegal chip allowed Justin to call anywhere in the world without it ever being recorded with the telephone company. He would buy the chip from his reliable source in New York City every six months to a year. That way, he could never be tracked.

"I know, Christina. Damn! Justin will have a record of the call."

"Shit! Sally B, you gotta get out now!" Christina was panicking.

"I can't, I wouldn't make it. Christina, you can't panic on me. Come on, you're not the one in the hot seat. Be cool. Besides, maybe I can help Corey." Sally B could hear Christina sigh.

"Listen! Once I find out what time, I'll call you. If you have to leave I'll put it on your machine. If I haven't met you or called one hour from that time, give the documents to the police. But give me one hour. It's important to give me one hour"

"But he could get away in an hour."

"Yeah, and I may decide to stay and work with him. What else is there?"

"There's always family . . . You always talked about wanting to start a family," Christina said.

"Look, I don't have time right now. You got everything?"

"Yeah."

Justin opened the door to the hallway area where Sally B was.

"What's taking so long?" Justin asked.

Sally B had to think fast.

"I keep getting static and they can't hear me."

Justin came to where Sally B stood, letting the door slam behind him.

"Let me see," Justin said, aggravated.

Sally B handed the phone to Justin. He dialed the number to the Harris residence.

"I don't hear any static," Justin said with a frown.

"There was a minute ago," Sally B said defensively.

It wasn't a sincere defense, but she didn't want to appear weak to Justin then. He might think something, since she always came across strong.

"It's ringing. Here."

Justin handed Sally B the cellular.

"But Justin, I don't know when to tell them to make the switch."

Justin looked at Sally B with contempt. It was a look Sally B didn't like. He took the phone from her. Sara answered the phone.

"Be at the Albany Airport, parking lot C, at 6:30."

Sally B looked at her watch. It read 5:30.

"What kind of car will you be in?" Sara asked.

"Don't worry, just be there. I'll find you!" Justin snapped.

Justin angrily clicked off.

"Get the car ready." Justin went back into the office area.

Sally B knew the airport wasn't good. After the switch, Justin could kill her, jump on a plane and be long gone before the police could stop him.

Inside her gut, Sally B felt the knots building up. She wondered how she was going to pull this off. She headed down the long staircase. She hurried to the bottom of the steps and ran to the nearest dark corner. She stuck her shaking hand between her legs and lifted her loose-fitting skirt. She put her hand in her crotch area underneath her panties and reached for her gun. She knew that if she showed any panic or alarm, Justin would suspect something. This wouldn't be good while he was in a killing state of mind.

Her hand no longer shook. She checked to make sure her gun was loaded. She put the gun back in its strap and ran to the front area of the warehouse. She uncovered the car parked in front of the black Maxima that they came in. She ran back to the stairs and ran up them.

Justin snatched the tape from my mouth. He watched over me.

"You know you're gonna get caught. You're not as smart as you think. I'm smarter."

"That's what you think," Justin said.

"I know how you think. You don't really want to kill me. There's something else going on. You would have killed me a long time ago."

"Shut up!"

Justin roughly put the tape back on my mouth.

At that moment I didn't care what I said to Justin. I figured he would do with me what he wanted anyway so why not.

I wanted to anger and frustrate him. I doubt what I said bothered him but it was my way to fight back.

I was scared but hoped that Mom and Dats were doing something to save me.

CHAPTER SEVENTY-ONE

THE PHONE RANG in the Harris house. Sara was in the kitchen. She answered it in a hurry.

"Yes?" Sara said.

"Sara, this is Rebekah."

"Yes, Aunt Rebekah, what is it? I gotta run out for a while."

"I just wanted to tell you about my great nephew. You said you wanted to know more about him. After all, he is your distant cousin."

Henry ran back into the kitchen with his Beretta 9 millimeter tucked in his front belt. Jim stood waiting with his .44 Special.

Sara waved them off.

"Aunt Rebekah, I . . . Okay, what's his name?"

"Al, Al Totten."

"Al what?"

"Totten."

This name sent a pounding in Sara's head. She had blotted out all the noise and everybody around her, and could only hear the name Totten echoing in her mind repeatedly. Her eyes shifted from Jim to the sketch on her kitchen table. She looked at it again. Jim began to shake Sara on her shoulder.

"Sara, come on, we've got to get to the airport. It's almost 6:00," he said.

Sara snapped back into the moment. She didn't want to believe what might be a reality.

"Aunt Rebekah, I've got to go. We'll talk about this later. Bye," Sara said.

"Bye," Aunt Rebekah said.

They both hung up. Sara was still stunned by the news from Aunt Rebekah as she made her way out of the kitchen back door. Jim pushed the automatic garage door button near the garage entrance, then hurried into the car and started the engine up. Sara got in the back seat, and Henry got in the front seat. Jim backed out fast, almost hitting Captain Lee as he ran up the driveway, carrying a fax. Jim slammed on his brakes, just missing Captain Lee. Mom pushed the automatic window button and her window opened.

"Yes, Captain Lee?" Sara asked.

He handed the fax to Sara. She read it to herself.

"We got this fax saying your son Corey was missing from school. I realize it was hours ago, but I was concerned since I was just here a short while ago and nobody mentioned it."

Sara immediately took over.

"Captain Lee, Corey is fine," she said with a forced smile.

Henry pulled the bottom of his shirt over his belt to hide his gun. Captain Lee's eyes shifted from Jim to Henry and back to Sara.

"Where is Corey?"

"He's with his aunt," Sara said.

"Earlier you told me he was sick," Captain Lee said with a fake smile.

"But he is sick, with his aunt. Please, Captain Lee, we're in a hurry," Sara said.

"Where's the fire?" Captain Lee joked.

"There's no fire. We just have to pick someone up from the airport?' Sara said.

"This fax was probably sent hours before we spoke to Father Donnelly. See, it's from Mrs. Hillzinger. There was probably a communication mix-up between them. And you've probably been gone all day. That's why you're just getting this. She probably called too, I bet," Sara said.

"Yeah, there was a message from Mrs. Hillzinger," Captain Lee said. "Okay, I'd better let you go before you're late."

Captain Lee stepped back a few steps from Sara's window. Jim forced a smile as he backed out of his garage onto Myrtle Avenue.

"She never told me Corey was sick," Captain Lee said to himself as he hastened his pace toward his car. He had set them up to find out information.

CHAPTER SEVENTY-TWO

SALLY B HAD FINISHED taking the cover off of the newly-remodeled 1967 gold Camaro. Justin loved classic cars. He kept them in separate warehouses throughout the state.

Sally B ran back up the stairs to the office. She remembered she had to call Tibby. Tibby still owed her some help, and she figured that may have been the time to call in those chips. Using Justin's phone again was a problem.

Sally B slammed open the door to Justin's office where he slowly paced and I sat. I liked watching Justin sweat, even though I was just as scared. I knew his life might be over in a very short time.

"We're ready," Sally B said, out of breath.

Justin grabbed me by my arm and escorted me to Sally B.

"Go to the car and wait. I'll be right down," he commanded.

Sally B hesitated a bit as she moved me toward the door.

"Put the blindfold on him," Justin said. She carefully put the blindfold on.

Sally B wondered why Justin stayed in the office. She hurried me down the steps and into the car, and opened the back door for me.

"Duck your head, Corey," she advised.

She helped me into the car, then got in the driver's seat and started the engine. She looked at the cellular, and contemplated her next move. She wanted to make sure she was covered at all ends. She leaned over to the passenger side window and looked up, making sure Justin wasn't coming. He wasn't. She quickly got back behind the wheel.

"Look, Corey, I'm gonna do everything I can to keep you alive. I'm tired of all the killing. I want kids one day, too. You remind me of a son that I would someday like to have. All this running and not knowing how long before we're caught is driving me crazy lately."

I wondered if she planned on taking me. She gently took the tape from my mouth, then carefully pulled the blindfold down from my eyes.

"Well, why do you stay? Just go," I said.

"It's not that easy. Justin has the means and connections to do whatever he wants. If he knew I was talking to you like this, I'd be dead."

"Don't you want a family though? You just said you wanted a son like me."

"I'm taking you with me, Corey."

"Then let's go."

Sally B slumped down in her seat and stared 'out'.

She had a look of doubt. I felt it.

"Corey, this life is all I know."

"Let's just get outta here!"

Sally B sighed.

"I do have some saved."

"Please, I know he's gonna kill me when he gets what he wants. Look."

My hands were still tied. I held up my severed middle finger "He's already cut my finger off."

Sally B kindly put my hand down on my lap and rewrapped it with the dry part of the partially bloody jacket.

"Not if you listen to me, Corey. I have a plan. Somebody is helping me. You just keep your mouth shut and you'll live. I like you, Corey, and I would never hurt you. Really I wouldn't let him hurt you. I've been a little bit of everything in my life, but I'm not a killer. I'll protect you."

Justin took another cellular phone from the desk drawer. He dialed a number. It rang once and someone picked up the phone. It was a female voice.

"Is everything set?" Justin asked.

"Yes."

"You have the package?"

"Yes."

"You know where to meet me, right?" Justin asked.

"Yes, the airport."

"Just bring the package. You won't need clothes. We'll buy some once we get to where we're going." Then he hung up. "It'll be me and you," Justin said to himself.

CHAPTER SEVENTY-THREE

CAPTAIN LEE WAS IN THOUGHT as he drove on Warren Street, headed toward the Division II Precinct. He slowed a moment and coasted, thinking about the turn of events at the Harris house.

"I never asked her his name," he muttered.

He slammed his foot on the gas pedal. Smoke rose from the rear tires as they made sudden contact with the blacktop pavement. As he sped past the precinct, he took his portable blue flashing light from the seat near him and placed it on the roof. He came to a red light at Warren and Pearl Streets and hooked a fast left, almost crashing into an oncoming car. The car stopped just in the nick of time. Captain Lee waved apologetically, and sped up the street to the corner of Pearl and Ferry Streets. He had a gut feeling that something was going to happen at the airport.

Jim drove fast on Route 87, bound for Albany Airport.

"I hope he's all right!" Sara said.

"He wouldn't hurt him as long as he knows we have the print-out," Jim said.

"Justin's crazy. He'll do anything to anyone, you know that, Jim," Sara snapped.

"Well, whatever the case, we need to know your game plan," Henry suggested.

"You're right, because Justin's going to want it his own way, no matter what . . . Whatever we do, we can't make any sudden movements, because Justin will start shooting. Henry you should wait for us at the airport entrance. Put yourself somewhere so that you can see everything. I'll wave to you if everything's okay. Otherwise, you gotta stop him from getting on the plane, somehow. Shoot him in the leg if you have to, but stop him."

They were held at the highway exit stoplight. Jim's nervous foot lightly pressed on the gas pedal, inching closer to one of the cars waiting in front of him. The light changed to green, and the four cars ahead of Jim slowly took left turns, the same way he was headed. Jim looked at the car panel clock, it read 6:15. He blew his horn several times. Sara looked at the clock.

"Jim, we're only five minutes away. We don't want to bring attention from the police," she said.

"There's no cops," Jim said.

"Look behind you," Sara said.

He glanced in his rear-view mirror. He saw a state police car pull up behind him.

"Now, c'mon, Honey, please, we're almost there," Sara said.

Jim tensed up a bit in his seat and lightly tapped his fingers on the steering wheel in rhythm. He was tailgating.

"Jim, you're too close. C'mon, calm down," Sara pleaded.

I was gagged, blindfolded and hog-tied on the back seat floor of Justin's Camaro. Justin sat in the back with his feet propped on me. He had a grey, wool blanket draped over my motionless body.

"Too bad for our little Corey," Justin said.

Sally B was at the steering wheel. We were parked in Lot C of the Albany Airport, in full view of anyone coming and going.

Captain Lee moved fast as he got off the highway onto Wolf Road. He pulled in front of a car and turned on his siren. Cars on Wolf Road stopped, allowing him to go ahead.

Sara, Jim and Henry drove at a safe speed, headed toward the airport.

"You hear that?" Sara said.

"What?" Henry asked.

The siren noise went faint.

"I thought I heard a siren," Sara said.

Captain Lee turned off his siren.

He drove fast on Albany Shaker Road, headed for the airport. He took off his blue flashing light and put it on the seat next to him.

Jim drove past an empty airplane hangar on the right side of Albany Shaker Road. Then he took the next right turn, and cautiously drove up Airport Row toward the medium-sized airport's main terminal.

Tibby sat in his old burgundy pickup truck in the far corner of Lot C. He could see Justin and Sally B sitting in the Camaro. Sally B inconspicuously looked out of the corner of her eye, trying to see who was around. It was difficult because the lot was full. It was hard for her to see from her point of view. She slowly began opening her driver's side door. She needed to check things.

"Where are you going?" Justin asked.

He wasn't about to let anyone screw up his plan.

"I wanted to check to see if Sara and Jim were here yet," Sally B lied.

"We'll see them from here. Get back in."

Sally B closed her door with caution. Parking Lot C's entrance was near the main terminal entrance. Jim slowly entered the parking lot, and took the parking ticket from the ticket machine. The one-arm gate closed behind him as he drove in and slowed almost to a stop.

"So what now?" Jim asked.

Sara looked around, trying to spot Justin's car. Henry did the same.

"I really can't see where he's parked," Sara said.

"Jim, maybe you should just pull over into a space. He'll find us," Henry offered.

"Okay, Henry, you go and wait inside the terminal. Find a spot where you can see the entire parking lot. Remember, if everything is okay, I'll wave to you. If not, stop Justin from getting on a plane. Once he goes into hiding, it will be hard to find him. He changes his whole look. He probably changes his name, too," Sara said.

Then it dawned on Sara about what Aunt Rebekah had told her earlier regarding her 'sometime' tenant.

"Pull in there, Jim," Sara said, pointing to an empty spot.

Jim backed his car into the parking space. It was a little easier to see who came toward them from this angle.

Twenty cars down, Sally B's friend, Christina, was parked in a new, black 300 Benz. She couldn't see who was there either. But she knew she had to wait.

Jim's clock said 6:38. The sun was setting, but there was still no sign of Justin, as far as they knew.

Captain Lee crept down Airport Row. He looked for Sara and Jim's car. Two aisles over, Sara saw Captain Lee's car driving away from them.

"What's he doing here?" Sara asked, frowning.

Justin got out of his car. He bent over to look in the front passenger side window.

"Wait here," Justin said.

"How long before you'll be back?" Sally B said.

"Shortly. Keep an eye out for me."

Justin headed toward Christina's car.

From a distance, Sara could see the figure of a man walking toward the corner of the parking lot.

"Who's that?" Sara asked, pointing.

"Who? Where?" Henry asked, frantically turning his head in every direction.

"Straight ahead, Henry, look through the car windows," Sara suggested.

Sara inched opened her door and got out of the car.

"Sara, wait!" Jim urged.

"Give me the printout. It must be him."

Sara saw Justin motion with his hand to someone in a car to the left of Sara's car. Sara looked in that direction. The car horn blew one time.

Justin kept walking toward the car. He was in plain view.

Sara could see that it was Justin.

"It's him, Henry, go."

Henry rushed from the car and went toward the terminal entrance. Sally B watched Justin get further and further away from her. This made her nervous. She gradually opened the car door and got out. She bent low and began walking between the cars, making sure Justin wouldn't see her.

Sara, with the printout in hand, began to walk toward Justin. Justin spotted her. They were about sixty yards apart. Justin cracked a small smile.

"Be careful, Sara!" Jim said in a low tone.

"Start the car!" Sara said. Jim started the car.

"I can't see Corey!" Sara said fearfully.

Jim pulled from his parking space and slowly followed Sara.

"Jim, stay back," Sara advised nervously.

Jim stuck his head out of his window to whisper back loudly "No."

Out of the corner of her eye, Sara saw Captain Lee driving in the parking lot. He hadn't spotted her yet, and she didn't want him to.

"Captain Lee's here, Jim," Sara whispered.

"Sara, hurry before Justin spots him," Jim said in a whisper.

Sara picked up her pace, and Jim sped up. Sara rolled the printout tighter in her grasp. The closer she got to Justin, the tighter she twisted the printout.

"Where's Corey?" she yelled.

Justin motioned over his shoulder toward his car.

"I need to see him," Sara demanded.

Justin smiled.

"*Now*, Justin, or I'm calling your friend," Sara said, pointing toward Captain Lee, two aisles over.

Justin's smile fell to the ground as he caught a glimpse of Captain Lee.

"That's right, Justin, I know everything," Sara said.

Sara was really bluffing, but Justin had no choice but to believe her because of Captain Lee's presence. Captain Lee was in plain clothes and a plain marked car.

"I told you, no police!" Justin said with anger.

"Oh, so you do know Captain Lee. Justin, I never saw that man in my life."

Sara lied again.

"My son!" Sara said.

Justin waved his hand toward Sally B for her to come forward in the car. Sally B saw Justin wave, but she was behind him on foot.

Sara watched, and waited for one of the cars to move from a space. "Nothing! Justin, I don't see Corey," she said.

"He'll be coming," Justin promised.

Christina could see everything from her vantage point. She waited for her signal.

Sally B wanted to escape, but she knew she needed to follow through with her plan. She'd made it back to the car, started it up and moved toward Justin and Sara. They were a short distance from Sally B.

Henry could see everything from the Terminal entrance. He stood on a concrete block that was on the grassy area off to the side of the entrance.

Captain Lee had made his way to the far end of the parking lot. He took a left, headed to the area where Sally B had driven from. He was about sixty yards away. Sally B had just pulled away from her parking spot.

"Stop" Sara demanded as she motioned with her hand. "I want to see Corey!"

Sara stopped. She and Justin were about twenty yards apart.

"You'll see your Corey. Sally B's right behind me," Justin said.

Sara could see Sally B following.

"How do I know he's all right? I can't see him," Sara said.

"How do I know that that rolled up piece of paper you have in your hand is the printout?" Justin answered.

Sara opened the printout and began reading it aloud.

"Mayor William Wales, payment of fifty thousand. Senator Harvey Houseman, payment of fifty thousand."

Justin cringed on every word. He looked around, trying to hide his nervousness. He kept one hand in the side pocket of his black leather jacket.

"Let's not get carried away, Sara. We wouldn't want the world to know our business, would we?" Justin shot back calmly.

Darkness had eased in. The sight of Christina brought an intrigued look to Sally B's face. Christina inconspicuously motioned to Sally B that everything was okay. Sally B knew it wasn't. She had instructed Christina not to surface at the airport. Suspicion clouded Sally B's mind. Christina always followed Sally B's instructions precisely.

Captain Lee spoke on his car radio. It was a female he was speaking with.

"Captain, that guy Jefferies from New York called back."

Lee pressed the intercom button and spoke.

"Did he leave a message?" Captain Lee asked.

"Yes, he said the name on the sketch that he sent you is a fake. His real . . ."

Noises that resembled gunshots were heard. Captain Lee instinctively stopped and ducked in his car. He pressed the intercom button.

"Yeah, we've got possible gunshots," he said.

The upper half of Captain Lee's body leaned over to the passenger seat. Two ten year old boys walked by with a cap gun. Captain Lee pressed the audible button on his car radio.

"Eighty-six that. It was only some kids playing.

Justin put his hand up, motioning for Sally B to stop the car. Sally B stopped, and Justin walked back to her driver's side window and spoke.

"I want you to back me up if something happens, no matter what. I'm gonna let Sara come to the car and get a look inside. Then I'm gonna snatch the printout. After I do that, get closer to the terminal entrance."

There was still no movement under the blanket in Sally B's back seat.

Captain Lee was not prepared to get distracted. He sighed in disgust as the precinct radio dispatcher kept him on hold.

Over at Justin's car, he motioned for Sara to move toward him. She twisted slightly to see if Henry was in place at the terminal entrance, and to make sure Jim was close behind in the car.

Sara quickened her pace to Justin's car. She was there.

"Hold it . . ."Justin warned.

She stopped. Her eyes cut to what appeared to be Corey.

"The printout first!" Justin demanded.

"No! Where's Corey?" Sara demanded.

Justin grinned a short one, then sighed.

"He's on the floor," Justin answered.

"I need to see him."

Justin took out his .45 automatic.

"I said he's on the floor. The printout or everyone dies," Justin threatened again.

Sara was between a rock and a hard place. She knew Justin would kill everyone in the end if he had to. She gambled with her next statement.

"Aunt Rebekah told me," Sara said.

Justin had an intrigued look.

"You know who I am, Justin. Why are you doing this?"

"You know nothing of what I've been through. You haven't lived my life," Justin said.

"I know, and I'm sorry for what I've done. But I was so young."

"Young? I started when I was young. You and your lover, Tibby, you had a choice. Why didn't you just let me stay? You sold me to the highest bidder."

"Justin, why all of this?"

"You deserve it. You're not a mother. You're a killer, just like me. You don't pull the trigger. You just break souls. You have no idea what I went through for all those years. Now you feel what I lived for my life growing up in fear! Now you want your son, just as I wanted life."

Sara wanted to embrace Justin. She raised her hands toward Justin to embrace him. Justin held the gun up to her head, directly between her eyes.

"Stop!" Justin yelled.

Jim stopped the car and got out.

"Jim, stay there. It'll be all right," Sara said.

Sally B watched, and slowly took her gun and held it ready.

Captain Lee was off of the radio and had turned down a few aisles from where Justin stood. He was about thirty yards away. He stopped his car and drew his weapon. He didn't recognize that it was Justin because it was too dark and he was wearing a baseball cap. He then got out and maneuvered toward Justin between the cars. Christina and Sally B made eye contact. Sally B suspected something was wrong with Christina.

"All I want is Corey. Please?" Sara begged.

"Corey's in the car," Justin said.

"But I still can't see him."

"Don't worry he's all right. Just give me my printout and I'll be out of your life. This time forever," Justin said.

Sara saw Captain Lee making his way toward the car.

"Justin, just step aside and let me have Corey"

"Lay the printout on the car hood and I will."

"But I don't know that Corey's okay"

Sara saw Captain Lee getting closer. She knew that he would expose himself and Justin would begin shooting. She knew Captain Lee would possibly kill Justin, and she didn't want that.

"The printout!" Justin demanded.

She was breathing fast and hard. She had to make a decision fast.

"You're my son and that's my son in that car. What I did was wrong, yes. Both of you are alive and that's what I want to keep you alive," Sara whispered angrily.

"You have no concept of what being a mother is," Justin gritted through his teeth.

"No, no, you're wrong, Alvin, Al or Justin, whatever your name is."

Sara moved closer. The gun touched her forehead.

"I do know! That's why I've been looking for you. And for the past twenty-some years I haven't stopped thinking about you. And I know somewhere in that hardened heart you love me or you wouldn't have stayed this close to me, knowing that I am your mother. You may not like me, and that's fine, but nothing can take away the fact that I'm your mother and that boy in that car is your brother. I'm not giving you this printout until I see Corey. That's my deal. So help me, if he isn't alive, all hell is gonna break loose."

Sara pushed Justin's gun away from her forehead, threw the printout on the ground, then quickly went to the car and opened the back door. Everyone was shocked. Sara checked to see if Corey was there. He wasn't. Justin picked up the printout. Sara panicked when she saw a sack of potatoes with a note attached.

Sally B hurried toward Justin with her gun drawn as Christina approached. Justin looked back at Sally B, then at Christina. Justin really loved Sally B, but he knew he had to make a decision. He knew Sally B had asked Christina to make copies of the documents that could destroy him. But Justin knew Sally B did it for her own protection. This is what Sally B had come to learn from Justin. So he couldn't blame her for this. He couldn't see how Sally B's best friend, Christina, could betray her. Justin knew someday Christina might do the same to him. Sally B would never betray him for money, only to save her life if he was going to kill her. Justin reached in his pocket and took out a silencer. He attached it to his gun.

Sally B and Christina were almost upon Justin.

"Christina was going to betray you," Justin said.

Sally B looked at Christina.

"No, Sally B. I did everything you asked me. Justin threatened me," Christina said. Sally B knew it was possible, but still wondered why Christina didn't tell her earlier. Sally B would have killed Christina herself.

Christina pulled out a small gun and pointed it at Sally B.

"Sally B! Watch it! She has a gun!" Justin warned. "Don't trust her!"

Then Christina aimed her gun at Justin. "You pig!" she shrieked.

Suddenly Justin fired his gun at Christina, twice hitting her in the head, killing her instantly. He continued walking toward the airport entrance.

Sally B stood over Christina for a few seconds.

"Sally B, are you coming?" Justin asked, knowing she would.

Sally B looked at him, then at Christina, then back at him. She started rapidly toward Justin. Justin saw Henry at the doorway. Henry saw Justin. Henry hadn't gotten Sara's signal. Henry saw Justin's gun by his side. Justin pointed it at Henry. Henry drew his gun.

"Henry, let him go!" Sara yelled.

Henry quickly tucked his gun back in his pants and turned his back on Justin. Justin put his gun in his pants. Sally B threw her gun in a nearby trash can as she entered the airport.

"Goodbye, Sally B," Uncle Henry said as he swiftly walked by her.

"Bye," Sally B said.

Back at the car, I was in the trunk tied up and almost unconscious, with blood all over me. Justin had put me there while we waited for Mom to arrive. Mom almost fainted when she saw all the blood. She tried to pick me up.

"Corey, oh, my God, wake up!" She vigorously shook me a few times. "What's all this blood?" Mom said as she began to weep. Dats and Uncle Henry arrived and got me out of Mom's hands, then laid me on the ground. They desperately tried to awaken me.

"Corey!" Dats shouted. They untied me.

Captain Lee stepped in. "Excuse me, please, let me take a look at him."

Everyone stepped back as Captain Lee checked for a pulse. Mom moved about frantically in one place for a few seconds, then glanced toward the airport entrance. She wondered if I was alive.

"I got a pulse," Captain Lee shouted.

"Thank God," Mom said, relaxing a bit.

Mom came back near the trunk with Dats and Uncle Henry, taking their hands and holding them tightly. Mom affectionately pulled Dats a few steps away from everyone and they passionately embraced. She began to whisper in his ear. "I lied to you earlier." Dats tried to pull away but Mom held firm. Then Mom slowly released Dats enough so that she could look him in his eyes.

"Corey *is* your son. I lied because I wanted to see if you would still protect us even if you thought he wasn't your child." Brief silence followed. They stared into each other's eyes. Then Dats pulled Mom close and held her tight and spoke softly.

"That's okay. I'm with you no matter what."

Justin hastily emerged from the men's room. He had dumped his gun. Sally B waited impatiently. She knew they could be caught if Mom let Captain Lee do his job.

Justin glanced at his watch.

"Justin, we're gonna be caught!" Sally B said.

Justin took her by the hand.

"Is Sara gonna tell after what you did to her son?"

They began walking toward the airport security area.

"Just smile. Corey's all right. Sara won't turn us in. And she won't let Jim or Henry. We've just got to get out. Our plane leaves in ten minutes. You dumped that little gun of yours, right?"

Sally B had a look of shock as they hurried through the security point.

"But . . ."

"I always knew I taught you well."

"Where are we going?" Sally B asked.

"You forgot about Richard Richards in Vancouver? You know, the hotel?" Justin said.

"Oh," Sally B said. This caught her off guard. She finally knew where they were going.

"We have business up there, remember?" Justin said. Sally B thought it was a good move.

I was becoming more conscious. I then slowly opened my eyes. Mom ran to me and hugged me. As I smiled, Uncle Henry approached.

In the far end of the lot, Tibby saw that Sally B was gone and out of sight, and hopefully out of his life forever. He started his truck and calmly left the lot without anyone noticing him. Sally B had positioned Tibby there in case her other plans failed. He was her safety net.

Captain Lee checked my eyes. "Are you okay, Corey?" He asked as he looked at my bloody hand.

I shook my head no, and held my bloody hand and cut off finger up to him in my other hand. They were shocked.

"We've got to hurry," Captain Lee said as he wrapped my hand tighter but gently with the same bandage.

"Sara, I need to know who that guy was. I have to call this in."

"Jus . . ." Uncle Henry started to answer. But Mom interrupted.

"Just a minute, Captain. You should be calling an ambulance for my boy, not worrying about someone who's gone. Corey could lose his finger!"

"He's a criminal, and he's mine whether you like it or not! It's my duty!"

"It's your duty to make sure my son gets immediate medical care. He'll be caught!"

Sara was concerned about Corey's finger, but also about her other son, Justin.

"Not if he's headed out of the country."

"Planes don't leave here bound directly for other countries," Mom said.

As they spoke, a plane roared past over their heads. On the side of the plane, lights shined on the Air Canada label.

"For Canada they do," Captain Lee said.

Sara was happy and sad. Happy because Corey was alive, and sad for a couple of reasons. The first was that she would probably never see her eldest son again. Only she and Justin would ever know who he really was, and she would keep it that way. The second was that she knew she had tracked a man who was guilty of cold blooded murder and he happened to be the son that she dumped. She felt guilty not only because she had dumped him, but also because she had let him get away knowing his crimes. But she knew this would be her way of making amends for her abandoning him to strangers years ago.

"I still need to report this. I'll call an ambulance while I call in," Captain Lee said.

Justin and Sally B sat together in the first class section. The plane was half full.

"How are you so sure that Sara won't expose you?" Sally B asked.

"Let's just say it's in our blood."

"What was all that about her being your mother?"

"I don't know. It sounded good, so I went along with it." Justin would never admit anything to anyone—not yet anyway.

Sara was indeed his biological mother, but he wanted to keep it to himself. He was able to locate her by going to the adoption agency in Albany. He paid a huge sum of money to Mr. Linton for the information, and for him to keep his mouth shut.

Justin hated the fact that Sara had given him up to the Summers, and he basically lived a life of hell. But with the Summers, he was forced to learn to survive, and out of the crash survival course came his psychotic ways.

He sought to make Sara suffer because of his years of anguish. He hated the fact that Sara had a happy home, and purposely sought to destroy it. To kill them would have only made it easy for them. No, he wanted them to suffer as he had. Once Corey invaded his privacy, it gave him the fuel to his fire to help with the destruction of the family.

Captain Lee ran to where he saw something laying in the parking lot aisle.

It was Christina's dead body. He took off his jacket and put it over her head. Then he ran back toward his car, stopping first at the car where I was with Mom, Dats and Uncle Henry.

"We've got a dead body over there. Somebody on that plane is a killer."

Captain Lee ran to his car. Mom, Dats and Uncle Henry knew who was responsible. They knew I knew, too. But nobody said anything. I was glad to be in safe hands, or was I? Still, it hurt that I didn't know who was molesting me.

I looked at Mom and Dats. They were happy to have me back.

"Are you okay, Corey?" Mom asked.

"Yeah, except for this." I nodded toward my cut-off finger.

"You'll never have to worry about him again," Mom said.

But I did have to worry about one of them, if Justin wasn't the one molesting me.

"As soon as you're okay, we're going fishing, Corey," Uncle Henry said.

I smiled and took advantage of the moment. I knew I didn't have to talk anymore, because they thought I was terrified at being kidnapped. But I wasn't. At least I knew if I was going to die it would be final. Being molested was worse, because it was painful and ongoing by someone I knew, but didn't know. I knew my day would come. They would slip and then . . . they would pay.

Sirens were heard, and police converged on the parking lot. The place was swamped with cops. Mom knew something I didn't, and I wanted to know, too.

A small traffic buildup had begun to develop in the middle of the parking lot. The lookie-loos were in the way. Soon morning would ascend on the entire scene and the event would be front-page news for the local 8:00 a.m. broadcasts.

CHAPTER SEVENTY-FOUR

SARA STILL WASN'T SATISFIED with the small amount of information she knew about her eldest son. As she made her way up Aunt Rebekah's steps, she knew time would tell what really went on with Justin at Aunt Rebekah's.

Aunt Rebekah opened the door after the bell rang twice. Aunt Rebekah was still oblivious as to what had happened the prior evening. All she knew was what she'd heard on the news. That was, as the newscaster reported, a shooting by an unknown assailant. One 'Christina' was left dead.

"How's Corey feeling, Sara?" Aunt Rebekah asked.

Sara wanted to tell Aunt Rebekah what had happened as she was led into the dining room. All Sara could do was stare at the back of Aunt Rebekah's salt and pepper hair and shake her head.

"Oh, he's fine. Still coughing a little, but he's taking his medicine," Sara said.

Aunt Rebekah sat in her chair at the dining room table and began to stir her black coffee. Coffee was Aunt Rebekah's eye opener every morning. Sara sat in the chair that was kitty-corner to Aunt Rebekah. Aunt Rebekah had a cup of Sara's favorite herbal peppermint tea waiting on the table in front of her seat.

"Is Corey in school today?"

"He went fishing with Henry. You know I would've brought him otherwise."

Sara thought about what she'd just said. She knew Corey couldn't stand going to Aunt Rebekah's. At the same time, Corey felt like he was on ball and chain from her constant badgering.

"Next time, bring him, okay? It's been a while since I've seen him. Seems like I see Randy and Tony all the time."

Aunt Rebekah paused and thought for a moment. She realized how long it had been.

"My God, Sara, it's been almost a year since I've seen him. By the time he gets over here, I could be dead and gone!" she said with a smile.

"I'll bring him over long before then, don't worry."

Sara knew it would be a frosty day in the hottest of hot days in the desert of Las Vegas before she would be able to get Corey to visit Aunt Rebekah. But fishing with Henry was another story

"So Aunt Rebekah, tell me about Al."

"But there's nothing to tell. He came and went so much I couldn't keep up with him. Why are you so interested?"

"Then just tell me about his comings and goings."

Aunt Rebekah paused in thought for a moment as she brought her coffee cup to her large, dark, wrinkled lips and took two long sips, swallowing hard after each drink. "He first came around five years ago. Actually, that was the last time I remember . . . As a matter of fact, I think that was the last time Corey really spent the night. Al came in later that night. He woke everyone up. We argued a bit."

"Why?"

Aunt Rebekah sighed.

"One of my friends was over that night. Al walked in and saw something he didn't like. It's not that I didn't enjoy the company of a man, but I always had this thing for this one particular woman who I was intrigued about. Oh, you don't want to hear about that . . . Al came in, saw her, put two and two together and we argued."

"Is that why you don't have any children?"

"No, never could have 'em. Don't get me wrong, I loved my husband. I just had a fling with a woman instead of a man."

"So what about Al?" Sara asked.

"Well, after he barged in and caught me in bed with that woman, he couldn't tell me what was really bothering him, because seeing me with her made him even more upset. He only told me that some horrible things were done to him while he was growing up, and that he needed to talk to someone about it. It broke his heart to see me kissing a woman, so he left."

"So did he ever tell you what the problem was?"

A long pause followed. Aunt Rebekah and Sara exchanged glances. Sara had an idea what Aunt Rebekah was going to say, but wanted to hear it directly.

"He was abused by his parents . . . sexually."

This last word hung in Sara's throat like a two-ton apple. Sara understood why Justin took Corey. Not to hurt him, but to make her feel what it was like to have something precious taken away and not know if you'll ever be normal again. The missing printout was just a reason. Justin would only act quickly if there was a solid reason. Stealing from him was the reason that helped him snatch Corey before he was really ready to. Sara understood why Justin showed up at the hospital the day Corey's eye was injured. He cared about his brother. He wanted him safe. Cutting his finger off was his way of saying to Corey that even though he cared, he wasn't going to lose control or go to jail for anyone. Justin wanted to be the one to cause Sara the discomfort for abandoning him.

Sara's mind had gone adrift. She had become deaf to Aunt Rebekah and all noise while malicious thoughts ran rampant through her mind. She remembered Corey wanted badly to tell her something. Could Justin have abused Corey five years ago at Rebekah's? Was that the real reason Corey wouldn't visit Rebekah? There were a lot of unanswered questions. For the moment, Sara felt secure about Corey since Justin was gone and he was fishing with Henry.

"But what was Al's real name?"

"It was Al Totten," Aunt Rebekah answered.

Sara knew that his adoptive parents named him Alvin Summers. Justin kept changing his name wherever he went. Sara realized it would be hard to track him if he moved frequently and changed his name. This was another reason why Justin left Albany for New York at a moment's notice.

Aunt Rebekah shook Sara's shoulder, trying to get her to 'snap' out of it.

"Sara, Sara . . ." Aunt Rebekah said.

"Huh? Oh, yeah, sorry I was just thinking about Corey," Sara said with a concerned smile.

"Oh, he's gonna be okay. Just a little cold, that's all."

"Rebekah, where did Justin—I mean, Al, stay when he came?"

"Mostly upstairs in his own place."

Sara was surprised to hear this. She stood in excitement.

"Can I look at it?"

"Why? There's nothing up there."

"I just want to look at the place. Somebody was asking about a room to rent."

Of course Sara was lying. But she had to lie in order to get Aunt Rebekah to show her the empty apartment. She helped Aunt Rebekah to her feet by holding her right hand. Her hand rubbed across a mole in the center of the palm of Aunt Rebekah's hand.

"I wonder why this mole got so big on you? Henry has the same one in the same place."

Sara held her hands up to show Aunt Rebekah hers. "Mine came on my left and right. Beauty marks, I guess."

As they both chuckled, Sara couldn't help but think about what Corey had told her.

The sun was all the way up. Me and Uncle Henry were in a small, black, wooden rowboat. Uncle Henry kept the boat in Ravena all year. During the winter, he kept it covered. He wouldn't let anyone use it anytime, except when they really needed it. He sat close behind me. My fishing line jerked a little. Uncle Henry saw this.

"Hold it steady. She's almost hooked. Keep your pole steady or she's gonna lose you."

"I got it, Uncle Henry"

My line went tight. I began to reel it in. It was getting away from me. Uncle Henry hands swallowed mine as he took a firm hold and helped me reel the fish in.

"I got 'em, I got 'em. He feels big, Uncle Henry. It must be at least five pounds, Uncle Henry"

"Yeah, yeah. Take 'er in slow now."

I noticed Uncle Henry was extremely close as he helped reel him in.

"I got 'em, Uncle Henry"

"Should've just shot the damn thing and got it over with," Uncle Henry said, smiling.

I glanced at Uncle Henry's Beretta that sat in the boat next to me.

"Okay, she's all yours. I know how you like to do things yourself," Uncle Henry said.

He sat back and watched me haul the fish in. It was a beauty.

With my hand bandaged, it was a little difficult maneuvering, but I managed. It would take some time getting used to being without a finger. I pulled the fish out of the water, unhooked him and threw him in the empty fish pail.

I stared at the flapping fish. He was struggling for air.

"Uncle Henry, how can you tell if fish are male or female?"

"You just feel under their belly. You might rub over his penis if it's a he."

We both started laughing.

"Uncle Henry, I gotta go to the bathroom."

"Ah, piss in the lake."

"That's not good. The fish could choke to death. I gotta go pee, Uncle Henry."

"Awh, Corey, can't you hold it? You're on a roll. They're bitin' now."

"I've been holding it for thirty minutes."

"Piss in the lake," Uncle Henry suggested again.

I frowned at this gross advice.

"People gotta eat those fish," I said.

"Oh, all right," Uncle Henry said.

Uncle Henry positioned himself between the oars and began to row toward the shore. I thought about what Uncle Henry said, then looked back at him with a strange look.

"Oh, come on, Corey, lighten up. We all say and do things sometimes that we don't really mean. You skinned that cat and fed it to us and thought it was the biggest joke, didn't you?"

A smile etched across my face.

"Yeah, yeah, come on now. You know what I mean. That'a'boy, have some fun," Uncle Henry said.

"I did it because I wanted you to have cat."

"But it still wasn't nice because you deceived us."

"I guess you're right."

"Okay, that's a sport. Oh, by the way, how's the finger?"

I looked at the cast for a second.

"It feels okay."

We reached the muddy shore. It had rained in Ravena throughout the night. I jumped in the mud and ran to a bush nearby. I quickly unbuttoned my pants, then unzipped them. They accidentally fell, exposing my butt. I began to chuckle as I peed.

"Don't look," I said.

Uncle Henry looked at my bare butt, then smiled, picked up his gun and got out of the boat.

"I won't," Uncle Henry said.

I glanced over my shoulder at Uncle Henry.

"You gonna do some shooting, Uncle Henry?"

"No, *we're* gonna do some shooting."

I finished my business and pulled my pants up, buttoning them as I walked toward Uncle Henry. He was aiming at different trees as targets. I knew this would be fun.

"Line up the cans, Corey."

I ran to where we kept the same cans we always used for target practice and set them up. This would be the fun part of our fishing trip.

CHAPTER SEVENTY-FIVE

SARA AND AUNT REBEKAH were still at the dining room table, chatting.

"You know, that night Al was in such a rage I didn't know what he was gonna do. I mean, we had argued in the past, but not like this. I really didn't like arguing with him, but I wasn't about to let him walk all over me either. He had a strong, overpowering personality. Was scary at times, too, but in the next instant he could be charming in his own way." Aunt Rebekah sighed. "Anyway, I haven't seen or heard from him since then."

"Now, can we take a look at where he lived, Aunt Rebekah?" Sara asked. Her reason was that she wanted to see where Justin had been living.

"Okay."

Aunt Rebekah opened a drawer near her and took out a set of keys. She stood and motioned for Sara to lead the way. They walked out the dining room door and headed up the long, dark staircase to the second floor.

"Sara, why are you so interested in Al? He was a distant relative," Aunt Rebekah said as she began to breathe heavily.

"I just like to try to know all my cousins, especially since he lived so close."

"Oh, I guess," Aunt Rebekah said.

Aunt Rebekah took each step up followed by a deep breath.

"I can't remember the last time I walked up these stairs," she said.

"Maybe you should get out more and do some walking. Exercise is good for you," Sara said.

"These stairs are about as close as I'm going to get to exercise. At my age, it pretty much doesn't matter anymore. The damage is done. There." Aunt Rebekah took a deep breath.

They reached the top step area of the second floor. The small walkway to the left of the door had three old ten-speed bikes parked there.

"Al used to ride those bikes all the time, when he was here long enough!" Aunt Rebekah said.

Sara gently caressed one of the bikes on the handle. Aunt Rebekah put the key in the door.

"Well, here it is," Aunt Rebekah said.

She turned the key and pushed the door open slowly. Sara stepped inside, followed by Aunt Rebekah. It was dusty.

"It's empty, Rebekah."

"Yep, that's how he kept it."

Sara slowly walked from one room to the next. Her footsteps echoed through the empty apartment. She was happy to be occupying the same space that her son did, even if it was for only a short time.

"But I don't understand. Where did he sleep?"

"Wherever and whenever. He did more sleeping on the couch in my place than anywhere else. The only reason he didn't sleep there that last night I saw him was cause Corey was asleep there. Which reminds me, Corey woke up that morning crying. He said something had happened, but he wouldn't tell me."

Sara stopped walking, and looked at Aunt Rebekah.

"Something like what?"

"Well he wouldn't say. I just figured he had a bad dream. But then he said something had happened a couple of nights earlier. I didn't think anything of it, because he was always thinking up stories and telling me. But this particular one must have scared him too much to tell. So I just let it go. He never told me another story after that night. He did say he didn't see how such a mole could grow on a person's hand. That was it. Oh, and that he didn't like them anywhere on his body."

Sara looked at her hand. She had the same mole as Henry.

"Henry has one, too," Sara said.

Sara went into deep thought, deafening herself to every noise around, wondering what Corey meant.

Pow, pow, pow, three direct hits. Uncle Henry was a good shooter. He knocked down three cans in a row. He blew the imaginary smoke from the end of the barrel of the gun, reminiscent of the cowboys of yesteryear. His broad smile covered his face.

"Here, your turn," Uncle Henry said.

I took the gun, aimed, took two shots and missed.

"Hold up. Let me help you."

Uncle Henry knelt down behind me and wrapped his huge arms around my entire body, meeting my hands and holding the gun steady. "Just remember what I told you. Never mind what you see on TV about allowing movement from the impact of the gun. Just aim straight and shoot."

Uncle Henry's lips almost touched my ear as he began to speak softer. His grip on me loosened, but was more affectionate. I didn't like it.

"Okay, Uncle Henry I got it. You can let go."

"I'll hold you up from the impact, just shoot," Uncle Henry said.

I got irritated.

"Uncle Henry, please let go!"

I wrestled away and fell to the ground, dropping the gun. Uncle Henry reached out to help me up. I brushed his hand away.

"I can do it. Just don't touch me, okay. I don't like that shit!"

"Don't curse, Corey, it's not nice."

"Well, neither is that."

"Corey, I was only trying to help you shoot."

"Let me do it myself. That's all."

"You know, you're very selfish. After all I've done for you."

"But you're my uncle."

"I'm a lot of things to you, Corey. Now let's shake."

He extended his hand, and I looked at the mole on it, then shook. He helped me up. Then he turned me around roughly into his arms. He covered my mouth, and I felt that mole on my face. It brought back horrible memories. Then I realized what was happening, but I couldn't believe it.

"It's time for you to give back."

He held me with his left hand, and began to undo my pants with his right hand.

"You! It's you! No, Uncle Henry, not you." I was shocked.

I was petrified at what was about to happen.

"I love you, Corey. You don't even know how much. Just be still and you'll like this, okay? I'll be gentle."

I was trapped and defenseless. I looked at the gun three feet away on the ground. Uncle Henry's grip was too tight for me to get to it. I had to break free. I looked at his thumb near my mouth. I immediately bit into it, taking out a plug. He yelled from the pain. He let me go. His pain still didn't match what I was feeling for the molestations that he had committed on me. I lunged for the gun, and Uncle Henry pushed me away from it. He jumped on me and started tearing at my clothes. I reached for a rock, grabbed it and hit him on the head. He was unconscious. His body went limp. I struggled from under him. He became conscious in seconds. I ran to the gun and picked it up. He stood and walked toward me.

"Stop, Uncle Henry"

"Put it down, Corey, I love you."

"No, you can't do that."

Uncle Henry got angrier.

"I said, put it down."

"No! You abused me. I swore the person would pay if I ever found out. I never thought it would be you. But it is, and you have to pay. Get back!"

"I'll kill you, boy!"

Uncle Henry ran toward me.

"You son of a bitch, Corey, I'll kill you for this."

"No, you won't. I got *you* with your pants down now. Goodbye, Uncle Henry!"

It was a shot to the head and instant death for Uncle Henry. He fell hard. I sadly stood over him not knowing what to do.

I slouched down on the ground, then dropped the gun beside me. Tears began to crawl down my cheeks. I was happy because I knew it was over. But I was sad because I killed someone. I loved Uncle Henry. We had good times together, but I guess he thought of me as more than just his nephew. I thought about our cat and how he died. After awhile I felt sorry for what I'd done to him. But I understand what drove me. It was being molested. I took out my anger and pain on our cat. I even began to feel sorry for what I'd done to Uncle Henry. I'm not a killer. I guess if anyone is pushed the wrong way, they're capable of anything. Uncle Henry pushed me too far. He was sneaking in my room to molest me when Tony was upstairs sleeping in Randy's room. It was always him. Always gagging me and pointing his gun to my temple. He had hurt me and I had hurt him, but deep down inside, I really didn't want to. Maybe if he had tried to tell me or get help, things would have been different. He didn't. I would have to live with it for the rest of my life.

CHAPTER SEVENTY-SIX

I AM EIGHTEEN NOW. It took me all these years to tell my story. It's been eight years since I shot my Uncle Henry. To this day, everyone thinks it was an accident. That's good. Everyone thought it was wrong for him to have been teaching me how to use a gun anyway, especially at the age of ten.

I miss Uncle Henry. I confided in him. Maybe if he had not attacked me that day, he would still be alive. Who knows.

With all the rage I was feeling because of being raped continuously over a five year period, maybe it's what was supposed to happen. As much as I wanted to know who was abusing me, when I realized it was Uncle Henry I felt sorry for him. I never really suspected him as much as I suspected the rest of my family. Even after the truth came out and I had shot him, deep down I still didn't want to believe it was him. It took a long time to digest.

At least Mom and Dats took that stupid padlock off their door. But thinking about it again, I realize that their lock wasn't a bad idea, since they had a cabinet full of sexual paraphernalia. They have since gotten rid of it. At least I can't find it. For me, what I saw Mom doing to Dats that day that made me sick was their business. But I know I don't want someone sticking their private parts in me.

For a minute there, I was wondering if Mom was a woman. But as I got older, I understood what she had on.

It took me eight long years of questioning my parents regarding the facts about their dealings with Justin. After finding out from Mom and Dats about what had been going on with Justin, I wanted to believe it was him and not Uncle Henry, even after I shot him.

I loved Uncle Henry as much as I love my parents. For the past eight years, I have felt like there has been something missing from our family. His confusion about his love for me and how he felt he should express it cost him his life, but I still remember the good things about him; his laughter, his energy, his overall good spirit. But I guess we all have a dark side. Mine came out the day I shot Uncle Henry.

One thing's for sure, the whole ordeal put a lot of attention on me. I can still remember very clearly what happened after the shooting.

I was laying in Mom's bed and she was rubbing my head, softly. Her giving me that much attention hadn't happened since I was a baby. I knew part of the reason for all the affection from Mom was that she wanted me to tell her what really happened at Ravena Lake. That's where I shot Uncle Henry. Thinking back, I really didn't blame her for wanting more information. After all, Uncle Henry was her only sibling.

During that time, I knew I couldn't tell Mom the truth because she would possibly become an accomplice. I couldn't have that. I knew I had to eat and have Mom take care of me. I wouldn't dare do anything to risk my mother going to jail. I never told the truth about it.

Shortly after the shooting, the courts assigned a shrink for me. They thought that I would have a mental breakdown. I thought they were the ones with a mental problem. As far as I was concerned, the shrink was just another way for them to try to get the truth out of me and put me away. I wasn't having it. I always went to my sessions, but I always showed them my upside. They felt because of this I could later be affected by the ordeal. I'm still sane at eighteen. I have since stopped going to my shrink, but I must admit, I liked going and talking to someone who I knew would always be somewhat objective. Plus, it got me out of the house.

A lot of my sessions were about how I felt after the ordeal. I remember telling my doctor that the affection from my mother felt good. Then he wanted me to explain the affection and what was being said. So I told him about the time I was resting in Mom's bed and she had my head in her lap and she just held me and we talked. It was soon after the shooting. I was still ten.

"I love you, Corey."

"I love you too, Mom."

"Mom, I was pretty scared for a while. I didn't know if I was gonna live or die."

"Yes, you've been through some very traumatic events the last few weeks. And I know you're going through a lot right now, Honey."

"Mom, are you just saying this to me?"

Mom raised her eyebrows and frowned before she answered. "No, of course not, Corey. You've had some very tough times." I could tell she was being sincere, but I also knew there was some patronizing going on, but that was okay. She knew I was full of it and wasn't really telling everything. I turned and looked at her in her eyes with a slight grin.

"Yeah, I guess most people would consider what I've been through pretty tough. But unless it happened to you, no one really knows."

"Mmm-hmm. But we know you're not like most people. In fact, as much as I know you're hurting, in some strange way I think you may have looked at the whole Justin thing as an adventure."

My smile got bigger. In a way, she was right. Then I got sad.

"Mom, are you gonna miss Uncle Henry?"

She looked to the ceiling and thought for a minute as she tried to hold back tears, then answered.

"Yes, I certainly will. But I know his good spirit will always be with us."

There was no way I would ever tell Mom what her brother had been doing to me, I thought.

"What about Justin?"

"What about him, Corey?"

"Do you think you'll ever see him again?"

"I don't think we will ever see him again."

For as much as Mom hated Justin for what he did to me, she still felt a motherly bond to him.

As I laid there with Mom, I always wondered how my ordeal would affect me later in life. I thought and realized that maybe some damage was done. My next thought was when my actions would start to reflect the abuse that I had endured, just as it had with Justin. I could understand his anger. But does that make it right for him to continue to abuse others? All I know is that I looked at my missing finger he cut off and wondered where he is, and what I'd do to him if I saw him.

I uncurled from my fetal position next to Mom, sat up and looked her in the eye with a slight grin.

"So, when are you gonna tell me what really happened on that fishing trip?"

I eased back down and cuddled next to her long, outstretched body on the bed.

"I told you already, Mom."

"No, you told them what they needed to hear. Your Uncle Henry is gone now. I know you told him a lot of your secrets, and everybody likes to be able to trust one person with what they're really thinking." She came closer to me and held me tight with a lot of affection. "I hope one day you can trust me and confide in me. I'll always be here for you, no matter what."

We grew silent for a moment and I began to think about Sally B.

"Sally B was really a nice person. I just think she got caught up."

"Maybe she likes it that way, Corey."

"Maybe. She was nice to me."

"Well, I guess she isn't all that bad, right?"

"No, not at all. Mom, why were you keeping Justin a secret from Captain Lee?"

"That's a long story. But to make it short, I'll just say, when you grow up, never forget about your family."

"But Mom, tell me the story."

She smiled at me and wouldn't give in.

"Someday I'll tell you."

"Maybe someday I'll tell you too, Mom." I closed my eyes and began to drift off to sleep.